RECORD *of* BLOOD

by

SABRINA FLYNN

ALSO BY SABRINA FLYNN

Legends of Fyrsta

Untold Tales
A Thread in the Tangle
King's Folly
The Broken God

Ravenwood Mysteries

From the Ashes
A Bitter Draught
Record of Blood

www.sabrinaflynn.com

to the fearless who act
and the children who survive

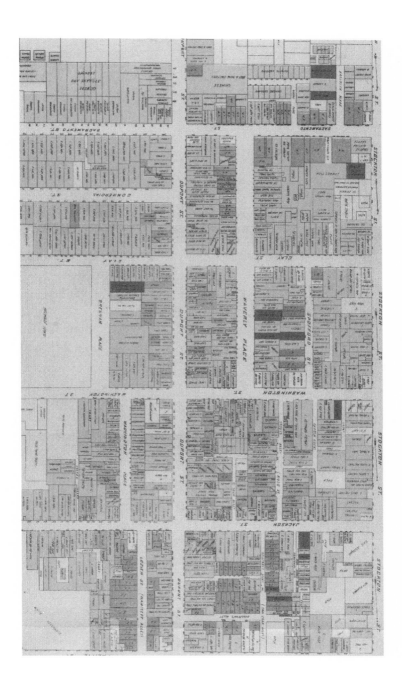

A number of Cantonese words can be found in this book. But using Chinese characters like this, 番鬼 or even Pinyin, would make English readers' eyes go cross. So for the simplicity of reading, *phonetic transcriptions of the Cantonese terms* are used. These vary from translator to translator and are for the benefit of English readers. A reader who actually speaks Cantonese may not even be able to tell what a transcription like Fahn Quai means.

Chinese names are from 'back to front', meaning the surname comes first and the given name after.

"These fragments I have shored against my ruins."
—— *T.S. Eliot*

1

Cruel Death

Sunday, March 3, 1900

THE OCEAN WAS IN a mood. A raging thunder threw itself at shore, and that kind of power frightened Edward Sinclair. All that water. As a boy, he'd seen a grizzly bear charge a man, and the sea and storm reminded him of that bear's fury.

He even fancied he heard the same screaming.

Rain and wind beat at his back, and he pulled his hat lower, hunching down into his slicker as if he could escape notice, just as he had as a child. But it was hard to shrink on horseback. His horse, Wilson, was nervous, too. The wind nipped at the gelding's ears, and the grass on the dunes looked like snakes in the poor light of the occasional lamp post.

Edward should have stayed at Annie's. Propriety be damned. He wanted to be inside, away from the thunder and crashing tide. He dreamed of a fire, and Wilson dreamed of dry hay. So when the horse tossed his head, and broke into a hurried trot, Edward gave him free rein.

As the lights of Ocean Beach fell away, phantom sounds came and went with the wind on the stretch of lonely road. Edward nudged Wilson into a run to climb the curving hill. Once they were safe in the sand dunes, the wind would lose its roar.

A streetcar's light shone bright over the crest. Edward cursed, and Wilson danced to the side as the car trundled past. Blinded by the light, Edward pulled on the reins. Wilson stumbled, the ground gave way, and the horse pitched forward with a scream, throwing Edward from the saddle. A hard weight rolled over him, a snap echoed between his eardrums, and pain came a moment later.

It was sharp. His leg didn't want to move. Wilson found his hooves, and bolted, and Edward yelled at him to come back through gritted teeth. But the frightened horse vanished into the night.

Yelling helped. And he threw a number of curses into the mix that would have heated his cheeks in the light of day.

Fighting down a wave of nausea, he lifted his head, and squinted into the dark. Distant lights shone from Ocean Beach like a beacon on the horizon, but those lights danced chaotically, and he squeezed his eyes shut, feeling sick.

Edward reached down a shaky hand, and probed his leg. The mere touch sent his nerves burning. Puffing out pain, he opened his eyes, and looked towards the dim lamp post light. There was a lump moving on the road, in the spot where Wilson had tripped.

Clenching his jaw, Edward dragged himself along the

sandy road. His heart pounded, his leg blazed, and as he neared he saw the jerking lump for what it was. A man.

The man's hat had tumbled off, and even in the storm, as the man gasped and gurgled, the glossy sheen covering his face was unmistakable. As the man convulsed, Edward tried to stem the bleeding, but death wasn't kind.

All of Edward's hopes and dreams for him and Annie caught in his throat—he had killed a man. With that thought, he fainted dead away.

2

The Murderer

A LITTLE RAIN AND San Franciscans went mad. So it seemed to Isobel as she watched the interns carrying in a badly mangled old man. There was a great deal of blood under the electric lights in the receiving hospital. His ribcage was off kilter, one rib protruding through his blood-soaked shirt.

Motorcar accident, she surmised in a flash. The Vultures, those noble knights of pen and ink called journalists, swarmed the carnage. But Isobel stayed where she was, sulking with boredom against a shadowed wall near a faulty bulb. She consulted her watch. It was near to eight o'clock. The night was busy, but the cases were mundane: one man bitten by a rattler; another man had tripped and fallen on a crack into an open basement hatch, hitting his head and dislocating a shoulder (the cappers were swarming that case); and, mildly entertaining, two old women who had beaten each other bloody. They were still screeching at one another from their hospital cots. Isobel pinned them as long-time roommates, or sapphic lovers.

The night looked to be a bust by all accounts. Certainly nothing that sparked her investigative instincts. She'd have to invent another story if she were to be paid.

As Isobel watched the chaos of physicians, police, and flustered family members, she began to wonder if it weren't the obvious crimes and accidents making her restless, but rather her own mind. Her thoughts kept traveling to a large chair by a warm fire, and a pair of warmer eyes across the way. And to two days before, to the hours spent with that distracting man Atticus Riot.

Her heart swelled at the memory, but as fast as it had come, the memory disappeared, as the weight of her life came crashing down on her shoulders. She was married for one; dead for another. Her life was a mess, and love was the most complicated, wretched tangle of them all.

"I'm telling you he was dying—dead. I killed a man! You *have* to go back." The frantic words snapped her out of bleakness. Ears bristling, she sought the source like a hound on the hunt.

What kind of man would confess to murder?

She pinned the self-proclaimed murderer in her sights, and sidled up to the attending physician.

"Calm yourself, Mr. Sinclair," the doctor ordered. "There was no one else on the road. The conductor already checked."

"I saw him," Edward persisted. "He was bleeding—in the throes of death. Look!" He lifted his hand, but it was only slick with mud and water. When he realized his proof had washed away with the rain, he tried to rise despite a broken leg, and the physician pushed him back down.

"If you don't calm yourself, I'll have to strap you to the cot."

"At least summon the police."

Mr. Sinclair was persistent. His leg was broken, but other than pain turning his voice raw, he looked a respectable sort—if drugged. The physician was about to make good on his threat, when Isobel inserted herself into the scene.

"I might be of some help, sir. Mr. Morgan at your service." She tipped her cap, and produced an official looking Ravenwood Detective Agency card. She carried an ample supply since she would never pass for anything other than a young man between hay and grass, and the heavy cards added respectability to her male disguise.

Edward latched on to the embossed card like a drowning man. "You'll go back? You'll look for him?"

"I've just finished up my business here," she said. "It's only neighborly. If I find anything I'll go straightaway to the police." Her offer seemed to calm the patient, so the physician let her be, while Edward unburdened his soul to her eager ears.

"Not a soul was out here, except that fellow with the broken leg," J.P. Humphrey told her. Isobel had met the conductor only two weeks ago, both as Mr. Morgan *and* Miss Bonnie. He ran the Park and Ocean line, and he was the sort of gentleman who was always keen to help someone in need.

"We nearly hit him," he said with a shake of his head. Even now, he squinted into the night like a sea captain at the helm as his streetcar rolled along the track. "Just over the crest as we were traveling west. It's a bad place to put a curve in the road, what with the slope and all. But I have good eyes, and know where trouble is likely to lie on my line."

The rain had lessened to a soft drizzle, and the streetcar lamp seemed to catch each drop and freeze it in the light for a breath. A gust of wind blew from the ocean, sending rain slanting sideways, until it released its hold and the drizzle ambled from the dark once again.

"The rider got out of the way, so I kept going, but when we came back, I noticed him lying in the road. He kept saying there was someone else when he came to. Simon and me looked around, but there wasn't anyone. The mind plays tricks in this kind of weather. For all I know it could have been the Beach Ghost come back to haunt the dunes."

"The Beach Ghost?" she yelled through a gust.

"Turned out to be a John Chinaman hiding out. There's lots of vagrants who live out here."

"What about his horse Wilson?"

"Haven't seen the horse. Probably shot off across the dunes, or it's already back home. Did you check there?"

The horse was of secondary concern. She brushed aside his question with one of her own. "If there wasn't a body in the road, then what do you think made his horse stumble?"

"The road is slick, and the wind harsh. Might have been anything," Humphrey yelled into another gust. "I reckon it could have been a piece of driftwood. Stop here, Simon!"

The brakeman pulled on his lever, and the streetcar rolled to a stop before a slope that curved sharply around dunes. The lamp illuminated the lonely stretch, and Humphrey took a hooded lantern from its peg before stepping off the runner.

Isobel followed. The drizzle was light, but gusts of

wind snatched at her cap and blew sand in her eyes. She kept her umbrella closed. This weather would snatch it right away. Between lulls in the wind, she could hear the angry surf—the crash and roar, and unrelenting power.

There wasn't much to look at on the road. Nothing at all save streaks of sand on wet earth, and trampled prints along the tracks. "Did you see a piece of driftwood when you found Sinclair?"

Humphrey thought. "Logs, boards, rubbish," he yelled. "All manner of things get dropped along the road. But if it's not on the track, I don't pay much mind."

A gust knocked her back. She clapped a hand over her cap, keeping it in place. "How long does it take to travel your route?"

"Forty-five minutes. From here to the end of the line on Market, thirty minutes, and fifteen to the Boulevard terminus."

Isobel appreciated a precise man. She thanked him, and told him she'd look for the horse. Humphrey left her with a spare bullseye lantern, and as the streetcar trundled out of sight, she was left alone with the howling wind. She kept the lantern's hood over the lens, and squinted into the hazy night. Distant lights from saloons and chalets shone along the shoreline: Seal Rock Hotel, Ocean Beach Pavilion, and the great monstrosity that perched on Land's End.

She shivered at the sight of the Cliff House. The case that had ended with her twin nearly drowning was still fresh in her mind, and she doubted she could ever look at that place without feeling a dread that clutched her heart.

Tearing her gaze from the lights, she looked to the dunes. The Outer Lands, as they were known, was a vast stretch of sand dunes considered uninhabitable. Civilization, however, had a way of spreading like a fungus.

Isobel removed the lens cover and shone her bullseye lantern on the road. Moving the light in a zigzag pattern, she walked slowly towards the curving slope. She didn't know what she hoped to find. If a dying man with his head caved in had been lying on the road, and now was missing, the storm was sure to have washed away the blood. There was nothing but confusion in the worn tracks of endless tourists traveling to Ocean Beach in their cabriolets and landaus. And puddles—a whole road full of water-filled potholes.

There was no body, and there was nothing that could be mistaken for a lump. Not even a piece of driftwood. Maybe the horse had tripped in a deep puddle and Edward had imagined the whole thing? A storm coupled with excruciating pain could do odd things to a person.

With the road clear, Isobel returned to the spot where Humphrey had discovered Edward. What did the throes of death look like? Had Edward seen blood, or simply mud in the night? He'd sworn it was blood, but with only an occasional street lamp lighting the road, how could he really be sure?

The moon and stars were obscured behind thick clouds. A drunk hermit flailing in the road could easily be mistaken for a dying man with this kind of light.

Isobel shone her lantern over a high sand dune. The road cut through a kind of shallow valley in the dunes. The rain had streaked the sandy slope, and the wind had given it a thorough sweeping. But there was a portion of caved-in sand, as if a good bit of it had slid down the slope.

She climbed over the crest, and shone her light like a methodical bumble bee, searching for prints, signs of life, or death. There were plenty of impressions, but she couldn't make heads or tails of most of it. The prints might be old for all she knew, and they were currently filled with water. Isobel sighed internally. She wished Riot were here. The man could read prints as if they were directions written in sand.

She searched for nearly an hour, and then finally looked towards the distant lights along the Great Highway. If Edward had been mistaken about the severity of wounds, perhaps the supposed-dead man had crawled towards those lights.

She turned west, towards civilization, and began climbing over crests and sliding down valleys. Ten minutes later, she stopped at a deep depression in the wet sand. It appeared as if someone had fallen, and then been dragged. Five feet away, she discovered a water-logged hoof print, and another.

Had the whole thing been a ruse? Had a man feigned injury to steal Edward's horse?

Something caught her eye in the lantern's light. It was a limp flutter in the wind, something foreign snagged on a bent grass. Isobel crouched, shining her light on the strange apparition. A bit of ribbon, or embroidery. She plucked it from the grass, and held it up to her lantern, but it was hard to tell the color. Turning it this way and that, she studied the intricate design. Blue, maybe?

Another gust howled, flinging rain and sand into her eyes. She tucked the ribbon into her breast pocket, and bent her head against the gust, shielding her eyes.

The gust released its hold, and a warning zipped down her neck—some primal intuition that screamed at her to flee. Isobel spun, swinging her lantern at a shadow. In the flash of flailing light, she saw a bowler hat and a snatch of flesh, before her lantern slammed into a man's head.

Sharp air zipped over her shoulder, and the crack of a bullet came a moment later. Isobel ducked, turned and drew her revolver. She squeezed the trigger, firing at a second shadow. It was aimed at a chest as broad as could be. But the man kept coming.

He slammed into her, knocking her clean off her feet. The air stuck in her lungs, and he was on top of her in a frantic second. His weight crushed her, and he wrenched her arms back, placing her square on her belly. An iron hand pressed her face into the ground. Sand filled her nostrils, and clogged her mouth. She couldn't even scream. And as she fought and struggled against his strength, air never returned to her body.

Isobel fought until there was nothing left, and still she struggled right up until darkness won.

3

A Wager of Life

A PHOTOGRAPH LAY ON a table like a snake. At least that's how Atticus Riot felt about it. He had not played this card lightly. Jim Artells, the man sitting across from him, stared at the photograph with narrowed eyes.

Riot was taking a gamble on the man. With every careful word, he gauged his client's reaction. "My men tracked your wife to a cabin in Santa Cruz. She's safe, Mr. Artells."

The photograph was of the cabin—a well-equipped retreat. It was situated along a river that ran to the sea.

Artells' face turned as red as his hair. "What do you mean, she's *safe?* My wife didn't go on vacation; she was abducted."

"This is the third time your wife has been abducted," said Riot. He hoped the real estate tycoon would come to the same conclusion that his agents, Smith and Johnson, had come to.

Artells shot to his feet. "Is she there with another

man?" His Irish lilt came through in his anger.

Riot shook his head. "No." And here was where he hoped his instincts would not fail him. "Sit down, Mr. Artells." His voice was quiet but commanding, and the man listened. Fairly bristling, Artells leaned forward with an intensity that promised violence if Riot stalled much longer.

"She abducted herself."

"What the devil?" Artells shot back to his feet, and took a threatening step forward. Rather than react, Riot sat calmly back in the chair, crossing his legs, and gestured at the ode to wealth that was Artells' study.

"Every time she's gone missing, what have you done?"

The man looked on the verge of lunging at him. "I've heard mixed reviews about your agency, Mr. Riot. But I never realized the extent of your incompetency."

At another time, Riot would have liked to find out what the man had heard, and from whom. But he remained focused. "How many hours a week do you work?"

"I'll ask you to leave now. I don't have time for this—"

"Just as you don't have time for your wife?" A well placed word at the proper time was like a blade to the heart. His question stunned the man. Slowly, the color drained from the Irishman's face, leaving him a pasty white. "You work nearly every day," Riot said. "And after work you spend your evenings at a gentleman's club."

"What are you implying?"

"Exactly as I say. In order to find your wife, we had to investigate your own habits, your associates, your friends, and enemies—I'm sure you understand the necessity. Along the way my agents discovered that you have a mistress."

"I do not."

"She is your work."

This made the man blink. Good, Riot thought. He hoped Artells would tip towards change rather than rage.

"The first abduction of your wife was legitimate," Riot explained. "What did you do when she disappeared?"

"I dropped everything to find her."

Riot nodded like an approving school teacher. "Your wife noticed. She was touched. She felt loved again. You even took a holiday with her. But then you went back to your mistress."

Artells sat down hard. All the hot wind taken out of him.

"The second abduction was staged, as well as this one. A close friend helped with the subterfuge—I won't divulge the lady's name. The rest of the players are hired actors who believed they were participating in an arranged charade on Pacific Street. One or two may have suspected more, but when cash is involved, even the most honest men are struck with acute blindness."

"Does she know your men discovered her ruse?"

Riot nodded. "I spoke with her today."

"And what did she have to say for herself?"

"That she loves you. That she misses the man she married, but holds little hope that you will forgive her."

Color traced Artells' unforgiving complexion.

"My agency is discreet, Mr. Artells. None of this will find its way into the papers—not from my agency."

"Reporters have been hounding my every move."

"You'll have good news for them—that your wife was found alive and in good health. Unfortunately, the villains escaped capture."

"Oh, it's as easy as that, is it? And I just forget all this— the heartache, the worry, the fear?"

Riot leaned forward and caught the man's eyes with his own. "Those emotions are exactly what you need to remember. How much you love her. You failed your wife. Whether you do it again is entirely up to you." With that, Riot stood, and collected his hat and stick. "I'll send my bill shortly. Agent Smith is waiting outside to escort you to the cabin, or to a divorce attorney. It's your choice. But either way, I'd stop toying with her heart."

He showed himself out, and climbed into a waiting hack.

Matthew Smith closed the door, and looked through the window. "How'd he take it?" the young detective asked in a low voice.

"Well enough, I think."

"What do you think he'll do?"

Riot looked at the large house situated in the Oakland hills. "I think you'll be taking another trip to Santa Cruz tonight. But just in case I'm wrong, have Monty keep an eye on things for another day." He had been wrong before. As a gambler, he had simply lost gold, but as a detective, he lost lives.

Instead of looking despondent over an evening of travel, the man brightened.

"Good work, Smith." The praise would go to Monty as well. The Pacific Street Case had been more complicated than any of them had supposed.

Matthew's chest swelled like a pigeon, and Riot extended his hand. The ex-patrolman had a firm shake. He liked the fellow. Matthew was genuine and kind, but far too trusting at times.

Riot knocked his stick on the ceiling. "The ferry terminal."

As the carriage rolled down the drive, a voice whispered from his past. *We are detectives, not magicians, my boy. We cannot be held accountable for the atrocities of others.*

"We're accountable for our mistakes," he murmured.

You are always too hard on yourself.

Riot wanted to shout at the voice. Ravenwood had been all cold logic, and had relied on Riot's uncanny knack for reading people. Ravenwood had trusted him. And Riot had failed.

His head gave a mighty throb. He rubbed at the scar tracing his skull. From dark corners in his mind, snatches of memory bubbled out like slick oil from the ground, tainting everything. As he rattled towards the ferry terminal, he looked out the window into the storm, and tried to make sense of his regrets.

4

Broken Blossoms

Tuesday, July 7, 1896

"THIS IS THE FOURTH girl, Ravenwood."

His stately partner was unperturbed. But the younger man was nearly fuming.

"Each death brings us closer to an answer." No emotion, no feeling, only simple fact. That was Zephaniah Ravenwood.

A muscle in Riot's jaw twitched. He shot his gaze over the water, and rubbed a hand over the day-old stubble on his chin. "It would have been better to find the killer after the first murder."

"Better *not* to find a body at all."

Riot glanced at his partner. Ravenwood was tall and solid, his white hair and beard immaculate, a pristine color compared to the dingy gray of San Francisco Bay. His shoulders slumped forward, not in defeat, but like an owl pondering a question from a lofty perch. *Who?*

Unfortunately, despite one murder every two weeks, they were no closer to finding the answer to that question. Eight long weeks of searching cribs and brothels for forgotten girls hadn't garnered a single lead.

"What do you see, my boy?" Ravenwood asked, as he bent over the body. His careful fingers searched through her hair, moving a strand here, and there, as if picking out lice.

What did he see? Riot nearly snorted at the question. He had started seeing the faces of slave girls in his dreams —their hopeless gazes, the life bleeding from their souls. And lately, he saw it in his own eyes when he looked in the mirror.

Riot couldn't bring himself to look down again. He knew her face would haunt him; instead, he turned away from the girl, and cast his gaze over the muck of low tide. The world spun as a cold rage chilled his bones. He ran his fingers over his revolver; the wood was familiar, and the steel cool. He itched to shoot the man responsible.

Two patrol men standing nearby shifted uneasily. They were waiting for the Deputy Coroner to arrive to take her to the morgue.

Ravenwood braced a hand on his silver-knobbed stick, and used it to stand. "If you keep avoiding the corpse, you won't learn anything new."

"She's a girl. She was alive," Riot said through his teeth.

"Not anymore."

Riot's fingers curled around his revolver stock.

"Shooting me won't help," Ravenwood said.

Riot put his back to his partner. A moment later, a strong hand gripped his shoulder. It anchored him to the ground, and Riot let his hand fall away from his gun.

"This was tangled in her hair."

Riot turned to his mentor, his friend, his compass. A small bit of wood sat on Ravenwood's palm.

"It could have gotten tangled in her hair while she was in the bay," Riot said.

"It might have," Ravenwood agreed.

"You're doubtful?"

"The corpse was meticulously cleaned, and wrapped in an oilskin tarp. I'll ask you again, what do *you* see?"

Riot took a steadying breath. Steeling himself, he crouched, and slipped on thin leather gloves to buy himself precious seconds. He flipped aside the tarp, and forced himself to look.

She looked no more than thirteen, but her short life had been as rough as her death. Branding marks, knife slashes, old wounds. And new. The cuts on the thighs were deep, severing both femoral arteries.

"The same," he said roughly. "The body is clean. The shift is new, and plain. A common variety from a ready-made store. The cuts..." His voice caught. "To the thighs, the stomach, pubic bone. She's been hollowed of her female organs, like the others."

The oilskin had protected her from rats, fish, and seagulls. Her eyes were glassy and wide, like most of the girls who stared from between their crib bars. But there was one difference—her face bore no lines, no grief. So unlike the misery in the eyes of the living that he encountered every night.

"She's peaceful," he murmured, expecting a sharp rebuke, or a chiding remark about logic over the heart.

Ravenwood tapped a finger on his silver-knobbed stick. It was heavy, and deadly. "The dead do not feel," he mused.

Riot didn't know if his partner was agreeing, or disagreeing. He waited. Silence stretched, and the gnats began to gather. Flies would come soon enough, and more aggressive vermin if the coroner didn't arrive soon. No doubt, a dead Chinese girl was low on his list of priorities.

Riot shifted the flimsy bit of cloth, knowing what he'd find. The same as he had found on three other girls—all Chinese. He tilted his head, looking at the pattern of cuts.

"The pattern of cuts is significant, don't you think?" Ravenwood asked, seeming to sense his thoughts.

"It's a deliberate sort of defilement." He rewrapped the oilskin tarp around her body. It looked like a funeral dressing, leaving a serene face, and eyes staring into the sky.

According to the coroner's previous reports, the cuts to the thighs had severed femoral arteries. He hoped that had been the first cut for this girl, but he feared that it wasn't always so—feared that the next victim would not be at peace, but that he'd find her face contorted in a scream.

Ravenwood folded his large hands over the knob of his stick. "Either our killer is dumping the bodies from a boat or transporting them in some manner."

"He could be tossing them in the bay straight from Angel Island."

"The tide would sweep them either to Oakland, or out the Golden Gate."

It was true. These girls had been found floating in the flotsam and rubbish around the dock districts.

"Or he's transporting his victims via the sewer," Riot said.

Ravenwood cocked his head like the bird of his surname. "A cumbersome task."

"But not impossible."

"Nothing is impossible," Ravenwood said. "Keep

searching. The dead always leave a trail."

"But not the forgotten," Riot murmured.

Fog and smoke, and paper light. The alley smelled of rot, and the men who came in and out of dark doorways looked as if that rot had taken root in their bones. Atticus Riot felt tainted by proximity; he feared the rot would soon infect his soul. He tried hard to forget his childhood— when these alleyways had been his home.

Tong watchmen were out in force as he turned down Stout's Alley. But long before entering the alley, white men and highbinders alike would have already decided if he were a threat to their undertakings, and if so given the signal to scatter. Dressed as he was in bowler and rough clothes, Riot looked no different than the other laborers sampling cheap flesh.

In the deeper shadows cast by a paper lantern, a highbinder stood outside a den. His queue hung over his right shoulder instead of his left. The tongs were fond of details, and Riot had learned to read a good many of them.

Riot paid the man no mind as he submitted to a quick pat down. When the man missed the Shopkeeper in his concealed ankle holster, Riot was allowed to enter. He ducked under a low doorway, and climbed the stairs to a cramped landing. A reinforced door at the top was scarred with axes and sledge dents.

He pressed a silent bell, and a slat slid to the side. Riot didn't smile into the mesh grate, he only waited. The door opened, and he stepped into a dingy den. It smelled of sweat and incense and pungent tobacco. Riot ignored the gambling tables, and went straight for the girls cloistered behind a curtain. Most gambling dens kept at least one

Daughter of Joy in case the gamblers tired, or became bored. It kept players in the house.

He dropped his quarter in their keeper's hand, and brushed aside a curtain. Two glassy-eyed girls sat on a dingy settee. They were sedated with opium, and wore thin cotton shifts. These were not a higher class of slave girl.

Riot removed his hat, and eyed both girls. He chose the younger of the two. Her eyes were clearer. He motioned her behind a screened off nook, and she obediently went.

A thin mat lay on the floor. She sat, lay back, and started to spread her legs, but he shook his head.

"No, not that," he said in Cantonese. It didn't seem to faze her that he was a white man speaking her tongue. She did not so much as glance at him, but rose, and reached for his belt.

He gently took her hand, and knelt. "I'm only here to talk," he said, keeping his voice low, careful not to alert her keeper. The girl looked at him for the first time, and fear crept over her glassy stare like ice over a window pane. He had seen that look in men about to be hanged.

"Have you heard anything about girls being taken, or disappearing?" he asked softly. It was a ridiculous line of questioning. These girls were cut and beaten on a regular basis. But what else could he ask? He withdrew four sketches, and showed them to her one by one.

She kept her lips firmly closed, and did not so much as glance at the sketches. There was distrust in that fear. A whole well of it. Riot waited, but patience rarely worked with these girls. They were beaten into silence, because no one needed them to speak.

He tried a different approach. "Do you want to leave this place?"

She stared.

"There's a mission at 920 Sacramento Street," he said. "A brick house with a big door on the corner of the hill. The women there will help you."

Not even a twitch of a lash.

"Here is what the numbers look like." He showed her a card he had prepared. "If you change your mind—show this card to someone who might be sympathetic to you, or run." As if she'd trust any man. Trust had more than likely gotten her here.

He left the card in her hand, and with an inward sigh he stood, placing his hat on his head. It would be a long night yet. A night of hopeless eyes, and silent tongues.

It didn't matter that it was night. The sun never touched the street in Baker's Alley. Cobbled-together balconies jutted from rookeries, and what slice of sky there might have been was hidden by a maze of laundry lines and lanterns. These lanterns were green.

The eerie light illuminated the cribs that lined the street. Small, cramped dwellings with heavy doors and iron grates on the front. Slave girls called out their price and flashed their flesh as he passed, while highbinders guarded either end of the alley, keeping a close watch on their investments.

A girl with clear eyes called out her price. She had a scar running along her cheek, and a burn on her bare shoulder. Her keeper leaned against the plank wall. He wore a wide-brimmed hat, and a loose silk blouse that likely hid a mail shirt and a wide array of armament.

Riot stopped in front of the clear-eyed girl. She pressed her breasts against the grating, and Riot stepped inside the crib. It was a small room. Three walls taken up by a double bunk, a small washbasin, and two curtains. Three other women occupied the crib, waiting their turn at the window.

The clear-eyed girl took his quarter, and held back the curtain. There wasn't even a hook for his hat. No self-respecting white prostitute would entertain a man while he wore his hat. It was obscene. But these girls weren't prostitutes; they were slaves.

Sounds from the other curtained cubby made him itch for his revolver. Riot removed his hat and sat on the bench. The girl stood in front of him, breasts bared, waiting for direction. Scars crisscrossed her tender flesh. She couldn't have been more than fifteen, but still within the legal age.

"I'm looking for information. I'm a detective; not a policeman," he whispered. As he spoke her tongue, a dim sort of curiosity entered her eyes. "There's been girls like you found in the bay. Do you know of anyone who has gone missing? Or anyone who has been offering to rescue you?" Slave girls weren't free to leave, but they frequently changed hands—bought, stolen, or traded from man to man.

"How do I know if they are missing?" she asked.

Riot produced the sketches. "These girls were murdered. Tortured to death."

A mad little smile spread over her lips, emphasizing her scarred cheek. "I am already dead."

"There's a way out," he whispered, and held one of his cards out to her. "There's a mission you can run to. 920 Sacramento Street. A brick—"

She backed away. "*Fahn Quai*," she spat. White devil. There was fear in her eyes. "There is your murderer. The white women eat us; they eat our shame."

"What do you mean they eat you?" Riot asked, taking care to pronounce the words. He wondered if he had heard her wrong.

"The men tell us. Now you tell me that girls are killed."

"There are kind women at the mission. I know them personally. The men only say that to keep you here."

Anger flashed in the girl's eyes. "You just told me it is true. Girls are being killed. Why should I trust you?" She stalked out of the curtain, and called for her keeper.

Riot was on his feet when the highbinder stormed in. The man started shooing him out with hard eyes and a string of insults. Riot left. But on his way out, he glanced at the girl. She was defiant—yet resigned. There was no life left beyond those rotting walls.

Riot had seen that same look in the eyes of his mother the day before she hanged herself.

Hei Lok Lau—the House of Joy—straddled China-town and the Barbary Coast. It was no crib, but a well-built building bedecked with bright lanterns and a sound balcony. Riot pressed his finger to a bell beside an ornate door, and after being patted down by a man who resem-bled a bull, he was granted entrance.

He stepped into luxury: teak and silks and beaded doorways; rich carpets and art, and plush chairs. On one side of the room, a bar shone with polish and glass. Men mingled with the women of the house, who came in all varieties. One of the girls slunk over to him. She offered a meek bow. Although painted and powdered, and wearing the slitted cheongsam of the singsong girls, she was white. Unlike the girls he had seen earlier that night, all of the women here were free to do as they pleased. And prostitu-tion was a profitable business.

"I'm here to see Pak Siu Lui," he said before she offered to show him the line-up.

"I am sorry—"

"I have an appointment."

The woman arched a perfectly sculpted brow, shattering her humble act. She asked for his name, and shuffled off on slippered feet.

While the scarred bouncer chewed the inside of his cheek by the door, Riot waited, absently watching the players at a faro table. A fast game with a lot of moving hands, and even more opportunity to cheat. The dealer's petite hands were deft, and her rings distracted the eye. The silk stretched over her breasts didn't hurt either.

An older gentleman, a typist by the look of his hands and slouch of his shoulders, sat at the table. His suit was tailored, but threadbare, and he kept adjusting his spectacles. The man was working up the nerve to cheat—likely a silk thread on a copper, but given the keen eyes of the beautiful 'lookout' the old man's night would end badly.

In a flash, without thought, Riot's quicksilver mind read the other players at the tables. There were some honest players, others drunk, and one fellow with a perpetual scowl who knew exactly what he was doing. He'd come away from the tables richer, and spend his winnings on women.

Atticus Riot knew these things for a fact. An intuition that he took as divine canon. He knew faces. As near-blind as he was, he had only been able to see three feet in front of him before spectacles. As a boy, Riot hadn't looked at buildings, the ocean, the carts and their horses—he had studied faces. Details. They had made up his world until Tim had threaded the first pair of spectacles over his ears.

And after, the world had been big. Too big. When it became overwhelming, he had comforted himself with familiar details: the look in a pair of eyes, the shape of an ear, the tilt of lips, the movement of an Adam's apple. Riot read people like an open book.

The meek woman returned, and gestured towards a side curtain. "Pak Siu Lui will see you." She parted it for him, and he followed her upstairs, and through a hallway of doors to the very last.

The woman left him there.

Riot squared his shoulders, and knocked. A call beckoned him inside. Pak Siu Lui, or White Blossom, stood in the middle of her boudoir. She demanded the eye.

Dressed in clinging red silk embroidered with dainty gold flowers, her hair was as black as ink, her eyes like deep pools, her skin as flawless as ivory. She reminded Riot of a black widow—a spider spinning her web over San Francisco. Her reach went far, and her ears were keen.

"Mr. Riot." Her voice was like the easy glide of a hammer cocking. It put him on edge. He had known many a madam in his lifetime. There were some who were maternal, offering men their warmth and love for an hour, while others relished the power they held over a man. Then there were the women who had been emptied of humanity, as if the years spent working their way through the ranks had stripped them of genuine emotion. Siu Lui fell into this last category. It was clear as day to a man like him, but most men bought into her act with the brain between their legs.

He forced himself to relax, to assume an easy confidence as she sauntered towards him. She was sinuous and unhurried, with a bite that could fell a man.

"I'm here to talk," he said.

Her fingers slid down his waistcoat, and those eyes of hers looked straight into his own. "Why should I speak with you?"

Riot reached into his breast pocket, and held up a gold piece worth ten dollars. Lady Liberty's head shone bright in the lantern light.

"I already have gold," she said.

"For your time."

"Men pay me for my body and discretion. Not for my tongue—not in that way."

"*The Broken Blossom Murders*," he said, tossing the subject between them. "There's been a fourth victim. She was found floating in the rubbish near the channel. I'm sure you've read the details in the newspapers. All four victims mutilated in a ritualistic manner."

Her red lips formed a taut line, and she turned towards a settee. "Do you know the slavers use hot irons on the girls when they show a spark of defiance?" she asked as casually as if she were discussing the weather. "A different death, a different kind of pain—what are four more girls in a well of misery?"

The last was meant to prod him into reacting, but he was a cool hand, and he aimed to keep it that way, especially in front of this woman. She took a seat, and gestured for him to do the same. Every instinct in his body shouted at him to remain on his feet, but Riot obliged, making himself comfortable, even as she did the same.

"The police haven't managed to identify a single girl. And neither have I. As far as I can tell no tong wars have started over these murders."

"And you think I know something?"

"I know you do," he said bluntly. "There's very little that goes on in the Quarter—in this city—that you don't know about."

"You give me far too much credit."

"Have you heard a story about the *Fahn Quai*—a white devil—who eats the girls?"

Rather than laugh, Siu Lui remained silent.

"A girl told me that the white women in the mission eat their shame. I hadn't heard that one before, but it sounds like a story to keep the girls from running."

"The most convincing lies are those rooted in truth."

"Are you implying the mission women are eating children, or that the tongs are killing their own girls to feed the lie?"

She smiled, sweetly.

Riot waited, but she was unconcerned. After a long two minutes of silence, he stood, hat in hand. "If you should hear anything. You know where to find me."

"That gold piece covers far more, Mr. Riot."

He stopped to regard her. With her dark eyes and full lips, and the silk over alabaster skin that looked as though no man had ever laid a hand on such purity, Siu Lui dripped with sensuality.

"I'm the son of a whore," he said, with a wry twist of his lips. "The way I figure, every whore I meet could be my sister." A lash fluttered, so slight he might have imagined it. "Ma'am." He nodded politely, and left. But it wasn't until cool air hit his cheeks that he breathed easy.

5

The Girl

Sunday, March 3, 1900

A STEADY SHEET OF rain fell outside the ferry building. Riot stood under the stone archway with a crowd of despondent travelers who had not brought umbrellas. He stared into the night. Carriages and cable cars glistened under the rain, and the cobblestones ran with water. Thick drops fell, illuminated by electric lights, and the usual thunder of bells, whistles, and rattling tracks was muffled by the rain. But Riot hardly noticed; his mind was trapped in events that had transpired three years before.

After his skull gave a mighty throb, he shook away melancholy and consulted his watch. It was well past ten o'clock. He wondered how Bel had occupied herself while he was tying up the last strings of the Pacific Street Case. She could be anywhere: at her boat, chasing a story, working at the Call building or in the Ravenwood office. And wherever she might be, who was she tonight? Was she masquerading as Miss Bonnie, Mr. Morgan, or was she using an entirely different persona? Isobel was an elusive woman. And extraordinary. More than likely she would find him.

With that hope warming his heart, Riot tucked his watch in its pocket, and began buttoning his overcoat, preparing to head home when he noticed a small figure in the crowd. A girl stood holding an unopened umbrella. There was a suitcase at her feet, and she stared at the blinding city lights. When a cable car pulled up to the terminus, a crowd of newly docked arrivals surged towards it, but the girl remained.

Riot dropped back to observe the child. She looked to be about twelve. Dark hair, an upturned nose, and a confident tilt to her chin. She seemed unattached to the few men and women who were left waiting under the ferry building arch. Her blue coat was buttoned and bright, but it was her knuckles that gave her away—she clutched her umbrella so tightly that they had gone white.

Tired, hungry, and skull throbbing, Riot came near to cursing his protective nature. Shoving down his own discomfort, he approached the girl, and tipped his hat.

"Excuse me, are you lost, miss?" he asked.

The girl looked at him evenly, with an unafraid, self-possessed gaze. "No, sir. Unless this isn't the San Francisco ferry building."

"It is."

"Then I'm right where I'm supposed to be." She had a nasal sort of twang to her words, and a habit of dropping her *R*'s.

"Might I ask what has brought a young lady from Tennessee to our silver city?"

The girl frowned, instantly on guard. She took a small

step backwards. "How'd you know I was from Tennessee?"

Riot produced a card. "I've a knack." He introduced himself, but her eyes were on the bit of pasteboard in her hands. It seemed to put her back at ease.

"Miss Sarah Byrne." She offered her hand, and he shook her fingers lightly.

"A pleasure. Are you waiting for someone, Miss Byrne?"

"Yes, my uncle, sir."

"Did he leave you here to get a newspaper, or secure a hack?"

"I'm to meet him here. Though I was told he'd be waiting for me."

"You traveled alone from Tennessee?" he asked, keeping the surprise and worry out of his voice.

"I did."

"And how long have you been waiting for your uncle?"

"An hour, or so."

"Did your parents put you on the train?"

"I've got no kin left. My uncle is taking me in." And instead of traveling to meet his orphaned niece, this uncle had her get on a train and travel over two thousand miles. Alone. Riot had no children (as far as he knew) but he could not imagine sending a child on such a journey.

"Did your uncle give you an address?"

Sarah handed him a letter from her pocket, and he bent it towards the light to read. The penmanship was crude, the contents impersonal, containing little more than step-by-step directions, and an obligatory social salutation and regards from a Mr. Lee Walker. It was written by a man bound by responsibility with no care or notion of what a child needed.

"I think we should summon the police, Miss Byrne."

"With respect, no, sir. I ask you kindly to leave me be."

"Is there a reason you don't want the police involved?"

"My uncle will be here," she stated. But there was a hint of desperation under her words. Sarah Byrne had to believe it; she had to believe that this man, her uncle, would not abandon her. Alone, with one lifeline, she couldn't consider the possibility that he wouldn't show.

"Then at least permit me to help you. We'll take a hack to the return address, and see if we can't find him."

"But what if he shows here?"

"We'll leave a note at his residence. And if we still don't get results, we'll put an advertisement in the papers."

Sarah frowned down at his Ravenwood Agency card. "Are you like Sherlock Holmes?"

"I am, although not near as brilliant," he said. "Now I won't hold it against you if you refuse my offer, Miss Byrne. It'd be the cautious thing to do, but you strike me as an astute young lady and you must realize that I can't leave you here unattended. Your safety is now my concern. You'll have to choose between me and the police."

She looked from the card to him. "I'll go with you."

Riot nodded, and stepped to the curb to hail a hack. When one pulled over, he opened the door, and handed her up.

"Salmon Street, off Pacific," he told the driver. It wasn't in the Barbary Coast, but it was near enough. As the wheels rattled over slick cobblestones, he turned to Sarah. "Have you ever met your uncle?"

"Once, I think. Don't remember him. He was a relation of my mother."

"Does he have a wife and children?"

The girl thought a moment. "I don't think so." Riot was liking this 'uncle' less and less.

Salmon Street was a narrow lane off Pacific with cramped Stick-style houses standing shoulder to shoulder. Saloons and bagnios lit up the street a few blocks to the east. Number forty-three was a well-maintained home, but the windows were dark and it looked uncomfortable squashed between its neighbors. A single light shone on the porch under the second-story turret window.

"If you'll wait here, Miss Byrne. It's cold, and there's no use in both of us getting wet."

The girl was frowning at the house, and she looked relieved by his offer. He ordered the hackman to wait, and walked up the steps to the door. Riot knocked, and waited.

He was about to give up, when the door opened. A silk-clad Chinese man with pock-marked cheeks and a long queue stood inside the door. He bowed politely, and stared at Riot with innocent eyes. The look immediately put Riot on guard.

"Is Mr. Walker at home?"

"No, sir."

"When is he expected?"

"Tonight, maybe." The word was heavily accented, pronounced 'toenight.'

"I'm Atticus Riot." He watched the man for a reaction, but there was no recognition in his eyes. "Was Mr. Walker expecting company?"

"What you want?"

"A relative of his came into town tonight, but he wasn't at the ferry building as they agreed. Would you tell him his guest is safe, and to contact me as soon as possible?" Riot handed over his card. The servant looked at the black raven on the heavy paper, and then at Riot.

"Understood?" Riot asked.

"Understand." The servant nodded, and closed the

door.

Riot didn't trust any of this. He climbed back into the hack and looked at the stray he had acquired. "Your uncle wasn't at home. I left my card with a servant with instructions to contact me."

"Is there a reasonable hotel nearby, Mr. Riot?"

"A number, but not any in which I'd stay. Is there any particular reason why you don't want the police involved?"

"I figure they'll send me back to Tennessee, or put me in an orphanage. After my gramma died, that's where they were keen on sending me. Then I remembered my uncle." Her voice was slow and easy, but there was a tremble in the twang.

"And you wrote him?"

"I did."

"Do you know how he makes his way?"

"I don't know anymore."

"What did he use to do?"

"Gramma said he ran off and joined a circus." Sarah pulled her suitcase onto her lap, and opened it. She handed Riot a photograph. A thin young man stood between a man that couldn't be more than two feet tall, and a woman who towered over the both of them. She had a beard. Sarah pointed at the man in the middle. He wore a swimsuit type garment that showed off his bony structure.

"Uncle Walker was an escape artist."

"Can I keep this until we find him?"

She nodded, and Riot tucked it safely away. "If I take you to a hotel, the police are sure to be involved. But I've a house in Pacific Heights. There's other children there, and there'll be a warm fire and a hot meal."

"I don't want to put you out, Mr. Riot."

"It's no trouble. We'll sort this out." One way or another.

❖

Sarah Byrne looked at the big house with surprise. Every light in the house seemed to be shining through the windows. "Detective work must pay well. I'll be frank, Mr. Riot, I don't have much cash to pay you for your services."

"This is more of a neighborly good deed, Miss Byrne. And I don't live here alone. It's a respectable boarding house. But if it will ease your pride, I'm sure the landlady wouldn't turn down an extra pair of helping hands."

"It *would* ease my pride," she said as they walked around to the grocer's entrance. The moment they climbed the steps, raised voices pierced the wood, and Riot regretted using the word *respectable*.

"...I put my foot down at lockpicking, Mr. Tim."

"It's a useful thing to know. Everyone ought to know how to open a lock."

"Not my boys, and not Maddie."

"Even better for a pearl like her to know. In case she has to get out of a jam. Those are right useful things to know," Tim retorted.

"I suspect you've been teaching my children how to pinch pockets, too."

"Only in theory," Tim hastened.

"Well, theory has a way of turning into doing. Tobias pinched my reading glasses from my pocket today."

There was a grumble, and an uncomfortable shift of a chair.

"You cannot be teachin' my children such things," Miss Lily stated.

"I taught A.J.," Tim shot back.

"We're negroes—police don't need another reason to

point fingers at us. You throw those kind of skills in, and a lawman won't think twice about accusing my boys."

Miss Lily always lost her properness when upset. Riot regretted coming around back. Before overhearing anymore of the argument, he quickly opened the door. As soon as it opened, the voices cut off.

Tim sat at the kitchen table looking dejected, and Tobias, Grimm, and Maddie wore similar faces. Riot might have laughed at the sight of an old man and three children sulking if it hadn't been for Miss Lily's anger.

"Mr. Riot." Lily turned to him, and was startled to see his young guest.

"This is Miss Sarah Byrne," Riot said. "She's just in from Tennessee. Alone," he added. The adults instantly took that bit of information in. "She's in a bind until we get a few things straightened."

"Pleased to meet you," Miss Lily said with a warm smile. She extended her hand.

"Ma'am." Sarah nodded, and hesitated, staring at the dark, outstretched hand as if she weren't sure what to do with it. Miss Lily only smiled, and kept her hand out. After a moment, Sarah shook it.

"She'll be earning her keep," Riot said, noting Sarah's hesitation. "Is there a room free that she could make up?"

"There is. Maddie and Tobias, go show our guest where the linens are. I'll heat up some food for the both of you."

Whipcord thin, fast as lightning and without much thought, Tobias White bolted from the kitchen. Maddie, as poised and stately as her mother, looked to the ceiling with a sigh. It took the boy a full five seconds to remember his charge. His footsteps returned, and he slid back into the kitchen, grabbed Sarah's hand, and motioned her to hurry.

She went. They might not have shared the same color, but they were close enough in age, and where children are involved, that generally breaks down all kinds of walls.

"You don't mind me teaching them other things like knots and woodworking," Tim huffed. He liked to teach. He knew just about everything, and took it as his sworn duty to pass that knowledge on to anyone willing to learn. Unfortunately, Tim didn't differentiate between what was proper and what was useful. To him, tatting and lockpicking were on the same level.

Before Miss Lily could formulate a rebuke, Tim stood and stomped off to his stable house. Grimm remained, looking as grave as his name.

Riot cleared his throat, and took the chair beside the mute boy. As he reached for a piece of bread on the table, a low voice stopped him dead.

"Mr. Tim teaches us good, Ma," Grimm rasped.

His mother spun on her heels, and looked at her son with wide eyes. Time seemed stuck, and Riot shook the shock from his bones. He didn't want to make anything out of the young man's decision to speak. It might chase him back from wherever he had just surfaced.

"He's a good teacher," Riot agreed. "Taught me most everything I know."

"Is he your father?" asked Grimm.

"More like a wayward uncle."

Grimm nodded, absorbing the information. Drained of words, the young man rose, and with a nod to his mother, left.

Miss Lily abruptly turned back to the stove. From the tilt of her shoulders, he knew she was crying.

"How long has it been?" he asked.

"Over six years," she said, her voice unsteady. "He

hasn't uttered a word in all those years."

Riot didn't ask why. She'd tell him when she was ready.

Miss Lily wiped her eyes, and composed herself. She put tea in front of him.

"I found Miss Byrne waiting at the ferry building," he said, adding his customary drop of milk.

"How long was she waiting?"

"She told me one hour, but I wager it was two considering the ferry schedule," he replied, and went on to tell her the whole of the story. "I'm hesitant to involve the police. Not yet, at any rate. The law is not always on a child's side."

"Amen to that," she said, setting down a plate of warmed pot roast and potatoes. "We've that extra room for now. And if Mr. Morgan or another guest should need a room, Sarah can stay with Maddie."

"Thank you, Miss Lily. That's very kind of you to offer."

She laughed. "It's *your* house. With the arrangement Mr. Tim worked out with me—it's in *my* best interest to manage it well."

Riot might have smiled, but his mouth was occupied with the results of her excellent cooking. When he had swallowed, he said, "Where Tim's stomach is involved, there's no price too high."

6

A Shiver of Sharks

COLD. SHE WAS SO cold. Isobel opened her eyes. And blinked. Her world was pitch black. A coarse fabric moved against her flaring nostrils. It smelled like old potatoes. She tried to swallow, but only coughed and choked on a parched tongue. Fiery needles burrowed into her shoulders. She shifted, trying to relieve the pain, but she could not move her arms. There were bonds around her wrists, and a hard rod pressed against the inside of her elbows and back. She was trussed as soundly as a hog.

Her attackers were not amateurs.

With that realization, her heart began to gallop, to flutter in its cage. Her breath came fast as she fought against the bonds. The world was crushing her, and she wanted to run.

After an excruciating minute of panic, Isobel slapped her mind back in order, and forced herself to relax. She thought of her cutter, and swimming, and she imagined Riot's calm eyes. She thought of their outing two days before, and an ache stabbed at her heart. She wanted to go back to that pond—to the memory and the man. To be anywhere but here.

Wishing was fine and lovely, but it did nothing to fix her current situation. And then she felt eyes on her.

Too late to play dead. "Hello?" she asked. She instantly regretted the question. Her throat croaked. Sand coated her lips from her struggle on the dunes.

How long had she been here?

Footsteps came quickly. There was little warning. She tensed a moment before a boot pounded her stomach. The kick drove the air from her lungs, and stunned her diaphragm. She tried to roll away, tried to curl into a ball, but it was useless with her hands wrenched behind her back and her ankles bound.

Rough hands grabbed the rod pinning her in place, and wrenched her upright and onto her knees. Isobel finally sucked in a desperate breath, and tried to stay calm. Her cap was absent, but the rest of her clothes, save her coat, remained. There was that, at least.

Whispers echoed dully in her ears. A hushed discussion that she strained to hear, but the snatches of sound were distorted.

"Where is the girl?" a heavily accented voice finally asked. The words were quick, and *the* came out more like *da* and girl was missing the *R*. English was not the speaker's first tongue. Chinese. Her mind reeled.

A boot slammed into her lower back, and she fell forward. There wasn't sand under her. It felt more like hard-packed dirt. Did the sack smell like potatoes, or was the moldy scent from her surroundings? All this and more came in a flash of pain. And it knocked her tongue into action.

"I was looking for a fellow's horse!" she quickly said, sensing the boot hovering over her head. She was wrenched back up by the rod, her knees barely touching the dirt. A new kind of fire laced across her shoulders.

She sensed movement, and something hit her forehead. Isobel flinched, but the impact was paper light. Again, something pegged her head, and bounced off. One by one, right after another, a dull whisper touched the sack over her face.

"Ravenwood Detective." The Cantonese accent was not kind to English *R*'s. Another whisper of air, and she felt the sharp point of paper. The agency's cards—her cards that she had been so proud of—the very ones she had handed out to give her an official air. 'Official' was the last thing Isobel wanted now.

"I don't know anything about a girl." For once, she spoke absolute truth. It came from her bones, and it felt odd on her tongue. "A fellow lost his horse on the road. I was looking for it—Wilson is the horse's name—but look, if you want the horse, keep him. I won't say a word."

She didn't say any other words—a boot knocked them right out of her. She tried to fall forward, coughing and gasping, but the rod at her back and a strong hand held her just off the ground.

As the shock subsided, and pain settled in, she became aware of voices arguing in Cantonese. There were at least two, maybe three. She tried to concentrate past the pain, but even she found it hard going. And her Cantonese was only passable for a dim-witted three-year-old.

"You work for Ravenwood." It wasn't a question.

"I'm new," she blurted out with a gasp. "I've only been there a week." Again, absolute truth.

The hushed conversation renewed, and Isobel strained

to understand. But the sound of a striking match made her knees goes weak. She couldn't fall, so she only hung there, shivering. The smell of cigar smoke wafted through the sack. It smelled familiar. Before she could place the scent, someone stepped quickly forward. She tried to retreat, but that was useless. Whoever had her by the rod at her back was strong and solid. It was likely the same man she had shot. The same who had held her face to the sand. That grip was as unyielding as iron.

The man behind her grabbed her hair through the sack, and wrenched back her neck, exposing her throat.

Heat taunted her through the cloth, and smoke filled her nose. "I'm looking for a horse! A man had an accident on the road. He said his horse tripped on a log. The fall broke his leg and the streetcar picked him up!" The desperation in her own voice sickened her. She was terrified.

A cool length of steel pressed against her throat, and then the blade tilted, the tip sliding beneath her collar. The razor-edge ripped through cloth, cutting waistcoat and shirt in one easy sweep. Hands gripped the edges of fabric and ripped them apart, exposing her flesh. Cold air brushed her breasts. And the room went achingly quiet as she knelt, head back, nostrils flaring, waiting for the inevitable. But Isobel was never one to wait for fate.

"You've heard of Ravenwood agency—you know their reputation. So you know Atticus Riot will be looking for me. That's not a man you want on your trail," she threatened. She would have spat if not for the hood over her head.

She felt a coward, tossing out Riot's name, but it held weight, and it was the truth. He *would* find her. And invoking his name was the only play she had left.

Hurried whispers flew back and forth like a tennis

match. One of the men hissed some words: *din gau.* She thought she recognized one of the words as dog, but couldn't imagine why they were talking about a dog. Did they plan to feed her to a pack of them?

Sharks would be easier.

Footsteps crunched, a feeling of movement made her tense, but instead of the expected blow, a heavy door opened. She heard the wash of waves for a moment. The hand holding her let go, and she fell forward. The men left, taking the smell of cigar smoke with them.

The door slammed shut, and Isobel was left gasping on the floor. Cold dirt was under her breasts, her abdomen throbbed, and she coughed into her hood, feeling as if she were about to retch. Every muscle in her body shook. Desperate, she fought and tugged at her bonds until blood warmed her hands.

7

A Tangled Web

"IS MR. WALKER AT home today?" Riot asked. The sun had risen half an hour ago, and although the rain had stopped, the sky was still a dismally undecided gray.

The servant shook his head.

"Were you informed that he'd be having a guest visiting from Tennessee?"

"*No sabe.*" The man shook his head. Then half-bowing, half-shuffling backwards with a smile on his face, he closed the door.

Riot stood on Lee Walker's doorstep, considering his options. There weren't any back doors in this narrow lane, but there was a basement entrance here in the front. As he walked down the stairs, he looked over the railing, eyeing the cramped little stone steps and the narrow passage that led to a small door. Two locks, easy enough.

Riot strolled to the waiting hack at the end of the lane.

Grimm calmly held the reins, and Tim sat beside the young man, chatting and smoking away as if it were a two-way conversation. Grimm didn't seem to mind the older man's company, and Riot was reminded of his own younger self. Quiet, hurting, and distrustful. There was no better man to bring a damaged youth out of his shell than Tim.

"Anything?" Tim asked.

Riot shook his head. *"No Sabe."*

"Does the Chinaman speak a different dialect?"

"No, but he spoke passable English yesterday." Riot spoke fluent Cantonese, but he was always reluctant to play a hidden card too early. "I think he's hiding something."

"For his employer, or himself?"

"That remains to be seen."

"Time for a distraction?"

"I had hoped you might be up for one. There's a basement door. Give me five minutes."

Tim hopped off the seat, and poked his head inside the hack. He rummaged under the seat, and brought out a suitcase of supplies. As Tim whistled and rocked back and forth on his heels, Riot looked over his shoulder. There was an assorted array of armament.

"Are you planning on selling a gun to the residents of a house I'm breaking into?"

"I don't have much else."

"Always caring."

Tim snorted, and eyed the street. "Hold on. A chimney sweep with a cart just passed." Before Riot could say a thing, Tim trotted off at a speed that defied his age. The man moved like a leprechaun, all bounce and energy.

In less than ten minutes, Tim returned with a chimney

sweep's cart. Riot didn't bother asking how he'd convinced the owner to part with his livelihood, but he suspected the chimney sweep would be found in a local saloon.

Riot strolled back down the narrow lane, keeping in the shadow of homes, and then ducked down the basement steps. He waited until Tim stomped up the porch, making a racket with brooms, poles, and char buckets.

The lock gave way to Riot's skilled hands, and as soon as the door above opened, he slipped inside the basement. It smelled of mold, but was clean and free of clutter. Voices came and went from upstairs, Tim being far louder than anyone—the old man's voice bounced off the surrounding houses. Riot got to work, trusting to Tim's stubborn persuasion.

The cramped basement was dark, and held little of interest. He walked up the stairs on soft feet, and cracked the door. He could hear the servant arguing with Tim, and based on the clatter of sound, could well imagine Tim bringing all his tools into the hallway.

Riot stepped into the hallway, and was struck by the finery. An expensive runner covered the polished floors, and a glimpse of fine furniture told him that the rest of the house was equally decorated. He walked towards the front door, and caught Tim's eye. He had his poles halfway inside, and when he saw Riot, he promptly dropped the whole armful.

The servant hissed, and started yelling. One didn't need to understand the language to get the gist of his words. Riot slipped past the servant's back as he bent to gather the filthy supplies, and disappeared up the stairs.

Whatever Miss Byrne's uncle did for employment, it seemed to pay generously. Although the house was not in Pacific Heights, any house in San Francisco was expensive.

And judging by a quick survey of the rooms, it seemed he lived here alone.

Riot entered Walker's office, and began rifling through a desk. He was meticulous, and careful, and not a paper's edge was out of place when he finished. Short of opening the safe that hid behind a painting, there were few things of interest: the card of an attorney by the name of Fields, receipts for restaurants and tailors, and a stack of collection notices for tabs at various saloons. Riot thumbed through the bank book. It showed a large sum of money deposited two years earlier, and a steady decline in funds since. The balance was less than two hundred dollars. Not near enough to settle his debts.

Riot hurried into the man's bedroom. Walker's suits were tailored, and he possessed as many polished shoes as Riot had hats. It seemed every well-dressed man had his passion.

Riot ran his hand under the mattress, and opened the dresser drawers. Silk handkerchiefs, fine ties, and postcards of naked women. The door downstairs slammed shut, cutting off Tim's rant. Stomping footsteps moved towards the back of the house. The agitated servant was likely going off to get cleaning supplies before the soot stuck to the carpets.

A red token caught Riot's eye. It was a faro token from a gambling den, but not from a low sort of dive—the Palm Saloon was one of the finest in the city. Riot knew the place. More club than bar, it was close to the financial district, and was a favorite of bankers and businessmen.

A soft noise alerted him. Slippered feet were climbing the stairs—the servant was on his way up. Riot quickly palmed the token, slipped out of the bedroom, and hurried down the hallway to the third-story stairway. It led to an attic room. It was cramped but clean, the walls newly papered in a floral pattern. A narrow bed was made up as if the house were expecting a new arrival, and a wilting bouquet of flowers sat on the mirrored dresser. Crushed between homes as this one was, there were no windows, save for a small round one at the front, at knee level, and a skylight.

Riot used a nearby stool to step onto a dressing table, then onto a dresser. He turned the skylight's latch, pushed open the window, and braced his walking stick across the opening. He was not as young as he once was, but regular fencing and boxing kept him fit. Using the stick, he hoisted himself up and out, and closed the skylight.

Cold, biting air embraced him, and he cast his gaze over rooftops. The Chronicle and Call buildings were lost in fog. Riot stepped over to the next house, and the next, until he found a neighbor's open skylight. He lowered himself inside, fixed his hat, and casually walked towards the stairs.

A door opened, and a woman in a lacy cap and robe stepped out into the hallway. Her mouth opened, her hand clutched her robe, and Riot tipped his hat.

"Pardon me, ma'am."

She stepped back into her room and slammed the door —likely going for a gun. Without waiting to discover what type of armament she favored, Riot swept down to the first level and out the front door. He hit the pavement with the click of his stick and an easy, unhurried stride, then climbed right into the waiting hack.

Tim's head appeared upside down in the window. "How'd you fare?"

"I think we'd best get going before the police arrive."

Grimm nudged the horse into action.

"Where to?" Tim asked.

"I doubt we'll get anything out of his attorney. Let's try his favorite saloon."

The Palm Saloon shone with polish. And palms. There were a great number of potted plants that sat between leather armchairs and hid the saloon's paneled walls. And each and every lamp was a work of art, done up in the popular French nouveau style, curling and twining metal, caught in a moment.

It was early yet, and the saloon was empty. Riot was dressed for death, and looked like a native of the saloon, so when he tapped his knuckles on the glass, the man sweeping the floor opened the door.

"Sorry, sir, but we're closed until eleven." The sweeper was in his late twenties, with a straight nose and fine eyebrows that had a perpetual tilt. He sounded as if he spoke through his nose.

"I understand, but a friend of mine left his best gloves here," Riot said in his plummiest tones. "He's in a meeting, and I promised to check for him."

"Oh, I see. Come in. We have a drawer for lost items."

Riot stepped inside. "Walker is always misplacing things."

"Many of our patrons do, sir."

The young man led him to the coat room, and opened the top to a basket. "What do his gloves look like?"

Riot frowned. "You know... he didn't say. I assumed there'd only be one pair here." He blanched, looking embarrassed. "Do you know him, perhaps? Lee Walker."

The sweeper's knuckles tightened around his broom handle. "You're not here for his gloves, are you?"

"I am not," Riot confirmed. His own hands were folded casually over the knob of his stick. All Riot had to do was shove him back a step and he'd be free to plunder the saloon. That realization was written all over the sweeper's face, along with the fear that the owner would hear of his blunder.

Before the man could act on whatever plan was brewing in his mind, Riot produced his card. "Mr. Walker has gone missing. A relation hired me to search for him."

"I'm not supposed to discuss our patrons."

"I imagine not," Riot said. "Not a problem. I'll call on the owner of your fine establishment. I'm sure he'll be more forthcoming. And I'll make sure to mention how hospitable you were."

The sweeper paled, and the tilt to his eyebrows seemed to droop. "I could lose my job, sir."

"Not if you tell me what I need to know."

"I don't know anything."

"You clearly know Mr. Walker."

Slim shoulders shrugged. "He frequents the saloon in the afternoon, when most of our clientele are here. He's run up his tab, and has yet to pay. The owner, Mr. Lloret, closed his tab, and sent a messenger with collections."

"Does Walker mingle much with the others?"

"Yes, he's friends with most everyone. Attorneys, bankers, real estate agents—everyone knows Walker."

"And what of his gambling. I take it he is a poor hand?"

The man's eyes flickered sideways, and he licked his lips.

"I've spent more than my fair share of time playing the odds. I don't care that your saloon runs a table or two in a back room."

"He plays faro. Really bad at it. The house didn't even
—" He cleared his throat.

"Cheat?"

"They would never do that."

"Of course not. Every house is as respectable as they
come."

"Especially *this* saloon." The sweeper's own lie seemed
to comfort him.

"So Mr. Walker socializes with patrons, has run up a
high tab, and now he's disappeared," Riot said. "Seems like
it's in your establishment's best interest if I find him. Do
you know anything about him? His profession, perhaps?"

The man opened his mouth, and then shut it. A puzzled sort of look confused his eyebrows. "I don't know what
he did. I think he frequents the racetracks. He is always
claiming he knows a fellow who can pick the winning
horse every time."

From the man's bank book, Riot had his doubts, and
he didn't relish the idea of combing the racetracks for
someone who knew Mr. Walker.

I never said a detective's job was an easy one, Ravenwood's
voice huffed.

Riot closed his eyes, and took a breath. Was he hearing
things, was his old partner haunting him, or was he just
plain mad? But Ravenwood had said something to that
effect during the course of his life, hadn't he? He had
always been quick to warn Riot of the hardships of the
trade—as if Riot hadn't been the one doing all the
legwork.

"Are you all right, sir?"

"No." He had stepped back from the coat room, and
had his back to the hallway wall. He glanced toward the
dining room, and wished he could sit down and nurse a

whiskey to drown his throbbing skull.

"Erm." Riot searched for his line of questioning, "When did you last see Walker?"

"The day before yesterday. He was here at peak time."

"Did he mention where this horse fellow was?"

"The place was down by the ferry building. It's popular with racing men. There are messengers that run to the telegram office across the street to place a client's wager in Sausalito. We provide the same service here, but he preferred his fellow." The sweeper thought a moment, and then snapped his fingers. "Park's Place, that was the name of it."

Everything is a tangled web—every fact and action—but not all the strands belong to the same web. Riot could hear Ravenwood's voice in his ear as if the man stood at his side. He wished that voice would stop whispering. It made him feel insane.

Did it matter if he was?

It mattered a lot. His hands shook, his knees locked in place, and he gripped his silver-knobbed walking stick as if he actually had need of it. Riot could not move. He was frozen on the boardwalk. Pedestrians flowed around him, wagons trundled past, and still he stood there, staring at Park's Place.

It was unremarkable by all accounts. A stout brick building with a facade front that transformed two-stories into three. It wasn't a dive, but it wasn't the Palm either. The front windows were clean, and, although it had only just opened, a few patrons had already entered. And yet Riot stood rooted in place.

The mind was a curious thing. Currently, he could no more make his feet move than stop his heart from beating.

A gun to the temple would suffice. Ravenwood's raspy chuckle was as irritating as sandpaper on wood. The man had always had a literal sense of humor, and the irritant spurred Riot to action.

Seeing Park's Place again was like stepping into the past. It was uncomfortable, and Riot wanted to flinch from it. For survival's sake, his mind had shoved the events leading up to Ravenwood's murder into the dark.

He was like a man with a broken leg who had a cobweb growing in some high corner. He hadn't been able to deal with it while he was recovering—so he ignored it. Not quite forgotten, but never acknowledged. It was a source of unease. And every time he stared into that dark corner, he was reminded of pain, of a web of events he could not change. And still others that he could not remember.

Riot gripped the door handle, and froze. The smell of blood and the bark of guns filled his senses. Flashes of movement and shadow, frantic voices, warm wood against his palm. And a grinning young man. His hand flinched towards his gun, but he stopped himself, and held on tight to the door handle instead.

As fast as the snippets of memory had hit him, they subsided. The urgency passed, and was replaced with a nearly overwhelming urge to turn right around and find Isobel, but he swallowed down his rising panic.

Why was he so reluctant to enter Park's Place? It wasn't as if the saloon had anything to do with Ravenwood's murder. Yet something nagged at his instincts. Some shadowed piece of information wanted to surface, but was caught in a tangled mess of facts.

Riot clenched his jaw, scowled at his severe reflection, and stepped into his past.

8

Park's Place

Wednesday, July 8, 1896

COOL MIST TOUCHED HIS cheeks. The streets were quiet, and only an occasional light flickered from a stubborn bagnio. It was the hour when barflies passed out and hoodlums stalked prey.

Riot needed a drink. But he didn't feel like returning to Ravenwood's house. The man would be waiting, and he needed to cleanse the brothels from his mind and body— to collect his thoughts. A stiff drink, or two, were needed before he could pass into oblivion.

Light cast deep shadows as he walked towards a familiar saloon. The weight of his Colt Shopkeeper in its hidden ankle holster was reassuring. Noise poured from the two-story building. He pushed open the door, and a man came barreling towards him. Riot stepped aside as a second man threw himself on the back of the first. Both men hit the planks. Fists and oaths were exchanged, a bottle was broken on an edge, and jagged glass flashed.

A sturdy woman grabbed the bottle-wielding wrist, twisted the arm behind the assailant's back, grabbed his trousers, and propelled the man out of her bar.

"You boys fight like kittens!" she yelled, as the man crashed through the swinging doors. The woman raised a cudgel at the second man, and he quickly scrambled after his wrestling mate.

"Evening, Mrs. Parks." Riot removed his hat. "Trouble?"

"What else but drunk men?" She turned to her patrons, and shouted, "Anyone else?"

A round of murmured 'no ma'am' rippled over the saloon, and she marched back to her bar. Riot cracked the front doors, and eyed the fighting men. Assuring himself that they would not come charging back in, he followed the proprietress to her domain.

"Your pleasure, Mr. Riot?"

"Whiskey." He tossed down a dime.

She studied him while she poured his shot. "That bad?"

He sighed, and tossed one back, then set the shot glass gently down. He nodded for another, and she pushed the dime back at him.

Her dark eyes softened. "On the house, A.J." Her words were heavily accented with French, and her voice was sultry and warm. He liked the way she talked.

He raised his glass to her.

"Does this have anything to do with those murdered slave girls? What are the papers calling it—*The Broken Blossom Murders*?"

"I'm afraid so."

"No luck?"

He swallowed down another bite of whiskey, and she poured a third, adding her own special combination of liquor. Mrs. Abigail Parks could mix a drink worthy of Miss Piggott herself.

"Not yet," he said, eyeing the shot glass.

"Well you look like hell."

"Just what a man wants to hear." He looked at the dark eyes across the bar. "You, on the other hand, are looking lively."

She laughed. "Don't I always on nights like this?"

"The cudgel suits you."

"You smooth-tongued devil." She leaned forward, displaying a fine décolletage. "I was about to close. Stay if you like."

"I'm afraid I need a good scrub."

"I still have a bathtub." She inclined her head towards a familiar door that led upstairs.

"Yes, ma'am."

The water had gone cold a second time, yet Riot still scrubbed, trying to wash the night from his skin. Unfortunately, he'd need to take the coarse brush to the inside of his skull to manage that feat.

How many girls had he questioned? How many had stared back with eyes numbed by opium, or dulled by hopelessness? How many had burned with anger and distrust? Too many. And all far too young.

The door to the bathroom opened, and Riot instinctively reached for his gun. It was cocked and readied before he stopped himself. Even near-blind, he knew those curves by heart. Abigail had auburn hair and generous breasts, and she was leaning on the doorpost.

"Still think I'm trying to kill you, A.J.?"

He set his revolver aside. "You're bound to get tired of me, sooner or later."

She sauntered in, and perched on the bathtub rim. "You have your uses."

"And what are those?"

"I'm fond of your gun." She bent forward, ran her fingers over his smooth chin, and kissed him deep and slow, while her fingers stroked the very thing of admiration. It wasn't on the chair.

Silver light cracked through the curtains. The bed lightened as Abigail rose, and padded across the floor to the bathroom. He admired her shape until she walked out of sight. When the door closed, he shook off his drowsy state and sat up, planting his bare feet on worn boards. Mrs. Parks' husband stared at him from the bedside table. Mr. Jim Parks was all cocky and sure, and as big as a man came. He had reminded his wife of that often.

"You seemed distracted tonight—this morning."

Abigail's voice snapped him from his thoughts. Riot looked up, but saw only a shapeless blur. "I apologize." He reached for his spectacles, and all became clear. She stood in the bathroom doorway, tying her robe, but the end result did little to cover her; it only managed to offer an enticing glimpse of her soft body.

"Feeling guilty?" she asked, nodding towards the photograph.

"Your husband's a brute."

"Don't I know it." She sat down beside him on the bed, and plucked the photograph up. Her robe shifted, revealing one of many puckered scars where Jim Parks had stabbed her. There were plenty of other scars, too—both internal and external.

"Why do you keep his photograph here?" Riot asked.

"Does it bother you?"

"No. I'm only curious."

Abigail frowned. She and Riot were lovers, maybe friends. Not much talking was involved in their relationship. He feared his question was too personal.

Setting the photograph down, Abigail tucked herself back under the covers. She was drowsy from a long night of work, and a good romp at the end. She'd sleep for hours yet.

"I don't know," she said with a yawn. "Habit? A reminder?"

"Of what?"

"He's my husband."

"He regularly beat you unconscious, and stabbed you multiple times."

She raised a shoulder. "But I loved him—still do, I suppose."

Riot nudged the photograph back an inch, to the precise location where it had been before she'd picked it up. He didn't like to disturb her room.

A smile curved her lips.

"What is it?"

"I am relishing the fact that your agency put him in San Quentin. It's a satisfying sort of revenge to bed you, especially after he refused to sign the divorce papers."

He studied her relaxed face. "You didn't think so fondly of me and Ravenwood at the time."

"No." Her eyes opened, and she looked at him. "I was terrified. I didn't know what would happen next. There's more fear in the unknown than any fist. No matter how bad things are, they can always get worse."

"Worked out well in the end," he said.

"It could have gone the other way—still can."

"I suppose." Riot's thoughts turned to the girls he had seen. He had wondered why more didn't run. The answer was in Abigail's words. The girls were in a foreign land, spoke a foreign tongue, and more often than not, their own families had sold them into slavery. In their eyes, there was no path to redemption, and those girls had only their slavers to look to—men who fed them horrors about foreign barbarians and their ways. The girls knew what was coming through their door—men with only one thing in their minds. But outside anything could happen.

"Truth is," Abigail murmured. "A man tells you that you're worthless enough and you start to believe it. I thought I deserved every blow he gave me." She quickly rolled over, putting her back to him.

"What happens when he's released next year?"

"At first I thought of selling this bar under his nose. But that seemed unfair. So I've tended it, and saved up a nice nest egg for myself. I'll be long gone by the time he sets foot in San Francisco. Maybe I'll go to Washington, or Canada—*merde*, maybe I'll visit my mother's family in France."

"I'm sure you'll make a life for yourself wherever you go." He leaned over, took her hand from beneath the covers, and kissed it. "Good night, Mrs. Parks."

As he stood to dress, a drowsy voice came at his back. "You're welcome to stay."

He glanced over his shoulder at the bed. The offer was tempting, but trust didn't come easy to a man like him. Sleep left a man vulnerable. And a shared bed was the most intimate kind of trust. Riot had never been able to breach that barrier. Not with a single woman.

"I don't sleep easy," he said. It was the truth. She didn't press him with questions, but drifted off to sleep.

As he dressed, a mirror caught his eye. His fingers stilled over his waistcoat buttons. It was a curio that Abigail had likely bought in Chinatown: a *bagua*. An octagon with eight edges and a mirror in its center. Chinese characters and patterns circled the edges. Although Riot had heard all manner of things about these mirrors, he didn't know much about them, only that they had to do with Taoism. He had heard that a *bagua* repelled evil spirits, that it brought balance to a room, or good luck. One thing he knew was that the Chinese were very particular about where they hung the mirrors. He suspected Abigail just liked the look of it.

And that's what had caught his eye. The look of it. In those eight sides, he saw the cuts to the girls' thighs and their hollowed out abdomens in the mirror. Riot shook the images from his head, grabbed his hat, and quickly left.

9

Bread Crumbs

Monday, March 4, 1900

AND NOW RIOT STOOD in that same saloon. He didn't know
what had become of Abigail Parks. That might be the
source of his unease—the unknown. And as there was no
threat waiting in Park's Place, and no reason to reach for a
gun, his earlier hesitation seemed a foolish overreaction.

A few patrons had settled in for a drink and an early
lunch. Not the kind of fare that came with a five cent
drink, but a solid meal. Abigail had worked hard to trans-
form her husband's dive into a proper saloon. Her efforts
appeared to have stuck.

Riot went straight to the bar. It was odd to see a thin
older man at the counter instead of Abigail, but he was
relieved it wasn't Jim Parks. He had no idea if the man still
owned the saloon, or if he had ever been released from
San Quentin. There hadn't been time to check.

"Fifteen cents for a drink and hot meal. Clam chowder

and fresh bread," the bartender said.

"As good as it smells, I'll pass," Riot said, sliding a dollar across the bar. "I'm looking for a regular of yours— a Mr. Lee Walker. He seems to have gone missing, and his family is concerned. I've been hired to find him." He left out his own name, for obvious reasons.

The bartender pushed back the dollar. "Keep it. Walker owes money on his tab. Far as I can tell, he backed the wrong horse."

"I take it Walker's sure-fire horseman steered him wrong?"

"That's about right," the bartender confirmed. "Freddy was full of piss and wind, and told him he had a banker. Walker believed him."

"When was this?"

"Three days back."

"When is Freddy usually here?"

"When there's a race."

Riot was about to ask for a description when the back door opened, and a solid man stomped in carrying a keg on his shoulder. He lowered it to the floor, and straightened. And now Riot was not looking at a photograph by a bedside table. He was looking at the man in the flesh. The very same whom he and Ravenwood had put behind bars. Jim Parks now had a missing ear, a nasty scar down his left cheek, and a crooked nose. Other than those injuries and a bit of gray, the man hadn't changed.

Riot's mind rippled, as if it were readjusting itself, like a mirage that was only now becoming clear. He felt suddenly light-headed, and his hand tightened on the knob of his stick.

"This fellow here says Walker's gone missing," the bartender said.

"Is that so." Jim Parks looked right at him. There was no sign of recognition—not even the flicker of a lash. "I'm not surprised. The man was always chasing dreams instead of rolling up his sleeves. But you know what, Jacob, if there's a man who will find Walker, it's this one here." A small sort of smile crept over Parks' lips. A satisfied one.

Riot kept an iron-grip on his stick. He stared back at Jim Parks, not backing down. It was the kind of staring match that generally ended in death.

"I swore I'd kill you," Parks stated plainly.

"Is that so?"

"For a good year, that's all I could think of."

"And now?" asked Riot.

A broad smile spread over the man's face, and he extended his hand. "I've made peace. Have you?"

Riot cocked his head. There was something in the man's voice—a knowing look, a smug tilt to his shoulders. On the outside Riot was all calm and collected, but the hand that held his stick trembled.

"I was only doing my job," Riot said. "Water under the bridge as far as I'm concerned." He shook the offered hand. Jim squeezed so hard that Riot thought bones might break. He pulled Riot's hand closer, threatening to yank him against the bar. Riot stood firm.

"That's very kind of you to forgive me. I'm a changed man now."

"I'm glad to hear it." Riot took his hand back.

Parks pointed to Riot's temple, to a streak of white hair. "I like what you've done with your hair. The beard, too. You're turning into that partner of yours. How is old Ravenwood?"

"He's dead."

Parks clucked his tongue, and gave a shake of his head.

"Happens to the best of us. You take care now, Mr. Riot."

"I plan on it."

"You look as though you've seen a ghost." Tim frowned, as Riot stood next to the hack, torn between climbing inside and getting on the first steamer headed out of port. Anywhere would do. He fully understood Isobel's tendency to run.

Tim hopped down, and stood in front of him. He gripped Riot's arm. "A.J.?"

"I'm fine, Tim." Wise blue eyes appeared to doubt his words. To shake off Tim's concern, Riot reached into his pocket. "Can you track down a horseman named Freddy? He frequents Park's Place, but don't let on to anyone what you're about. He told Walker about a banker, and the backed horse lost. He may have had something to do with Walker disappearing."

"What's he look like?"

Riot opened his mouth to reply, but stopped short. He hadn't gotten a description. "I don't know."

"Now I know something's wrong."

"My head hurts. I need to walk." It was nearly a snap. Even now, he was resisting the urge to rub that side of his skull where the bullet had left a deep rut. His heart felt as if it were trying to claw its way out of his throat. Without another word, he turned and strode away.

Walking helped. It always had. He had walked himself to exhaustion more than once in the months after Ravenwood's death.

His feet took him to a wharf, where a sea of masts bobbed in a world of gray. Noises were dulled, even the shift of rigging and the knock of hulls. Far off whistles and mournful horns came out of the fog. The simple sounds and smell of salt soothed his head.

As he walked down the wharf, the grizzled dockmaster raised his first bottle of whiskey of the day in greeting. He tipped his hat in return, and wondered when the man had last been sober.

He was relieved to see that the Pagan Lady was still in her berth. He had not seen Isobel since their outing across the bay. The Pacific Street Case and her own work had kept them apart.

"Ahoy there," Riot called, before stepping on deck.

A head popped up from the cabin hatch, and a blond person waved a cap at him. "Welcome aboard."

It took Riot a moment to place the person. At first he thought it was Isobel in disguise, but the golden hair tied back gave her twin away. Lotario.

A tabby cat darted from the hatch and whined at Riot, threading its beefy body around his legs. "I'm surprised to see you here," he said, as he bent over to scratch the feline behind the ears.

"I'm probably not the twin you were hoping for," Lotario said, as he joined Riot on deck.

"Not the one I was expecting, especially dressed like that." Lotario was dressed in rough clothes fit for the sea. With the cap covering his head, he looked exactly (and eerily) like Isobel dressed in her Mr. Morgan guise, with blond hair instead of black.

"I always dress the part." They shook hands, and Riot discovered that Lotario didn't just dress the part—he be- came it. Dressed as he was, his handshake changed from languid to firm. "I was hoping Bel would be with you."

"She's not here?" Riot asked.

Lotario shook his head. "We were supposed to meet for

lunch, and sail the bay this afternoon."

Riot climbed down the companionway ladder, and walked into her cabin. Watson came bounding on his heels, yowling for attention. Everything appeared to be in its place. Even the bedding on the berth. He went to the Shipmate stove, and opened the door. The ashes had been scraped, and the inside was cold.

"Did you clean the stove, Lotario?"

"Yes, right after I scrubbed the deck and scraped the hull." A voice drawled at his back. And then Lotario's breath caught in realization. "The stove wasn't lit last night, was it?" It had been a cold night.

"No." Riot stood, and turned to the berth. He opened the trunk underneath, and rummaged through her belongings. Her revolver was gone. And so was her male clothing.

"I was about to try her boarding house, but that Mrs. Beeton is about as useful as Watson for keeping track of her."

"Precisely why Bel rented the room."

"She does this a lot, you know," Lotario said. "It's common for her to disappear for days, even weeks."

"But she usually keeps her appointments."

"Except for the time she told mother and father she'd be home for Boxing Day, and faked her own death."

Both men frowned.

"Maybe she sent a telegram to your agency?" Lotario suggested. "I'm as hard to find as she is at times, what with my obligations as Paris and Madame de'Winter." Like his twin, Lotario had many names. Paris was a dancer at an upper-class brothel, and Madame de'Winter was a talented opera singer. The twins swapped gender and personality as often as they changed clothes.

"I'll check at the agency." Riot started to climb the

companionway, but stopped midway. He had a shadow. He looked over his shoulder to find Lotario trailing after him.

Lotario looked up, and batted his eyes. "I was promised lunch."

"It will be difficult to inquire after 'Mr. Morgan' when you look exactly like him."

"Oh, yes." Lotario tapped his smooth chin. The twins were identical in every way save their gender. It did not appear that Lotario had need of a razor. "Wait a moment."

As Lotario disappeared into the forward cabin, Riot stood on deck and waited, scrutinizing the surrounding boats. In less than ten minutes, Lotario reappeared—sporting a cocky bowler, a short blond beard, and a flashy green waistcoat. "Sean Murphy at your service. A bit o' the flash and Irish charm distracts the keenest eye."

Riot blinked at the man. He had completely transformed himself from sailor to swell. "Where does she keep all that?"

"In the secret compartment."

Riot started towards the hatch, but Lotario shut it. And Watson squeezed his bulk through an open porthole, yowling at both men for food. "You'll have to hunt, you lazy beast," Lotario muttered.

After Lotario locked the hatch, he glanced at Riot, a look of devilish amusement ruining his guise. "You don't know where the compartment is, do you?"

"I don't suppose you'll tell me?"

Lotario laughed softly. "Only if you let me hold your stick."

"No."

"I meant your walking stick."

Riot planted his coveted stick on deck. "I'll find the

compartment myself; otherwise Bel will accuse me of cheating."

Lotario sighed. "Have your way. But no Irish swell is complete without a stick."

"I'm sure you'll manage," Riot said. "Let's hope no one decides to test your Irish fighting spirit."

Lotario flashed a grin. "That's why I have you."

The door to Ravenwood Agency offices was unlocked. Riot walked in, expecting to see Matthew Smith manning the telephone, but the main office was empty. As quick as a blink, Riot drew his revolver, and Lotario jerked in surprise. With revolver cocked and ready, Riot glanced in the open conference room. Finding it empty, he moved to his office, and nudged the door open.

A man was leaning back in Riot's chair with his boots propped on the desk. His Stetson was pulled forward, hiding his eyes.

"Enjoying yourself?" Riot asked.

Montgomery Johnson pushed back his hat, and eyed Riot. Then his gaze drifted beyond Riot's shoulder. "I didn't realize you had company." The detective sat up, leaving dirt on the desk.

"You're supposed to be in Santa Cruz keeping an eye on Mrs. Artells."

"I'm not a damn mammy," Monty said, and stood, smoothing his waistcoat.

"Did Smith stay behind?"

"He did. That boy looks up to you like a puppy."

Riot ignored the jab. "I wanted you to stay for a reason. There's no telling how Artells might react."

Monty took a few threatening steps forward, until he

stood within a foot of the smaller detective. "You don't tell me what to do, A.J. You left us high and dry, and we've done just fine without you these past three years."

"This isn't about me; it's about Mrs. Artells."

"Maybe you should have thought about that before you told the husband how she made a fool of him." Monty leaned close. "But it's nice to see you're finally doubting your cocksure attitude."

"If you have something to say to me, then say it."

"I would have said it three years ago, but you ran," Monty growled. "That personal little vendetta of yours got Zeph killed—so goes the story. But I've started to wonder who benefited the most from his death?" The man stared long and hard, and Riot stared back, threat crackling between the two.

"That's an excellent question," he said calmly. "Why don't you look into it?"

"You sure made out well when you inherited his estate."

"Are you accusing me of murdering my mentor and partner for his money?" Riot asked.

"As far as I'm concerned, you did. And all for a bunch of filthy chinks." Monty bumped past Riot, knocking him aside. "There is a stack of telegrams on your desk."

Riot turned on his heel, and raised his voice. "If you don't care for me, then quit."

Monty stopped. "I'm here for Zeph—not you. This was his agency, and he would never have abandoned it for three years."

"You don't get paid to sleep."

"You got a job for me that doesn't involve your mistakes?"

Riot sighed. "I'll give it to Smith." Shoulders bowed, he

walked towards his desk, and shuffled through the telegrams.

"Fine. I'll pass the job on when he gets back." It was a grumble, but some of the anger had blown out of the man.

"I need to locate a woman by the name of Abigail Parks, formally Laurent. She used to run Park's Place for her husband while he was in San Quentin. Now he runs it."

"I know the place."

"Discretion is key," Riot explained. "We put him behind bars, and he knows me. Stay clear if you can—he's a dangerous one."

"I remember the case, and *that* fellow. Is this one of your past mistakes?"

"It is." Suddenly tired, Riot sat down and ran a hand over his beard. "There's not a day that goes by that I don't regret my choices, Monty," he said softly.

Monty glared at him. "Well, too bad Zeph's not around to say I told you so."

"He is." Riot smiled. And Monty froze. A few uneasy seconds passed before a glimpse of madness sent the larger man hurrying out of the office.

I did say it was a dangerous game. Ravenwood's voice rattled around his skull.

"And I said that life is full of risks," Riot answered the voice. "Only I didn't think you'd be the one at risk."

"What was that?" a voice asked.

Riot blinked, fearing another incorporeal had joined the tumult in his mind. But flesh and blood stood in the office, not a memory. Lotario was rooted in place. His gray eyes were narrowed, so like his sister, possessed of the same analyzing glint.

"Nothing." Riot shook himself. "Something I said to a friend long ago."

"Ah." The prim expression conflicted with Lotario's swaggering appearance. He gently closed the office door, and sat in an empty chair. "I feel as though I shouldn't have witnessed whatever that was."

"Likely not." Riot cleared the grit from his throat, and tried to focus on the yellow telegram slips.

"Well, as long as I did—who is Zeph?"

"My mentor and my friend. He was murdered three years ago."

"Sorry to hear it," Lotario said soberly. "Was it your fault?"

The telegram blurred. Riot removed his spectacles, and rubbed at his eyes. "It was," he said.

Lotario's eyebrows shot up. "You killed him?"

"No."

"Oh. Well, that's very arrogant of you to take responsibility."

Riot jammed his spectacles back on his nose, and looked sharply at the man. "Monty has every right to hate me."

Lotario sat back, crossed his legs, and idly brushed a speck of dust off his trousers. "Just because someone has a right, doesn't make it righteous."

Silence descended, of an uncomfortable sort. Lotario shifted like a school boy in his chair, but he didn't back down. His comment had surprised Riot. For all Lotario's flippant disregard, there were hidden depths to the man, each layer revealing something more. Just like his twin sister. The twins were like chameleons, ever-shifting, ever-surprising—never stagnant.

Riot had no answer to Lotario's observation. He focused on the Western Union slips, hoping this distraction would ease the ache in his head. There were replies from inquiries regarding current cases, messages from attorneys, and—Riot paused.

HAS YOUR AGENT FOUND THE BODY? —SINCLAIR

It was sent from the county hospital. Riot passed the telegram over to Lotario.

"I take it your agency is not involved in a murder investigation involving a fellow named Sinclair?" Lotario asked.

"I'd wager every penny to my name that Mr. Morgan has made us involved."

Lotario narrowed his eyes. His lashes were long, his cheekbones high, and his nose straight. He resembled a sleek feline with twitching ears. "Bel is always chasing cold bodies," he sighed. "I, however, prefer them warm."

10

Intersecting Trails

LOTARIO RESISTED THE URGE to wrinkle his nose as he walked into the county hospital—Sean Murphy would not be so sensitive to the chaos and odors. Instead, he hooked his thumbs in his waistcoat, and followed after Riot.

It wasn't that the hospital was dirty, only... used. Like an old theatre that was low on funds, but whose cast went to great lengths to keep the old girl polished up. That's what Lotario told himself, at any rate. He tried hard to ignore the underlying smell of death.

Patients, standing and lying on beds, lined hallways: immigrants and miners; the confused and fearful; the poor and desperate. It was chaos.

Riot navigated the mass with ease, and located a nurse. Her eyes flickered to the card in his hand, then to his face, and something about the soft-spoken man made her smile. And blush.

Lotario would have liked to hear what Riot said, because of the smile that lit up her face—even as harried and exhausted as she was. She pointed down a hallway indistinguishable from the rest, and hurried away to her next patient.

"Sinclair is in recovery," Riot explained.

Lotario fell into step beside the detective, as he led the way to the ward. Atticus Riot had an easy, unhurried gait, as if he were out for a morning stroll, and Lotario wished he could feel as relaxed. No matter how much he told himself not to worry, he was worried about his twin. She was his other half. And he hoped, he prayed, that he would at least know if she died. He glanced at Riot, who appeared unconcerned, and wondered if the distress he had glimpsed in Riot's office was imagined. This was not a man who kept his emotions on his sleeve. It wasn't an act; it was who he was. Atticus Riot reminded Lotario of the sea. Calm on the surface, with a current that would sweep the unwary away. Deep waters, as they say. Small wonder Isobel was so drawn to the man, even if she wouldn't admit it to herself.

They found Edward Sinclair in a row of beds separated by thin partitions. His leg was cocooned in plaster and bandage, and he was of the same age as Lotario. He had an honest, open face with eyes that were dazed and dreamy. But whether this was from morphine, or the woman at his bedside clutching his hand, Lotario didn't know. She was a cheerful looking woman, with kind eyes and a healthy glow. And Lotario felt a pang for the pair—they looked as innocent as doves in love.

"Mr. Sinclair?"

The intrusion slowly dragged Edward out of his dreamy stupor. "Yes?"

"I'm Atticus Riot. You contacted my agency inquiring after a corpse."

Edward's eyes flared, and all the blood rushed from his face, turning him as pale as a corpse. He abandoned his lady love's hand in favor of Riot's. "Have you found him? The man I killed?"

Lotario blinked, and glanced uneasily around. Who the hell would admit to murder? But Riot didn't miss a step. Never taking his eyes off the man, he calmly asked, "Are you going to introduce me to your friend?" It was a simple, every day question, and Edward responded automatically to propriety.

"Oh, yes, of course. This is Miss Annie Wade—my fiancée." The introduction seemed to soothe the man.

"A pleasure." Riot lightly shook her hand. "Now, Mr. Sinclair, I can tell you are an honest fellow, but I'd advise you to keep your guilt to yourself for the time being."

"But—"

"If you love Miss Wade, you'll be careful with your tongue."

"But I killed a man," Edward hissed.

Lotario looked at the ceiling.

"That remains to be seen. Wouldn't you agree, Miss Wade?"

She nodded, emphatically. "I think the man was already hurt. Wilson would have seen him long before, if the man had been standing upright."

"Wilson?" Lotario asked.

"My horse," Edward said.

Riot held up a hand, and perched on the side of the bed. "Start from the beginning, and tell me what happened."

Edward told all. And when he was done, Riot sat in silence—waiting.

"Was Mr. Morgan looking well?" Lotario could not

help himself. Riot's eyes flicked over to him, but aside from a brief flash of irritation, he betrayed nothing.

"What?" Edward asked, trying to work through his fuzzy mind.

"Mr. Morgan," Lotario repeated. "Did he seem... well?"

"I suppose," said Edward. "He was certainly keen to help me."

Lotario nearly snorted. Isobel's motives were far from altruistic. She simply wanted to poke at a dead body.

"What did the man on the road look like?" Riot asked.

Edward frowned, and reached for Annie's hand for support. "It was so dark—and the rain. I don't know."

"You'd be surprised what you can recall when you think on it," said Riot. "Was he wearing a hat?"

"No, I saw the wound on his head, remember?"

"Was the blood pouring down the front of his face, or the side?"

"Why would that matter?"

"Every detail, no matter how small, is relevant."

"The front, I think. It was raining, you see, and I'm not sure it was blood."

"But that was your first impression?"

"Yes—definitely. He was in the throes of death."

"Have you ever seen a man die, Mr. Sinclair?"

The man's shoulders sagged. "My father. Death isn't a pretty thing, is it?"

"No, it rarely is."

Lotario quickly looked away. Sean Murphy would not be seen tearing up. He shoved thoughts of his own father out of his mind. Lotario would never be welcome at his father's deathbed.

"You said you crawled back to him because your leg

was broken. Did you clutch his collar when you looked into his face?"

"I did actually."

"Did he have a beard?"

Edward shook his head. "Smooth chin. Square jaw. And a..." Edward felt his own fingertips. "His waistcoat was silk, and he wore a fine sort of coat. Far nicer than mine. Not coarse wool—not a peacoat."

Riot was silent, and this time, Lotario did not make the mistake of speaking. He waited, curious to see how all this would play out.

"He was a strong man, too. Not big, but not thin. I remember the girth of his chest when I checked on him. Strong, like..." Edward trailed off, and closed his eyes. After a time, he opened them again. "I'm sorry, Mr. Riot. That's all I can remember."

"That's more than you thought you remembered, now isn't it, Ed?" Annie asked.

"I don't see how it's much help."

Riot didn't reply, but reached into his breast pocket and pulled out a photograph. "Was this the man?"

Sinclair studied it long and hard, and Lotario leaned forward, wondering where on earth Riot had found a photograph of what had become a missing corpse—or better yet, why he supposed a circus performer was the man, or maybe it was the bearded lady.

Edward shook his head. "I don't know. Maybe? He looks familiar."

Annie was frowning mightily at the photograph. "He *does* look familiar."

All three men looked to the woman in surprise.

"Were you with Mr. Sinclair?" Riot asked.

Annie shook her head, then her eyes brightened. "I

know why he's familiar. He's right over there." She rose, stepped between the row of beds, and pointed down the line. All eyes followed her finger.

A man was propped against the pillows. A murder of reporters stood around his bed, taking notes. His arm was in a sling, bandaged heavily against his body, and there was another on his head. He was a thin, wiry fellow. Just as in the photograph.

"I'll let you know what I find, Mr. Sinclair. In the meantime..." Riot leveled a hard gaze on the man. "I don't want to hear the words 'murdered' or 'killed' leave your lips. There are any number of explanations for what happened."

"But—"

"I don't doubt what you think you saw. But that doesn't mean it *was* what you think." Riot looked to Annie. "Try to keep your fiancé from incriminating himself. The police are always on the lookout for a willing confessor. They'd be happy to pin something on him."

Before Edward could object, Riot walked down the row of cots, and stopped in front of the circus fellow. Lotario followed, wondering how this man could possibly be tied to whatever it was that Isobel had gotten herself into.

"Mr. Lee Walker?" Riot asked.

All conversation stopped. Riot was prim rather than large, slim rather than powerful, but all the same he possessed an unmistakable aura of command.

The reporters parted for him.

"That's what they call me," Walker rasped. There was a slow drawl to his words, and an amiable smile on his lips.

"May I speak with you in private?" Riot asked.

An older man stepped forward from the mass. "You

may not. Whatever it is you'd like to say, you'll have to say to me as well."

"Mr. Fields, I presume."

The reporters scribbled.

"You presume correctly. I am Mr. Walker's attorney."

Riot smiled, while Lotario bit back a comment about the obvious. If Riot knew the man's name, then it stood to reason that he'd know the rest. But there was no need to draw attention to himself while the pack of reporters was present.

"And you are?" Fields asked.

Instead of answering straightaway, Riot produced his card, and handed it over.

The attorney seized on the opportunity. Having an audience made him even more robust. "Atticus Riot. A detective from Ravenwood Agency," the attorney read aloud. There was a murmur from the gathered reporters. More furious scribbling in notebooks, and a good number of whispers. "I suppose Mr. Claiborne hired you to intimidate my client?"

"He did not." Riot turned to Walker. "A Miss Byrne hired me to find you."

Surprise, dread, and remorse transformed Walker's features all at once. "Good God, I'd forgotten all about her!" He started to reach for Riot's wrist, but winced with pain, and collapsed back on his pillows.

"Who?" asked a reporter.

"My niece. She was orphaned, and was traveling from Tennessee to come live with me. I was on my way to meet her when I fell into that basement hatch."

Lotario imagined he could see dollar signs in the attorney's eyes. The man latched onto that. "Amnesia, too. That blow to the head you sustained could have lasting damage. And the child could have been abducted by slavers while she was waiting for you at the ferry building."

Riot tilted his head slightly, and regarded the attorney.

"How did you—" Lotario started to ask, but Riot whacked the side of his leg with his walking stick.

"Well, Mr. Walker. It seems you have some recovering to do. In the meantime, your niece is in my care. You may contact my office when you've recovered."

"Surely you can bring Sarah to see me?" Walker said.

Riot looked at the expectant reporters. "I think the young lady has been through quite enough. She needs rest. Good luck with your endeavors, Mr. Walker." Without waiting for more, Riot turned and walked briskly out of the ward. Lotario had to trot to keep up with him.

"What was all that about?" Lotario asked.

Riot's eyes slid to the side. "Why don't you ask our reporter."

Lotario blinked, and glanced over his shoulder. There was a slim young man on their heels. A shock of blond hair and a patch of sunburnt skin showed beneath his cap.

Since he'd been discovered, he introduced himself. "Cameron Fry."

"Tell me, Fry. Who is Mr. Claiborne?" Riot asked.

"I'll tell you if you grant me an interview with Walker's niece."

"No," said Riot, tapping his stick on the floor. "And there went your only chance to be of use for the day. I'll have one of my agents find out in due time."

"It's not that I don't want to be helpful, sir, but I *need* a story."

Riot stopped so suddenly that the young reporter ran into him. He turned. There was a stillness to the detective that put Lotario on edge.

"You can refuse to help a twelve-year-old girl who was made to travel halfway across the country, only to be left standing in front of the ferry building for two hours in the rain. Alone. Or you can be a gentleman, and tell me who Mr. Claiborne is."

Fry swallowed. His fingers nearly itched to write that morsel of information down. In the end, he relented. "Vincent Claiborne. The silver baron and developer."

"And I take it Lee Walker fell into the basement of one of Claiborne's properties?"

"Yes, he did. Twenty feet down. Dislocated his shoulder and blacked out."

"Sounds like Mr. Walker fell into a pit of money."

"He sure did," Fry said with a grin. "Luckiest man alive. His attorney has already started filing the lawsuit."

"That's fast work."

"He's up against some tough men. Alex Kingston is Claiborne's attorney."

"Is he, now?"

Fry bobbed his head. "It'll make the headlines."

"You'd best get back in there, then," Riot said, as they exited the hospital. "Good luck to you, Mr. Fry." Riot slipped on his hat and hurried down the steps. Lotario walked after him, leaving a disappointed reporter.

"You don't think Kingston has something to do with Bel's absence, do you?"

"I don't know, Murphy." Worry tinged his voice. Lotario appreciated that Riot remembered to use his assumed name. Such slip-ups could be disastrous. He had certainly done it often enough with Isobel, although some of their best stories involved him forgetting his sister's *nom de plume*.

"Let's hope it's a coincidence." Lotario was ever optimistic.

"I'm not one for coincidences."

"They do occur," Lotario said. "It's a small world. Even so, if there's a man I'd like to murder, it'd be Kingston."

"You and me both," Riot said under his breath.

"To Ocean Beach?"

"Yes."

"You know I was only going to ask how the attorney knew that the girl was waiting at the ferry building." Lotario rubbed his thigh, even though Riot had tapped his calf.

"I know."

"But didn't you want to know, too?"

"I know how he knew."

"You do?"

"Yes."

"How?"

Riot glanced over at him. "Walker didn't forget about her."

"I don't follow."

Riot showed him the photograph of the circus performers. Lotario smiled at the sight. He had loved the circus, and a pang of regret stabbed his heart. But he would never join again without his twin. That, and the circus had only accepted them for their identical faces rather than any sort of talent.

"What do you think Lee Walker did in the circus?" Riot asked.

"I don't know. He certainly wasn't partnered with the bearded lady, or the strongman."

"Take a guess."

Lotario frowned in thought. And then the pieces clicked. "Oh. What are you going to do?"

"I don't know," Riot sighed, and hailed a hack.

11

A Cold Trail

"I DROPPED MR. MORGAN off right here." The streetcar rolled to a stop in the middle of wind-swept sand dunes. Lotario could hear the distant surf, and smell the salt in the air. A lamp post stood to the side of the muddy road, and a few wagons sloshed past, making their way to Ocean Boulevard. "There wasn't a body in the road. I'd have known. I told Mr. Morgan the same. Only fellow I saw was Sinclair."

"I appreciate the information, Mr. Humphrey," Riot said, as he and Lotario stepped off the runner. "I won't keep you any longer."

"No trouble at all." Humphrey sucked on his teeth. "Hope Mr. Morgan didn't get himself into trouble. The young are always finding plenty of that. You let me know as soon as you find your agent, now."

"I will." Riot tipped his hat, and the streetcar rolled away on its track.

Lotario frowned at the dunes. "I'd say that I can't believe Bel would venture out here in a nighttime storm alone, but I know my twin far too well. She's done it plenty of times before.'7 If Riot hadn't been there, he'd have felt unsafe in these vast dunes—exposed and lonely—even in the daylight. Lotario did not like to be alone.

But he was now. Riot had disappeared. Lotario spun, then saw where sand had been disturbed. He hurried up the dune, slipping back with every step. The crests were in the sun, but fog still clung to the dips between them. Riot stood in one such depression, hazy in the silver light and slightly bent, his gaze fixed on the ground. Lotario quickly slipped down the dune.

"Stay behind me," Riot ordered.

Lotario did as he was told, frowning at the indentations in the sand. They all looked the same to him. "Are you following tracks?"

"Yes."

"Consider me impressed."

"It's a simple exercise in observation and deduction."

"Ah." Lotario searched the sand. It looked uneven and messy, and he couldn't decide if the sand held the print of every foot that had ever walked over it, or if a herd of children had recently rampaged across the dunes.

"You know, I had hoped she'd be spending her nights with you," Lotario said after a time. He was bored. Following a bespectacled man, no matter how well-tailored his suit, up and over sand hills was tedious. And Lotario was cold.

"I'm not even going to acknowledge that comment."

"Haven't you just?"

"No comment, Lotario."

Half an hour in, Riot stopped at an unremarkable spot. Abruptly, he dropped to the sand and lay on his belly to examine yet another indentation. Lotario watched, mesmerized, as Riot brushed his fingers in the pockmarked dip.

"What is it?"

"I think it's Bel's boot print." Riot sprang up, and quickened his pace, disappearing over another dune. Lotario stopped to examine the spot. He frowned, wondering if Riot were toying with him. He hardly knew the man, but Riot didn't strike Lotario as a jokester, especially where Isobel was concerned.

They walked for a time, and finally Riot stopped again. Even Lotario could see that the ground was churned. There was a large mess of agitated sand that had been flooded by rain, then swept by wind, and hit with more rain.

He watched as Riot circled the area, and then slowly worked his way outwards, examining every shrub, every inch of sand. Finally the man straightened. "There was a struggle here."

"Bel?"

"I can't say for certain," he said. "You see pockmarks, there? That's from the rain. So we know this struggle happened while it was raining. These aren't fresh. Unfortunately, when rain fills up tracks, it makes them nearly indistinguishable."

"Do you think she may have run into the same thing while she was looking for her corpse?"

"Possibly." Riot said, absently dusting off his trousers.

Lotario looked to the distant waterfront, at the ramshackle dwellings and the sturdier buildings to the north, towards the Cliff House. The sight of the tottering chateau made him shiver with memory. Duncan August had been transformed from a handsome, charming gentleman to a cold-hearted lunatic in a flash. He feared he would never again trust a handsome face as long as he lived.

"There are prints heading towards the shore."

"Bel's?"

Riot shook his head. "The stride is too long."

"Her trail led here, but not back?" He couldn't keep the worry out of his voice.

"This *might* be her print. The storm didn't leave much for me. This," he gestured at the mess of wet sand, "is too large to completely erase."

"So she might have doubled back?"

"Possibly, or gone on." Riot frowned at the marks.

"Or?"

"This print here is deep."

"Meaning?"

"Either the man was large, or he was carrying a load."

Lotario's heart began to flutter.

"He may have been carrying Sinclair's missing body," Riot said thoughtfully.

"I know," Lotario said. The wind nearly snatched his words from the air. "I only worry that Bel found the body along with the murderer."

"Her revolver was gone. She was armed."

"And yet she's missing." Lotario could not keep the tremble out of his voice.

"We'll find her, Lotario," Riot said calmly.

"Of course we will."

"You'd think I'd be past this." Lotario wiped his eyes. "She's a difficult woman to love, you know. Do you have any idea how often I've spent worrying the night away?"

Riot waited for Lotario to answer his own question.

"Too many. She disappears for days—weeks—without a word, never thinking of the people she leaves behind."

Riot started walking towards the shoreline, keeping his gaze moving back and forth, searching for another sign. Wind snatched at their hats and coats, and flung sand in their eyes. Lotario barely noticed his next words. "I don't think it's intentional, Lotario," Riot said at last.

"Intentional or not, it's damn annoying," he said with feeling. "Don't ever expect to tame her."

"I wouldn't dream of it."

"Good," Lotario said. "No man who tried would ever be worthy of her."

"She's lucky to have a brother like you."

"I'm her twin; not her brother. And I can't bear to think of her trapped. In any sense." He bit his lip, looking to the buildings scattered along the shoreline, worrying over the heavy prints. "You seem very calm about all of this."

"I am not," Riot said.

"You look it."

"Part of the trade."

"As a detective?" Lotario asked.

"I was a gambler first."

This was not reassuring in the least. "Can you identify the make of these bootprints?"

The edge of Riot's lip quirked. "This isn't a detective novel, Lotario. The storm erased most of the evidence, including the tread. Only a portion of the impression is left."

"If the storm hadn't erased it, could you have identified a person based on their boot's tread?"

"With ready-made stores and shoe factories? Unless the suspect has money for a cobbler, treads are nearly identical now. But it is possible to garner a few telling details. Plaster impressions of prints are mostly useful for placing a suspect at the scene of a crime. You can match the size, the wear, and tread."

"Let's hope there was no crime involving my twin." They both knew this was unlikely. "What do we do next?"

"I'm hoping the storm simply washed out her prints, and she headed for the saloons to question the patrons about a missing corpse. With luck she's staying at one of the hotels, or might have already returned to the Pagan Lady."

"And without luck?"

"Do you really want me to answer that question?"

Lotario didn't respond.

"We'll ask a few discreet questions along Ocean Boulevard," Riot said. "You helped Bel question the theaters on the last case—can you manage saloons and hotels?"

"Anything involving people, I can do."

"We'll split up, then."

The horizon was ablaze with the setting sun, but Riot did not stop to appreciate it; instead, he watched a well-dressed gentleman dismount from his horse, hand the reins over to a stable hand, and walk inside a large, brick, chalet-style building. It sported lamp posts, a gymnasium, cultivated grounds, and a carriage house.

It wasn't as opulent and out of place as Seal Rock House or Cliff House, but it was solid and well-maintained. The thing that stood out most was the lack of advertisement. There was no sign, no name, only a simple numbered address and a wrought-iron fence around a spacious yard. While there were no physical words, 'exclusivity' was written all over its austere brick walls.

The building had not been there when Riot left three

years before. As he walked through the gate, he decided he'd place a fair wager on it being a clubhouse for yet another one of San Francisco's social clubs: the Odd Fellows, the Olympic Club, the Free Masons, the Falcons... the list went on. If there was an interest, there was a social club for it.

Instead of going straight to the front doors, Riot walked around back, to the carriage house. The stable hand had already removed the horse's saddle, and was running a brush over its shiny coat.

"Excuse me," Riot tipped his hat, but the stable hand didn't look up. He continued on with his business. He was a mousy man with a balding head and a pointed nose. His ears flapped out attentively, and he looked at the horse with kindly eyes.

"Sir?" Riot stepped into his line of sight, and the man started, spooking the horse. The horse danced nervously, but the man reached out with a sure hand, and soothed it with soft noises. He had a small, tight mouth with a jaw that seemed to pain him.

The man nodded, keeping a hand on the horse.

"I didn't mean to startle you. I wondered if you might have seen a stray horse roaming around this area? A friend of mine lost it last night. He might have come by looking for it—a youngish fellow with black hair?"

The stable hand's gaze was fixed on Riot's lips. He shook his head in answer. Riot described the horse, and again the man shook his head.

"I see. Thank you for your time. What kind of club is this? A horseman's club?"

The stable hand lifted his sloped shoulders.

"Send a telegram here if you find him, would you?" Riot produced his card, hoping the man could read and write. The stable hand looked at the card, and tucked it inside a pocket.

As Riot left the man to his work, he eyed the phaetons, and the other horses in their corrals. There was money here. He glanced over his shoulder, and when he saw that the stable hand had turned his attention back to his work, he lifted up a saddle flap, searching for a name tag. Brody.

Riot strolled from the carriage house, and walked to the front of the main building. He applied his stick to the door. It opened to a silk-clad Chinese man. Riot started to step inside, but the man did not step aside.

"I'm a guest of Mr. Brody," Riot said in his plummiest tones.

"There are no guests allowed, sir." His English was as impeccable as his attire.

"That's not what he told me. If I could just speak with him?"

"That is not possible," the doorman replied.

"There must be some mistake. This is his club, isn't it?"

The man shook his head, and started to close the door in his face. But Riot thrust his stick in the way, stopping it halfway. He smiled like a wolf. "Is there someone I can speak to about joining your club? Money is no concern."

The man looked to the right, and stepped aside. A white man with a cocky tilt to his shoulders and a cigar in hand came to the door.

"This is a private club, Mister…?"

"Atticus Riot. And you are?"

There was a slight change in the man's stance. A shift to his shoulders, a tensing as if he were a pugilist preparing for a fight. As fast as it came, the man relaxed again.

"Parker Gray, at your service." He had a careless hand-shake. As if the man had better things to be doing.

"Are you the owner of this building?"

"Only passing through."

"Then you won't mind if I speak with Mr. Brody."

Gray smirked. "No guests allowed. House rules, which makes me think you don't know Brody at all."

"You caught me red-handed," Riot said. "A friend of mine was looking for a man's missing horse. I thought since you kept a stable here, the horse might have wandered in and been picked up."

"What's your friend look like?"

"A thin young man. Black hair, sharp nose, a few inches shorter than me."

Gray looked to the doorman in question. He shook his head. "It seems he didn't come here."

"What kind of club is this?"

Gray thrust the cigar between his lips. "We all share a passion for riding." The man lifted his eyebrows suggestively.

"I see," Riot said. "And how does one go about receiving an invitation to join? As I told the man here, money is no object."

"It's by invitation only. Long-time members keep an eye out for prospective members. You never know, someone may already have an eye on you."

"Of that, I'm sure."

Gray nudged Riot's stick out of the way with his boot. "I hope you find your friend."

"Well, if he doesn't turn up, you'll be seeing me again. I'm a persistent fellow, and Land's End won't like me poking my nose into its business."

Gray's teeth tightened around his cigar for a moment. He nodded, and shut the door.

✣

Riot found Lotario walking down Ocean Boulevard. His persona, Sean Murphy, had the gait of a Irishman with a chip on his shoulder. Short, and ready for a fight. But all the swagger left when he came to a stop. There was concern in his eyes. Isobel had those same eyes. A gray so light it reminded Riot of a mirror, their eyes picking up the closest color nearby. In this case, Lotario's eyes possessed a greenish tint from his waistcoat.

"No one I questioned knew anything about a missing horse, nor had they met a young man or woman who fit Bel's description. By the look in your eye, I'm guessing your own inquiries were less than fruitful."

"Nothing," Riot admitted. "However, I didn't like the hospitality of that brick building. It's some sort of club. Invitation only. Do you know it?"

Lotario didn't even glance down the road. "It's a sporting house for the elite. As you said, by invitation only, and very secretive." Lotario dropped any vestige of his swaggering Irishman. He seemed to shrink, and he clenched his jaw against a shudder that swept over his body. "I worked there for a night as Paris. Hera contracted me out for a special request. I won't go back."

Riot took a step closer. "What happened?"

Lotario glanced around to make sure that none of the strolling tourists were within earshot. Still, Riot gestured with his stick, and they started walking away from the club towards the side of the road.

"I don't want to offend you," Lotario said quietly.

"Are you worried about *my* delicate sensibilities?" Riot asked with a wry twist of his lips.

"Yes."

"I'm a detective; we tread into the darkest alleyways for breakfast, and then head into the sewers for lunch."

Lotario met his gaze, and looked away. There was anger, but mostly fear, and a vulnerability that awakened every protective instinct that Riot possessed.

"I don't know much about the club," Lotario said. "As far as I know they don't keep regular prostitutes, but they act as a sort of middleman so their members don't dirty their hands."

"That would explain the secrecy."

"And if any sordid little rumors should find their way out to the public, the club acts as a buffer for its members. Hera told me very little. I'm not sure she knows anything more than I do. They pay extravagantly, however. And the madams are all too happy to act as suppliers."

"Was Paris specifically requested?"

He shook his head. "A client wanted a virgin boy." Lotario's lips curled with distaste. "Hera has standards, and wasn't about to fill that order. But requests for virgins are commonplace. Every brothel has their 'virgin' prostitute. When I wish to I can shed years, and I don't mind a bit of playacting. So I went." He snorted. "They picked me up in a carriage. All very secretive, and under the cover of night. The windows were draped, but I have a wonderful sense of direction, and I know my city's roads."

"Good to know."

"Bel is the same way. I'm sure you knew that."

"I didn't."

"Oh. Well, you need to spend more time with her. I think it comes with sailing," he mused. "At any rate, the client became rough. Luckily Hera had negotiated for my bodyguard to accompany me. But when Bruno tried to intercede, he found the door locked. The key didn't work. And I couldn't open it from the inside."

Lotario stopped walking, and looked back at the distant

building. He waited for a strolling couple to pass before continuing. "But while I was waiting for my client, I noticed a switch along with what I suspected were peepholes. I'm sure you know that brothels and gambling halls are riddled with secret passages and dummy locks." Riot nodded. "I was able to get to the switch and unlock the door."

"What happened when Bruno barged in?"

"The client calmed right down. They always do. He said he was only playing."

"Did you leave?"

Lotario pressed his lips together. "A slick sort of man cornered me. The owner maybe—I don't know. Blond-haired, blue-eyed, and thick lips. He threatened to shut down the Narcissus if I didn't go back inside the room."

"So you went back."

Lotario gave a slight nod. "Aside from Bel, the Narcissus is my family now. I couldn't risk it. Not with the kind of money and power floating around that hell-hole." He shifted in the silence, and his next words were faint. "Most days it's all right. Enjoyable even, but sometimes—in quiet moments—I wonder why I do it." In the blink of an eye, his mood changed, and a mischievous lip curled upwards. "So I make sure my life is never quiet."

Riot would not be diverted. "You're not a slave, Lotario. You can leave any time you want."

"Can I?"

"If you want to."

"What do you know of my life?" The words were sharp and guarded.

"I know you're not chained to a bed like some of the Chinese slave girls I've come across. The only chain, as far as I can tell, is in your mind."

Lotario made a disgusted sound. "God save me from a

man of the world. It's not near as entertaining when I can't shock you. How does Bel put up with it?"

"I'm serious, Lotario."

"I know. That's the issue." Lotario started to wave a languid hand, but thought better of it; instead, a barely perceptible change in his stance transformed him back to Sean Murphy. He spit on the ground, and readjusted his hat. "Do you think Bel is caught up with this club, some-how?"

"It certainly raised my hackles, but given the nature of the establishment, that isn't surprising."

"What do we do now?"

"I'm going to check at the room she lets from Sapphire House again. I'd like you to wait at her boat. We could have simply crossed paths."

"And if she's not there?"

Riot looked towards the brick building. "Then I'll tear Ocean Beach apart until I find her trail."

"That's the problem with my twin; she's never where you think she is. Bel could be halfway to Oregon by now."

12

Fish on a Hook

Three days earlier

"YOU HAVE TO GET *into* the water before I can teach you to swim." Isobel regarded the man on shore. He stood well away from the rickety dock.

"It looks like rain," Atticus Riot said.

"You don't have your spectacles on. You can't see the sky." It *did* look like rain and the bleak gray was keeping the local children away from the swimming pond in the East Bay. With no one present save Riot, she could hardly offend anyone with a male bathing suit on her feminine form.

"The water is freezing," he argued.

She snorted. And lazily kicked the water. Her elbows were resting on the dock, while her legs floated in the pond. "It's warmer than the air." She could tell he wasn't affected by the temperature, because she was busy admiring the way he filled out his bathing suit.

When he did not budge, she scooped up a handful of water and splashed it at him.

"That's hardly going to lure me closer, Bel."

"Likely not, but it's entertaining. If you're terrified to get near me in a bathing suit, you could take lessons at the Sutro Baths. And they have a hot water pool."

Riot walked slowly forward, as if approaching a wild animal. Eyeing her warily, he carefully sat on the edge of the dock. His thigh brushed her elbow. The scattering of his dark hair was warm, and the brief touch like a static charge to her skin.

"I refuse to have a rope put under my arms, so some young man can reel me around like a fish," Riot said.

"Well, hell, there goes my next plan."

"You're not a young man." Closer now, he could see her clearer. His gaze dipped down to where her breasts and nipples pressed against wet fabric, and back up to her eyes. "And you're lying. You *are* cold."

"So observant. Are all 'tells' so pointedly obvious?"

"Considering the men with whom I've gambled, I'm eternally grateful they aren't."

The edge of her lip quirked, as she lifted up on her elbows and stretched towards him. "We really should just get on with this, Riot."

"You could teach me chess until summer comes around."

"I wasn't referring to your swimming lessons."

Riot looked at her, long and hard. Her flippant remark took on weight until every fiber of her body felt charged with electricity. It was thrilling, and terrifying, and like a spooked animal she took flight. With a flash of teeth, she slipped into the water, floating backwards across the rippling pond. The water cooled her skin and slowed her heart. As she did a neat backstroke across the pond, she could feel his eyes on her.

Riot was perplexing, and she couldn't account for it. She glanced towards the dock, and stifled a smile as he dipped a foot in the water and grimaced. Riot quickly withdrew the foot. After she had completed a circuit of the pond, she returned to the dock, propping her elbows on the wood.

"You're the strangest man I know," she mused.

"Why is that?"

"Most men wouldn't hesitate to accept an invitation from an amiable woman."

"I'm not most men."

"So I've noticed." She left the question of *why* sitting between them. They had dined twice together since she'd agreed to work for Ravenwood Agency. Conversation had come as naturally as breathing, and silences came like the beat of a heart. But he had not managed to catch her off-guard, and as he had said in her mausoleum, he was indeed a patient man.

Riot looked down at her with a quiet thoughtfulness. "I have a parable in mind, but I'm fairly sure you'll seethe at the comparison."

"Does it involve a man and a fish?" she asked.

"Why, yes. It does indeed." There was genuine surprise in his voice.

"You'd best keep your tongue still. I'm no fish."

"To a starving man, a fish is his whole life."

"Are you starving, Riot?"

"I didn't know I was, until I met you."

"Why don't you catch your fish, then?" she asked. "You can't keep her on the line forever."

There was a playful light in her eyes, but when Riot

spoke his voice was grave and honest. "I'm afraid I'll spook her, and she'll disappear under the sea."

Isobel lifted herself up, leaning in close, until her lips were within inches of his own. "Then dive in and join her." Her eyes flashed in challenge, as she dropped back into the water.

"Right." He took a breath, braced himself, and pushed off the edge of the dock. Cold water shocked his body, and he came up with a gasping oath. As fast as he had hopped in the water, he gripped the dock and pulled himself out.

"That's cold as hell!"

Isobel started laughing so hard she feared she'd drown.

Isobel was not laughing now. She had closed her eyes. Only for a moment, or so she thought. Now she was cold and tired. And still tied up. She wanted to go back to that pond, to that day, and that man.

Terror had long burned away, leaving determination. And boredom. Struggling with bonds required patience—a quality that she lacked in spades. But there wasn't much else to do, and while her body struggled, her mind roamed. Captivity left her alone with her own thoughts, and her mind kept churning over the few facts she had gleaned. Who was the girl her captors had asked about? How was the dying man Sinclair found connected? Where was that man? Why were these men roaming the dunes? And why did they think she was involved? The main question being —involved in what?

There was a flood of questions with no answers.

"*Data, data, data,*" she muttered under her breath. "*I can't make bricks without clay.*" She felt her favorite detective's frustration. But Sherlock Holmes was never captured and trussed up like a pig. And if he had been, he likely would have escaped hours ago. Surely Atticus Riot had never been so soundly beaten. But then Isobel doubted that the fictional detective or the real one had ever shot a man at point blank range in the chest, and had him keep coming.

Isobel frowned under her hood. Considering Raven-wood's murder by the tongs, maybe Riot had. Her captors spoke Cantonese. Had she stumbled on some tong affair? According to rumor and newspapers, the highbinders wore body armor of some sort. But what would they be doing at Ocean Beach? Their activities were usually limited to Chinatown.

Isobel growled with frustration. Captivity was irritating. Clenching her teeth, she gathered her failing strength, and applied herself to escape. As she wrestled her way onto her side, she puzzled over the reaction that Riot's name had evoked in her captors. If she were to put a name to it, she would call it fear. But if they were tong members, why would they fear Atticus Riot? Hatchet men had chopped off his partner's head, and nearly killed Riot in the process.

"Forget the clay," she rasped. "I don't even know what a brick is yet."

Riot had not elaborated on the murder; he had avoid-ed the details. But then neither had she asked.

How little she knew of the man. And how she ached to find out more. But Isobel couldn't even assure *herself* that she wouldn't bolt like the figurative fish he feared. He had a right to be cautious. The last thing on earth she wanted to do was hurt Atticus Riot. And her dying would certainly do that.

On her knees now, with her arms wrenched behind her back, she felt triumphant. She was upright. Again. This was not the first time in the previous hours (days?) that she had struggled to this position.

Isobel leaned carefully to the side. It hurt her bruised stomach, and she swayed like a strand of grass in the wind, trying to control her descent with abused muscles, until she felt the tip of the rod catch on the dirt.

Taking a breath, she flexed every aching muscle in her body. All she needed to do was loosen *one* strand, and the rest would follow. That was her hope, at any rate.

She rested there for a time, catching her breath, letting her weight be supported by the rod behind her elbows. It was uncomfortable, but so was lying on her stomach.

Bracing herself, Isobel tensed, and with abdominal muscles feeling like tenderized meat, threw all her weight to the side. The action jammed the end of the rod into the dirt. It caught for a moment, slipped, and Isobel fell forward, landing on her stomach, and then her chin. She bit back a groan, and lay panting against the coarse sack over her head.

As children, she and Lotario had tried to follow their older brothers everywhere. Merrik and Vicilia were particularly plagued. And in their efforts to keep the twins at home, the brothers had taken to tying them up whenever they were ready to sneak out. As a result, Lotario and Isobel had learned to escape almost everything. Eventually.

Isobel wrestled herself onto her knees once again. Her bladder was near to bursting, and if this attempt failed, she was not keen on lying in her own urine.

"*Once more unto the breach, dear friends, once more,*" she muttered.

This time Isobel lifted off with her knees, performing a little hop, before throwing herself to the side. The rod gave, and she hit the dirt hard, head and shoulder banging against the ground. Dazed, she rolled onto her back, and nearly shouted with joy. The rod between her back and elbows had been pushed from the ropes.

Working quickly, Isobel slipped her bound wrists around her tied ankles, and whimpered as the blood rushed back into her arms. Her fingers were numb, but her hands were in front of her. She yanked the sack from her head.

Removing the bag didn't improve her view. It was still dark. But light seeped from a crack under the door. Dim, yet bright compared to a bag over the head. As she applied her teeth to the ropes around her wrists, she gazed around the dank room. It was a root cellar; an empty one, or so she thought at first. Before she saw a lump by the far wall.

The strange smell was not rotting potatoes.

Grimacing, she looked away, and focused on her bonds. When the ropes dropped to the ground, blood rushed to her limbs, sending tingling needles racing down her arms and legs. Isobel tried to stand, but she stumbled. Her feet were asleep. She braced herself on a wall, and pulled herself up on the rough stones. Arms and legs trembling, she took turns stomping each foot, trying to restore feeling.

When her feet were more reliable, she picked up the rod. It appeared as if it had served as a broom handle in another life. She used it now as a cane to shuffle over to the door.

There was no handle, no lock. It was likely barred from the outside. Still, she pushed it—one never knew. But the door did not budge. Escape was never so simple.

Isobel pressed an ear against the thick wood. She listened for longer than was necessary, avoiding the inevitable. She was all too conscious of the lump in the corner. Her fingers tightened around the broom handle, as thoughts and strategies flew through her mind, mapping each possible outcome and the probability of survival.

All was silent. Not a peep reached her ears. Steeling herself, she turned towards that lump, and hobbled over to it. Even without the faint light seeping from under the door, she knew what she'd find. The lump was wrapped in a tarp, and the shape was suggestive. She crouched, and the world swayed. Isobel caught herself.

When the walls stopped heaving, she moved the folds aside, knowing what she'd find. A corpse. Once a man; now cold flesh. Rigor mortis was well and set in. He had longish hair and square features, a mustache, and thick sideburns. He had a broad chest, and a stocky build. But the skin looked stretched, like a shrunken skull she'd once seen at a carnival.

With a sigh, she moved to the far corner to relieve the pressure on her bladder, hoping her captors wouldn't decide to walk in on her. When she was through, she moved back to her cellmate, and crouched by his head. Light from beneath the door offered a view of the gruesome wound to his scalp.

Squinting, she parted the hair, and probed the wound with numb fingers. The gash was long, a groove that bit into his skull. It was deeper towards the crown of his head. This was not a wound caused by a hoof, but by a cleaver-like weapon or a hatchet.

Isobel picked up the mixture of dirt and sand on the ground, and washed her hands. She turned to the man's pockets. No revolver, but there was a clasp knife, billfold, and a token. She slipped the knife into her own pocket, and opened the billfold.

Isobel blinked. It was full of cash. One hundred dollars to be exact. Whoever these people were, they were not thieves. His calling card was inside as well: Mr. Lincoln Howe.

She looked to her companion. "Now why would they leave all your information in your pockets?" she whispered. He did not answer. What were her captors planning to do with the body?

Isobel slipped one of the calling cards into a pocket, and added the cash as well. It wasn't as if *he* needed it any longer. The print on the token was too small to read in the dim light, so she added that to her growing inventory.

Further searching of the body revealed very little, save that his clothes were tailored and his shoes expensive. From a mushroomed ear, crooked nose, and the scarring on his knuckles, she surmised that he was a pugilist.

What would a pugilist be doing on the dunes at night, and why was he killed with a knife—a hatchet or cleaver, she corrected—and then brought here (wherever *here* might be) along with herself?

Isobel sat back on her hunches, and promptly fell on her backside. Her legs were shaky, and her muscles still cramped. She cursed under her breath, and climbed slowly to her feet. As she paced the perimeter of the cellar, trying to work out the kinks, she swung her broom handle, testing its weight. She could fashion a slungshot out of the rope. She had a knife, too. But the memory of being held down face first in the sand was all too recent. All her struggling had been useless.

She could attack directly... or she could bide her time and use her wits like a good 'possum. As attractive as the first option was, there were too many unknown variables. How many men were there? Where was she? And even if she managed to get past the men at the door, how many more would she face, and how far would she have to run, to escape them all?

It would have to be wits, then. Isobel stopped, and looked at the discarded rope. All she needed now was to figure out how to get back *into* her bonds.

13

Catch and Release

THE DOOR OPENED, AND Isobel fought down an urge to bolt. She was prone, lying on her stomach, head in a bag, with wrists bound behind her back. Only there was one difference. A quick tug on a strand of rope, and the entire thing would unravel. She hoped her captors wouldn't notice her adjustments.

Rather than cut a small hole in her hood, she had taken the coarse sack and rubbed the fabric against brick until it thinned. Now she could watch through a gauzy layer as a pair of feet approached. They weren't covered in boots, but in slippers.

"Scream, and you die," said a heavily accented voice. The man stepped behind her, and as casually as lifting a sack of potatoes, he wrenched her off the ground and slung her over a shoulder. The pressure on her bruised stomach nearly made her retch. Spots danced in her vision, and she fought against the wave of nausea, squirming in pain on his shoulder.

Two others moved into the room. One wore slippers, the other boots. She heard a grunt, and shuffling. The man carrying her walked out of the room. Her view was limited to a silk tunic, but she could feel his thick queue brush against her shoulder with every step.

Brick steps passed under her line of sight. A narrow hallway, more steps, and finally carpet. It smelled... rich. Flowers and cologne, tobacco and cigar smoke mingled with the moldy sack over her head. But the hallway didn't last long. Another door opened, and a blast of cold ocean air hit her. And darkness. A fleeting feeling of freedom gripped her, and she bit back an urge to struggle, to tug on the rope that would unravel her bonds, and take her chances here.

Isobel tensed, but before she could give into fear, she was tossed onto a hard wooden surface that groaned. It felt hollow. She heard the stamp of a hoof, the shift of rigging, and felt the floor give as her stiff companion was laid beside her. She was in a wagon bed.

Through thin fabric, she tried to study her surroundings, but the night was dark and foggy, and she could see next to nothing. The wagon sagged, slippered feet crouched beside her, and a tarp was thrown over her body. The wagon jostled forward.

Isobel began counting, softly to herself, keeping track of turns and curves, of bumps in the road, and committing them to memory. Sooner or later they'd leave the wagon, and she would be marched off to some lonely spot to die. She needed to know her way back.

The wagon slowed, but did not stop. The tarp was ripped away, and a strong hand grabbed her by the hair through the cloth over her head. She could make out a large, thick face, with narrow eyes gleaming in the dark.

"The horse you look for is tied to tree. Your things are in bags," the voice said. "You leave. You forget. You tell *Din Gau*—Atticus Riot—nothing, or *chun hung* will be plastered on all walls with your names. You die; he dies."

Before the words had fully settled, the ropes behind her back were sliced, and she was tossed from the moving wagon. She hit the hard-packed dirt, bounced once, and rolled far too many feet before she stopped.

She gasped for air, but her lungs would not fill. So she relaxed and waited, and when the shock had finally receded, she sucked in a breath. Isobel wrestled free of her tattered bonds, and yanked loose the rope around her ankles. She tugged the sack off her head, and hopped up, ready to give chase.

But the wagon was already out of sight, its trembling wheels echoing in the night. Isobel spun, searching her surroundings. Trees, a wide dirt road, plants—Golden Gate Park? A horse stood calmly near a tree with its reins tossed over a branch. She buttoned her coat over her gaping shirt, and limped over to him. It was hard to put a color to the horse in the dark, but the stripe down his nose fit a familiar description.

"Wilson?"

The horse's ears angled forward. She put a hand to his nose, and pressed her forehead gratefully against his. Isobel took a shuddering breath, and briefly considered climbing into the saddle to give chase. But fear (and bruises) shook her body.

Swallowing, Isobel put her foot in the stirrup, and pulled herself onto the saddle. Feeling sick, she bent over the saddle horn, clutched the horse's mane, and prayed the world would stop spinning. When the darkness stilled, she nudged the horse with her heels, and plodded slowly in the opposite direction of the wagon.

14

Night Terrors

A GIRL RAN, BLACK hair floating like a ribbon behind her, in and out of pools of light and dark. Her bare feet pattered in frantic flight on wooden planks. But she was like a bird with clipped wings, unable to leave the ground.

It was dark with fog and smoke, and shadows deeper than any dream. The paper lanterns felt her passage with a stir of air, but their flicker did not illuminate her path. A plank gave way—a rot, like the room she had fled. Her toe caught, and she tripped. Rough splinters dug into her knees.

Shouts followed her, bouncing through the murk and maze of alleyways. Her heart quickened. She scrambled forward to her feet. And ran.

920. The foreign numbers burned in her mind. *920.* She could taste their shapes on her swollen lips. *920.* She would find her wings there.

A shadow disturbed the mist, and she turned sharply, skidding on planks, lost in the rotting maze of her prison.

A door opened, and she flew into the dark portal. It shut.

"You are safe now, child," a voice whispered in her ear. She had heard that voice before.

Slowly, light from a red lantern crept into the dank room. It smelled like a slaughter house. Of blood, and bowels, and fear. The girl stood, shivering. Frozen. The lantern was not red from paper; it dripped blood. And instead of a rectangle, it was the head of an old man with a white beard that had turned grim. The head hung in the dank room, swaying back and forth with a creak. Slowly the bloody light cast a shadow on another man—a faceless man. He held a butcher's knife.

The man stepped forward, and the girl stepped back. A macabre sort of dance, until her back pressed against a wall that dripped with human waste. The man's face passed into the red light, and Atticus Riot smiled like a sickly wolf.

Tap, tap, tap.

The sound woke Riot from a worn nightmare. His arm flew out and fingers curled around a familiar weight. With a click he held his revolver close, trying to make sense of shadow and smoldering cinders.

A volley of heartbeats drummed against his ears. His hand trembled, and he swallowed down bile in his throat, as he listened for the *tap, tap, tapping*. The sound did not come again; instead, he heard a soft scraping.

Quick as a snake he flung the covers free, and slipped to the window. With a finger he flicked the curtain aside. A shadow fiddled outside the glass. A blade slipped through the crack between window and sill, and nudged the lock aside.

The latch moved.

Riot wrenched the window up, and pressed round steel to a forehead. The cat-burglar yelped, lost a precarious perch, and slipped. Two hands latched onto the sill like a cat's claws on wood. A cap flew off, fluttering three stories into darkness.

"Bel?" Relief transformed her name into a whispered prayer.

The woman in question looked up, annoyance flashing across her eyes. "Are there any other women who'd climb into your window at night?"

He stared at her, mind reeling from the aftereffects of his dream.

"Are you going to pull the trigger?" she asked.

Riot could hear her kicking feet as she tried to find purchase. With a muttered oath he uncocked his revolver, reached over and out, and hauled the woman into his bedroom by her coat. She flopped onto the floor.

"You're going to break your neck." His words came out like a growl.

"Haven't yet," she shot back. Isobel sounded winded, and she seemed disinclined to pick herself up off the floor.

"Is something a matter?" he glanced out the window.

"No." Isobel slapped a hand on the sill, and pulled herself upright. "I had a time dodging Miss Dupree and her gentleman callers though."

Riot closed the window and curtains, and turned to his cat-burglar. "Who knew a resident prostitute would keep crime to a minimum. Were you planning on stealing my pocket watch?"

"No. Your virginity."

The comment caught him off guard, like so many other things about her. Isobel Kingston unbalanced him, constantly. And that was the last thing he needed right now.

He started to holster his weapon, and realized he was wearing a thin white union suit. But only just. The upper half hung around his waist, and he was drenched in cold sweat. Riot shivered, and carefully set down his revolver on a side-table. He walked over to the washbasin, dipped his hands in cold water, and drenched his face. The water cleared his mind.

After he had slipped his arms through the underwear and tugged on his trousers, he turned to find Isobel holding out a glass of brandy for him. She had one of her own, and a thoughtful kind of look in her eyes. As if she were plotting her next move in chess.

He accepted her offering.

"You look the worse for wear, Riot."

"Finding an intruder at one's window does that to a man." He looked at her for the first time—with sharp eyes and a clear mind. Her peacoat was buttoned up to her neck, and she wore kidskin gloves. She looked dingy and worn, as if she'd been doing hard labor all day.

"You don't look much better yourself," he noted.

"Cold steel to the head will do that to a woman." Glasses clinked, and they both took a fortifying drink, nearly downing them in one. Warmth flooded his veins, chasing away his night terrors.

"Are you fortifying yourself with drink to steal my virginity?" he asked.

She swirled the brandy in its glass. "I think I'd like to be sober for that."

"Someone beat you by a few decades," he said dryly.

"There goes that plan." She took another draught, and when she moved to pour another, he threaded spectacles over his ears. She came into sharp focus, and he noted the vibrations in her brandy as she brought it to her lips. She was trembling.

Riot stepped over to her. "Where have you been?"

"I was looking for a horse," she said casually.

"Wilson."

Her eyes narrowed. "Were you looking for me?"

"You were supposed to spend the day with Lotario."

"So you followed my trail?" Her voice was hoarse. "That's an annoying habit, you know."

"We were worried."

"Lotario came with you?" There was something close to panic in her voice, but then she caught herself. "How far did the trail take you?"

"To Ocean Beach. There appeared to have been a struggle on the dunes, but the storm erased the trail. I was worried you were involved."

She took a small sip, and casually turned, placing the glass on the sideboard. With her back to him, she said, "I'm sorry I missed it. Whatever happened might have made for a good story. The recovery of a missing horse is hardly newsworthy."

Riot noticed she did not mention Sinclair's missing corpse. "What happened, Bel?" His words were soft, a mere brush of a deep purr on an uneasy night.

"Why do you think something's wrong?"

"Did you have another reason for tapping on my window at," he glanced at the mantle clock, "three in the morning?"

She turned to face him. "I couldn't sleep."

"Couldn't you?" He reached out, and gently gripped her wrist. Her whole body was shaking.

"A question was plaguing my mind," she said.

"What question was that?"

"You asked me what I thought of your beard, but I never asked what you thought of my kiss."

Another comment to throw him off track. He thought of cornering this elusive woman. He ached to corner her. To demand a direct answer and play his cards, but that, he knew, would be a sure fire way to never set eyes on her again. Isobel Kingston was a feral, wild thing, and the only way to befriend a creature like that was to let her come to him.

He rubbed a hand over his trim beard. "I was drowning at the time."

She smirked. "You were not."

"Close enough."

"So how was it?"

His own pulse quickened in memory. She had not yet taken her wrist away, but neither had she stepped forward, nor back. She was on the verge of one or the other, and while he could play along with her game and take her bait, Riot was more concerned with her condition than with his own lust. She was clearly frightened.

"Are you going to tell me what force drove you up the side of a house to my bedroom window?"

"I asked first."

"I'm hammering out the rules of the game, Bel."

"Well, I thank you kindly for the drink, Mr. Riot." Her eyes strayed to his chest, to exposed flesh, and the swath of dark hair. Before he knew it, Isobel removed her hand from his, and slipped out the window. He rushed to the sill, and watched her scramble down the drain pipe.

"Bel," he hissed.

She stopped, and looked up. Eyes wide, and face pale.

"Your kiss breathed life back into me."

"That's what I was afraid of," she called back in a whisper. She touched ground, and the fog swallowed her.

❖

"Dammit," he swore. She was not escaping that easily. He turned, and raced out of his room. He ran down the stairs on bare feet. When he hit the first floor, he skidded on the carpet runner, scrunching it and sliding halfway down the hall before he shot out the front door. The air was wet and cold, and it cut to the bone as he ran down the steps.

A slim figure walked under muted lamplight.

He raced to catch her. She glanced over her shoulder, and seemed about to bolt. But then stopped. "You've ruined my dramatic exit," she said.

"I'm hoping you won't attempt another."

"Was it that bad?"

"Worrying, more like."

Water dripped from his hair onto his face, clouding his spectacles, and leaving his beard glistening in the half-light. Blind from the soft drizzle, he removed his spectacles and wiped them hastily on wet linen. When he returned them to his face, the lenses were streaked.

Isobel's gaze traveled from his bare feet, to the suspenders hanging around his waist, and finally to his soaked union suit. Frowning, she opened her umbrella and held it over his head. "I'm not good at... *this*," she blurted out.

He shivered slightly. "You're holding the umbrella just fine."

His comment didn't lessen her frown. The gas lamp at the corner was only a dim beacon in the cold night, and he wished he could see her eyes better.

"I mean sharing," Isobel explained. "Things in my life."

"There's a hot bath and warm food waiting for you

inside. That's all, Bel. You don't have to tell me a thing."

She took a step closer, and looked up into his eyes. He could feel the heat of her body, see her breath misting in the cool night. The umbrella handle was the only thing that separated them.

"What does *din gau* mean?" she asked.

The question was like a kick to his stomach. He took a step back. His hand jerked towards where his revolver should have been. He glanced around the empty street, feeling exposed without it.

"Where did you hear that name?" It was a demand, not a question.

Isobel raised her brows. "I didn't say it was a name."

He clenched his jaw. "What have you gotten yourself into?" He gripped her hand, fingers curling around the umbrella handle over her own. But there was no gentleness. He held it like a man clutched a lifeline, his knuckles stark in the night.

"It appears I'm not the only one who has difficulty sharing."

"What happened?" It was a plea.

"I'm fine, Riot." Her voice was soft. "It's over now." He didn't believe her for a second.

Riot forced himself to relax, to loosen his hold, to breathe. "Stay with me tonight."

"Oh, now that's low."

"You were more than eager the other day," he said.

"You just want to keep an eye on me."

"And my arms around you." He slipped his finger under her glove, and traced her wrist. She winced with pain, and pulled away, but not before he felt the raw patch of flesh circling her wrist.

Isobel made an exasperated sound. "That's precisely

what I mean. You're a scoundrel. You did that on purpose."

"I'm only employing your own tactics."

"What does *din gau* mean?" she repeated. "Why do the Chinese call you that?"

He stood frozen. His tongue heavy, and his throat parched. Words got stuck in his throat, as she waited, eyes searching his own in the dark. Flashes of light burst in his mind. Screams. Guns. And blood.

A touch brought him back to the present. There was concern in her eyes, and her lips were moving, but he barely heard her words. "…you're the last man on earth I want to hurt, Riot. I'm sorry. I shouldn't have asked. I made a mistake coming here." She withdrew her hand, leaving him holding the umbrella. "I left Wilson in your yard. Can you see him stabled, and returned to Sinclair?"

She didn't wait for an answer, and as she turned to leave, Riot closed his eyes. He hadn't answered, because he didn't have one to give her.

No, you're hiding from the answer, Ravenwood corrected.

15

Bricks Without Clay

Wednesday, July 8, 1896

920 SACRAMENTO SAT ON a hill which would strain the hardiest of legs. As Riot climbed the steps, he noted a man lurking in an archway across the street. A common sight around the Presbyterian Mission home. Brick walls protected its runaway slave girls from the outside world as sure as the women who ran the mission.

Riot banged the knocker against its plate. A small grate opened in the door, and an eye peeked through. Caution was always required at the mission.

"Atticus Riot for Miss Culbertson."

The eye shifted to either side of him before the door opened. A black-haired girl of fifteen with bright eyes welcomed him. He removed his hat and stepped inside the front hall, offering a traditional bow in return to hers.

"You are growing like a rose, Miss Ling."

She smiled. "A weed or hay is the proper term, Mr. Riot."

"It hardly suits you."

"A rose has thorns; hay is useful."

"Then you're definitely hay."

The girl beamed, and gripped his hands.

"How are you?" he asked, squeezing her hands gently.

"I'm well. And you need rest, Mr. Riot. You always need rest."

"I'll have plenty of time for that when I'm in the grave."

She paled. "Spirits do not always rest easy."

"I'm hoping to be a lethargic one."

Ling laughed, and hugged him briefly. It was a beautiful sound, that laughter. She had come a long way since he first met her.

"Then your lazy spirit can wait here. I will tell Miss Culberston." She left him in the front hall, and walked off on light feet. Peaceful sounds of children playing, soft singing, and waves of conversation in both English and Cantonese drifted down the halls.

A few minutes later, Ling returned with Miss Donaldina Cameron.

"Atticus." She shook his hand heartily.

"Good to see you, Dolly. I apologize for calling so early."

Donaldina waved a dismissive hand. "There's no such thing as early here."

In her late twenties, Donaldina was a force to be reckoned with. He had escorted this woman into dark dens, then watched her charge through windows and climb through skylights in pursuit of a slave girl. She was a kind gentlewoman who had arrived at the mission a year earlier as the sewing teacher, and quickly dived headfirst into Chinatown rescues.

Riot looked up into her eyes. "How are you doing?"

"As sleep-deprived as you appear. Margaret is in her office."

"There's a fellow across the way with his eye on the home."

"Yes, we know. We had a new arrival a few days ago. It feels like the mission is under assault of late. The police came by with a writ of *habeas corpus*. We had to hide the woman under a sack of rice in the basement. I suspect that fellow is hoping she'll look out a window."

As she spoke, he followed her to the office. A rail-thin, middle-aged woman sat behind the desk. Miss Culberston smiled in greeting. But it quickly fell. "You do not have the look of a man bearing good news, Mr. Riot." Her voice was clear and crisp, and as matter-of-fact as they came.

"I'm afraid not."

"Would you like tea or coffee?" Donaldina asked.

"No, thank you."

She reached for a waiting tray, and poured two cups, handing one to Miss Culberston.

"I haven't had a chance to look at the newspapers. Has there been another murder?" Miss Culberston asked.

He produced a sketch of the most recent victim, and both women leaned in to study it with hard eyes, as if committing the nameless girl's face to memory, branding it on their hearts so the girl might live on in some form or another.

"Ling, please show this drawing to the others," Miss Culberston instructed. "See if any of them recognize her."

Ling looked at the sketch, and hurried off.

When she was out of earshot, Riot continued, "Last

night, when I mentioned 920, a girl told me that the women here eat their shame. She referred to you here as *Fahn Quai*—white devil."

Miss Culberston nodded. "I've heard a similar story before. Their handlers tell them that we drink their blood and eat their organs. They make us out to be evil spirits."

"Dolly, you mentioned that you feel like the mission is under assault of late. Why is that?" Riot asked.

Miss Culberston glanced at Donaldina, and the two seemed to hold a silent conversation. Miss Culberston opened a drawer, and slid a slip of paper across the desk. "This note was delivered two days ago, on the heels of our newest arrival."

It was a hastily scribbled note from a slave girl in need of rescue. It was rare for the girls themselves to write a note. Pleas for help were usually written and delivered by a sympathetic client, with instructions on how to find the den.

"I left at once," Donaldina said.

"Without an escort?"

"There wasn't time." There rarely was. She waved off his concern. "The door to the room was open, and when I rushed inside, I found it empty. Very nearly. An effigy of me was hanging from a beam. There was a dagger in its heart."

Riot frowned. "Miss Culbertson has been rescuing women and girls for years. Why now?"

Miss Culberston cleared her throat. There was a twinkle in her eyes. "It's the first time they've encountered a fearless Scotswoman, with a stubborn streak as hard as steel and the vigor of youth."

"I think the steel runs through her spine," Riot said.

Donaldina made an exasperated noise. "If the dynamite they planted outside the building when I first arrived didn't deter me, a straw woman dressed in doll's clothes won't either. But Margaret has the right of it. We've been pressing the slave dens hard of late. The newspapers are even starting to take notice."

"There may be another reason for the trap," he mused.

Both women waited, expectantly.

"The newspapers are pointing fingers at the tongs for the murders. But barring an obscure ritual, it doesn't seem likely that the tongs are to blame. Why draw attention to themselves? It'd be a simpler task to dispose of a corpse in a less public place."

"What are you implying?" Miss Culberston asked.

"Maybe the tongs have started believing their own rumors. Maybe the tong threat had to do with these murders."

"You think the tongs might actually believe that we're slaughtering girls?" Donaldina asked. Indignation warred with repulsion in her eyes.

Riot waited, and slowly the idea took shape in their minds.

"There *is* a lot of superstition in the Quarter," Miss Culberston said. "Hatchet men eat the meat of a wild cat before an assassination or a fight. They think it will imbue them with the cat's powers."

Riot nodded. "And they pay well for that meat. Have your informants turned up anything?"

"Not a whisper," Miss Culberston said.

"Do you find that unusual?"

Donaldina took a sip of her tea. "Last month a hatchet man charged up a stairwell and shot a slave girl in the mouth for accidentally tossing water on him from an upstairs window. I heard of that through the police. The tongs are a blight on Chinatown, and death is a constant here. What is another nameless girl without family or clan?"

"*The green reed which bends in the wind is stronger than the mighty oak which breaks in a storm,*" he recited.

"Eloquent as always, Mr. Riot," Miss Culberston said with a smile. "It's the philosophy of survival for a populace that live in constant fear of tongs, white hoodlums, and police. What I do find odd is the lack of skirmishes. The shooting of that slave girl last month triggered a cascade of fighting between tongs, but these murders haven't caused a ripple."

A piece of the puzzle clicked into place. "These murders aren't the only thing that doesn't cause a stir," he realized.

Donaldina's eyes widened a fraction. "A war is never triggered when a girl runs to a mission."

Riot nodded. And Miss Culberston looked across her desk at him. "Do you really think the missions are involved in some way?" she asked.

"I don't know," he said. "Do you keep a list of your contributors and mission workers?"

"I do, but these are good Christian people, Mr. Riot," Miss Culberston said. "I can't imagine any of them doing something like this. Besides, it would require a knowledge of Chinatown that most don't possess."

"There's a mind—as twisted as it may be—behind this, that's for certain. These murders are precise, ritualistic in nature. We have to explore all avenues."

Zephaniah Ravenwood sat in his consultation room. His customary chair was aimed at the fireplace. His long fingers were steepled, and the embers gave his white hair a fiendish glow. He looked like a gargoyle ready to spring on some hapless victim.

Riot hung up his hat and coat, and stopped to study a map that was spread on the desk. Red dots marked where each girl had been found floating in the bay. Small, neat notations accompanied each mark, along with dates, tide tables, and currents. How many others had been swept out the Golden Gate?

He tried not to think of that. But then maybe that was the killer's (or killers') intent. The killer *wanted* the children found.

The police assumed that the girls were wrapped in an oilskin tarp for transportation—for ease of disposal. But maybe the reason was twofold. The tarp could also serve as a barrier between scavengers and the killer's gruesome work, a way for him to preserve his masterpiece.

Riot lowered himself into the second chair, and let his head fall back. He felt drained, not only physically, but mentally. An endless stream of hopeless eyes and young faces looked at him from the darkness behind his lids.

He opened his eyes, and squinted towards the window. Sunlight shone through a gap in the curtains. Riot blinked, and stirred. Pain shot up his neck. He grimaced as he adjusted his spectacles. He thought he had only closed his eyes for a moment, but he must have fallen asleep.

The feeling of being watched brought him around. Ravenwood's eyes glittered from across the small table. Waiting.

"Productive night?" asked the man.

Riot rubbed at the kink in his neck. "Not especially."

"There was something." Ravenwood's eyes missed nothing.

"Most of the girls I question are either fearful, silent, or full of anger. But last night a girl told me that the white women in the missions eat their shame." Riot pulled out his deck of cards and began squaring their edges. "So I paid a visit to a madam by the name of Siu Lui—White Blossom—a woman who runs a brothel in the Quarter."

"Why her? Why now?" Ravenwood demanded.

Riot shuffled his deck, considering how best to answer.

"Pray tell me it wasn't simply due to the inclusion of 'white' in her name?" Ravenwood drawled.

Riot smirked, and shot half his cards to the other hand, making a perfect fluttering bridge of cards. "Maybe so."

Ravenwood's eyes narrowed. "She's an acquaintance of yours." It was not a question, but an observation.

"Something like that."

Ravenwood grunted, and sat back. Riot was sure his partner had his own opinion of their relationship. But correcting the man's assumption would only lead to questions that Riot wasn't willing to answer. They might be partners, but that didn't mean Ravenwood needed to be privy to every intimate detail of his past.

"She has her fingers everywhere in the city."

"Why did you wait so long?" Ravenwood demanded.

"Because she has strong ties with the tongs."

"Ah, you were worried she'd inform them of your search, and the tongs would bar you from their dens."

Riot nodded. "And truth be told, she's a woman to be avoided."

"I find that true of most members of the *gentler* sex." He twisted the word into a sardonic bite. "What made you go to her now?"

"I'm at a loss," Riot admitted. "Call it the act of a

desperate man. I'm not sure there's any use in questioning more slave girls. It's gotten us nowhere."

"We're dredging deep waters, my boy. It will be muddy, but our efforts will eventually turn up something." Ravenwood waved a languid hand in dismissal. "Was this risk of yours worth the reward?"

"When I mentioned the rumor, she neither confirmed nor denied it."

"Is that suggestive?"

Riot frowned at his deck of cards. "She said the most convincing lies are rooted in truth."

"Ah, I see." Ravenwood scowled at the fireplace. "What did *you* make of her words?"

"She could have been trying to throw me off track. It's an old rumor, and as enemies of the tongs, the missions are a convenient scapegoat."

"Then you think she was protecting the tongs?"

"It occurred to me that a sacrifice of a few might keep the majority cowed."

"An accusation of the newspapers," Ravenwood reminded. "That one of the tongs is killing a few select girls to keep the others in line. Do you believe it?"

"I don't know," admitted Riot. "Handlers have been known to beat a slave girl to death in front of her crib mates after an attempted escape—an example to the others of what will happen if they run."

"The key being 'in front of the other girls'."

Riot acknowledged the observation with a dip of the chin and a neat shuffle of cards. "I'm not even sure the girls I questioned were aware of the murders. None of them recognized the sketches I showed them."

"That they admitted," Ravenwood reminded. "But I think you'd know."

Riot spun a card on his finger. "I think you put too much faith in my intuition."

"You're a gambler, my boy. You wager gold on that very same intuition; I wager lives."

Riot frowned at the man. Ravenwood valued Riot's uncanny ability to read people. He had seen something in a young cocky gambler twenty years ago, and had been convinced a wild, unrestrained gunfighter would make a fine detective. After twenty years, Riot still wasn't convinced.

Ravenwood sat back. "I've been pondering the significance of thighs."

"I enjoy a more hands-on approach."

Ravenwood scowled. "I'm sure you will appreciate the subject, then. In biblical terms the upper thighs often refer to the sexual organs due to close proximity. The cuts on the victims—the precision of the wounds, the hollowing out of the female organs—all point to an obsession."

"It's also perfect tinder for the 'white women' rumor."

"Which leaves a question that begs answering: which came first?"

"According to Miss Culberston that rumor has been around for a long while."

"Why assume that the murderer hasn't been butchering girls for an equal amount of time?" Ravenwood asked.

Riot frowned. "That's a long time, and a lot of bodies. I can't believe that none of them would have been discovered before now." It made him sick to say it out loud.

Ravenwood clucked his tongue. "Perhaps our killer— or killers—have tired of secrecy, and desire infamy. Or something may have changed in the murderer's life—a change of environment, a death, an illness."

"We're back to our needle in a haystack."

"Do you think the missions are involved in this?" Ravenwood asked.

"I hadn't considered the possibility before the girl mentioned it." Riot idly began rearranging his cards, following the edges with sensitive fingertips, memorizing, counting—an old pastime of a near-sighted boy. "But now that the idea is there, I can't get it out of my head. That's why I paid a visit to the missions before coming here." He squared his deck, and handed over a neat slip of paper. "Miss Culberston supplied a list of backers for various missions and charities in San Francisco."

Ravenwood accepted the offer, and perused it with a quick eye. "Did anything at the missions strike you as odd?"

"Aside from the fact that the missions even need to be there—no. The superintendents I questioned mentioned that there seemed to be fewer girls seeking refuge of late."

Ravenwood absorbed this information silently. After committing the names to memory, he set the list aside. "I spoke with the Consul General yesterday evening. There hasn't been a tong assassination in connection with any of these murders. I believe we can discount this being the work of rival tongs. If these girls were being abducted by a resident of the Quarter, the tongs would handle it themselves or turn it over to their attorneys."

"I thought the same," Riot admitted. "One thing that strikes me is that the tongs are accustomed to girls running to the missions."

"Yes?"

"It's the perfect cover for an enterprising murderer."

Ravenwood's eyes glittered with pride. "It is, isn't it?"

Riot slipped his deck into his pocket. "You know those cuts…"

Ravenwood arched a sharp brow.

"They remind me of a *bagua.*"

His partner stared at him blankly.

"The little red octagons that the Chinese hang over doorways. They usually have mirrors in the center. They're connected to Taosim."

"The slanted cuts and the hollowed out abdomen," Ravenwood realized. "Is there a significance to the position of the cuts and the *bagua*?"

"I intend to ask the Consul." San Francisco boiled with anti-Chinese sentiment, and the Consul General had heard too many cries of '*The Chinese Must Go!*' to think the newspapers' habit of lumping tong criminal activities with the Six Companies wouldn't stir up trouble. Since the police could hardly be trusted where slave girls were concerned, he had hired Ravenwood Agency to investigate the murders quietly.

"I'll speak with him again tonight, and inquire after the *bagua* for you," Ravenwood said. "I'd like you to sniff around the customs house and quarantine station on Angel Island."

"Why?" asked Riot.

"I'm not convinced the murdered girls ever set foot on American soil."

"What do you mean?"

"The custom agents are accepting bribes."

Riot looked at the man. "Do you have proof?"

"No," said Ravenwood. "It's a logical assumption."

"Logic tells me that the majority of politicians in San Francisco are corrupt, but it doesn't do me a lick of good."

Ravenwood looked at him over the tips of his fingers. "It's a starting point."

"A very *wide* starting point."

"It's far more focused than you imagine." Cryptic as ever.

"Have you narrowed down the selection?" Riot asked.

"Of course." Ravenwood's gaze flicked to the ceiling. It wasn't quite an eye roll, but it was close. "One agent is deep in his drink; another has betrayed signs of an opium addiction; and a third sports a pocket watch that you would envy."

Riot smirked. "But not you."

"Never." Ravenwood took out his own watch, and checked the time. "I do admire a timepiece that performs its function, however." He wound it methodically and clicked it shut. Riot knew, even before he spoke, that his partner had come to a decision. "I'd like you to see if you can find a connection between the missions, the customs office, and steamer ships."

"Before or after I sleep?"

Ravenwood looked sharply at him. "You've slept, my boy. I was here."

"Of course," he muttered. Ravenwood did not believe in sleep… or food.

Ravenwood stood, and reached for his silver-knobbed walking stick. He rarely carried a revolver, but he was never without the heavy stick.

"Where are you off to?" Riot asked.

"There may be another possibility."

"I'd say there's a whole city full of possibilities," Riot said dryly.

"I'll tell you when I know more."

Waves of carbolic acid assaulted Riot's senses, sharp and searing. He grimaced, and pressed on, walking down the narrow steamer ship passageway.

Tim inhaled the fumes, and beamed. "This brings back memories."

Riot glanced at the impish man with the eternal spring in his step. He wondered how long he had worked as a quarantine officer.

A middle-aged man backed out of a cabin. His blue uniform was crisp, and he held a bucket of disinfectant. Riot doubted the mask over his nose and mouth softened the overpowering smell.

"Mr. Cook?" The man paused at the entrance to the cabin. His eyes held a questioning look. "I'm Atticus Riot. Here on behalf of Ravenwood Agency." He produced a card.

Cook set down his supplies, but not his mask. With his mouth covered, it'd be difficult to read him. But there were so many 'tells' to a person. The tilt of the shoulders, the arch of a brow, the flicker of a lash, or the stillness of fingers.

"What can I do for you gentleman?" Cook asked.

"Do you recognize this girl?" Riot showed him a post-mortem photograph. In death, her face was serene. She looked nearly alive—only asleep. The man studied the photograph for a good many seconds, but in the end he shook his head.

"I may have seen her in passing. There's hundreds of Chinese coming in on every steamer. They all look rather the same, don't they?"

Riot did not answer. He tucked the photograph into his pocket. "What is it that you do here?"

"I disinfect." He nodded to his bucket as if the sharp, noxious fumes billowing around the trio weren't answer enough.

"The cabins?"

"Anywhere I'm needed, but mostly the lower cabins."

"Do you ever come across people still inside their cabins?"

"On occasion," Cook said with a nod. "They'll be asleep—drunk. And some people just don't like crowds, so they wait until most have disembarked. Sometimes they're sick."

"What do you do if they're sick?"

"I report it to my superior officer, and we cart them straight to the quarantine physician."

"Were there any sick on the S.S. *Australia*?"

"I'm not sure."

"Seems like it's a *yes* or a *no* type of answer."

Cook sighed, and started to run a hand over his face, but stopped himself. "The ships run together—like the faces. Am I under investigation?" Concern shone in his eyes. Open and honest. A little too honest for Riot's taste.

"No, not all. We're trying to find out more about the girl in the photograph."

"You might ask Howard."

"And who might that gentleman be?"

"Howard Belmont. He does the same as me. Inspects the cabins and disinfects."

"I'll be sure to speak with him," Riot said. Cook nodded, and started to pick up his things. Riot waited until Cook had his bucket in hand and was headed to the next cabin. "You made a sizable donation to the Society for the Prevention of Cruelty to Children a few months ago."

Cook stopped, and those shoulders tensed. The swath above his mask turned pink. "Yes, I did. Why would you know that?"

"We're thorough. And I think it's notable."

"Well, not as notable as the people who run such organizations. I think it's real noble what those ladies do."

"In regards to the Chinese?"

"No, sir. American children. It's not right, them being abandoned, beaten—what have you."

"It's definitely not right," Riot agreed. "Thank you for your time, Mr. Cook. If you should remember anything, please contact me." He left his card, and left the man to his work.

"What do you think, Tim?"

"I think Zeph gave us a splinter in an ocean sort of task."

Riot's lip twisted ruefully. "Why don't we split up, then."

16

Graft and Pain

Thursday, July 16, 1896

WILLIAM COOK HURRIED FROM the ferry. He had the gait of a man on a mission, and as rushed as he was Cook failed to notice his shadow.

Riot followed at a distance. He wore a bowler, and a silk waistcoat, and people parted for his confident stride. Perhaps it was the leather strap crossing his waistcoat and the telltale signs of a revolver stock.

It was nearly dark when Cook plunged into the Barbary Coast, and entered the first gambling den he came across. Riot watched the saloon for five minutes, before venturing in after. Riot knew every dive on the coast, and almost everyone who worked there. He nodded to the bouncer, and went to the bar, tossing down a nickel. The beer here was watered, and he only pretended to drink while he watched Cook lose badly at Faro. It would, he feared, be a long night.

When the game lost its thrill, Cook disappeared upstairs with a lady, and Riot turned to the bartender. "Is that gentleman a regular here?" He pushed a dollar forward to loosen the man's tongue.

The bartender hesitated over the dollar. "You investigatin' him for adultery?"

Riot shook his head. "Nothing so mundane, Abe. It's more serious in nature."

"You know I don't rat out my customers."

"My only aim is to find out who's murdering children and dumping their bodies in the bay."

Abe frowned. He was a thin, bony fellow, with a pointed chin that he tended to rub. He did so now. Riot didn't mention the race of the girls. There wasn't much sympathy for the Chinese in San Francisco.

"That right?" Abe asked.

"If he's not involved, I'll leave him be," Riot assured.

Abe pushed the dollar back. "I don't care for child murderers. Consider this on the house... not that there's much. But that fellow who just disappeared with Kitty always comes in flush with cash. He makes his rounds, but he's bad at his habit."

"That's plain."

Abe smirked. "The dealers are lucky you shook the habit, A.J."

"I never shook it. I only found more important matters. Does he have a regular woman?"

"Not that I can tell. He likes to sample all the ladies. But I reckon this is his first stop. We get a lot of fellows who are eager to get the gambling rush straight off the ferry."

Riot inclined his head. He knew that thrill, but it

wasn't the quick money, the flutter of cards, the prestige, or thrill of winning that got his blood pumping—it was the challenge of looking into a man's eyes and knowing in his bones when an opponent was bluffing. Riot had discovered that detective work offered far more of a challenge.

After an hour, Cook returned, and Riot resumed his reconnaissance. He trailed the man to two more dens. A quick game of dice, a poor bet on a rigged roulette table, and Cook disappeared into a Sullivan's Alley crib. This struck Riot as odd. Cook hadn't seemed the type of man to visit a crib whore—one of the lowest class of prostitute there was. And what was more, he was out in less than five minutes. Considering the quickness of the visit compared with the length of his stay with the last woman, Riot grew suspicious.

Cook hurried away from the crib, as if seeking to put as much distance between himself and Dupont Street as he could.

Riot eyed the three-story rookery behind the crib. White men stood at either end of the alley. Hired sentries, if he were any judge.

He had a choice to make.

Riot turned towards Cook, and quickened his pace. The quarantine officer was a safer bet. Cook hailed a cab at Jackson, and as the hack slowed to let him inside, Riot stepped up his pace, climbing in after.

"What the—"

"Mr. Cook," Riot said in a friendly manner. As friendly as a purring panther. He pushed up the brim of his hat. "What a coincidence."

Cook made a sudden move, but Riot was quicker, and drew his revolver in one smooth motion. "I wouldn't."

Cook froze, and slowly placed his hand on his thigh.

"You haven't told the hackman where you're headed."

Cook remained tight-lipped, so Riot called out directions for him. Directions to the man's home—to his wife and children. Cook squirmed in his seat.

"You didn't make a donation to the Society for the Prevention of Cruelty to Children. Your wife did," Riot said, as the hack rattled over cobblestones. With his free hand, Riot patted the man's coat, and plucked out a billfold and gun. Keeping one eye on Cook, he rifled through the bills. Riot whistled low. "Five hundred dollars—far from the weekly pay of a quarantine station employee." The cash also confirmed Riot's suspicions. "I watched you go into that crib in Sullivan's Alley. The Quarter loves its trapdoors and passages as much as the Barbary Coast. What tong is bribing you?"

Cook crossed his arms. He looked like a defiant six year-old.

"Mr. Cook." Riot smiled like a shark. "I'm not above telling your wife about Kitty, or about your gambling habit."

"I won't say a thing," Cook said. "I can't. If I say a word there'll be a price on my head, and I'll be gunned down by a highbinder in cold blood."

"Doubtful. Hatchet men don't usually target white men. And it's not like I'm asking you to testify in a court of law." Yet, Riot added silently. "How about you just nod real easy like, if I get near to the target."

Cook nodded.

"Would it be the Hip Yee Tong?" The Temple of United Justice mostly dealt with slavery. A twitch in Cook's bicep confirmed Riot's educated guess even before the man nodded.

"How'd you find me out?"

"Your pocketwatch," Riot answered. "The house you keep. Any number of things. You practically left a trail of bread crumbs for me to follow."

"Everyone takes bribes," Cook spit out. "How else are we supposed to survive. Breathing in the Lord only knows what, day in and day out. I don't have much time for this earth."

"Question is... where you're headed in that afterlife."

Cook sucked in a sharp breath. "We're both gentleman. You... you wouldn't tell my wife? Surely?"

"Wouldn't I?"

"Please."

"That entirely depends on your answers." Riot let his words sink in and his stare burrow deep. Cook closed his eyes, and nodded. "Did you recognize the girl in the photograph?"

"I don't know. She looked familiar, but I'm not sure. I really can't tell Mongolians apart."

"That's all very convenient for you, but it won't help you. Tell me who you *think* she might be."

"The girls... they stay behind—pose as sick—dressed as white women, or even a young man sometimes. All I'm paid to do is say I'm escorting them to the receiving station on the island. But instead of doing that I hand them over to their relatives."

"Relatives?"

Cook shrugged. "They look like kin to me."

"Because 'they all look alike'," Riot quoted dryly.

"That's right. Who am I to keep family apart?"

"Whatever eases your conscience."

"I do as I'm told."

"After you take the money."

"If I didn't take their money, someone else would."

"Who else is involved?"

"My supervisor, Mr. Quiver."

"I see."

It was hard to read Cook in the dark, but Riot could feel him quivering. Not with rage, but the kind of shake that made Riot fear for the man's bladder. "This girl that you may or may not recognize, what did her family look like?"

Cook tapped his finger on his thigh in thought. "Pig-tailed, slanty-eyed, silk blouses."

"Same fellows you get your money from?"

Cook shrugged.

"Well, Mr. Cook, you are a singularly unobservant fellow, and what's more, you've been very uninformative. You haven't told me a thing that I didn't already know." Riot let those words sink into the man's thick skull. "I'm looking forward to meeting your wife."

"Wait now." Cook jerked, and Riot jabbed the barrel of his gun against his ribs. The man froze. "I told you all I know."

"You'd best think harder, because earlier you said that the Chinese girls are sometimes disguised as white women. I think a Chinese man picking up a white girl would draw attention."

Even in the dark, Riot could see the man pale. He licked his lips, and when he spoke, his voice was hoarse. "There's usually a different lady who comes for them. American. But we only do a few like that. It'd raise suspicion otherwise. Most go through the interpreter."

"At the customs station?"

Cook nodded eagerly. "The girls are coached with answers to give to the agents, but some agents just let them right through, as long as they have forged papers."

"As interesting as that is, I'd like to go back to the subject you're trying to avoid: the girls who stay behind in the cabins. Why don't they go through the customs office? Seems easier. Why do some pretend to be sick?"

"I don't know. I figured it was so customs doesn't get suspicious of certain agents."

"The bribes don't always work?"

Cook hesitated. "I don't know."

"How do you know the girls are pretending to be sick?"

"They aren't moving."

"So they're drugged."

"I said they're pretending."

"Sounds like they're drugged to me. Unwilling. That would certainly explain why they don't make it to customs," Riot said with a click of his teeth. "Or maybe too young to memorize the required information?"

"Look, I don't ask questions."

"I imagine not," Riot said.

"I have a family to support."

"And it's far easier to go home to your own daughter and pretend those girls don't exist." As long as Riot walked this earth, he'd never understand men like Cook. "If a white woman is posing as their kin, who carries the unconscious girls?"

"A big chink. He has a long, thick queue. As thick as my wrist."

"With a scar hereabouts?" Riot traced a line from the edge of his lip to his ear.

Cook nodded.

Riot had encountered the man before. A notorious hatchet man known as Big Queue in Hip Yee tong. He sometimes acted as a guard for the House of Joy. White Blossom's brothel.

❖

Painted ladies entertained a room full of men in the House of Joy. The women's eyes sparkled, and their tongues dripped with smooth lies, while the men drank every drop of their act.

White Blossom stood in the center of a knot of men. She had a way about her that made every man feel special, even in a group. A brush of fingertips, a suggestive look, a flattering smile had each man believing he was the only one. It was her gift.

Riot smoothly interjected himself into the group, and wedged himself between two of her admirers, who tried to nudge him away from the object of their desire. Riot didn't budge. He might be on the smaller side of the male sex, but he was wiry and quick, and men often made the mistake of underestimating him.

"We need to talk," he whispered in White Blossom's ear.

She didn't glance at him. "I'm entertaining."

"I'm sure you can excuse yourself."

"I'll call the guards," she warned in an undertone.

"I'll blow my whistle and summon the squad of patrolman waiting outside. Loud or quiet, Siu Lui. It's your pleasure."

He did not have such a squad waiting outside, but Riot could weave a lie as convincing as any madam. She chose quiet, and led the way to her boudoir. She sat down, looking like an irritated feline.

Riot did not sit; he faced her square. "You know something about the latest girl who was murdered."

"Do I?"

"One of your women helped transport her from the

quarantine station. I know you too well to believe you're ignorant of that fact."

She regarded him with serene patience, as if he were an unruly child. Riot forced himself to relax. He took the chair opposite, crossed his legs, and adjusted his spectacles.

The silence was broken by her smile—one tinged with sadness. "I remember how you used to sit and watch a hole as a child," she said. "You'd sit there for hours, as still as a statue, waiting for an animal to poke its head out of its den. I liked to watch you. You were so intent, so focused, as I never could be."

Riot didn't say a word. He listened, and waited, making a conscious effort not to clench his jaw.

"And do you know what galled me the most was the look of utter satisfaction on your face when the animal revealed itself to take a morsel of food from your hand. This isn't one of those times. There is no kindly creature in the hole you're staring at."

"This animal is killing children, Jessie." He used the name he had called her from their childhood. If the sound of it affected her, she hid it well.

Siu Lui shook her head. "Were we any older than they were when I collected cash from my first john, or you pinched your first billfold? All for a scrap of food and one more day of life."

"Somewhere between grass and hay still isn't old enough. No man or woman should end up like those girls."

"I've told you all I can," she said, with an honesty that he had not seen in her since they were children.

"You haven't told me a thing."

"I know you're not a stupid man. You can read more in what someone doesn't say than in all the lies of the world. If I tell you anymore I'll meet the same fate as those girls.

But for you I'll say it plain: look to the missions."

Riot calmly regarded her, waiting for more.

"I remember when you used to smile, too," she said quietly, looking at him from beneath mournful lashes. But it did nothing to humanize her. Siu Lui was surrounded by empty beauty, in a hollow home that was a mirror of her soul.

"Despite what you think of me, I'm not killing those children, A.J."

"You're selling them for the Hip Yee Tong."

"I'm transporting them," she corrected.

"Straight to the Queen's Room," he returned.

"I don't work for Hip Yee. I do, however, pay them for protection, and the right to do business in their Quarter. I also pay rent to the *owner of this building.*"

There was emphasis on that last. Realization dawned, and Riot stood. She blew out a long breath. "You can be absolutely obtuse at times."

"I've never denied that fact," Riot said, putting on his hat.

"And A.J.?"

He paused.

"Do try to look satisfied when you leave. I wouldn't want to spoil my reputation."

Broken Silence

Friday, July 17, 1896

ATTICUS RIOT RUSHED THROUGH Ravenwood's front door to be confronted by the man himself. He was on his way out, and didn't pause, only gestured sharply for Riot to follow. Riot turned on his heel and caught up to the limping older man in no time.

"The building owners—"

"Yes, yes," Ravenwood huffed, as he climbed into a waiting hack. Riot stopped, stunned. "Get in, my boy." The order snapped Riot into action. He climbed in after.

"920 Sacramento," Ravenwood barked at the driver.

Riot looked at his partner in question.

"We've been summoned," Ravenwood explained.

"We've been focusing on the members and contributors of the missions—"

"Not the building owners."

"How did you—"

"It occurred to me that there was a third party we had not yet considered—the owners of the missions themselves." Ravenwood uncurled his hand. A small bit of wood, the very same he had pulled from the fourth victim's hair. "This is bamboo. A piece of wicker from a chair or basket. The Chinese Mission Church on Stockton and Sacramento is owned by a man who also owns a lumber yard and a basket weaving shop. A Mr. Jones. A retired physician who spent five years in Canton."

As usual Zephaniah Ravenwood was a step ahead— without the tedious leg work and endless questioning that seemed to plague Riot. He didn't ask how he had found all that out. Riot knew that his partner would simply wave his hand at the bit of bamboo wood, and declare it obvious.

Miss Cameron answered the door to the mission, and Ravenwood swept past the woman, stepping into the front hall. Riot nodded politely, and waited for her to invite him inside.

When the door closed, Ravenwood spun on the woman. "What is it?" No greeting, no formality, right to the point as usual.

Donaldina was familiar with the man and his eccentricities, and took no offense. Deep down Zephaniah Ravenwood cared greatly for people. Or so Riot liked to believe. Even after twenty years of working together, Riot found the man difficult to read. He was like a puzzle box.

"A girl came last night," Donaldina said. "She wouldn't speak to me, but she finally opened up to Ling. A dark-haired man told her to come here. She said he had a warm voice." Donaldina smiled at Riot.

Ravenwood made an impatient sound. "And?"

"There was another man who told her he'd help her

escape weeks ago. Only she didn't like the sound of his voice. A 'preacher man' who came in much the same manner as the second man, which I believe was Atticus. Another girl *did* trust him, however. And arranged to be rescued the following night."

"I want to speak with this child," Ravenwood said.

"I'm not sure that's a good idea, Mr. Ravenwood."

Riot had to agree; his partner tended to loom.

"Perhaps she'll be more at ease with me?" he asked.

Ravenwood grunted, and sat on the bench in the front hall, folding his hands over the knob of his stick. With the gargoyle settled, Donaldina sent Ling to fetch the newcomer. She returned shortly, holding the new arrival's hand.

The girl kept her head down, staring at her feet. And Riot immediately recognized her. She was one of the girls he had visited last week—when he first heard the story about the white women. She had been the silent one behind the curtain in a gambling den. Unresponsive. Staring, as if drugged with opium.

She glanced up, her eyes darting between men. When she caught sight of Ravenwood, she stopped, and took a step back.

Riot adjusted his stance, ever so slightly. To appear less threatening. He caught her attention with a nod. "I see you made it here. Are they treating you well?" he asked in Cantonese.

The girl's eyes returned to her slippers, and remained. She nodded.

He introduced himself, and asked after her name.

"Wong Hai," she said. Her voice was so very faint. And he feared the slightest mistake would send her back into silence.

"A pleasure." He pressed his palms together and bowed

slightly. She automatically returned the gesture. "My partner and I are trying to help other girls. Miss Cameron told us what you said about the man who came before me—the one your friend went with."

He didn't take out the photographs or sketches. Not yet.

"Do you remember what he looked like?"

She shook her head. And he could well imagine what she was thinking. How many men had used her since she came to San Francisco? Had she even looked at his face?

But this girl who ran from her captors and risked torture and death to escape was made of sterner stuff than he thought. She pointed to Ravenwood, and made a gesture around her chin.

"He had a beard?"

Hai nodded.

"White?"

Hai shook her head. Ravenwood shifted, but Riot shot him a warning glance, and he subsided, scowling at his shoes.

"Blue like Miss Cameron's skirt?" Riot asked.

At this Hai smiled—the faintest of expressions. "No, yellow," she said.

"Young and handsome like myself, or old and grouchy like that one?"

Again a light entered her eyes. "Thin. Tall. He had wrinkles around his eyes and silver in his hair."

"Did he give a name?"

"Mr. Jones."

"How was he going to help you escape?"

"He told us that the Chinese Mission Church right before the big hill would help us. That we would be saved from our life of shame, and that he was a preacher man."

Ling translated all of this for the benefit of the others.

"Did he tell you all this in Cantonese?"

She nodded.

"And you were to run there?"

"He would come back for us," Hai said. "Through the hole in the roof."

"*Did* he come back?"

"Not that night."

"When did he come for your friend?"

"I don't know. I was sold to another man."

Riot nodded. "Thank you, Miss Wong. I am going to show you some sketches of other girls. I need you to tell me if you recognize any of them. Would that be all right?"

She nodded. And he took out the sketches. Hai frowned as she sorted through each. Four in all. "Here is my friend. Where is she?" The third victim.

Riot did not immediately answer. "Where did you first meet her?"

Hai began to tremble violently. Her eyes turned inward, and Donaldina placed her hands on the girl's shoulders.

"You don't have to tell me," Riot said.

Hai didn't have to, but she did, her words tumbling from her lips in a rush. "I did not want to go. I would not learn the names of the family they told me to memorize. So the man gave me something. It made me sick and dumb, and I was picked up from the steamer cabin. I was taken to a place—a big room where a white woman put me on a crate. There were other girls. And we were all stripped. The white woman and another Chinese woman looked us all over—our teeth, our tongue, our... legs.

"Over the next day, more men and women came to look at us. The girls who resisted were beaten, or burnt with iron. Then one day a woman shoved a gold coin in my hand. After she cut hair from my body, and pricked my finger, she had me sign a paper. She told me I was marked, that bad things would happen if I did not go with the man. That is where I met Lun Foo."

Hai did not cry. Her eyes were dry, but her body quaked as if the ground itself were moving her. "Where is Lun Foo?" she repeated firmly.

Riot took a breath, and squared his shoulders. "She was killed. We're trying to find the person who killed her, and with what you've just told us, I know we'll bring her murderer to justice."

Tears dripped down Hai's cheeks. "There is no justice; there is no peace for her."

18

Saintly Suspect

ZEPHANIAH RAVENWOOD BASHED HIS heavy stick on the door. It left a dent in the wood. The man might be as hard to read as a slate of stone, but that didn't mean he lacked emotion. His anger was the slow, dangerous kind, and once he made up his mind, those who got in the way were crushed.

An old Chinese woman bent with time and wear answered the door.

"Ravenwood for Mr. Jones."

Her milky eyes traveled up, and farther still, to the face of Ravenwood. She took a step back.

Riot cleared his throat, and nodded politely. "If Mr. Jones will see us," he said in a softer tone.

She ushered them into the sitting room. The furnishings were in an oriental style—teak woods, reds, and scrolling gold work. Spartan, yet rich. Riot's gaze flickered to the *bagua* hanging above the front door, but this one was turned around, the mirror facing the wall.

Mr. Jones was a hearty, older man. His light hair and beard might have been blond once, but gray had long since taken over in the way that particular color blended with the other. He had sloped shoulders, and one twisted arm that ended with a hand plagued by arthritis. The fingers resembled a talon.

As usual, Ravenwood left the pleasantries to Riot, while he scrutinized the room. Riot made introductions, and extended his left hand. The older man shook it with his good hand. It was a strong grip, and his eyes shone with warmth.

"Your reputation precedes you, of course," said Jones, gesturing at a chair. "To what do I owe this honor?"

"We're investigating some recent murders. Have you heard of the Broken Blossom Murders?" asked Riot.

Jones nodded grimly. "It's a shame. A true shame. But then, it's really only one more crack among many in that dam."

"How so?" asked Riot.

"Have you ever traveled to China?"

"A brief visit."

"The poverty among the lower classes is extreme, and the value of a girl is so low that the parents themselves sell their daughters."

"And men of all sorts have no issues using them," Riot said.

"True, true, the problem is pervasive," Jones admitted. "I've always thought if there weren't such strict immigration laws—if men were allowed to bring their wives here— that we'd not have thousands of unmoored bachelors in the Quarter. As I said, it's one crack in a failing dam."

Riot waited politely, to see where the man would go next. Most people had a need to fill silence, and Riot was content to wait to see what Jones would fill it with.

Ravenwood was not content. He rapped his knuckles on a modest piano. "Do you play, Mr. Jones?"

The man grimaced. The question called attention to his claw-like fingers. "I haven't been able to for years." There was true grief in his words. "My son plays, however. And my wife did. God rest her soul."

"Do you have a photograph of your son?" Ravenwood asked with a flash of teeth. It was a far from reassuring smile.

Riot shot his partner an irritated look. It was lost on him. If there was a sure way to close a man up like a clam, it was to put him on guard about his kin. But Mr. Jones appeared not to mind. Quite the opposite, he appeared pleased that someone had asked. He left, and returned with a photograph. Jones Jr. was the spitting image of his father. Tall, thin, sparse hair, but with two good hands. Although one couldn't tell from a photograph, Riot would wager his hair was blond, with a few gray threads.

Ravenwood snatched the framed photograph.

"Is there something wrong?" Jones asked.

"We're questioning everyone connected to the missions. To see if they might have seen something," Riot lied smoothly. "You own the Chinese Mission Church?"

"Oh, yes, of course. I help where I can. I'm not a man of great wealth, but it's a good place for the mission."

"Are you active at the mission?"

"I stop by now and again."

"Do you rescue slave girls?"

"I'm afraid those days are over." He rubbed his crippled hand with his good one. "But I used to visit dens in an attempt to convince the girls to run. I tell them of a kind Christian God, and talk to them about seeking safety in his arms. Unfortunately the guards know me by sight now, and I'm never allowed entrance." Mr. Jones paused, and sighed. "As awful as these murders are, they've raised awareness for the slave girls. Before the killings, the newspapers and general public would scarcely acknowledge that slavery of this kind was taking place in the city. People don't like to be reminded of unpleasant things."

"Acknowledgement brings responsibility," Ravenwood grunted. "Your son," he set the photograph down with a kind of purpose that Riot knew well, "Does he follow in your footsteps? Does he rescue slave girls?"

"He has nothing to do with mission work. He's a business man." The disapproval was plain in his tone. "He concerns himself with worldly possessions rather than spiritual."

"Does he manage your properties?"

"Not exactly," Jones said. "But he does manage a lumber yard on a property of mine. It's on the edge of the Quarter."

Mr. Jones Jr. was an unremarkable man. His shoulders sloped like his father's, and his spectacles sat on the end of his nose. His eyes were perpetually squinting with strain. Everything about him screamed accountant. Except for his hands. They were large and calloused, and his sleeve protectors were taut around his forearms. There was strength in those arms. He smiled amiably, and shook hands. Riot glanced at the pin on his lapel. A gentleman's fishing society.

"A fellow sportsman, I see," he said after introductions were made. The man started with surprise, and Riot glanced pointedly at the pin.

"Oh, yes, of course," Jones said, smoothing his beard. "Are you a fisherman yourself?"

"I am," Riot said, adding silently 'of a human sort.' He could well imagine Ravenwood's internal snort. "But it's a hard thing to do without a boat."

"River fishing, then?"

"Mostly. I don't have the strength for ocean fishing," Riot said.

"It only takes the right equipment. As do most jobs. I enjoy the challenge—a man and the sea. It gets the blood pumping."

"Indeed. Nearly biblical."

Jones Jr. paused in thought. "I suppose so. The apostles were fisherman after all. What can I do for you gentlemen?"

Riot took the offered seat, but Ravenwood remained on his feet. The looming, white-haired bird of prey didn't seem to bother Jones Jr. His eyes were all innocent inquiry.

"We're questioning residents in and around the Quarter about the girls who have washed up in the bay. I was hoping you, or some of the other residents, might have seen a fleeing girl, or heard screams."

Mr. Jones Jr. chuckled. "Aside from the regular gun shots, screams, and arguments of the Quarter?"

Riot inclined his head in acknowledgement. San Francisco was far from peaceful. Gun fire barely elicited the flutter of an eyelash in the Barbary Coast.

"I've heard nothing out of the ordinary," Jones Jr. said. "We would have whistled for the police if we'd heard anything. These murders are unfortunate. A terrible, terrible tragedy."

"Are you involved with your father's mission work at all?" asked Riot.

Jones smiled. "I'm not much of a church-going man. Numbers keep me occupied—" Mr. Jones Jr. blinked. "Er, where did your friend go?"

Riot glanced over his shoulder. For a tall man with a limp, Ravenwood could be surprisingly swift. "Fresh air," he said smoothly. "Do you mind if I question your workers? Do you have a night watchman?"

"I'll put you in touch with him, or you can come back tonight. His name is Seaward."

"I'd appreciate it."

"You should think about joining our society, Mr. Riot. Jolly good fun. We'll get you out on the ocean for some fishing in no time."

"Do you have a boat?"

"Yes, a modest one," Jones Jr. replied. "But it's not a requirement. That's the beauty of a club. What one doesn't have, others share. There's never a weekend goes by that someone isn't out on the water."

Riot thanked the man, and excused himself. He found Ravenwood scowling at a stack of baskets. They were the type of baskets that Chinese laborers used to carry large loads on their shoulders. These were full of wood scraps.

Ravenwood knocked a basket with his stick. They were certainly large enough to stuff a limp girl inside.

"We could be grasping at straws," Riot said under his breath.

"Puns are not lost on me, my boy."

"The comment was more on the serious side."

"If we are, then it is a very large straw. What do you make of the son?"

"He's hiding something," Riot said. Most people were. Brandish a detective agency card and people tended to get nervous.

"Find out who delivers the lumber shipments from the docks."

Riot strolled around the yard, and stopped to introduce himself to four dogs basking in the sun. The smallest mutt growled, but Riot went straight to the largest, and scratched behind the dog's ears until his companions became jealous. "I'll bring food next time," he said softly, dodging an eager tongue. After a round of head pats, he went in search of the delivery man. The dogs followed.

He wasn't hard to find. A broad-shouldered Chileno with hands that looked like tree roots picked up a board, flung it over his shoulder, and carried it to a waiting wagon. The unloading made the wagon shudder. When the man turned, Riot touched the brim of his hat.

"Atticus Riot."

"What kind of name is that?" the bull-sized man asked.

"Depends on yours."

"Jim Mason."

"What kind of name is that for a Chileno?"

Mason grunted. "I tan easy."

Riot offered his hand with a quirk of his lips. His grip made Riot wince. When he recovered his hand, he shook out his numb fingers behind his back.

"What can I do for you?" Mason asked, as he hefted another staggering load onto a shoulder. The boards passed right over Riot's head.

"Do you handle all the deliveries?"

"Most," Mason said. "Why, did I cut off your cabriolet? If I did, there's nothing I can do about it, and I wouldn't start a fight with me if I were you, being as small as you are."

"I prefer to walk rather than take a hack, but thank you for the warning."

Mason paused with the load of lumber easily balanced on a massive shoulder. "Now that's rare in this city. What do they say? Why walk when you can ride? Not of fashion to walk, or do they say uncivilized?"

"It's unfashionable," Riot answered. "And you're correct. I'm practically a savage."

"You use the wrong tailor for a savage," Mason grunted. A racket of noise signaled another unloading, and the wagon shuddered again.

"Same could be said for a certain mule."

Mason chuckled. "I take what jobs I can get. I do the work of two men for half the pay of one." Mason frowned. "You're not a union man, are you?"

"I am not."

Mason looked relieved.

"Do you pick up the lumber from the wharves?"

"I do."

"Alone?"

"Is there a point to your questions?"

He'd get nowhere at this rate. Given Mason's size, Riot couldn't imagine him spiriting away slave girls without someone remembering a Chileno giant. "I'm investigating a number of murders. The victims were Chinese girls. Their bodies were thrown into the bay."

"You think I did it?"

"No," Riot said truthfully. "I was hoping you might have seen or heard something. Here, or down at the wharves—anything out of the ordinary."

Mason shrugged. "I hear talk of those murders. It's all over the wharves. Lots of things are ordinary in San Francisco, but if I saw a child in danger, I would not be reporting it to you now. I'd smash the bastardo's head in."

"Likewise, although I'd put a bullet there."

Mason nodded.

"What time do you generally make deliveries?"

"When I'm needed."

"Does anyone help you?"

"Michael, Little Bill, and Johnathon. And the night watchman rides down with me most mornings."

"Seaward, isn't it?"

Mason nodded. "Timothy Seaward. He has a place down by the water. It's too noisy during the day to sleep here with the mill."

Riot glanced around the lumber yard. It was hemmed in by a U-shaped fence of buildings, with a real fence at the mouth. The gate was currently wide open. "Does the night watchman keep a shack here?"

Mason nodded towards the south of the yard. "There's a stove inside. No sleeping though."

"Thank you, Mr. Mason." Riot started to leave him to his business, and then stopped himself. "Do you ever transport anything in baskets?"

"Baskets?" Mason looked at the large stacks of lumber.

"Like nails, tools, scrap wood, and the like."

Mason unburdened himself of another load. He looked at his palm and started picking a splinter from the leather-like skin. "Timothy always takes Mr. Jones' fishing supplies with him—back and forth. The boss doesn't like to leave them unattended on his boat."

"How much do those supplies weigh?"

"Not much. Maybe eighty pounds or so."

"That's a lot of fishing supplies."

"Ocean fishing isn't for the weak."

"Are you a fishing man?"

Mason shrugged. "From solid ground. I don't like boats."

"I don't either."

19

The Lumber Yard

SMOKE AND INCENSE MINGLED with fog, as a drone of quiet voices drifted from high windows. A voice raised from one of those windows, only to die down after a frenzy of words had been vented.

Atticus Riot looked from that angry window to the lumber yard. Three sides were penned in by high buildings, and laundry hung from every window and balcony. The fence that closed the mouth of the yard was high and solid and topped with crude iron railroad spikes.

"Any one of those buildings could have a passage into the yard," Riot said to his companions. They stood in the mouth of an alley. Riot's horse gently snorted puffs into the night. "There aren't any, according to my maps," Tim whispered.

"Farwell's maps focus on the Quarter, not the white businesses," Ravenwood murmured. "It's only logical to assume that there are secret passages that remain secret."

Tim glared up at the man. "I have more than Farwell's

maps, you know."

"Even a particularly dull-witted simpleton can knock bricks out of the side of a building to make a new passage," Ravenwood retorted.

"What would you know about knocking anything from anywhere, Zeph? Takes more than a good bash."

Riot sighed, and mounted his horse. The two could argue back and forth for days. Ravenwood might have cold logic, but Tim had hard practicality and experience. The two older men butted heads like rams in rutting season. He suspected they enjoyed it.

Leaving his partners arguing at his back, he casually rode up to the lumber yard fence. When he was close enough, he swiftly gripped the horn and stepped onto the saddle. He tossed a sack over the fence, reached for the iron on top, and hoisted himself the rest of the way up. Riot slipped between the iron spikes, and landed on the other side with a thud. He staggered to his feet in time to see swift, growling shapes barreling towards him.

"Hello there, friends," Riot whispered. He tipped back his hat, and smiled. The growls turned to wagging tails. He picked up the sack, and dumped its contents in the dirt. "As promised," he murmured, patting the closest head.

Tense and listening for the cock of a shotgun, he moved deeper into the lumber yard. Riot puffed warm air into his hands as he walked. The fog was thick, and the chill bit down into his bones. It was ideal weather for breaking and entering, and as he sulked past the watchman's shed, the firelight spilling through drafty cracks was reassuring.

Riot kept his eyes away from the glow, and crept to the tool shed. It was the only outbuilding that had been locked. He slipped a tension wrench into the keyhole followed by a pick. Applying a slight pressure to the wrench, he gently nudged each pin. The padlock gave way with a click.

The shed smelled of cold metal and mineral oil. It was also dark. He eased the door shut, and pulled out a small candle. Dim light touched a murderer's arsenal, or a carpenter's, depending what business one was in. Saws, hammers, bins of nails, clamps, and sharpeners were neatly arranged along the walls of the shed. And a line of baskets.

Riot lifted the top of the first. It contained an array of chisels. The second held rags for varnish, and the third gloves, carpenter belts, and harnesses. The last held fishing supplies. Not the small reels and lines used for river fishing, but the heavy equipment required to snag a shark.

The back wall of the shed stood against one of the surrounding buildings. It was devoid of supplies, save for a bench that held a pile of tarps. Riot crouched, and held his candle closer to the floorboards. A faint, curving mark had been scratched into the wood.

Riot picked up one side of the bench, and set it over the marks. It was an exact match. He turned his attention to the wooden wall, and knocked about gently, listening. Part of the wall was solid, but the part behind the bench was hollow. Riot pushed on the wood. A panel moved back an inch, and he slid it up like a window in its groove.

The darkness beyond smelled of sewage and rot. Dreading what he would find, Riot thrust his candle inside. Finding it empty of life, and death, he crawled into the secret room, and the source of the smell became apparent. It wasn't from leaky pipes, but rather a board in the middle of the floor.

Riot slid it aside, and grimaced. Putting his sleeve to

his nose, he carefully edged his candle closer, wary of the risk of an explosion. His dim light caught dingy brick, and an egg-shaped passageway below—the sewers. A crude ladder led down to a makeshift platform. Not an uncommon sight in the sewers. He had once tracked down a criminal who had been hiding in a space like this for a full week.

He replaced the board and turned his attention to the little room.

A thin pallet lay against the far wall, and baskets identical to those in the shed lined another. He lifted the first lid. It contained a medicinal bottle of laudanum, water, a rag, and rope.

"Lovely," he muttered. The second basket was empty, and the third contained fishing supplies. And at the end of the line of baskets was a pair of rubber boots.

A sound whipped him around: boots crunching on gravel. Riot blew out his candle, and hurried over to the open panel. He reached through and moved the bench back to its place. The crunching grew louder. He quickly slid down the panel, and moved to the side, crouching in the hidden room with revolver drawn.

The door outside opened, boots thudded on the floorboards, and light played through the cracks in the wood. The watchman did a circuit of the shed, and then left. Riot heard the click of a padlock, and muttered an oath. Short of taking a sledge to the door, he would not be leaving the same way he had entered.

Riot holstered his revolver, and looked down at the board on the floor. Ravenwood was going to owe him a new suit.

❖

"You smell like shit." Tim wrinkled his nose.

"I'm surprised you can still smell at all," Riot retorted. He looked to Ravenwood, and was about to explain what he'd found when the man stole his triumph.

"You found a hidden room that led to the sewers."

"No," Riot said dryly. "I fell in an outhouse."

Tim guffawed, and quickly clapped a hand over his mouth.

"There's a hidden panel in the tool shed that leads to a small brick room. A hole in the floor leads to the sewers." He described the room's contents.

"Why are there two sets of ocean tackle?" Tim asked.

"For obvious reasons," Ravenwood said.

Tim shot him an irritated glance. "So, should we barge the gates, and go question the watchman?" He tensed like a dog about to go in for the kill.

Ravenwood gave a shake of his head. "It may put Mr. Jones Jr. on guard."

"We don't know it's him," Riot said.

"No, we don't," Ravenwood conceded. "But he lied to you about not being involved in mission work. Wong Hai's description was more than suggestive. Regardless, someone in this lumber yard is using that room to kill, and if we spook him, he may not strike again."

"We can't leave it unguarded, Ravenwood. He might drug the girls and do the cutting right there," Riot said. "He could toss the entrails right into the sewers." His own words made him sick.

"The rats would snatch that up right quick," Tim agreed, rocking back and forth on his heels.

"Possibly," Ravenwood conceded. But doubtful, said his tone of voice. "We'll put a guard in the room. I assume you exited the lumber yard via the sewers. Can you find your way back?"

"I can," Riot said.

Ravenwood looked at Tim, and smiled.

"God dammit," Tim spat.

20

Denizen of the Night

Saturday, July 18, 1896

THE LUMBER WAGON RATTLED over cobblestones, through the busy streets of early morning San Francisco. The sun had not yet pierced the fog; the Silver Mistress was still heavy with sleep. She'd not stir until midday, if Riot was any judge.

His hat was pulled low, and he rode his horse at an easy pace, lagging behind so as not to attract attention. Mason and the night watchman, Seaward, rode on the seat. The wagon was empty save for a basket in the back.

Ravenwood followed in a hack, at a slower pace. He could no longer comfortably ride a horse due to an injury some years before. But that was just fine with Riot. The tall, stately older man tended to attract attention on horseback.

Mason pulled the lumber wagon to a stop at the Folsom Street wharf. Seaward hopped down and went to the back of the bed, hoisted his employer's fishing tackle over a shoulder and headed towards the wharf.

Riot dismounted, tied the reins to a post, and followed at a discreet distance. The man boarded a moored steam trawler. Since black smoke would signal Seaward's intention, Riot waited for the hack to roll to a stop. Ravenwood looked out the window, eyes searching the masts.

"He took the fishing supplies onto that little steam trawler," Riot said. "I don't think there's a need to follow Mason."

In answer, Ravenwood stepped out of the hack, and told the driver to wait a block away.

"I'll take a look first."

Ravenwood nodded. "Remember we need him alive, my boy."

"So little faith in me."

Ravenwood offered him his weighted walking stick, but Riot declined. It was an old exchange between mentor and apprentice. A remnant of his early days working with Ravenwood. Twenty years ago the man had recruited a cocky young gambler with two lightning-quick triggers. Time and persistence had refined him, but sometimes he wondered if Ravenwood still worried he'd fall to his gunfighting ways, which generally left a trail of dead men.

Riot strolled down the wharf towards the boat. It appeared that Seaward was inside the cabin. Keeping clear of the windows, Riot stepped over the rail.

"Ahoy, there!" Ravenwood's voice boomed over the water. Riot's heart leapt out of his throat. Footsteps stomped up the companionway, and Riot scrambled around to the port side of the cabin as Seaward stuck his head out of the hatch.

"Yes?"

"Are you the captain of this boat?" Ravenwood presented a stately figure. Tailored suit, tall, fine hands, and a gentleman's stick. His shoulders were slightly slouched giving an appearance of aging fragility.

"No, sir," called Seaward. "I mind it, is all."

Ravenwood cupped a hand to his ear. "What was that?" he yelled. The show was repeated once more before Seaward climbed onto the wharf.

The two fell into conversation, and, taking advantage of the distraction, Riot slipped into the cabin. He went straight for the basket. Preparing himself for what he might find, he opened the lid. Fishing supplies. To see if a girl might be hidden under the tackle and line, he carefully shifted it to the side. More fishing supplies.

While Ravenwood had Seaward distracted, he searched the rest of the boat. Berths, a small galley, a head, rods and lines, and cold storage. He eyed the ominous stains in the fish locker. No one could tell the difference between human and fish blood.

As he searched, he pondered the basket. Why carry a basket back and forth every morning and evening when it could just as easily be stored in the locked shed during the day? It made sense for one of his employees to lug the thing back and forth if Jones Jr. planned a fishing trip, but why every day?

Riot hurried back to the basket. This time, he did a more thorough search. His fingertips brushed something foreign, something leather. He pulled it free. It was a thin leather book.

Ravenwood raised his voice. "Surely you wouldn't mind showing me the way?"

The deck shuddered, footsteps clicked on the boat, and

Riot spun, drawing his gun. "Stay right there," he ordered.

Seaward froze in the cabin door. His pale face turned white as a sheet before sense slammed back into the man. He bolted.

Riot's finger twitched, but he ground his teeth and stopped himself from shooting; instead, he lunged after the man. Seaward was quick. But the moment his boots hit the wharf, the slouched elderly gentleman straightened, and casually swung his stick. The knob caught Seaward in the gut. He doubled over, and the stick cracked down on his back. He fell onto his knees, and Ravenwood nudged him forcibly onto the dock.

Ravenwood pressed the tip of his stick against the man's back. "Stay," he warned. Seaward wisely decided to stay.

Timothy Seaward sat on the berth looking ill and dejected. Detainment aside, he had an unhealthy appearance about him: thinnish brown hair, dark circles around his eyes, a grayish tint to his complexion, a red nose, and a tremor to his hands. Drink had aged him prematurely. He looked to be in his forties, but Riot wondered if he was yet thirty.

Riot stood guard as Ravenwood flipped through the leather book. Riot had his gun holstered, but his jacket was tucked back, displaying the weapon for Seaward's benefit. Riot leaned to the side, and eyed the numbers with one eye while he kept the other on the night watchman. It looked like an account book.

The records appeared to be of lumber shipments. Had Jones Jr. taken the account book along on a fishing trip, and left it behind by accident? He wouldn't be the first man to take his work home.

"It's time you talked, Mr. Seaward," said Riot.

Seaward looked confused. "I don't know what you want."

"I've just said what I want," he replied.

"But what do you want with *me*?" Seaward's eyes rolled from Riot to Ravenwood, and back to the man with the gun.

"You can start by telling me why you ran," Riot said.

"You pointed a gun at me."

Without looking up from the book, Ravenwood clucked his tongue like a disapproving mother. It took effort not to glare at the man.

"Is this your boat?"

"It's my boss's boat," Seaward said. "Mr. Jones. He lets me sleep here during the days 'cause boats have a way of disappearing."

"Why do you transport the basket back and forth?"

"Mr. Jones says it's expensive fishing gear. He has me take it from the lumber yard every day. I don't mind. The arrangement helps me save money on room and board."

"Why not leave it in the locked shed at the lumber yard?"

Seaward picked at his teeth in thought. His gums were angry, and he looked in need of a dentist. "I don't honestly know. I do what I'm told. Sometimes he goes fishing after work. But I figure he's never sure. Just likes it here in case he decides to go."

"Do you fish with him?"

"I've been," Seaward said, with a nod. "But if he goes out in the afternoon, I head to the lumber yard early."

"Why is that account book in the basket?"

Seaward eyed the leather book, and shrugged. "Maybe Mr. Jones was going to do some work? I don't know. I can't read, sir. I just do what I'm told."

"Then you don't listen well," Riot said. "I told you to stay right there, and yet you bolted. I'll ask again, Mr. Seaward, and this time I'd like the truth—why did you run?"

Seaward ran a hand over his head. He was nervous. "I figured you'd kill me anyways."

"Now why would you think that? Are you a wanted man?"

He winced. "No, sir. I thought you were a hired gun come to collect."

"Do you have a bounty on your head?"

"I figured I might."

Riot tilted his head. "Why would you think that?"

Seaward pressed his lips together. And Riot crossed his arms, waiting. Silence deepened. Seaward shifted, and finally Ravenwood shattered the quiet. He slapped the book closed, and his voice entered the fray. It was a low, dangerous sort of purr—like a cat sidling up to a mouse before the strike.

"As it stands right now you'll be pinned with multiple murders lest you start talking, Mr. Seaward. If you are hanged for murder, I have no doubt that the real murderer will count himself lucky, and stop slaughtering girls. We benefit either way."

Seaward's mouth worked. His tongue seemed stuck in place, and then it started moving. "I don't murder them!" Seaward burst out. "I *rescue* the girls. I thought you were hired by the tongs to kill me for stealing their slave girls. That's why I ran."

"If you rescue the girls, why drug them and stuff them in a basket?" Ravenwood asked.

"It's easier to transport them that way—to get them

away from the Quarter safely. Most of them are too frightened to keep calm."

"Where do you take the girls?" Riot asked.

"Here," Seaward answered. "And then Mr. Jones takes them across the bay in his boat. It throws the tongs for a bit of a loop."

Ravenwood arched a brow. "Does he?"

Seaward nodded. "That's what he told me."

"Who does he entrust the girls to?" Riot asked.

"I don't know. I just do as I'm told."

Riot reached into his breast pocket, and pulled out the post-mortem photograph of the fourth victim. "Do you recognize this girl?"

Seaward squinted at the photograph. "I'm not sure."

Riot was tired of hearing that answer. "Yes or no will do."

"It's dark when I help them escape."

Ravenwood interlaced his long fingers. "How do you know what girl to rescue?"

"Mr. Jones tells me where to get the next girl. I go and get her that night—if she's still there—and then I take her here in the basket in the morning."

"We'll just have to confirm your story with Mr. Jones, then."

Seaward paled. "I'll lose my job."

Riot took a breath. He wanted to throttle the man. "Children are being murdered. And so far you're looking like our prime suspect."

Seaward looked him straight in the eye. "I'm not murdering no one, and Mr. Jones isn't either."

"And how do you know that?"

"He's a good Christian man with a wife and children. And he's well off. Why would he do all that?"

"Why, indeed." Ravenwood frowned. "The most ruthless person I've known was a church-going Sunday school teacher. God has nothing to do with the likes of evil. And evil often wears a saintly mask."

Riot studied Seaward. He couldn't quite pin the man down. He hadn't expected loyalty. "Regardless," he said. "There's a way to put the question to rest without him knowing you talked with us."

"How's that?"

"You're going to help us."

"What do you want me to do?"

"Same as you always do."

21

Hindsight

Tuesday, July 21, 1896

THOSE LAST WORDS RANG in Riot's ears as he sat, days later, on the trawler waiting for the delivery wagon that would deposit Seaward and his load.

The days had not been spent idly. Jones Jr. was indeed a family man, and the fishing society had nothing but praise for him. But the account book revealed a suspicious amount of money passing through the yard. Jones Jr. was not without stain, and he appeared to be reaping the benefit of ill-gotten gains. The question of where the money came from, and where it was going, would have to be determined later.

Tim and Ravenwood waited with a boat at the end of the wharf, and another agent waited inside the hidden room at the lumber yard. It was left to Riot and Monty to stow away on the trawler.

They needed to catch Jones Jr. in the act.

Riot crouched outside the cockpit, pressed against the bulwark. He had a view of the wharves looking through the windows, and easy access to the trawler's saloon. Monty was in the hold. They were taking no chances.

A wagon rattled on the wharf, and Riot poked his head around the cabin, watching its approach. It was the lumber wagon. But only a single man sat in the seat. Dread hit Riot full in the gut.

Jim Mason drove the wagon. He was as large as a bull, but his hand with the horses was gentle. He clucked them to a stop, and climbed off the seat. Mason reached over the side and hoisted a basket out of the bed, then lugged it towards the boat. He hopped on the rail with a shudder of deck boards, and disappeared into the cabin. Timothy Seaward was nowhere in sight. This was not the plan.

Riot drew his gun, and stepped into the hatch. "Hands up, Mason," he ordered calmly.

Mason put his hands up, then spun. But his left hand wasn't empty. A knife whizzed towards Riot's face. He ducked under the missile, and fired, but the shot only grazed, and in the next second a bull of a man rammed into him. He was thrown against the bulkhead. A fist came crashing down next. Pain stung the side of his face, his spectacles flew off, and his gun clattered to the floor. A volley of fists followed.

Stunned, Riot struck blindly. He landed a solid punch to the man's face. It felt like hitting a stone wall. A lethal fist drove towards him, and he ducked under and behind the man. Mason twisted, throwing another punch. Riot retreated, trying to put space between them. His heel hit the basket on the cabin floor, and he lost his balance.

Mason charged, and when he hit, it felt like a stone

wall had thrown itself at him. Three hundred pounds of muscle landed on him, and a smell of blood and death assaulted his senses.

Mason raised his fist, and Monty Johnson leapt into the fight. The big brawler threw himself on Mason's back, wrapping his arms around the thick neck in a chokehold. Mason's fist paused in midair, hovering over Riot's face. The combined weight of both men was crushing the air from his lungs. Riot could not breathe.

"*Mi Dios*," Mason breathed. He didn't seem to notice Monty on his back, attempting to choke the life from him. Mason's eyes were wide, and they were fixed to the side.

With a surge of strength, Monty pulled the man off Riot. They both fell to the ground, and Riot gulped in a breath. He choked on blood, and spat it out. The cabin was blurry. He scrubbed the blood from his eye, and squinted with the one that was still functioning. What he saw made him sick. The basket had overturned, the lid had rolled across the cabin floor, and its contents were laid bare. A girl's butchered body lay on the cabin floor.

There was clear shock in Mason's eyes. And his mind finally caught up with the scene. Riot could see the wheels of his mind turning. He had brought the basket. A dead girl lay inside. No matter his innocence, any jury would be more than happy to hang a Chileno with circumstantial evidence like that.

"Wait!" Riot barked, holding up a halting hand, before the man exploded into action. "The night guard Seaward —where is he?"

Mason was so stunned that he answered in Spanish, which was well and good because Riot could speak it just fine.

"He said he had to get groceries, and asked me if I

could take the fishing..." Mason trailed off. Pale and bloodless, he couldn't take his eyes off the girl. His body convulsed, and he had the look of a man about to be sick.

Monty wisely let go of him as he retched.

"Where did you drop him?" Riot demanded.

Mason wiped his sleeve across his mouth. "End of Market."

It was near the vegetable markets and fish vendors, but it was also by the ferry building—the gateway to every train leaving California.

Riot snatched up his spectacles and gun. The world came into cracked focus. "Signal Ravenwood," he said as he hurried out of the cabin.

"Where are you going?" Monty yelled.

"The ferry building!"

The streets were clogged with wagons, lumber carts, pedestrians, and everything in between. A hack would have been useless in the morning rush, so he ran. Heedless of his own safety, he sprinted through the crowds, not caring whom he jostled on the way.

The ferry building was caged in scaffolding, a skeleton of construction, its planned tower and clock not even close to completion. There was no time to check his watch, and the sun was blanketed behind thick fog. He ran, pounding through travelers moving towards the docks. He took a guess, and headed towards the ferry terminus for Oakland.

Riot nearly ran into a knot of policemen. He skipped to the side, and blinked through the cracks in his spectacles. A knot of uniforms surrounded a tall, stately gentleman. Ravenwood. What the hell was he doing here?

Riot opened his mouth to shout at the man to help him

look for Seaward when the knot of men parted for the briefest of seconds. Timothy Seaward lay cuffed on the dock. Riot skidded to a stop, and pressed a hand to the stitch in his side.

The police parted for Ravenwood. "Slowing down, my boy?" There was amusement in his voice. And it drove Riot over the edge. He was not amused. Not after what he had seen. He launched himself into the break, throwing himself at Seaward. Fists fell, flesh pounded, blood filled his vision. He reached for his revolver.

"Atticus!" Ravenwood's voice cut through the haze, and an iron hand locked around his arm. His fingers brushed the stock. As Ravenwood pulled him off Seaward, the butcher started laughing. Spittle and blood dripping from his chin.

"I'm dead already," Seaward wheezed. "Those chinks gave me the French Pox. This will speed things along."

Riot shook free of his partner's restraint.

"A crime of convenience, then," Ravenwood said. "And vengeance. The cuts were simply intended to point a finger at the tongs."

"Don't matter," Seaward said. "These Chinese are like rats. Diseased, foul, stealing our jobs." He spat on the ground. "You thought you were all high and mighty. Smart like, but I had you both fooled. Lowly little me felled the great Ravenwood."

Riot tensed, his fingers twitched. The iron hand returned, locking around his wrist.

Orders were shouted, and Riot heard himself telling the police about the girl in the basket, and then he left. He found himself walking. San Francisco moved around him in a haze, but his blood blazed. Slowly he became aware that he was not alone. Though walking must have pained the aging detective, Ravenwood limped alongside, relying heavily on his stick with every step.

Conscious of his friend's limitations, Riot slowed his pace. He glanced at the streets, and realized he was walking up California, towards Chinatown—towards the dark cloud of smoke that hung over the Quarter.

"You suspected," he bit out the words.

"Tim was on the boat. I saw no reason to be there. All other avenues were covered, so I simply waited at a less likely possibility. I thought he might try to escape."

"I looked that man in the eye," Riot growled. His words were full of rage, and anger, and a whole heap of regret.

"Seaward felt justified. Given his prejudice, I doubt he considered it murder. Perhaps he felt that he was ridding the world of the disease he contracted."

Riot did not answer; he didn't trust himself to answer. He felt out of control, and that was never a good thing. He didn't say a word until they reached the lumber yard. Ignoring the protests of the workers, he stalked up to the tool shed, and when they became persistent, he brandished his gun. Mr. Jones Jr. called his men away, and Riot opened the secret door.

The agent who was guarding the room was dead. His name was Clark, an experienced man who had met a brutal end. There was blood and entrails, and a racial slur written in blood on the stone. Seaward had butchered the girl here, knowing full well he would be caught.

Ravenwood poked his head in, and grunted. "I'll summon the police."

As his partner walked away, a cold rage gathered in Riot's blood. He'd be damned if he'd fail another child.

22

Strike of Lightning

Tuesday, March 5, 1900

ISOBEL CURSED HER RASH decision. She had let emotion cloud her judgment. Why on earth had she thought Riot would already be in danger? But there had been something in her captors' voices that spooked her. She had been filled with an irrational fear for him.

It may have been the numerous kicks to her gut.

Cold, sore, and hungry, she stomped back to the Pagan Lady. Light seeped from the portholes. Suppressing a sigh, Isobel braced herself for yet another worried face as she opened the hatch.

The shipmate stove was blazing, and the cabin sweltered. Her twin hopped up the moment her foot touched the ladder. His golden hair was undone, brushing his shoulders. Lotario looked luminous in the fire's light.

"Bel!"

Isobel slammed the hatch, already regretting her

choice to come here instead of going to her room at Sapphire House. Lotario always fussed over her. "I'm fine."

Lotario rolled his eyes. "Aren't you always? I told Atticus you would be. Where did you run off to? You were supposed to meet me."

"I was looking for a horse."

She rummaged through the galley, produced a tin of hard biscuits, jerky, and an apple, and tossed them on the table, sitting down to stuff everything she could into her mouth in the least amount of time.

"I'm glad to know where I stand." Lotario hovered over her. She could feel him frown. "You look terrible."

"I feel worse than I look. The horse gave me issues."

"I hope he was worth it."

"I found him." She shrugged.

Lotario walked over to the galley, filled a large kettle with water from the stores, and set it on the stove. "You need to clean up. I can't stand it when you're filthy; it makes me feel dirty, too."

She looked at him as she gnawed on a biscuit. The moment he sat down on the berth across, Watson jumped on his lap, and preened until Lotario started petting the tabby.

"When did you get a cat?"

"I didn't. He volunteered to guard the Lady."

Lotario smiled, stroking the feline's back. "I like him," he said with a yawn. He leaned on a pillow, and pulled the blanket over him. "So where did you go?"

"To Ocean Beach."

"Atticus and I followed your trail there," Lotario drawled. "It was exhilarating, to say the least."

"Atticus?"

"Yes. I can't call him Riot, too. That would be odd."

"Because there's nothing odd about you and me already?"

Lotario fluffed his hair. "We're a perfect pair," he agreed.

"What did you two do at the beach?"

"We asked questions. I felt like a real detective... you know, I could get used to this sort of work."

"Except there's usually an element of danger involved."

He wrinkled his nose. "Oh, yes, of course." Lotario tugged the blanket closer, as if taken by a sudden chill. "I could be an armchair detective. You know like Sherlock Holmes' more brilliant brother Mycroft."

"You *are* lazy."

"I know, it's perfect," he said. "But don't think I missed your exclusion of brilliant."

"You know you are, Ari."

That soothed his wounded ego.

"For example," he said lazily through half-closed lids. "From the way you're sitting, I know your stomach is hurting. You sat the same way after you fought off that pack of dock boys who were bullying me."

Isobel sank her teeth into a hard piece of jerky.

"And you're wearing gloves to hide some other obvious injury."

"The horse kicked me. I'll be pissing blood for a few days."

Lotario clucked his tongue. "Naughty horse."

"Where did you and 'Atticus' go on the beach?" she asked.

"Oh, everywhere. He sent me to the more civilized venues by the Pavilion, while he traveled south along the shore. We couldn't find a trace of you. Only some tracks of an apparent scuffle. The rain, you know, made a mess of everything. He's a very useful man to have around, though."

"Yes," she said faintly. Abruptly, she stood, grabbed a pot, and poured hot water into it from the kettle. She disappeared into the forward cabin to wash. Not that she was the modest sort where her twin was concerned—the pair had formed a bond in the womb that was nearly tangible to this day, and she was never quite sure where she left off and Lotario began. But she didn't want him to see whatever bruises had blossomed.

"You should let him know you're safe as soon as possible. He was ready to storm the gates."

"The gates to where?" she called back. As she peeled off her clothes, she grimaced at the angry boot shaped bruises stamped on her abdomen. She tried not to look at the rest of the bruises.

"Oh, you know…" he drawled vaguely.

She clenched her teeth. "No, I don't know."

"If you were the more brilliant part of the pair, then you would."

Isobel poked her head into the saloon. "Enlighten me."

"Nowhere in particular. All of Ocean Beach." She could tell when Lotario was lying. And she said as much.

"As if you're not?" he shot back.

Isobel sighed, and applied herself to scrubbing. When she was clean and dry, she pulled on a union suit. The garment reminded her of Riot, and she could not quite shake the memory of him in his own union suit, disheveled and in a state of undress. But it wasn't lust that preoccupied her; it was the cold sweat, the way he shook, the wild fear in his eyes. And finally the hard mask that had slipped into place when she had asked him about *din gau*. She shivered, and buried herself in a thick sweater. It had felt as if a door had slammed in her face—a wall had been erected, and she hadn't known what to do. So she fled.

She certainly didn't like others prying into her past. Why should he tolerate it any better? She had become too comfortable with the man.

Isobel had intended to tell him everything, but the moment she saw his distressed state she changed her mind. The bullet scar tracing his skull was known to her. Along with his headaches and night-terrors, and the talking dead man. What demons might she stir awake if she told him of the tong threat? And how could he expect her to share when he clearly would not?

She frowned as she walked into the saloon. Lost in thought, she plopped on the same berth as Lotario, and the two curled up like a pair of cats for warmth.

"You should tell Atticus that you're safe," he repeated. "He is worried."

"I already did. I left Wilson there."

"Oh. I thought you might have stayed."

"I'm tired, Ari," she said into his hair.

"Of course." There was a long stretch of silence. And as her lids grew heavy, she heard her twin's distant voice. "You should tell him—whatever happened. He loves you."

Isobel sighed. "Would you stop using *that* word. We've scarcely spent a week together."

"Father proposed to mother the day he met her. It was the *colpo di fulmine*, as the Italians say." Love that came like a strike of lightning. Isobel would not admit it to Lotario, but that was exactly how she'd felt when she met Riot— only she'd been hit by a weighted walking stick.

"Mother and father couldn't even communicate. They didn't speak one another's language," she pointed out. "And they *still* argue in their native tongues."

"Even better, they can't understand each other. Besides, who needs to talk when you're in love?" Lotario asked.

"I tried that, it didn't work."

"That gondolier in Venice doesn't count."

"I'm dead, Ari," she reminded.

"You're awfully warm for a corpse."

She sighed. "I don't want to hurt him."

"Silence hurts worse. I should know." His tone was wounded.

Isobel glared at the back of her twin's head. "I shot a man at point-blank range who kept coming. I was hog-tied, repeatedly kicked, and kept in a cold basement for a day. They threatened to kill Riot if I told him, and then threw me from a moving wagon."

"Oh, is that all?" His voice caught, and he settled his back more firmly against her. She could feel a tremor passing through his body. "Seems like something he should know."

"He should," she agreed. "But I fear he might do something foolish."

"As if you won't?"

"Riot isn't as prim and cultured as he appears."

"Of course not, he's attracted to you."

Isobel slapped her twin's chest.

23

The Hunt Begins

SHARP NAILS DUG INTO her skin. Isobel was trapped under a heavy weight. The scent of her ex-husband filled her memory, and she jerked awake, unleashing her rage. Something thumped to the floor. Claws sank deeper, and a warning growl stilled her fear.

Isobel blinked at the cat on her chest. Watson retracted his claws, and fell into a gentle kneading. His growl turned into a purr. She scowled at the beast, and he flicked his ears in return.

"Damn you, Watson," she muttered, scrubbing her face. A wet nose and whiskers tickled her chin in apology. "It's too early." Or too late. Sunlight was fighting its way through the porthole.

She looked at the floor. Lotario glared up at her from where he had landed. He picked up his blanket with all the dignity he possessed, and fell into the opposite berth. He was back asleep in seconds.

Isobel tried to sit up, but the cat on her chest proved

too much for her abused stomach. Everything hurt. With the purring heater, she was tempted to follow her twin's example. But it hurt to lie down as much as it did to move. She carefully extracted Watson's claws, and nudged him to the side. He flicked his tail in her face, and melted off the berth to continue his nap on Lotario.

She pushed herself upright, and leaned against the cushion. While she caught her breath, she reached up and opened the hinged window above her berth. Sunlight stabbed its way through the misty canopy. It'd be a sunny afternoon in San Francisco.

Her thoughts traveled to questions with no answers.

"Ari?"

He didn't move.

She picked up a newspaper and chucked it across the saloon. It hit him in the face, and he yanked the blanket over his head. She called his name again.

"What?"

"What does *din gau* mean?" Lotario was far better with languages than she was. While Isobel spent their childhood impatiently plotting her next escape from the family home, her twin had shadowed Hop, their family butler, and learned passable Cantonese.

"It's too early," he said.

"It's important."

He nudged down the blanket, and squinted at her. "Will you take me with you today?"

"No."

"Will you take Atticus?"

"I don't know yet," she said honestly. "I need more information—hence my question."

"Will you tell me where you're going?"

"I'm going to hell."

"I'm sure to meet you there," he drawled, and then sobered. "I'm serious, Bel."

She relented. "Yes, I'll tell you as soon as I figure out where I'm going."

"If you're not back by dark, I'm telling Atticus."

"Never mind," she growled. Both Watson and her twin were traitors. Anger spurred her into action. She stood and lifted the berth cushion up, rummaging through the underneath storage as she pondered her clothing options. Mr. Henry Morgan was known to her abductors, but then they also knew she was a woman. However, they didn't know what she looked like in women's clothing. She'd have better chances as Miss Bonnie today.

As Isobel began shedding her long johns, she heard a hiss. It wasn't the cat.

"Good God, Bel!"

She glanced at her twin. His gaze was fixed on her black and yellow stomach. "I told you they kicked me." She tugged on her chemise, and reached for her sports bodice.

"But your wrists—did you clean those cuts?"

"Yes," she sighed.

Never one to trust her first aid protocol, Lotario tossed off his blanket and bolted over to the medical supplies as if he feared she would run. She would have if she'd been dressed.

"It's fine, Ari."

He ignored her.

Resigned, she sat down and started emptying the pockets of her male guise from the day before. She laid the items out on the table, and gritted her teeth as Lotario began cleaning her injuries with diluted carbolic acid. There were a number of wounds that she didn't know she had.

"Are you going to tell me more about what happened?" he asked.

Isobel debated his question for a full minute, before he began roughly scrubbing the dirt out of a large scrape on her back. "Ari!"

"If only I had a story to distract myself with, I wouldn't be so impatient," he lamented dramatically.

A growl worthy of Watson escaped her throat. But in the end, she told him all.

"You stole a hundred dollars from a corpse!" He nearly dropped the bottle of diluted acid on the floor.

Isobel snatched the bottle from his hand. "It's not stealing; it's a retainer fee for finding his murderer."

"You *are* going to hell," he huffed. "Sooner rather than later if you don't drop this business."

"Those men were after a girl," she reminded. "Whoever that girl is, she needs my help and I intend to find her before they do."

Lotario sighed. He knew better than to try and argue with her when someone was in danger. "*Din gau* means mad dog, or maybe rabid dog."

"Rabid Dog?" She puzzled over the meaning. The night before, Riot had asked her where she'd heard that name. It was an uncharacteristic slip on his part. He had been charmingly flustered, and then all at once his gentle eyes had turned to stone. She had whittled away his defenses, stripped him of his armor and blindsided him with those words. He had a right to be angry. But why would the tongs give him such a nickname?

"I don't know," Lotario answered. She didn't remember asking the question out loud. "Hop used to call us *Siu Wai Daan*—little rotten eggs—all the time."

"And here I've been thinking it was a term of endearment."

Lotario rolled his eyes. "It was. When he was really upset, he called you *Wu Lei Ching*—a fox spirit."

"I'm flattered."

"It's not flattering in his tongue."

She shrugged. "A matter of perspective."

"I've heard *choi chi*—dog whelp—before, but a rabid dog is..."

"To be feared. Not an insult," she finished.

He nodded as he dabbed at the rope burns on her wrists.

"They're afraid of him, Ari. The room went dead still as soon as I said his name."

"We were questioning everyone in Ocean Beach," Lotario pointed out. "He may have questioned your captors. It probably spooked them."

"Maybe so."

"Did you know he picked up a stray girl?"

"Who?" she asked.

It was Isobel's turn to listen. And she did, as Lotario told her about Sarah Byrne and her uncle in the receiving hospital. But in the end she dismissed the information.

"It's a small world, but it's not that small, Ari. This isn't the girl they were looking for. Riot's stray was waiting at the ferry building when I met Sinclair in the hospital. And why would the tongs be searching for a white girl from Tennessee?"

"How do you know the men were part of a tong?"

Her gaze fell on the bit of embroidery that lay on the table. The very one she'd found on the dunes two nights before. Dried, and sitting in the light, she could see the color clearly: turquoise. It was part of a floral pattern with an intricate maze-like design. Isobel knew that design. She had seen the style before—during her dangerous adolescent wanderings down unsavory alleyways.

She pointed to the embroidery. "Because of that."

Clicking, clacking, bells and deep voices slammed into Isobel as she stepped off the elevator. Newspapers never slept. She threaded her way through an obstacle course of desks, and made her way to the Sob Sister's enclave.

Questions poked at her mind like a cattle prod. Who was Mr. Lincoln Howe? Why was his body in her cell? Where had those men taken Howe's corpse? And where was the girl they were looking for? Who was she?

The myriad of questions mixed with the jumble of emotions that were clouding her mind.

"A crack in the lens; a tear in my sail," she said under her breath. The crack was Atticus Riot. And she felt as if she had just dragged him into a rattler nest. Only he didn't know it yet.

Common sense told her to leave well enough alone, but Isobel had never listened to sense; she rebelled against its every principle.

Clara Sharpe sat at a desk in the Sob Sister's office. The older woman stared at a blank piece of paper in her typewriter. A thin line of smoke rose from a cigarette between her lips; it seemed forgotten, the ash growing by the second.

Isobel walked across the room to her preferred desk by the window. She took out the red token and the bit of embroidery, and laid them down in front of her. The token distracted her eye—its vibrant red mocked. She swept the cloth away, and moved the token to dead center where it sat like a bloodstain.

The Palm Saloon. It sounded expensive. Of course *palm* could mean something else entirely where the Barbary Coast was concerned.

A single question swam to the forefront of her mind: where to start? This investigation required care. She was known to at least one party involved. And she had no wish to mark Riot for death (or herself for that matter). Asking after Lincoln Howe would do just that.

Her eye kept being lured back to that bit of embroidery. A symbol of a girl being hunted. The question remained: where to start?

She glanced at Cara Sharpe, whose cigarette had dropped ash on the desk. Cara was a veteran reporter—direct, self-assured, and quick with a laugh. Isobel liked the older woman. She was everything opposite of hesitation, and her current stillness was profound.

"Start with a detail?" she asked the reporter. Advice that Cara had given her only a week before.

Cara plucked the cigarette from her lips, and smashed it into an ashtray. She turned in her chair and looked straight at Isobel. "It's the details I don't like." The woman's eyes were as sharp as her name, and Isobel felt like a fish in a bowl. "You look the worse for wear, Bonnie."

"Rough night," she said. "Do you know who generally handles affairs in Chinatown?"

"Mack McCormick."

Isobel groaned. It would be *him*. She did not feel like dealing with a misogynistic, womanizing sportsman. No matter, she thought as she reached into her handbag for a mirror. She had dealt with Kingston for months. Only, Cara was right, Miss Bonnie was looking positively frumpy today. More harried college girl than seductress. She clicked the mirror shut, and sighed.

"Don't sell your soul to the man," Cara said. "What do you need to know about Chinatown? Is it about the murders this morning?"

"Murders?"

"There was another tong shootout. Mack is writing up the article now."

Isobel leaned back, pushing her chair onto two legs, and looked into the corral. The big man was bent over his typewriter, glaring at the keys. She dropped back down. "I had a question about an old story."

Cara waited.

Isobel realized that the veteran reporter had been with the Call for years. She had the editor's ear. Cara was also sharper than Mack by spades.

Tread carefully, warned an internal voice. Isobel wondered if she had her own ghost haunting her. Maybe that was where her sense had gone—she'd killed it long ago.

"Do you know anything about Zephaniah Ravenwood's murder three years back?"

Cara didn't hesitate. "I remember it."

"Did Mack handle that story?"

"Anything with grisly details attracts him like a fly to dung."

Isobel had been in Europe when Ravenwood was murdered, and it only earned a three line mention on a back page. But she had recently dug through the Call archives for the story. Hip Yee hatchet men had hacked Ravenwood to pieces in his own home. The assassination had somehow triggered a tong war (so the article claimed), and the Hip Yee leader was gunned down by Suey Sings.

August Duncan had claimed that Ravenwood's head was placed on a platter, but the article made no mention of it. And while the coroner might simply have been trying to distract her (a ploy that worked), the article lacked the kind of detail that Isobel had expected; instead, it had deteriorated into a long, drawn-out exposition on the Chinese threat to San Francisco, and the poor victimized white man.

"Do you have a story brewing?"

"It's near to boiling."

"Aren't you acquainted with Atticus Riot?" Cara asked.

"I am," she said. There was no use denying that. "But it never hurts to be armed with more information before angling for an interview."

Cara smiled, her eyes nearly disappearing. "Good girl."

If anyone else had addressed her as such, Isobel would have bristled. But Cara exuded motherliness—the kind of mother who would sell her own daughter for a story.

"What do you remember about his murder?" Isobel asked.

"That there was too little information."

That's exactly what Isobel thought. She decided to play dumb. "But why?"

Clara cocked her head. "Mack isn't the most thorough investigator. But if I remember correctly, the editor wasn't interested in any more articles on Chinatown."

"Do you find that strange?"

"The tongs are old news," explained Cara. "There's not a week that goes by that some lurid story isn't published. And the Quarantine Station Scandal was old news. There was probably another story that caught the public's attention at the time." Cara lit another cigarette, and took a thoughtful drag. "Besides, half the men in San Francisco likely use those slave girls. I don't think they much care to be enlightened."

Prostitutes were there for a man's pleasure. Anything beyond that was far too complicated for most men to ponder. Accountability was a bitter pill to swallow when one could use a woman for twenty-five cents. Using a slave took the same level of commitment as slipping a penny into a Mutoscope, being entertained, and walking away.

"The article said that his partner, Atticus Riot, was injured in the attack—nearly killed. It seems like there must be more to the story."

"There was." Cara studied her through a haze of smoke. "Rumor said Atticus Riot was ambushed and dragged over to Chinatown. I heard he was tortured, and dumped at a Chinese undertaker's to die."

A lump rose in Isobel's throat. She quickly looked out the window, and tried to keep her voice from shaking. "Seems newsworthy." Her voice cracked.

A Chinese undertaker worked differently than an American one. The sick were taken to an undertaker while they were still breathing, to lie on a cot in a back room and listen to the hammering of the undertaker constructing their wooden overcoat. Because it was bad luck to have someone die in your home.

Cara smiled. "One would think. You'd have to ask Mack about the particulars."

Isobel thanked the woman, and returned to the evidence. But her thoughts kept traveling back to Riot, to the scars on his body, and the one that ran along his temple. She could almost imagine the bullet tracing the bone; a millimeter to the left and he'd be dead.

Isobel shivered, and for the first time in her life she wondered if she should walk away and be grateful that she had escaped with nothing more than a bruised stomach. But her eyes drifted to that bit of embroidery. There was a hunted girl out there.

Snatching up the ribbon, she put on an amiable face and walked into the corral to confront Mack McCormick.

❖

Mack ripped out a sheet of paper, crumpled it up, and tossed it into a growing collection of discarded words. His big, scarred hands fed a virgin sheet between the type-writer's paper table and platen. His red hair was thinning on top, and his neck seemed to have been swallowed by his massive shoulders years ago.

Isobel stood to the side of his desk. "Do you have a minute?"

"I usually need at least five," the man said. But the response seemed more automatic than sincere. He glanced over at her. "Were you hit by a wagon, Bonnie?"

"My friends call me Charlie."

Mack scratched the dimple in his square chin. "Is that what you tell your husbands before you murder them?"

"I never said it was murder—only accidental poisoning. I'm absentminded. I can't help it that cyanide looks just like salt."

"Call me Mack." He showed his teeth. "Now that we're on intimate terms, why don't you have dinner with me? Only we can skip the dinner part."

"You appear busy." She nudged the wastepaper basket with her shoe.

"I am." He looked at the blank sheet and blew a heavy breath past his lips.

She looked at his work so far. "*Butchery At The Butchers?*" she read.

He snatched the paper away, but she was a fast reader, and had already glimpsed the words underneath. Five

Suey Sing Tong highbinders walked into a store and gunned down two members of the Sam Yup Society, adding more names to a growing list of tong murders.

"It's a working title."

"I'm sure."

Mack leaned back in his chair, and crossed his arms. "What's the trouble with it?"

Isobel raised a shoulder. "Answer a few questions, and I'll give you a better option. One that will catch the desk editor's mousy eyes."

Mack glanced at the man behind a horseshoe-shaped desk. "I'd rather have dinner with you."

"I'd rather be escorted to a boxing match."

"I knew I liked you."

"I think you like every woman."

Mack snorted. "I can tell you don't think very highly of me."

"Do you blame me?"

He chuckled. "I can be charming."

"I thought you were already making the attempt," she retorted.

"That tongue of yours makes up for your 'run over by a wagon' appearance."

"I'm flattered." She smiled, and meant it. And he leaned forward. Mack was a big man with a Scottish accent that he worked hard to keep, and even sitting he was nearly at eye-level with her.

"Are you all right, Charlie? If someone roughed you up, I'll clean his plow." Mack cracked his scarred knuckles. And Isobel wondered how many noses those knuckles had broken.

"I appreciate the offer, but there's no plow in need of cleaning at the moment. I have some questions about an old story of yours."

"Which one?"

"The Ravenwood murder."

Mack grunted.

"The article seemed brief."

"That's 'cause the editor butchered it as sure as the hatchet men chopped up that old fellow."

"So what was taken out?"

He crossed his hands over his stretched waistcoat, and thought a moment. "I can't say off the top of my head. Details mostly. I described the scene in all its gory glory, but that was axed." He paused to see if she appreciated the pun; she did not. "Then there was a bit about his partner. I forget his name. Odd name though. Matty Wild, or some drivel."

Isobel nearly choked. She cleared her throat. "What bit was that?"

"The fellow got ambushed, captured, tortured, and left for dead with a bullet in his head. Only I couldn't get the story, because the bullet rattled his brain so thoroughly that he couldn't remember a thing."

Amnesia. It sounded like a lurid romance novel. She said as much, and Mack barked out a laugh. "That's why I didn't press it. It was crossing into Sob Sister territory. Why do you want to know?"

"One can never have too much ammunition before an interview."

"I prefer a good pair of fists."

"Speaking of fists," she said. "Have you heard of a pugilist by the name of Lincoln Howe?"

"Can't say I have. I can ask around."

"I'd rather you not, but I'd appreciate it if you kept an ear to the ground."

His bushy red brows shot up. "Dangerous fellow?"

"Something like that," she said dryly. "Now, do you want help with your article?"

"I doubt I'll use your suggestion. *Butchery At The Butcher* has a nice ring to it."

She offered her suggestion, and he looked like a child tasting a new food. Slowly, the flavor of the words grew on his tongue. Mack grunted, scratched out his own title, and added hers: *Record of Blood.*

24

The Falcons

A MOB OF BOYS loitered outside the Call building. Every single one of them was a waiting explosion of energy. Excitement flashed across quick eyes, and Isobel knew that their feet were even faster.

She motioned the smallest over. He was thin and covered in so much dirt that she wasn't sure what color lay beneath. But his eyes were bright, and the curly mop on his head lent him a mischievous air. His hair currently had a dusting of ash on the top. He called himself Bill Cody, and lived up to his name by charging at the other cappers, runners, and snitches like a wild buffalo when pickings got slim. Small, fast, and fierce, he reminded Isobel of herself.

"'Ello, Miss Bonnie," he said with a dip of his head. "I got a accident on Market, a lady who jumped off a ferry, a cigar store robbery, and another carbolic acid drinker." He fired off the growing list like an auctioneer, while he chewed on the stub of a cigar held between his lips. Isobel had recently hired him for exclusivity, but truth be told, she felt sorry for the boy; no one else would hire him. The other reporters went for the ones with longer legs and less smell.

"Keep your ears out for anything about a missing man, or one found dead with a wound in his head. I'll either come by and find you tomorrow, or you can leave a note at the telegram office for me." She dropped a quarter in his hand.

"Right then, Miss."

Isobel bought a paper from a newsboy, and planted herself in a cafe. She scanned the articles for any mention of Lincoln Howe, an unidentified dead man, or a runaway slave girl. There was no mention of any of them, but she found two articles that mentioned Atticus Riot: the safe return of an abducted woman, Mrs. Artells, and another story involving the girl who'd traveled from Tennessee. He had been busy.

She read *A Careless Injury*, and thought that the girl's uncle, Mr. Lee Walker, was a lucky man, indeed. If one were going to stumble and fall into an open street cellar, then best make it a property owned by a silver baron. She was about to put the paper down when a small paragraph caught her eye. She choked on her coffee, and stood, glaring down at the article.

AN ARGUMENT BETWEEN DETECTIVES

A passerby witnessed a confrontation between famed detective Atticus Riot and an unknown man in the early morning hours before dawn. The distinguished detective charged out of Ravenwood estate in a state of disarray, dressed in nothing but suspenders, union suit, and trousers. He stood in the rain without hat and shoes, and exchanged heated words with another man believed to also be a detective. Mr. Riot then stalked off in stony silence. The witness was unable to hear what was said, so one can only speculate on the nature of their disagreement.

Isobel muttered a crude oath at the article. If one could even call it an article. Slowly she became aware of eyes on her. A whole cafe full. Gathering herself, she primly sat back down and made an effort to sip her coffee. Ravenwood house was being watched. At the time, she'd assumed the fellow in the yard was visiting Miss Dupree, the resident prostitute, but it appeared he was a reporter.

A wave of relief rocked her. Thank God it was dark. The article could have been far worse. Better a fight than a tender exchange between Riot and a young man on the street. More care would be needed in the future.

In an attempt to calm herself, Isobel gazed out the window into the brightening day. There was a freshness to the city, and the promise of a crystal sky. Hay and lumber wagons trundled by, while cabriolets and phaetons bounced towards Golden Gate Park.

A single detail clamored to the forefront of her thoughts. Those men had been searching for a girl on the dunes. If the girl was a slave as Isobel suspected, then she wouldn't be familiar with the city. The Outer Lands stretched for miles, and a lone Chinese girl would attract notice.

Where would a lost girl run to in a foreign land?

A bicyclist narrowly missed colliding with a cable car, and an idea lit her mind. She tossed down her coins, and went off to send a telegram and spend her retainer's fee.

Wheels sped over gravel with abandon, as Isobel wove in and out of carriages and horses in Golden Gate Park. She was not the only bicyclist enjoying the sun and the crisp, cold air. Others, men in tweeds and women in split skirts and cycling costumes, rode at varying speeds.

Isobel made full use of her horn as she sped past most of them. She gripped the handles tightly, and clenched her teeth. Every bone in her body protested the exertion, but her mind would not leave her alone. No matter how her body ached, spending a day lying in a berth bunk was out of the question. Whether resting or moving, bruises still hurt, and Isobel preferred to be on the move. Fresh air, a brisk ride, and some snooping were called for.

Isobel hit the brakes on her Roadster, and skidded to a stop in front of a tree. If she had followed her mental map correctly, this was the same that Wilson had been tied to. She studied the ground, and saw his hoof prints stamping over the ground. Her own footprints were there, too.

In the light of day, the park felt friendly. Children played and couples strolled arm in arm. Women displayed their finery, walking like peacocks, in broad, high hats, clinging jackets, and skirts. Isobel's terror the night before seemed a childish overreaction, and her harried flight to Riot simply foolish.

Isobel sighed as she walked her bicycle along the hard gravel road. She stopped at the spot where she estimated she'd landed. But any marks had been erased by a maze of wheel tracks and footprints.

A burst of laughter caught her attention. Sounds of unrestrained joy were accompanied by horns and bells, and a cacophony of shouts. A group of women on Racers peddled furiously, in competition with two men on similar bicycles. The women wore caps, riding bloomers, and high leather boots, and were bent over their handlebars.

A cabriolet jerked to a stop as a bicyclist cut in front of

it. The horse danced nervously, narrowly avoiding a rosy-cheeked woman. A barrage of ungentlemanly cussing followed the woman, and she yelled back a lackluster apology. The group sped off, and Isobel thought she'd be hard pressed to keep up with them in her current condition.

She gazed after the women with longing. Her own life had once been that carefree as she'd jumped from one thrill to the next. But as she climbed back onto her bicycle, Isobel could not help but think of her despicable ex-husband Kingston. Of the constant strain, the toll those months in his company had taken, and the threat those same shadows still held. Death had severed their matrimonial ties, but then she wasn't really dead. And that left her in a vulnerable position.

She shoved that mess aside. If she could help even one soul—keep a single girl from being cornered as she had been, she would.

But at what cost?

Isobel pushed on a pedal, and let momentum speed her away. The carriage had traveled a winding course, which she followed—in reverse. It was satisfying exercise, both mentally and physically, and it distracted her from her own life. The route crisscrossed and doubled-back through the pathways of Golden Gate Park—just as she'd suspected while bouncing under the tarp.

A sheen of perspiration coated her skin as she shot onto Ocean Boulevard, and the sharp ocean breeze brought welcome relief.

The wagon carrying her the previous night had turned north, towards the Cliff House, but then it had turned around at a roundabout she knew well. Still, to be thorough, she followed the attempted ruse, counting seconds as she kept an even pace.

But that proved difficult. The sun was shining, and no matter the time of year, a sunny Ocean Beach attracted visitors. The Sutro Baths, the Cliff House, the Pavilion, and the Pacific tempted city-dwellers, and the road was packed. So she turned south at the roundabout, rode past the Lurline pier and the life-saving station, then headed towards Carville.

A host of abandoned street cars had been turned into vacationing cottages, clubs, and cafes. And sitting in the middle of Bohemian glory was a brick building guarded by a wrought-iron fence.

Isobel swerved to avoid a pothole—the same that the wagon had hit when it exited the brick building's drive. She did not stop, but kept cycling towards the glistening, Saharan-like dunes. In the distance, lonely tangles of Acacia trees rose, leaning against the wind, their branches and leaves swept back, shaped by an ocean's fury.

She glanced back at the three-story brick building. As an eye sore, it was worse than the Cliff House. And knowing what lay beneath—the cellar where she'd been hogtied for a full day—made her shiver.

She peddled into a sandy lot, and stopped in front of an old horse car that had been converted into a clubhouse. A sign over the roof proclaimed it *Falcons Bicycle Club*. A lean-to housed six Racer bicycles, four women's and two men's, and under a shelter sat a long table that looked like it could seat a banquet. The bicyclists were sipping drinks on a porch extending from the beached railcar.

"Hello there," she called as she walked her bicycle up to the porch. "I saw you riding in the park. Racing, more like."

"I hope we didn't cut you off," a tall, broad-shouldered

woman said.

"No, not at all, but I was impressed." Isobel kicked down her stand, and walked up the steps. "Charlotte Bonnie."

Handshakes were exchanged along with names, and a drink was placed in her hand. In no time at all, Isobel found herself sipping sherry with a group of men and women who seemed game for most anything.

"How does one join the Falcons?" she asked.

"A love of bicycling, and membership dues to help with food and upkeep," answered Margaret. She was blond and tall and had a boot propped on the railing, relishing the freedom of riding bloomers. Muscles played through the leather of her high boots, and she wore her hat at a jaunty angle. The puffed sleeves of her blouse looked comically feminine on her, and clashed with everything else about the woman.

"That, I can do," said Isobel.

"Do you swim?"

"I do. Sail, too."

A round of gasps traveled around the group. A few eyes glinted with plans for future excursions. Her membership was secured.

Margaret leapt to her feet. "Come see the inside."

Isobel followed the woman into a Bedouin paradise of luxury in the dunes. "It reminds me of a ship's cabin," she said. "I wouldn't mind living out here." And she meant it. With the constant waves and salt in the air, she didn't feel so claustrophobic here. Land usually made her itch; it made her feel trapped.

"It's splendid here. I stay over at night sometimes. And we swim when no one's looking." Margaret flashed a grin, making it clear that traditional swimming costumes weren't involved. "We play cards and host dinners—artists, musicians, writers, and even a mayor or two. Are you a working woman?"

"I'm a reporter for the Call."

Margaret's eyes widened a fraction. "Have I read anything by you?"

"Did you read *The Mysterious Savior?*"

Margaret gave a high-pitched squeal more suited to a school girl. She stuck her head out the door and told the club. At once, Isobel found herself the center of attention.

"Was it true, then?" a gentleman asked. Victor was thin and muscular, and wore his riding tweeds like a second skin. Everything about him seemed to be shaped by the wind.

"Course it was," Isobel replied. Most of it, at any rate.

"And the other story where he rescued the opera singer?" asked Gertrude. She was dark-haired and stout, and the daughter of a lumber yard owner. 'Lumber is as good as gold these days,' Gertrude had confided.

"Yes, that one too."

"Minnie, here, has it in mind to meet that detective—even if it's to be her own murder," Gertrude said.

Minnie was a quiet, petite woman who didn't look much older than seventeen. She blushed pink. But Isobel found little humor in the jest. What had once been a fascination was now her reality. Behind every murder was a face, a life. Both victim and killer. And sometimes killing was perfectly justified. It wasn't a game. She wondered what she'd uncover in this investigation.

A barrage of questions about the mysterious detective followed, which she skillfully deflected, giving only minimal answers. Isobel had no idea that her stories about Riot had generated so much enthusiasm—mostly among women it appeared. That had been her intention, she just hadn't realized how successful she'd been. It was both flattering and alarming. San Francisco had a way of building up legends, and then ripping them apart.

"Are you working on a story now?" This last question came from Ed, a brawny English gentleman who seemed more interested in Minnie than in cycling.

"I'm always looking for a story," Isobel said, flashing a grin. "But I'm mostly enjoying the sun today." She glanced slyly at the group. "You wouldn't happen to have something stronger?" The bold question was answered with grins, and a bottle of whiskey was brought out.

"I had a feeling you did." She raised her glass, and took a sip. "I should do a piece on your club. I'd never have found you if it weren't for your sign."

"We have something of a reputation," Gertrude said proudly. "We can't let the Fuzzy Bunch outdo us." It was another club in the area, full of long-haired Bohemians. Lotario was a regular of that club, and ran with its members.

Isobel glanced down Ocean Boulevard, towards the first signs of gentrification. "That brick building doesn't seem to fit in with Carville."

Margaret rolled her eyes. "It *doesn't* fit. And it ruins the character of Carville. We come out here to get away from the snobs, and then they plant their foot right in the middle of our territory."

"We're not *all* snobs," said Gertrude. "But it does put a damper on things."

"Is it a clubhouse? A residence?" Isobel asked.

"We aren't sure," admitted Victor.

Ed crossed his arms, displaying muscles that bulged and stretched the fabric of his sleeves. "It's a horseman's club. And boxing, I wager. Nothing more than a gentleman's retreat."

"You've been inside, then?" Isobel asked.

Laughter erupted—the laugh of shared mischief between friends.

"We dared Ed to try and get inside," Victor explained. "The Chinese doorman knocked him flat."

Ed hit Victor in the shoulder—a good-natured punch between brothers.

"Minnie thinks it's a Hellfire club," Margaret said when the laughter died.

Minnie blushed furiously.

"Why do you think that?" Isobel asked.

Comforted that she might be taken seriously, she answered, but avoided eye-contact with her peers. "I saw a woman looking out one of the windows once. She looked haunted, and… I've heard screams on the dunes."

"That was the storm," Violet said. She had an unearthly look to her, swathed in scarves, wisps of nearly white hair curling around pale features. She was the only married woman among the bunch, and though she carried herself with a certain amount of reserve, she rode like a fury. "I've talked to a few of the gentleman who were riding to it, or just coming away. They're charming enough."

"All men are charming to a pretty face," Gertrude said dryly. She downed her whiskey and poured another.

Isobel looked at Minnie. "When did you hear screaming?"

"Two nights ago. The storm came on suddenly, so I stayed the night."

"Alone?" Ed asked, concern plain in his voice.

"I wasn't about to ride home in that rain," Minnie

defended. "But I know what I heard."

"Dear," said Margaret, patting her hand. "You're always afraid when you stay over in the clubhouse, even with us."

Minnie's spine stiffened. "That was last year."

"It was probably the Beach Ghost," Victor said.

Glances were exchanged, and it was Margaret's turn to be put on the defensive, only instead of a blush, she turned red with anger. "So it turned out to be a person. I still saw something."

"Beach Ghost?" Isobel asked. The conductor, J.P. Humphrey had joked about the same thing.

"It was two years ago," Victor answered. "Margaret claimed she saw a ghost roaming the dunes."

Margaret sat back and crossed her arms. "Others saw it, too. I even tried following it one evening, but it disappeared."

"A reporter tracked it across the dunes, and it turned out to be a John Chinaman hiding from the tongs in a cave he'd dug out of a dune," Gertrude finished.

"The dunes *are* haunted," said Minnie.

A collective sigh traveled through the group.

"Did you hear anything else two nights ago?" Isobel asked.

Minnie shook her head. "I saw a light—a wavering light. It reminded me of a will-o'-the-wisp."

"They were probably lanterns," Ed said, in a comforting manner.

"But who would have been out in that storm?" Minnie looked at each in turn.

Isobel's thoughts churned. "Did the screams come before or after the will-o'-the-wisp?"

Minnie stood to leave. And Isobel reached out, taking

her hand. "I'm serious." She resisted the urge to drag the girl off and interrogate her without the others listening in.

"Are you a spiritualist, Miss Bonnie?" Violet asked. Her eyes were very nearly the same as her name.

"I'm more like an inquirer, and as curious as a cat. But back to the Beach Ghost. Screams aren't very ghostlike, are they? There's a lot of lonely territory out here."

"Miles of it," said Ed. "That's why I cringe at the idea of Minnie staying out here alone." The girl clenched her jaw. "One practically needs a pith helmet and camel to traverse the dunes."

"How'd the Chinese man survive?" Isobel asked.

Gertrude poured another shot of whiskey. "I heard he fished in the ocean at night, and picked up stray bits of vegetables and other things that washed ashore from passing boats."

"Is he still living in the dunes?"

The group exchanged puzzled glances. The thought had never occurred to any of them. "I don't know," said Margaret. "There's plenty of hermits living in the dunes, or nearby caves."

Half the populace in Carville could be considered hermits. Some of the abandoned horse-pulled railcars were little more than an amalgam of salvaged driftwood.

"Honestly, with the way the fog clings to the dunes, and the wind... I don't think there's a soul in Carville who hasn't been spooked," said Margaret. She thrust out her chin, defying anyone to disagree. No one said a word.

Isobel gazed across the dunes. A dusting of sand clouded the air, picked up by the ocean wind. The answer came to her like a gust. With a group of men hunting her, where else could the girl go?

She leaned forward in a conspiratorial manner. Isobel

had six game people filled with sherry and whiskey. She wasn't about to pass up an opportunity like that. "We should go ghost hunting."

25

Uneasy Rest

A KNOCK INTERRUPTED THE quiet. Silence answered. Tobias shifted in front of the tower room door. The morning breakfast tray sat in the hallway, the plate still covered, the tea cup untouched.

Tobias glanced at the yellow envelope in his hand. He *could* slip the telegram under the door—he probably should, but he had been told to hand it to Mr. Riot directly. As the boy stood debating with himself, a boarder, Mr. Löfgren, walked past and smiled broadly at the boy. Tobias returned the greeting, clutching the telegram close. It was meant for Mr. Riot, and he would guard it with his life. But nothing so drastic was required; the cheerful Swede walked by without stopping.

Tobias knocked again. Nothing. He glanced right and left, and tried the handle. The door gave way, and he poked in his head.

The room was dark; the bed rumpled. But no one slept in it. An entire deck of playing cards littered the floor around the fireside chairs. There was a bottle on the floor, too. A hand hung limp from the big throne-like chair. It was fine and tanned, and it sparked terror in Tobias, being as still as it was.

Heart in his throat, he rushed towards the man. Mr. Riot was slumped in the chair, chin on his chest. He wore his union suit and trousers, his suspenders hanging around his waist.

Tobias stared at him. He'd seen dead men before, but Mr. Riot wasn't dead—not yet. It was more of a shock to find him so disheveled. Overcome with worry, he began to shake him as hard as he could. But as soon as Tobias laid hands on the man, Riot came alive like a snake. There was a click, and Tobias' eyes crossed as he looked straight into the barrel of a gun. His world went suddenly black.

"God dammit, Tobias!" Atticus Riot nearly threw his revolver across the room. He uncocked his gun, and started to stand, but pain stabbed at his temple. The world tilted, and he nearly pitched forward. He sat back down, hard. And leaned forward, planting his elbows on his knees.

Riot pressed the side of his revolver to his temple. The cool steel helped, but the feel of the revolver so close to his head brought a flash of memory. A grinning young man, and the bark of a gun. He fought for breath, fought for control. Fought to steady his hands and his mind. But the harder he struggled, the more he slipped. Tobias. The thought of the boy gave him strength. He set his gun on the table, and dropped to his knees to check on the boy.

Only a faint. He gave Tobias a gentle slap, and the boy's eyes snapped open, wide and fearful.

"Sorry, I don't sleep easy," he muttered. "Sit up slow—that's it." Riot needed to follow his own advice. His stomach flipped.

The empty bottle was evidence enough without the wool in his head. Once Tobias was sitting upright, Riot eased himself over to the washbasin and dunked his head in cold water. He grabbed a towel, and dried his hair as he walked back to the door.

A tea tray waited outside. When he picked it up, the delicate porcelain and cutlery chattered along with his hands. He set it down on a table, and grabbed his left hand with his right to steady it. The shaking had started three years before, after his head wound. It came and went with the flashes of memory. And he hated when his hands shook; it reminded him of unsteady men with ready fists. When two cups were poured with minimal spillage, Riot placed one in Tobias' hands. "Drink."

He followed his own orders, sitting beside the boy on the floor. When nothing but dregs were left in his cup, he reached back, feeling for his spectacles on the table.

"There's a telegram for you." Tobias held up a crinkled yellow slip.

Forcing his mind to action, Riot took it, and ripped it open.

NOT MY STORY -B

Riot grabbed the newspaper on the tray, and searched its pages while Tobias occupied himself by collecting the scattered deck of cards. The account of the argument in the street brought to mind Isobel's mention of Miss Dupree's gentleman caller.

"Mr. Fry," he muttered under his breath.

"Who?"

Riot shook his head, instantly regretting it. He glanced at the empty bottle, and closed his eyes against a stab of regret. No problem was ever fixed at the bottom of a bottle. And all he had to show for his night was wool in his skull. Isobel, on the other hand, had likely landed herself in more trouble. He should have answered her last night, should have followed her... But he hadn't.

A squared deck entered his line of sight. "I'm sorry, Mr. Riot."

"No need to be. You did right." He looked up at Tobias, and accepted the deck of cards. "Next time throw something at me from a distance first."

"Grimm's the same way," Tobias said, as he refilled their cups. "I throw a pillow at him, but he don't have a gun. And he don't talk, so I don't know why he's the way he is."

"Silence isn't always a good thing." Sooner or later the mind started to crack. Riot folded the telegram slip, and tucked it in his pocket. A bit of hope in the bleakness. It was proof that Isobel cared what he thought of her. He only cringed at what she'd eventually think of him.

Tobias shrugged. "Maybe it's all Grimm can do. Do you talk to people about why you don't sleep easy?"

Riot glanced at the boy, and promptly changed the subject. "Thank you for delivering the telegram."

Tobias hopped to his feet. "Sarah was asking after her uncle this morning."

"Who?"

The boy made a face. "Sarah Byrne. The girl you brought here yesterday."

"Of course." Riot pressed his fingers to his temple, scratching at the scar beneath his hair. "I'll uhm... talk to her shortly."

As soon as the door closed, Riot let his head fall back against the chair, closed his eyes, and wondered if another bottle laced with laudanum might silence his ghosts for good.

❖

Hat in hand, Riot walked downstairs. The house was quiet. Still. It felt empty. He stopped at the bottom of the stairs. The dining room doors were closed, and he stared at them until girlish laughter burst from the level below. It shattered the quiet, and made him shiver. Joy felt wrong in this house.

Riot turned towards the front door, not knowing where he'd go. He needed to walk, but he didn't get far. Tim's voice stopped his flight.

"Tobias claims you are near to dead." For an old man, he moved on quiet, quick feet that possessed an eternal spring in every step.

Riot smirked. "I'd likely feel better if I were." He turned to regard the man. "Have you ever thought of wearing pointed slippers, and a hat with a feather on top?"

Tim glared. "Last man who said that to me ended up on his ass." The little man rocked back and forth from heel to toe, itching to move.

"It can't leave me with a worse headache than I already have," Riot muttered.

"There's tea in the kitchen."

"Is Miss Lily in there?"

"No, she's gardening."

"Outside?" Riot asked.

Tim shook his head. "Greenhouse."

The word was like a trigger. Flashes of memory hit

him: a trail of blood and footprints, and a headless corpse. He couldn't look at the dining room doors; instead, he focused on his shoes. "You said you found me at a Chinese undertaker's," Riot said. He might have been speaking to Tim, or to the ghost of a memory that hounded his every step.

Tim's gaze flicked between Riot and the dining room. "That's right."

"How'd I get to Chinatown?"

"Ambushed, far as I can tell. You were in bad shape."

Riot clutched his walking stick; his hand was still shaking.

"I read the paper this morning," Tim said, deftly changing the subject. "Did Mr. Morgan turn up last night?"

A pang of regret stabbed Riot—he had moved too fast, and she had fled.

"Bel asked me what *din gau* meant."

Tim stopped rocking. "Shit."

Indeed, Ravenwood rasped.

Riot inclined his head. There really wasn't a polite word for it. The name that followed him was accompanied by furtive glances and whispered words uttered like an oath to ward off demons. Just as the tongs called Donaldina Cameron *White Devil*. They called him Rabid Dog. Riot feared that dark corner in his mind; he feared what he would find when he stared into its depths.

"What's she got herself into?" Tim asked, slowly.

"I don't know yet."

"Is she here?"

"No."

"Where'd she go?"

Riot spread his hands, hat in one, and stick in the

other. "Your guess is as good as mine, Tim."

The man spluttered.

"As much as I'd like to scour the city for her again..."
Ravenwood chuckled in his ear, and Riot forced himself to
keep talking. "...I have other responsibilities."

That woman of yours is an intriguing distraction.

The comment caught Riot off-guard. He could think
of only one other woman whom Ravenwood spoke of
favorably.

"Those being?" Tim asked.

"I'd like to speak with Miss Lily and yourself." He
sounded tired, even to his own ears.

Tim shifted from side to side, studying him with concern. "You want me to ask her to come into the sitting
room?" Tim well knew his aversion to the greenhouse.

Stop running, Ravenwood urged.

Riot shook his head. "No." He walked purposefully
towards that wing of the house. And in his mind's eye, with
vivid recollection, he saw a trail of blood as he had three
years before. A flash of memory—of blood, a caved-in
skull, and a frail woman, limp in her nightdress. Bruises
covering her face, neck, and arms.

"A.J." A hand grabbed his arm. "You're white as a
sheet. And that's saying something for you."

Riot blinked. His heart hammered as if he had just run
clear across the city. He pulled away from the old man,
and kept walking, passing into warmth, sun, and a green so
bright that it struck the inside of his skull. It smelled of
earth, and life—as if the man who died there had left all
his vitality behind.

Miss Lily White greeted the gentlemen with a pleasant
smile, and clippers in hand. She stood by the roses, gently
holding a stem between thorns, clipping off shoots until

only three leaves remained.

Tim cleared his throat. "Don't mean to interrupt you, Miss Lily."

Riot looked to the long table. Ravenwood had used the greenhouse as a laboratory, much to his old housekeeper's consternation. The beakers and tubes, glass and chemicals were gone, replaced with sprouts and seedlings, and an array of tools that would coax life from the ground.

"You have a green thumb, Miss Lily." There was a tremor in his voice.

If she noticed, she didn't say. Lily was too polite; instead, she smiled. "I like my ingredients fresh," she said, setting down her clippers. She pinched off a stem of rosemary, rubbed the soft, needle-like leaf between her fingers, and inhaled the scent. "They say food is made with love, but it starts with plants. I can grow them all year round here, and it saves on the grocer's bill, too."

Her voice was soothing, low and calm, and while she was talking, his gaze traveled to an empty spot on the earthy floor. Only in his mind it wasn't empty. A headless corpse lay there.

Why was Ravenwood killed in here? With as many cases as the agency had been involved in, he should have been in his consultation room reviewing his notes.

Question everything, the man rasped in his ear.

"Can I help you with something, Mr. Riot?" Lily's voice brought him around. But he didn't answer her question. He walked over to a glass panel by the door. The one that had been shattered to gain entry. Had Ravenwood heard the glass, and hurried to confront the intruder?

Riot tapped his walking stick in thought. It had once belonged to Ravenwood, and he'd found it clutched in his dead partner's hand, covered in blood. If Ravenwood had heard a noise, and been drawn to this observatory, why hadn't he grabbed one of the guns? And if he had been working, why did he have his stick here with him?

"A.J.?" Tim's voice sounded at his side. "You had something you wanted to talk to us about?" It was more reminder than question.

"Sarah Byrne," he said absently.

"She's been a big help," Lily said. "Been no trouble at all."

Riot suspected that the gentlewoman would say that if he brought a pack of wild dogs into the house. She'd likely have them calm and settled within an hour.

"I found her uncle." His voice was hoarse; his mind conjuring phantom images. A broken pane, silenced with a cloth. Ravenwood hunched over in his laboratory working —on what? Had he turned to see the man approaching from behind with a knife? Yes, most definitely. There had been bruises on his body. He had put up a fight.

"We read that in the paper this morning," Tim said, bringing him back to the present. The old man was perched on a low wall. Blue eyes regarded him with no little amount of concern. As they should be; Riot was concerned as well. His feet no longer felt attached to the ground.

"There were two reporters who came by already. They asked to see her," said Lily. "I sent them both away, and told her to keep clear of the windows. I hope that was all right."

Riot nodded, and ran a hand over his beard. The gesture focused him, brought him back to the ground. But this room still nagged at him, picked at his brain like an itch.

He cleared his throat. "I'm not sure what's best for her.

I have reason to believe that Lee Walker, her uncle, staged the whole accident. Specifically targeting one of Claiborne's properties with the intent to sue him for damages. I think he timed it with Sarah's arrival. A recently orphaned niece left alone at the ferry building was sure to add fodder to the reporting frenzy."

"But he's hurt, isn't he?" Tim asked. "A twenty foot fall could have killed him." Tim took out his pipe, and made to light it, but Lily gave him a pointed look. She only tolerated smoke in a boarder's own room, or the smoking room. He flashed his gold teeth, and stuck the stem between his lips unlit.

"This is the only photograph that Sarah had of her uncle." Riot showed the postcard to them, and Tim whistled. "She said he was an escape artist in the circus," Riot explained for Lily's benefit. "It's a profession that requires special skills."

"Skills like dislocating the shoulder," Lily said, catching on.

Riot nodded. "He's now a horse betting man with no sense, and he's up to his nose in debt."

He had nothing against gamblers—he'd be the largest hypocrite in the West if he did—but his professional pride drew the line at a bad gambler.

Lily considered the photograph. "And you're wondering if you should look into the matter more?"

Riot gave a slight nod. "I don't know what would be best for her. An uncle who is a con man, or no kin at all."

The statement was answered with silence as both adults pondered the conundrum that had plagued him since he met Walker. It wasn't his affair. He had no proof, only suspicions—all easily confirmed if he decided to poke his nose further into Walker's business. And if Riot's instincts were correct, this wasn't the first time Lee Walker had feigned an injury. His bank book had shown a large deposit—money that Walker had burned through.

From the moment he engaged her at the ferry building, she had become his responsibility, and Sarah Byrne's future now rested on his shoulders. That didn't set well with him; Riot had enough blood on his hands to give him pause in deciding her fate.

"For what it's worth, he had a room prepared for her. It was clean and warm, in a fine house."

"The bast—scoundrel," Tim corrected hastily, "left her waiting at the ferry building in the rain. She might have been snatched."

"I'd say pneumonia was more likely," Lily said. "Have you told her about your suspicions?"

Riot shook his head. "She's terrified of being an orphan. That fear drove her clear across the country alone. If he's arrested, she'll go to an orphanage."

"Well, she's been asking after him," Lily said. "Wants to visit him in the hospital, and if you ask me, she's the type of child who will go with or without you."

She was right. But Riot knew beyond a doubt that Walker would have a mob of reporters waiting to write down every word.

Tim poked his boot at the dirt. "You weren't hired to investigate the fellow."

"There's the temptation," Riot said with a quirk of his lips. "We could stop right here. All I have is a suspicion."

"There might be more to the man. More than him just being a con man," Tim said.

"There could be," he agreed. "I hate to pass this off to you, but Smith and Monty are tied up with other matters, and I have business of my own." Tim didn't need an explanation; he well knew that Riot's business involved a certain cross-dressing young woman.

"I'll poke into his past. Shouldn't be difficult." Tim scratched at his beard. "I'm... uhm, still searching for Walker's sure-fire horseman named Freddy."

"You haven't found him yet?" Riot asked with feigned surprise.

"I'm getting old, boy. Don't push it."

"Mr. Riot?"

He looked expectantly at Lily. She clipped a dead bulb from the stem, and placed it in a pot as she chose her words. She was a graceful woman in everything she did, and there was a kind of magic to her movements that slowed down even the most hurried mind.

"Sarah's a bright one," she explained. "Children are more perceptive than most adults give them credit for. Maybe she won't much care for her kin, and all this might come out in the courts anyhow. Some battles aren't our own."

"I won't leave a child to fight alone."

Lily smiled, displaying two dimples. "I think you have your answer, then."

26

The Snitch

LEE WALKER'S EYES LIT up when his niece walked into the infirmary. "The spitting image of my sister," he breathed.

It might have been a touching reunion if not for the mob of eager reporters. Walker stretched out a hand, and winced, falling back into his pillows. "I'm sorry I wasn't there for you, Sarah."

Sarah stared at his weak, reaching hand, and then at his face. She stood beside Riot, rooted in place.

Walker noticed her hesitation. "I was on my way to fetch you, and I fell down an open shaft. A property owner's negligence at its finest. I'm so sorry you were left out there, in the rain, the cold—you might have been abducted." This was said in a slightly elevated tone. Journalists scribbled, and the attorney beamed, while Riot tightened his grip on his walking stick.

He waited to see what Sarah would do. She moved slowly towards her uncle, clearly made uncomfortable by the audience. She offered her hand in greeting, and Walker took it warmly.

"Mr. Riot saw that I was well taken care of, sir."

"And I'm indebted to him for it," Walker replied. There seemed to be truth in his words. He spoke with real feeling, likely due to dealing with a well-known private detective rather than a run-of-the-mill policeman. Far better for the newspapers.

"Call me Uncle Lee, won't you?"

Sarah nodded. "Will your arm mend?"

"The doctors say so, but I'll be laid up, and there's my head, you see. There's still gaps in my memory."

"Losing memories of bad things might be a good thing," Sarah said, with a gravity that surpassed her tender age.

The reporters chuckled, and her uncle laughed. Riot could only silently agree. Three years had passed, and there were still gaps in his own memories. He didn't want to know what happened. He feared to know, because it would only confirm his growing suspicions.

"I suppose so," Walker agreed. He winced again, and looked suddenly tired, lids drooping, eyes fixed on Sarah. It was a dramatic performance. "You bring back so many fond memories of my sister. She died a terrible death, and you being left all alone—except for my mother."

"How'd her mother die, Mr. Walker?" a reporter asked.

A cool kind of rage charged through Riot's veins. He stepped forward, and placed a hand on Sarah's shoulder. "You look as though you could use some rest, Mr. Walker. We don't want to tax your recovering mind. I'll see to it that Miss Byrne is looked after until you recover. If that's agreeable with you, Miss Byrne?"

Sarah backed up, moving closer to Riot, giving a silent but clear answer.

"Of course," Walker said. "You're right. I'm thankful for your kindness."

"It's no trouble."

"Goodbye, Uncle Lee."

"Give your ol' uncle a kiss on the cheek now."

Riot felt the girl's hesitation, and promptly gave her a way out before she felt forced into politeness. "Movement, Mr. Walker," he reminded, slipping Sarah's arm through his. "It's best you stay immobile." He gently steered the girl away from her only kin, the mob of reporters, and one elated attorney.

"What did you think of your uncle?" Riot asked.

Sarah's head was turned away from him as she looked out the window of the rattling hack. "I wasn't expecting all those others." Her voice was nearly lost in the racket of springs and wheels.

Riot waited.

And as if lured by his patience, she looked away from the window, and turned towards him. "Maybe if I could speak to my uncle alone. Why did his accident attract so much attention?"

"The man who owns the property is wealthy," Riot replied. "Your uncle is suing him for negligence."

Sarah's brows drew together with concern. "Are my uncle's injuries bad? The doctors say he'll live, right?" Here was a child who had already experienced loss. She well knew the precarious perch of the living.

"I'm told he'll make a full recovery. Although memory loss can be… It can take longer to recover."

"I suppose he's lucky he wasn't hurt worse."

"Very lucky," Riot said dryly.

The girl didn't miss his tone. She frowned, weighing matters that no child should have to contemplate. Her black hair was still in braids, and her dress was a child's, but she was already pushing at the boundaries of womanhood. Clean, fed, and well-rested, she looked like a proper young lady. However, the green smudges on her stockinged knees hinted at a child underneath the facade.

"You don't like him," she stated plainly. She was a sharp one, too.

Riot regarded her. There was no use denying it; not to her. And he suspected that she felt the same. She was only looking for permission to feel that way.

"I'll be frank with you, Miss Byrne. I'm not entirely sure your uncle is of the best character."

A girlish laugh escaped her lips. "Of course, he isn't, Mr. Riot," she said with practical Southern politeness. "He ran off to the circus. Mamma always said that you can't trust such folk. She called him the black sheep of our family to her dying day, and for as long as I can remember everyone told me that I wasn't to have anything to do with him."

"Do you know why he ran off?"

"I do not. Do you know?" There was worry on her face. The way she sat, the way she'd seemed to shrink when she asked the question. It was one that she had no doubt been asking herself the entire train ride across the country.

"No," he admitted. "And that concerns me."

"I don't know what I expected." There was a tremor in her voice. "But it wasn't that. I didn't much like him either. He seemed..." She shrugged.

"He seemed to be putting on a show?"

Sarah nodded. "A bad one, but he's the only kin I got

left." Tears shimmered, but did not fall. She scrubbed a hand across her eyes, and clenched her teeth.

Ravenwood made an impatient noise. *This isn't your affair.*

The voice was so real, so urgent in his mind. He could see that shadow of the man turn his back on the child—as he had done so many times when faced with a distraught client. Always an unmistakable signal for Riot to take the reins of an interview.

Riot reached over, and took both of her hands in one of his. "Sarah," he said her name softly. He waited until she met his gaze with misting eyes. "I'll do everything in my power to see that you don't end up in an orphanage."

When the hack pulled up to Ravenwood manor, the front door opened. Tobias skipped down the steps, and hurried over to the window.

"Get off my hack!" the hackman snarled, raising his whip.

"Strike him, and I'll strike you!" Riot barked.

Sarah jumped with surprise, and Tobias hopped backwards off the carriage, scrambling out of range. Riot quickly opened the door and stepped down, staring hard at the driver as he helped Sarah out of the hack.

"I don't tolerate niggers in my hack," the hackman growled.

"And I have no tolerance for bullies."

"You're lucky the lady is there, fellow."

"Indeed." Riot flipped the man his fare, but no more. With a hand on each child's back, he ushered them up the stairs towards the house.

"There's a visitor for you, sir," said Tobias. "Says he's a

friend of yours. Been waiting this whole time."

"Does this friend of mine have a name?" As they walked up the steps, Riot noticed a man lurking by a lamppost. It wasn't Mr. Fry, and most of the other reporters had been at the hospital for the meeting. The man was casually smoking, unhurried and unconcerned.

Riot paused on the steps, and stared across the street at the stranger. When he saw Riot looking, he tipped his bowler. Wearing a ready-made suit with mustache and long sideburns, the man was the type that blended in with any crowd.

The complete opposite of Riot's visitor. As soon as Riot stepped into the entryway, a familiar face rushed out of the sitting room. He wasn't wearing his Sean Murphy disguise, or Madam de'Winter (she had taken a retreat to France after her abduction), or the foppish Paris in an electric-blue, velvet suit. No, Lotario was dressed in a bespoke suit today. And from the cut and quality of tailoring, it could only be from *Steed and Peel*—Riot's own tailors.

Riot looked at him in question.

"Just me, today," Lotario smoothly supplied.

"Ah, may I present Miss Sarah Byrne." Riot made introductions.

Lotario took her gloved fingers. "A pleasure, Miss Byrne. You know how to make an entrance in this city. You've barely set foot in San Francisco, and your name is already in the papers. Only a very few can claim that distinction."

Riot cocked his head, marveling at the man's range of voice. Today, it was even and smooth, not quite deep, but not high either. A carefree tone that was all charming humor.

Sarah smiled. "I assure you it wasn't intentional."

"Ah! A natural talent, then. How is Mr. Riot treating you?"

"He's a fine host."

"Without a doubt. And how do you find our silver city?"

"I've hardly seen it." Her disappointment was plain.

Lotario clucked his tongue. "That will have to be fixed. Patience, I'm told is a virtue, but I've never found it very fun." Lotario gave Riot a pointed look.

"It never is," she agreed.

"I was kept waiting for ages in that sitting room. Have you ever been locked in a sitting room?"

"We didn't lock you in," said Tobias indignantly.

"But you were spying on me," Lotario said.

"You were juggling teacups," the boy retorted.

"Goodness, no."

"And then knives."

"Your story gets more fanciful by the second. Next you'll be claiming I was jumping on the furniture."

Sarah giggled. And Tobias darkened. "You *were*."

Riot cleared his throat. "If you will both excuse us, I need to speak with Mr. Amsel."

Tobias spluttered, and Lotario plucked a coin from the boy's ear. He rolled it over his knuckles before flipping it to Tobias with a wink. A gasp of delight came from Sarah, but before the children could beg for more tricks, Riot ushered Lotario into the sitting room. He grabbed both doors, and looked hard at the children. "I'll know if you try to eavesdrop."

Both of them blushed, and hurried towards the kitchen as he slid the doors together.

"What a charming young lady. She reminds me of myself at that age."

Riot paused, and turned to meet the other half of the two-headed chameleon. And just like that ever-changing creature, Lotario transformed from charm to a high-strung thoroughbred about to bolt.

"Did Bel stop by?" Lotario asked.

Riot drew him away from the doors, to the opposite side of the room. This house had sprouted very inquisitive ears.

"Yes, she did."

Lotario glanced at Riot from under his lashes. He was waiting for something.

Riot took a gamble. "I see you talked with her."

Lotario deflated. "You know," he breathed with relief.

"I agree, it's worrisome."

"Worrisome? I'd say it's terrifying. She should have told you straight away, but she was worried about you. *You*, of all people. Never mind that she was attacked on the dunes by three men. Being hog-tied, beaten, and kept in a basement for a day couldn't have been enjoyable, even for my twin."

Riot swallowed down a cool rage.

"Bel hides her fear well, you know, but I've never seen her so frightened. The threat of a *chun hung* on your head rattled her."

It took effort to keep his voice steady. "As well it should," he said.

"I'm more rattled by the possibility of one on *her* head," Lotario said. "I hope you weren't angry with her for not telling you right away. She panics, and bolts. And she has an awful protective streak. Always has. Do you know whenever I was bullied, she'd jump into the fray and take the beating for me? I hated it. And I loved her for it." As Lotario prattled on, he unclasped a leather carrying case.

"That's why I'm worried. She tried to hide this..." He yanked out a shirt and waistcoat that had seen better days. "I found it while I was cleaning up her cabin."

Riot took it, moved a vase aside, and laid the garments out on a table. The outline of a boot print was clear, but his eyes were drawn to the blood stains, and the perfectly sliced buttons down the front. He had wondered why she'd kept her peacoat on, and why it had been buttoned clear to the collar in the heat of the room.

"Do you know anything about this? She said they only kicked her..." Lotario's voice rose a notch, close to Madam de'Winter's perfect soprano.

Riot held up a hand, stopping the man. "This might not mean what you think."

"How on earth can you be so calm?"

"Because I have to."

"But I'm sure she's gone off to look for the girl the men were after."

Riot wanted to demand the whole story, but he worried Lotario would seal up like a clam when he realized Isobel hadn't told Riot a thing. So he continued his bluff. "Bel may be foolhardy, but she's no fool. Her guard is up now."

"She shot a man point-blank, and he didn't even slow," Lotario reminded. "What good is her guard when a revolver is useless?"

"I intend to find her first."

"I'm coming with you, then."

"No, you are not," Riot said firmly. Lotario started to protest but he cut him off. "I need you to do something for me so I can corner your twin."

"How are you going to find her?"

"The same as I always do."

"What do you want me to do?"

"I need you to escort Sarah around San Francisco. She's traveled all the way from Tennessee, and I think it only fair that she see the city."

Lotario snorted. "Why do I feel like I'm being shoved off to the side?"

"You can feel however you like, but you're the only one I'd trust this to. There have been reporters lurking around the house, and I'm sure they'll hound her for an interview the moment she steps outside."

Lotario arched a thin brow.

"You are more than adept at dodging reporters," Riot said, stroking his ego.

"Well, there is that."

"Besides, I'm sure you won't want to be anywhere near Bel when she finds out you told me everything."

Lotario casually glanced at his nails. "I can hardly be blamed for being tricked by a scoundrel such as yourself."

Riot had not been the only one bluffing. "In that case, tell me the rest of the story."

27

End of the Trail

LAUGHTER FLOWED UNDER THE sun. It was a reassuring sound to Isobel. The Falcon's ghost hunt had only lasted until the words 'food' and 'hungry' were uttered. Then they had headed straight for Mrs. Gunn's Home Cooking, a restaurant made up of three railcars tacked together into an L-shape that hugged a patio. With baskets in hand, the group set out across the dunes, laid down a blanket, and promptly stuffed themselves to bursting.

Isobel was no exception. Later she walked arm in arm with Margaret across the wind-swept sand. She could see the top story of the brick building, but she didn't feel exposed. Although her captors knew she was a woman, they wouldn't look twice at someone from a local club known for its social gatherings.

"…truth is, I don't know what I want to do with myself. I win every woman's race, but it's not as if a woman can be a professional bicyclist." Margaret gave a sigh.

"I don't think there's much future in that for men

either," Isobel pointed out. Her voice was casual, with the kind of closeness that came with new friends exploring each other. But even as they walked arm in arm, Isobel searched the dunes for signs of life. Unfortunately, the wind had a way of wiping the sands clean, leaving only rippling marks.

"How about college?" she asked.

"My father is very ill. It's only because of a nurse that I'm able to escape at all. Besides," Margaret wrinkled her nose, "I'm not one for book learning. I like to use my hands."

That was clear as day. "What do you like to build?" Isobel asked.

Margaret started in surprise. "How did you know?"

"Your hands are rough," Isobel explained. "Your palms, and the area between thumb and index finger are thick with callouses from holding a hammer. I noticed faint stains when I shook your hand—an attempt to remove the varnish that I smelled on you when we first met."

"Oh." Margaret studied her hand. It seemed obvious now. "It's not a very womanly pastime, but my father has a small shed of tools where he used to tinker before he became ill. I mostly build birdhouses, dollhouses, and smaller types of furniture." There was sadness in her voice. "I really want to build houses."

"You could at least design them. Women have graduated from the University of California with an engineering degree."

"I don't think anyone would hire a woman architect."

Isobel raised a shoulder. "You never know until you try."

"I suppose it couldn't hurt. It would at least be interesting." Margaret smiled ruefully. "I know I'll never marry."

Her eyes flickered sideways with a question. "What about you?"

"And let a man ruin all my fun?" Isobel clucked her tongue, and Margaret laughed. As far as anyone was concerned, Charlotte Bonnie was an independent single journalist with no plans to settle down. The guise warmed Isobel's heart; it made it easier to forget her months with Kingston.

"What are you up to anyway? I didn't buy that sunbathing story for a hair's breadth."

Isobel leaned in conspiratorially. "Do you know where the Beach Ghost was hiding?"

"Not precisely," Margaret admitted. "The reporter said he found the prints a half mile south of the bend in the Park and Ocean line, then followed it for a mile, but the Ghost doubled back and such. But that was years ago. I'm sure the tunnel has caved in by now. I tried to build a smaller version, but the sand was impossible."

Isobel arched a brow. That was definitely close enough to the brick building, and not far from the Falcon's clubhouse. She ran her eyes over the horizon. The distant patch of acacia, stunted and windblown, pricked her instincts. Roots offered stability.

"Why are you so curious about it?"

Isobel debated whether to lie or not. Lying, she decided, was generally a good idea. "I'm looking for my next story, but the city was stifling. I need fresh air," she said with feeling, because at that moment it was true. They were walking farther from the others, whose laughter was dying in the sand hills. The slanted acacias grew closer, and a mark caught Isobel's eye. A small, smooth impression of the ball of a foot.

"Are you only here for the day?"

"I'm not sure." Isobel tore her eyes from the print, and looked to the ocean, to the shacks and railcars. "Are those more clubhouses?" Carville hadn't existed when she'd been shipped off to Europe in disgrace five years before.

"The railcars have been turned into cottages for vacationers. You can let them for a few nights. Mostly, erm…"

"People use them for illicit dalliances?"

Margaret grinned with relief. "I was hoping you weren't a prude."

"A woman riding a bicycle in bloomers can't be too proper."

"True," said Margaret. "But one never knows. We try to keep things tame when Minnie is with us. And don't let Violet fool you. She's the wildest of us all."

Isobel laughed.

"You know, now that you're a member, you can stay in our clubhouse. There's even spare clothes in the trunk."

"I just might, but—"

"Yes?"

Isobel chewed on her lower lip for effect. "I want to check on the availability of those cottages—in case." The two women glanced at each other, and both fell to laughing.

Isobel paid her dues, received a neat little falcon pin that she proudly attached to her lapel, and parted ways with her new friends.

Every time she spent Lincoln Howe's money, she thought of him. He was bound to turn up as either unidentified, or the unfortunate victim of a robbery.

So she hoped.

As she walked her bicycle along Ocean Boulevard, she

wondered how many other detectives had been abducted by murderers, had found a corpse, and then lost it. The thought depressed her, and left her feeling that she had taken the coward's way out of the situation.

With a sigh, she eyed the line of railcar cottages along the shore. A massive wall of fog roiled on the horizon, coming in like a slow tidal wave towards the little cottages. She never tired of watching the blanket of gray creeping ever closer, until it crashed on land and washed the city clean. By the time she reached the railcars, San Francisco had gone from sunlight to shivering mist. Isobel kicked down her stand, and shrugged on an overcoat.

She walked around back, eyed the water tower and numerous footprints, and then gazed east, towards the grove of acacia, but the stunted trees were lost to her now.

She returned to the main cottage, spotted a sign on the front 'Cottages for Rent' and knocked. A weather-worn woman answered the door. She wore scarves and enough jewelry to make a gypsy spiritualist envious. There was paint on her fingers.

Isobel shivered, letting her teeth chatter. "Do you have any cottages available for the night? I don't much care to ride back in this cold."

"Caught you by surprise, didn't it? Always does to city folk and tourists. I can tell you're not a tourist though. You're from the city. I can tell that by the coat. Outsiders never think to bring a coat when it's sunny. But the weather has a mind of its own on the coast, doesn't it? Another storm is coming." The woman stopped to breathe.

Isobel thought not, but nodded politely. San Francisco was fussy about its rain. Before the woman could ramble on about the weather, she said, "I have money."

"That's all you need, dear. And you don't have to worry

about being alone in my cottages. I keep a ready shotgun. There's only one other boarder, and he's quiet enough. Winter is never very busy. Although it doesn't make much sense, since summer can be just as cold—"

"Do you have a recommendation for a particular cottage?"

"Well, the green one is pleasant. Closest to the water tower and outhouse."

"Are there any thieves about? I'm worried about my bicycle," she said, as the woman led her to the converted railcar.

"I can't guarantee a thing," the woman said. "I've a shed you can lock. Never had much issue though. Clothes, knickknacks—they sometimes disappear, and I don't mind folks using my water. We're a community that looks after one another."

"Nothing has gone missing of late?"

"Well, my bucket disappeared," the woman admitted. "But it was a battered old thing. I might have left it on the ground, and it blew off during the storm, or the ghosts that haunt the dunes took it." The woman gave her an exaggerated wink.

The cottage consisted of two rooms. Simple but clean, with a decidedly bohemian decor. Paintings filled the wall space with an explosion of color. Isobel tilted her head at a bright blue and orange splattering. She didn't quite know what to make of it. "Are these your own?" she asked.

"They are," the woman said proudly. "And for sale."

Isobel searched for a suitable compliment. "It certainly adds color."

The woman beamed. "Not many appreciate that. It's nice to have color with this never-ending fog. Speaking of that, you have striking eyes. The color reminds me a bit of the fog. What with your bone structure, you could be an artist's model. There's plenty of artists in Carville."

"Maybe when the stress of the city has worn me down." Isobel set down her bicycle basket. The cottage was perfect, and she said as much.

"I'll light the stove for you. You'll be warm as toast. There's a diner that's not far from here. Mrs. Gunn's."

Isobel thanked the woman, and excused herself to head over to the water tower. Animals, even hunted and terrified, always came to water, and they always left tracks.

Footprints crowded around the spigot, and the woman's spare bucket, well dented, hung from a hook. She spotted the strange, heelless print that she had seen on the dunes, and followed it away from the water tower. It had not rained today, but the sand was still damp, holding the prints well.

Night would come quickly, and the thought of being stuck out on the dunes in the dark made her shudder. A lantern would be a risk. But if the girl had come here and taken a bucket, she might not be back tonight. Isobel was never one to wait anyway. She grabbed a hooded lantern from the cottage, and checked the cartridges in her revolver, before heading across the dunes.

Tracking, Riot had explained, *is simply an exercise of observation and interpretation.*

She studied the smooth half-prints. The spacing between prints was not very long. She might think it was an adult tiptoeing across the sand, but the footprints were too small, too narrow for an adult's. Foot-binding was a popular custom with the Chinese, but binding the feet made for difficult walking. Isobel had once watched a woman with bound feet walk across the street. Her steps had been small, and careful, and she could not imagine that same woman attempting to traverse sand. Therefore, this was a child wearing slippers, and she'd very likely been running.

A girl on her own in a strange place wouldn't stray far from the lights of civilization, but neither would she risk exposure. Armed with that knowledge, Isobel mentally divided the terrain into three parts, as if it were a nature painting. The foreground, the mid-distance, and the far ground, as Riot had taught her. As she walked, she swept her gaze left to right, and right to left, moving her search from far ground to foreground.

The footprints zigzagged back and forth, never cresting a hill, but winding through valleys. When she neared the acacia grove, she caught sight of a long wisp of black hair fluttering on a strand of grass. She followed the footprints inside the grove to where they stopped.

Isobel frowned at the smooth sand. It didn't look brushed, only wind-blown, like everything on the dunes. A thirty-foot dune could disappear overnight in the Sahara of San Francisco.

As the fog caressed the branches, she made a circuit of the clearing, widening her search. Stillness thundered in her ears. Dusk was gone, and the sun was setting somewhere beyond the gray haze. She was loath to light a lantern. The thought made her stomach flip.

The cottages were obscured, but her keen sense of direction and the distant surf guided her. She returned to where the prints stopped, and looked up in the trees. There were no ready branches or roots to climb (unless the girl had the leaping ability of a tiger).

She squatted next to the prints, and narrowed her eyes. The prints were deeper than before and a little wider. The girl had doubled-back, she realized. She followed them back to the last large dune. The trail passed near a clump of grass on a hillside.

Isobel stepped near the tangle, and then on top of it. A piece of driftwood lay half-buried nearby. She stepped onto that too, and then took a step to another patch of grass. She could practically see the girl skipping from place to place. On the other side of the rise, the trail began anew. And then stopped. Again. It was like following a sparrow in near dark.

Isobel backtracked, and stood in a valley so thick with fog that it might as well have been night. She felt exposed. Horribly so. She strained to listen past her hammering heart. Fear eventually triumphed, and Isobel darted for cover, scrambling over the crest of the dune. She drew her revolver, intending to aim for the head this time.

Lying on her stomach in the sand, she waited with the silence prickling her spine. Isobel glanced over her shoulder, into a swirl of gauzy air. She braced herself for a fight, but no one emerged.

Slowly, she edged up the dune, and peeked over it. She stared into the murk, and out of the corner of her eye, in that blur between reality and imagination—the half vision of intuition—she saw a darker spot. She did not look directly at it, but studied the surrounding shrubs. It seemed out of place—more of an arrangement than natural.

Isobel moved quickly to the side of the darker spot, grabbed the grass, and yanked the clump away, revealing a burrow. A swift form darted from the dark—a girl. And Isobel gave chase. With braids flying, the girl seemed a bird, flitting over the dunes. Hampered by split skirts and a bruised body, Isobel had no hope of keeping pace. On the crest of a dune, she launched herself at the small girl. A brush of hair touched her fingertips, and she clamped down tight, grabbing a braid.

As Isobel tumbled, the girl was wrenched backwards with her. The ground came fast. Isobel landed on her stomach, taking in a face full of sand. She raised her head in time to have a diminutive foot slam into her nose.

Isobel reeled back, her vision watered, and the braid slipped from her fingers. The girl scrambled forward, and Isobel lunged after, catching her ankle. A blade flashed silver. She caught the little hand before it could break flesh. With a surge of determination, Isobel pinned the girl's arms to her side, and plucked her off her feet. Heels kicked furiously at Isobel's knees, and the girl threw back her head, catching Isobel on the lip. And then came the teeth.

"God dammit, I'm trying to help you," Isobel hissed. This didn't reassure the girl. Her head slammed against Isobel's chin, and an elbow hit her ribs. Isobel dropped the feral child to the ground, and promptly sat on her.

"*Bong*," Isobel said in Cantonese. She hoped it meant 'help'. Blood poured from her nose, but she dared not pinch it. The girl would go wild. She pulled Cantonese words from her mind. "*Ngor bong nei*." I'm trying to help you.

The girl stilled, and a suspicious pair of black eyes looked up at her. The girl said something in Cantonese, and Isobel wished she had a larger vocabulary. Her mind drudged up more words, "*Wai yan*." Bad men.

"*Faan tung*," the girl spat.

Isobel had no idea what that meant, but the girl's voice was hushed. She was well aware of the danger. Isobel bit a button off her cuff, and tore the sleeve back with her teeth, exposing her wrist. She held the raw, rope-burned flesh in front of the girl's eyes. "*Wai yan*," she repeated.

The girl's gaze moved from her wrist to her eyes.

Isobel gestured at herself. "Help you."

Reason replaced wild rage, and slowly, Isobel loosened her hold. She pinched a handkerchief to her nose, and when the girl did not fight, she climbed off, freeing her completely.

Quick as a snake, the girl reached for her dagger. Isobel let her keep it.

"I'm Charlotte Bonnie," she said. Her voice came out a muffled, nasal mess.

The girl stared. Her lips were pressed tightly together. She was thin and underfed, and a scar cut across her cheek, just under her dark eye. Another slashed diagonally across her jaw. It was difficult to assess her age in the dark, but Isobel thought that she could not be more than ten.

In the fading light of dusk, the girl looked menacing, a seemingly impossible feat considering her size and the girlish braids. Maybe it was the knife.

"Fine, have it your way," Isobel said, and staggered to her feet. "I thought you were in trouble, but you can clearly handle yourself against the 'bad men'."

Isobel turned to leave. She got halfway up the dune when the girl spoke.

"*Dang dang.*"

Isobel stopped, and turned.

"*Nei tai*," the girl said, gesturing at the hole in the dune. Keeping an eye on the pint-sized fury, Isobel limped over and poked her head in the hole. It was dark, and with cold, shaking hands, she struck a match.

"The devil hang me," she muttered.

28

Out of Darkness

ISOBEL HURRIED ACROSS THE dunes, heading straight for lights she could not see. Fearing detection, she relied on her sense of direction as she waded through the fog.

Shadows moved, and a breeze bent the grass, blowing the mist farther inland. The air was a mash of shadows and storm clouds, with mournful noises swimming in the haze. Out of that darkness came imagined phantoms, and men who were immune to a bullet's bite. She clenched her jaw to keep from jumping at every shadow.

She walked, keeping her revolver firmly in hand, until the water tower and a dim light swam into view. A lonely bulb pushed at the shrouded night, and she focused on the warm light seeping through her cottage shutters. The cottage offered heat and safety, and she hurried towards it, preoccupied with the items that she'd need.

A shadow detached itself from a cottage wall. In a flash, Isobel assessed the rough cap, coat, and predatory air, and brought her gun to bear. She aimed right at her attacker's face. Only she never finished the movement. An iron hand clamped around her wrist, pulled her forward, and spun her around as smooth as a dance. Her back hit wood, and her hand was slapped against the wall, pinning her solid. A flash of silver near his eyes put her at ease.

Relief made her knees go weak. "Riot," she breathed. She was torn between hitting and kissing him, or both. But before she could act, he clamped a hand over her mouth.

"Are you being followed?" The words were barely a whisper in the dark, but his voice was hard. And his eyes glinted. She could feel the heat of the man, the wiry muscle under his clothes, the press of his body against hers.

Isobel glared up at him, and stuck her tongue out, licking his palm. She could hardly answer with his hand over her mouth. He loosened his hold, but not his proximity.

"Apparently by you," she said in hushed tones.

"It's fast becoming an addicting habit, Miss Bel."

"You should find another; I'm likely to get you killed."

"Speaking of which, the next time there's a threat on my life, I'd appreciate being informed. To say nothing of the threat on your own." His words hit her like a slap.

"I—" A dozen arguments rose to the tip of her tongue, and died right there. The mere thought of him dead made her body go numb. Impulsively, she wrapped her arms around his neck.

Riot tensed with surprise, but only for a moment, before responding in kind. His arms were reassuring, and pleasantly crushing, and she savored the strength of him. He felt like a safe harbor after a storm, and in the murky darkness, they clung to each other. All her anger and fear calmed in his arms.

"I was terrified," she whispered. Isobel had never uttered those words to another soul. "They threatened to kill you."

"A regular occurrence for me," he said after a time. "What would you have done if our positions were reversed?"

She drew back, only slightly, enough to catch his eyes. "I doubt I could sneak up on you. And I sure couldn't pin you so soundly."

"You're changing the subject."

"I'd likely walk away," she said casually.

"Nice try, Bel," he drawled. "I'll hardly leave when I've only just found you."

"How *did* you find me?"

"Carefully," he said. "How did you escape those men?"

"With difficulty," she answered. "Now what? Are you planning on lecturing me about my reckless behavior?"

"I wouldn't dream of it," he whispered against her ear. "I came to return your umbrella."

"Is *that* what's pressing against me?"

His lip quirked, and his fingers slipped around her neck, following her jawline in a gentle caress that sent shivers down her spine. He leaned closer, his beard teasing the corner of her lips, promising more, and then he stopped, drawing back. "Your lip is bleeding."

"Dammit, you were thinking of kissing me, weren't you?"

"I wasn't just thinking about it." Riot turned her face towards the light seeping through a shutter. "Who attacked you tonight?"

"A hellion." She sucked on her swollen lip, and tasted blood. "I'll explain later. Right now I need your help." The truth of it was, she was glad to see him. Overjoyed, even.

"I'm at your service, Miss Bel. On one condition."

She arched a brow.

"Try to remember that you have a partner."

She smirked. "Not an easy thing for me."

"We're both learning, then. How can I help?"

Isobel reluctantly untangled herself from his arms, and walked over to the shed. A tarp, she decided, would be preferable to a rug. The key was with the landlady, and she still hadn't mastered picking a padlock. "Do you have your lock picks?"

Riot produced his tools, and opened the lock in under five seconds. If she hadn't felt so harried, she might have been annoyed with the man.

"I need help carrying a wounded man," she whispered, as she rummaged through the shed in search of a tarp.

"At least it isn't a body," Riot muttered.

Isobel glanced back at him. "How much did Ari tell you?"

"For the record, I twisted his arm."

"I had hoped he'd wait at least twenty-four hours."

"He found your shirt." There was a question in his voice. And a good deal of concern.

"My virtue is as tattered as it's always been." Next time she'd dump her clothes in the bay. With the tarp tucked under her arm, the two set out across the dunes. Riot had his electric light box, but the fog only amplified and scattered the light, so they relied on their senses.

"I found the girl those men were looking for," she whispered. "She's been caring for a wounded hermit in a sand cave. He's in a bad way, and the girl won't leave his side. You didn't charge around Ocean Beach again asking after me, did you?" Dread rose in her throat.

"Give me more credit than that, Bel. Although I might have if Lotario hadn't told me what happened."

She bristled. "I didn't ask you to look for me."

He said nothing. Isobel quickened her pace, and that silence he wielded like a weapon hit her over the head. Anger, frustration, and pride beat at her heart, until his mere presence melted her defenses. "I'm glad you found me, Riot," she whispered into the stillness.

"So am I," he said easily.

They walked in silence, and when her unerring sense of direction warned her that she was approaching the right valley, she slowed her pace. "Try the light."

He clicked his electric box on, and light flooded the small valley, illuminating tendrils and puffs of floating mist. The last thing Isobel wanted to do was surprise the hellion in the hole again. She moved through the drifting fog banks, and crouched by the hole. Riot shone his light inside.

The small cave was reinforced with driftwood and salvaged lumber. Roots curled around the ceiling and poked between boards. The missing bucket was there, a bowl, a mat, and a small fire, shielded in a sand pit. Despite the tiny source of warmth, the cave was cold, and the dampness didn't help the man lying on the mat. He was an alarming shade of pale, and he burned with fever, while murmuring in Cantonese. The girl raised a hand, shielding the light from her eyes.

"I've brought help," Isobel explained. "We'll carry him in this."

Language was as much about body language as speech. Isobel pushed the folded tarp inside the cave. But the girl only glared. She was looking beyond Isobel's shoulder. At Riot.

He said something quick in flawless Cantonese. Isobel gaped, but the girl kept her lips firmly sealed. Riot repeated his words, and pointed at the tarp. Finally, the girl wrung out the rag she'd been using to mop the man's brow, and began unfolding the tarp, spreading it beside her patient.

"You never told me you spoke Cantonese," Isobel whispered.

"There are a number of things I haven't told you." There was little humor in his words. She wanted to drag him back to the warmth of the cottage and hear every single word he had for her and then some, but there was other business at hand.

Isobel shooed the girl out of the cave, and crawled inside. Working in the tight space, she wedged part of the tarp under the feverish man. He was dingy, covered in blood, and his long black queue laid on his chest. She slid her hands under his arms, braced herself, and moved him to the side. He stifled a scream with gritted teeth.

Nearly three days wounded. Not good, not good at all.

There was no assessing his wounds there, so Isobel shed her coat, and laid it over the man. Riot handed his light box over to the girl, and grabbed the edge of the tarp. He dragged the man outside, and moved over to his head, while Isobel moved to the lighter end. Together, they lifted, and began carrying their awkward load over the dunes, slipping on sand with every step.

It was a grueling journey, and Isobel had to stop and rest frequently. The man wasn't heavy, but the long days had taken their toll on her, and her bruised stomach protested the work. Every time they stopped, the girl stood glaring at her.

Moving in a daze, Isobel was dimly aware of a door opening, the sound of her footsteps shuffling over wood, and finally a wave of warmth sweeping over her. As they shuffled the man towards the bed, she realized Riot was speaking to the girl. She looked at him as he carefully carried their load while navigating the cottage backwards. Perspiration covered his brow, his glasses were fogged, and the foreign tones flowing from his throat seemed surreal. It was a decidedly one-sided conversation, however.

On the count of three, they lifted the man onto the bed, and Isobel sat down by his legs, and rested her elbows on her knees. Riot repeated a question. And finally the girl spoke, with clipped brevity and iron in her tones.

"What did she say?" Isobel asked in a breathless wheeze. In the light of the cottage, the girl looked even more severe. The scars were stark against her malnourished face.

"Her name is Sao Jin," he answered, removing his spectacles to wipe them clean. "She claims this is her brother, and some men shot him on the dunes while they were fishing."

Isobel grunted. She swiveled towards their patient, and began unbuttoning the toggles of the man's padded jacket. A wad of blood-soaked bandages had been stuffed against his chest. She frowned.

"I don't suppose you know a trustworthy surgeon?" She glanced up at Riot, and stopped. The room had gone deathly silent. Riot was taut as a bowstring, and as pale as the man he stared at.

"What is it?" She moved instantly to Riot's side, and looked down at the hermit, as if the new angle would reveal something more. Free of the dim cave, she studied the man for the first time. He was young, and handsome. Still possessed of the fine bone structure and near beauty of a young man who had yet to fully mature. A scar, like a tear, dripped from his right eye. But the disfiguration only added to his beauty rather than distracted. She thought him no more than nineteen.

One moment Riot stood stark still, and the next he snapped. He surged forward, and grabbed the man by the collar, half lifting him off the bed. His knuckles were white, his hands shaking, and his voice was chillingly cold.

"*Hei san la nei, chap chung!*" Riot growled.

Isobel was too stunned to move. Her brain tripped over the Cantonese words, but the demand in Riot's voice was unmistakable. The young man opened his eyes. They grew wide, and he fumbled at his side, muttering, half-dazed.

Riot caught his wrist in an iron grip. And Jin started yelling, her distress clear, fast with a growing tinge of anger.

Riot let the man's collar go, but kept him pinned while he patted his jacket with the other hand. He reached into the voluminous garment and pulled out a hatchet-like weapon with a very short haft.

Riot bit out words in Cantonese, and Jin charged, knife in hand. Isobel cursed, snatching the girl up and earning another bruise from a well-placed slippered foot. She wrenched the blade from the girl's hand, and plopped her into a chair.

"Stay," Isobel ordered.

The command in her voice stunned Jin to silence. She turned in time to see the hermit clutch Riot's coat. He rasped out desperate words, and then went limp. Riot's hands tightened; he was on the verge of shaking him back awake.

"Riot," Isobel said, putting a hand on his shoulder. "He's close to the grave already. Push him there, and you won't get your answers." She might not understand the words, but she knew an interrogation when she saw one.

The hatchet was damning enough. Now she wasn't so sure who killed Lincoln Howe.

Riot let the man go, passed the hatchet to her, and finished searching the young man. There were no other weapons on him. As soon as Riot finished, he stepped away, and stood staring at the man as if he were a ghost.

Isobel inserted herself in his line of sight, and looked up into his eyes, but they were so very far away. "Talk to me, Riot," she whispered, placing a hand on his chest.

Slowly, his deep brown eyes focused on her. They were hard, and full of pain. "He's no hermit," he said hoarsely. "He's *boo how doy*—a hatchet man."

Out of the corner of her eye, she saw the blood drain from Jin's face. The girl went very still.

"How do you know?" she asked. Anyone could take a cleaver and chop off the handle.

Riot's gaze flicked to the man, and then he quickly looked away, half turning his back as if he'd been struck. "He put a bullet in my head."

29

Into Light

WHAT DID ONE SAY to 'He put a bullet in my head'? Isobel stood frozen in shock. This sort of silence was as thick as it came—like a quagmire that swallowed time.

Isobel glanced at the hatchet man. Wounded, feverish, near to dying, he looked a world away from the type of man who'd put a gun to another's head, and pull the trigger at sixteen. Jin was quiet, her eyes wide, her gaze dancing from the man she had cared for to Riot who had moved to the sitting room. And Isobel looked, too. To the head of slightly curling black hair, and the strong shoulders, and the narrow back that was currently as stiff as a rod.

Tired, sore, and reeling, Isobel closed her eyes, and smothered emotion, reaching for the comforting embrace of thought and reason. *Tracks*, her mind shouted.

"Riot," she called. She didn't know if he was on the verge of revenge or bolting, but she wasn't about to find out. She hurried to his side. They needed focus; he needed a task. "We've left a trail that a man full in his cups could follow. We need to get them out of here. Tonight. We can sort the rest out later."

Closer now, she saw him better. And what she saw alarmed her. Atticus Riot shook from his head to his toes, as if his past were bleeding from his body. That look had returned. Haunted and wild, and so unlike him.

She interlaced her fingers with his own. "The girl needs your help. *I* need your help, Riot."

The admission broke through whatever hell he was reliving. She knew it would.

"I'm not the man you think I am." His voice rasped like a dry wind.

"You're the man standing in front of me," she whispered. "That's all you need to be. And right now I need you to find a wagon."

A simple task was enough. His fingers tightened for an instant, before he grabbed his hat, and stepped out into the night. She only hoped he'd return.

The fog stayed thick and low, clinging to San Francisco like a lover, as they bumped through the night in a borrowed wagon. Isobel hadn't asked where Riot found it, and he hadn't offered an explanation. Without a word, he had loaded the hatchet man into the wagon, and climbed onto the seat.

Isobel hunkered under the tarp with Jin and the wounded. The girl sat with her back against the farthest board. Isobel could feel a cool glare in the darkness. Was there hate, or fear, behind those eyes?

She remembered Jin's reaction when Riot had said the hermit was a hatchet man. Despite what Jin claimed,

Isobel didn't believe her story for a moment—that they were attacked while fishing. So why had she lied? Who was she protecting? And what was a hatchet man doing on the dunes?

A tumult of questions rattled around her head. Unfortunately, both girl and hatchet man were unfit for interrogation.

The wagon rolled to a stop, and she peeked out from under the tarp. A dim light flickered over the doors to the carriage house at Ravenwood estate. They had decided his house was the best place to conceal the pair. It was closer than her boat, and also less conspicuous than carrying a half-dead man down the dock.

Riot hopped off the seat, and gently coaxed the horses inside. Scents of fresh hay, oiled springs, and the tang of metal filled the air.

Isobel climbed over her bicycle, and slid off the wagon bed. She hit the dirt, staggered, and caught herself before falling. She was stiff with cold and bruises, and irritated by it. She looked out into the night, searching for any lurking shadows. With a shiver, she firmly shut the doors.

Riot flicked on the electric lights.

"What's going on?" Tim whispered. The old man currently stood wild-eyed at the bottom of the stairway with shotgun in hand, and wearing nothing but his long johns. It was a sight Isobel could have lived without.

Riot didn't answer. He simply stood, looking at his old friend. Tim's eyes flickered to Riot, and he shifted, nearly shrinking back a step. Isobel was tired of not knowing what was going on. She felt like she had picked up a book, and started reading from the wrong end. And all the dialogue was scratched out.

The air felt like a storm about to snap. And she didn't

want to find out what would happen when it did. Clearing her throat, she stepped up to the side of the wagon, and ripped the tarp back with a flourish. "We've brought you one guest, and one prisoner in need of a discreet surgeon."

The announcement broke whatever silent standoff the two men were having. Tim moved quickly to the wagon's side, and stood on his toes to peek over. He barely passed the rim. "I'll fetch a surgeon."

"Do you have one that will keep his mouth shut?" she asked.

Tim looked at her, eyes dancing with wild amusement. "This ain't our first dance, girl." He stomped over to a bench, shrugged into a heavy coat, stuck bare feet in rubber boots, and slipped through the doors.

Isobel looked at Riot. "He's forgot his trousers."

"Not the first time." He sounded tired, defeated. But he held out a hand, and spoke quick words in Cantonese. Jin stood in the wagon, said something in return, and jerked her chin towards Isobel, and then hopped over the side, ignoring his offer of help.

During the exchange, Isobel caught the words *faan tung* again. "What does that mean?"

"It translates into 'rice ladle' or 'rice bucket'." Noting her confusion, Riot explained, "It means 'worthless' or 'eats and contributes nothing.' She's given you a nickname."

Isobel snorted.

Jin reappeared, standing just to the side, glaring around the corner of the wagon. Isobel had not given her back the knife. But she fiddled with a leather bracelet woven with beads, turning it round and round her wrist. A sign of fear, or a nervous habit?

"*Wai daan,*" Isobel said to the girl, and promptly stuck out her tongue.

"Like two peas in a pod," Riot quipped. "My stray is far more civilized."

Isobel sighed. It was just her luck to find a wildcat instead of a girl. But then those scars crisscrossing her young face were hard to ignore. Sao Jin had not had an easy life. Far from it.

Without another word, Riot grabbed the edge of the tarp, and pulled the hatchet man out. Together, they carried him up the stairs into Tim's workshop-cum-living area.

Jin gawked at the machinery and tools. The array of knickknacks and oddities. Isobel hoped that there were no loaded revolvers lying around, but then the various blades, sharpeners, shears, and crowbars would do just fine as a weapon. As they shuffled through Tim's clutter, she tried to catch Riot's eye, but he was half-turned, watching his steps as he walked backwards.

As soon as he deposited the patient on a cot, Riot left the room. Too fast, as if fleeing. She soon heard him rummaging about Tim's small kitchen, and the knot between her shoulder blades eased.

Isobel sat by the hatchet man's side, and began poking at the bandages. The jacket he wore was heavy. And something clinked when she moved it. She looked at the lining, and rubbed it between her fingers. Chainmail and padding.

Jin swatted her hand aside, and glared, until she scooted over. The girl skillfully peeled back the dressing. A wound lay just below his collarbone. The skin around the hole was angry and red, and it was smothered with a green ointment. Isobel was no physician, but given the jacket's lining, she wagered it had slowed down the bullet. Since there were no bubbling or sucking noises coming from the wound, it had likely missed the lung, and lodged in a muscle or against bone.

"What is that?" Isobel pointed at the ointment.

Jin took out a delicate jar from her voluminous tunic, and dabbed more of the green gunk over the wound. It smelled of herbs. She replaced the bandages, and the jar disappeared up her sleeve. Jin sat, stoic and aloof, pointedly ignoring Isobel.

No matter. Isobel turned her attention to the cleaver. A weapon like that could have easily put the dent in Lincoln Howe's skull.

Riot returned with tea, bread and butter, and two pieces of pie that Tim had no doubt snatched from Miss Lily's kitchen. He set down the tray, handed a cup to Jin and Isobel, and then put his back to a wall, as far from the hatchet man as he could get.

Riot gestured to the food, and Jin began stuffing it in her mouth. When the girl had licked the last of the crumbs from her dirty fingers, Riot asked her a question, and Jin froze.

Again, Riot repeated the question. Jin finally spoke, quick and brief.

"She insists he is her brother, and that they were living on the dunes," he translated for Isobel's benefit, and continued to do so. "Did you know your brother is part of Hip Yee tong?"

The girl's eyelashes twitched, but other than that small reaction, she remained stone-faced.

"What did the man look like who shot him?"

Jin shrugged. "It was dark."

"What's your brother's name?"

"Wong Kau."

"Why were you out on the dunes?"

"Fishing," she repeated again.

Isobel rolled back her cuff, and brandished the raw flesh. "The men who did this—the ones who shot your brother, they thought I knew where to find 'the girl'. Any idea why they are after you?"

As Riot translated this last, he started rubbing his temple. His fingers sinking into the white hair over the rut in his skull.

Jin pressed her lips into a thin, stubborn line.

They would get nowhere like this. "It's clear she's lying, Riot."

"We'll give her some time," he said. "Would you trust us if you were in her place?"

Isobel glanced at the scars, the dark circles under Jin's eyes, and finally looked into her fierce, glittering eyes.

"I don't think I'd trust anyone."

The next hours were a blur. It took Riot's considerable powers of persuasion to convince the girl to rest. Finally, Jin warily planted herself in Tim's plush chair by the stove and fell asleep in a matter of seconds. Isobel tossed a blanket over the child, more to hide her from sight than from any sort of maternal instinct.

The physician soon arrived—a short-haired Chinese man with round spectacles and a mustache. He introduced himself as Ewan Wise in impeccable English, and greeted Riot with a hearty handshake. With swift decisiveness, he began rolling up his sleeves, and promptly sent Riot and the others away.

Tim was standing outside the door, and Riot pulled him aside. "Strap that man to the bed as soon as Ewan is through," he ordered through clenched teeth. "And put some guards around the house."

Tim's bushy white brows shot up. "Do you want trustworthy men, or do you want hardened men?"

"I need them to protect lives."

"I can't guarantee the silver, but I have a few who'll do. Miss Dupree might want to close shop for awhile though. What the hell kind of trouble did you bring home?"

"He's a hatchet man."

Tim sucked on a gold tooth. "I'll keep both eyes on him. What about the girl?"

Riot looked at the sleeping child. "I don't know," he sighed. "She'll likely bolt, but I won't keep her here against her will."

"Bribe her with food," Isobel suggested.

Tim chuckled. "Miss Lily's cooking would make anyone settle down."

Riot was in no mood for humor. He brushed past his friend, moving towards the stairs.

"You plan on tellin' me anything more, A.J.?" Tim tossed the words at his back.

The question halted Riot, and he turned on the stairway. "I don't know, Tim. Were you ever planning on telling me?"

"Telling you what?"

"That you've been lying to me for three years."

The blood drained from Tim's face. Riot waited, the silence was thick in the air, and the tension practically crackled. Isobel remained perfectly still, her mind reeling, trying to answer the questions that wanted to burst from her lips.

"I did it for your own good," Tim whispered.

"You fed me lies, Tim!" There was anger and betrayal in that vehement whisper. "How could that possibly benefit me?"

Tim walked down the steps, until he was of the same height as Riot, and stared him straight in the eye. "If I had told you the truth, you'd have turned yourself in."

"You're damn right," Riot said.

Isobel held her breath, watching the standoff with equal parts curiosity and dread.

"They killed Zeph," Tim bit out.

"*One* person killed him."

"You don't know that."

"Don't I?" Riot asked.

"*Do* you?" Tim leaned forward. Pale blue eyes inquiring.

Riot clenched his jaw. "The man who shot me in the head is currently lying in your bed."

"Is he now?" Tim whistled low. "I suppose seeing him knocked your memory back into place. Were you there when Zeph was killed?"

Riot appeared surprised by the question. Tim didn't know as much as he had imagined. Isobel knew next to nothing, and she wanted to shake both men and demand answers.

"No, I wasn't," Riot said.

"Look, A.J." Tim held up a hand. "Whatever happened, or didn't—that tong was dealing in slavery a long while, using girls up until they died. That's abduction and murder of the innocent. You saw to it justice was done."

"It wasn't justice; it was vengeance!"

"As if you'd never killed a man before that night." Those words fell like a brick in the space between the men. Riot retreated a step, and put his back to the wall as if he'd been struck. He breathed heavily, his chest rising and falling, perspiration beading his brow. Finally he pushed off the wall with a slap, and hurried down the stairway, taking the stairs two at a time.

"Shit," Tim hissed.

Isobel cleared her throat. "I'd say something stronger is called for."

The wizened man looked at her. "Then why the blazes are you still standing here?"

His question knocked sense into her. Without a word, she trotted after Riot, and caught him halfway down the driveway. Visibility was low in the mist, and she hoped keen ears weren't lurking.

"Riot?" she said softly.

No answer. His eyes were fixed ahead, his pace quick and hurried. It was clear he wasn't much for company, but she wasn't about to leave him alone. Ignoring the cries of her protesting muscles, she kept pace.

Despite her discomfort, the cool air was a welcome relief after the heated conversation in the carriage house. She matched his pace step for step, and soon relaxed, appreciating the peace of the night.

The silence deepened, occasionally interrupted by a distant foghorn. Soon the houses grew farther apart, and died out altogether. She could smell the salt in the air, and hear the steady bells of the bay. After a time, a barely perceivable change came over her silent companion—his footsteps slowed and he drifted closer.

"Do you have a particular destination in mind?" she asked.

His shoulders slumped. "I generally walk until I exhaust myself. I find it helps." From the sound of his voice, she surmised he had reached that point. "I apologize, Bel."

"There's no need for an apology. I understand." She

slipped her arm through his as if they were a couple out for an early morning stroll. "I've always found the fog comforting." It muffled her voice and enhanced it all at once. "It's always quiet—peaceful-like. I feel like I'm drifting in an ocean."

"She's the city's mistress," he said, tucking her arm close to his side.

Isobel glanced at him. The words were soft, barely uttered.

"A moody one?" she asked.

"Very." There was pain in that word. "I'll say it again, Bel. I'm not the man you think I am."

"And there's plenty you still don't know about me. Anyhow, from what I overheard, you're not the man you thought you were either."

He chuckled, a bitter, dry sound that put her on edge. "I'm a thief, a gambler, and a gunfighter. And I've sent enough men to the undertaker to be considered his friend."

Isobel sighed. "I killed my own brother, Riot. We both have a record of blood. Do you want me to turn myself in?"

"No."

"Then that option is off the table for you, too."

"You don't know what I did."

"I don't know much of anything at the moment," she countered. "There's a conspiracy of silence as thick as this fog."

"It's not an easy thing for me to talk about."

"I can see that," she said softly. "It's why I haven't pressed you, but I'm beginning to feel like I'm caught in an idiotic Shakespearean play where the characters refuse to communicate with each other. I'm guilty of it, too. Leaving the other night was a foolish mistake."

"It wouldn't be much of a mistake if it wasn't foolish."

Isobel slid her eyes to the side, and wished she could see him better. But she couldn't see much of anything at the moment. "You didn't have to agree with me so readily," she muttered.

"I was referring to my own actions that night. I gave you every reason to leave." Riot stopped, and sighed. It was the sound of a man who carried an unbearable weight. "Your question the other night stunned me. I haven't been able to remember that day for a long while. I didn't know how to answer you."

"Amnesia?"

Riot pushed his hat up, rubbing at his temple. "The days leading up to Ravenwood's murder are a blur. I was accompanying the Chinatown Police Squad on raids at night, and spending my days in court. I had been running myself into the ground for months. Ever since—" he came to a grounding halt, and quickly looked away. She gave him a moment to compose himself, and when he started again, she felt as if he had skipped over what he'd found difficult to say. "The day Ravenwood was murdered comes in flashes. As if someone keeps closing the shutter on a lantern and reopening it over and over again."

"But not anymore?"

"Seeing the… boy, his face, it shed some light on a few dark corners."

Standing still, in the early morning, Isobel shivered, more from the despair in his voice than the cold. "You don't have to tell me a thing, Riot. Not if you can't."

"I need to tell you."

"Why?"

"A small hole not mended in time will become a big

hole much more difficult to mend."

"Disastrous at sea," she agreed. "I've not heard that bit of sailing wisdom before."

"It's a Chinese proverb," he said. "Silence isn't always a good thing, and I'm afraid this hole has gotten too big for me to fix alone."

"*A união faz a força*," she quoted.

Riot cocked his head. Portuguese was not one of his languages.

Isobel reached up, gently halting his fingers, and drawing his hand away from the scar tracing his skull. She interlaced her fingers with his. "Strength made from union," she whispered.

"I could use a great deal of that right now."

"Then you have it," she said with feeling. "I'd offer you a hot bath and warm food, but my boat is a long walk away and it's likely cold as this air."

"My offer from the other night still stands."

"Arms and all?" she asked.

"You'd best hear me out first."

"I'm cold and hurting, Riot," she admitted. "Nothing you say is going to keep me from a hot bath."

Concern spurred him to action; it gave him something to focus on. Riot tucked her arm under his, and turned back towards Ravenwood manor.

"Besides, I've already made up my mind about you," she said.

"So have I."

"What's the verdict?" she asked.

"Ladies first."

Isobel snorted. "I'm no lady."

"Well, that's a relief. I wouldn't know what to do with a proper one."

Isobel's sharp laugh bounced in the muffled silence, and a number of dogs barked in answer. "Your turn," she said. "What have you decided about me?"

"You never gave an answer."

"So perceptive," she said. "I can see I'll have a time trying to manipulate you for any future schemes."

"*Please* works well with me," he said.

"I'll keep that in mind."

"Since you're still avoiding my question, I'll answer for you."

She arched a brow. "Oh, really?"

Riot made a contemplative sound. "There's the facts, of course. I have a superb selection of hats, which is always impressive to the gentler sex, I'm sure." A smile tugged at her lips. "I worked as a galley cook. You're in dire need of one, by the way. But I'm double your age, so that makes me a bit long in the tooth."

"*A vida começa aos quarenta,*" she said. "Life begins at forty."

"And here I thought it was because I met you."

"You are too charming, by far, Riot."

"It's not charm; it's simple truth."

"*Pure* charm," she persisted.

"Was that your answer? That I'm *too* charming?"

"I suppose, for now." Her voice held a smile, and she leaned into him as they walked. "Now what have you decided about me?"

"That I love you." The words were calm and matter-of-fact, leaving no doubt, but then she already knew it in her heart. Those three words were simply an answer; not a declaration.

"You must be delirious."

"You told me to jump in, Bel," he said easily.

"These waters are treacherous; my life is a mess."

"And mine isn't?" he asked.

"I'll reserve judgment until after you tell me what happened."

"Fair enough, but I feel like I'm treading water here."

"You'd sink," she quipped.

"You have that affect on me." It was nearly a purr.

She glanced sideways at him. "I never said I'd make it easy for you."

"I hardly expect you to."

In the dark, in the fog, alone in the world, they strode arm in arm, comfortable in the lost hours before dawn.

"We have a bit of a walk left," he said into the peaceful night. The gentle humor was gone from his voice, and she felt a shivering tremor shake his body.

"There's no rush, Riot."

"I know, but if I don't tell you now—" He cut off, and changed tack. "I'd rather be moving when I tell it." And he did, starting with a mutilated girl.

30

Fifty-two Cards

Wednesday, September 2, 1896

ZEPHANIAH RAVENWOOD SAT ON his throne, impassive as ever, watching his partner shuffle a deck of cards without his customary finesse. It would make the second deck he'd ruined that evening.

Atticus Riot was neither impassive nor calm. While emotion was regrettably commonplace, unrest was not, and consequently troubling to Ravenwood.

"The deck will remain the same no matter how many times you shuffle. It will still contain fifty-two cards."

Riot stopped his restless shuffling. He looked into the humorless eyes across from him. The light from the fire danced in their dark reflection. As always, Ravenwood's words held deeper significance. Riot tapped his abused deck square, stood, and placed it on the mantel.

"You are angry," Ravenwood noted dryly. The severe

man interlaced his long fingers in thought. "We solved a case, brought a murderer to justice, and yet you appear dissatisfied. Usually you are eager to celebrate, while I am not. I need no company, my boy, go do whatever it is you do—I suspect women."

"There's no cause to celebrate," Riot murmured.

"As I have been saying these past twenty years."

Riot bestowed annoyance on his partner. "With this case," he clarified, knowing full well that Ravenwood knew it too. "As you said, no matter how many times I shuffle the deck, it won't change the cards."

"Not my precise words but—"

"We haven't changed a thing, Ravenwood. Those children are still dead!"

The large man in his throne was unruffled by Riot's frustration. "The dead have been avenged."

"It doesn't change a thing," Riot repeated, running a hand over his face. "I'm tired."

"Sleep would remedy your ailment."

"Of this? Finding the killer *after the fact?*"

"We have, on occasion, prevented a crime—including murder."

Riot closed his eyes briefly. There was truth in his words, but today, of all days, truth wasn't enough. He took a calming breath and resumed his seat.

"You will recall, I am sure, the day we met."

"Don't patronize me, my boy."

"I had a certain reputation as a gambler: The *Undertaker's Friend*. You said if I was a friend to death, then you were his avenger. Well, I'm tired of avenging. I'd rather save people while they're still breathing."

"We took a brutal murderer off the streets. He'll soon hang because of our efforts. Preventable measures have their own rewards."

"And what of the others?" Riot asked. "All those children being peddled like cattle."

"You can join Father Caraher's war and attempt to blockade the brothels and cow yards. You'll be the first ex-gambler, ex-detective, turned preacher."

"Don't mock me, Ravenwood," he warned.

"We are detectives, we see to justice. We don't change the world. That's a job for the preachers, police, and politicians."

"They're not doing their jobs."

"Have they ever?" Ravenwood asked, gripping the armrests and leaning forward. He resembled a snowy owl about to swoop on its prey. "You are allowing emotion to cloud judgment. As I have often reminded you through the course of our partnership—that is never wise."

"I'm tired of finding mutilated corpses of children thrown into the bay."

"While I admit this last case had a number of unpleasant aspects, balance has been restored. The rest of this…" Ravenwood waved an impatient hand at his partner. "…is clearly a personal vendetta."

"It's not personal."

"Your history strongly indicates otherwise."

"My mother has nothing to do with this," Riot said through his teeth.

"Did I mention your mother?"

If there was ever a man to get under his skin, it was Zephaniah Ravenwood. Riot stared at his partner, resisting the urge to pummel him with his walking stick. Instead, he stood, recovered his deck of cards, and resumed his shuffling. This time the cards whispered in his skilled hands.

"I'll humor you, Riot," Ravenwood stated, leaning

back in his chair. "Let's consider your proposal. The Tongs run the slavery and opium markets. Both lucrative, both supported by politicians and police officials who benefit from graft. Chinatown's own Six Companies have long worked against both the slave trade and vice, providing the police with needed information about criminals. But the police only make token raids, as money finds its way into their pockets."

It was the bitter truth, and Riot had no answer.

"I'll say again, we are not lawmen; we are detectives. Have you forgotten why we left Pinkerton's?"

"This isn't about strike-breaking."

"What do you propose to do?"

"Sever the head," Riot stated coolly.

"It's a twelve-headed beast. Sever one and another will take its place."

"Then I'll bring them all down."

"Alone?"

"I'll find honest patrolmen."

"It's a dangerous game."

"Life is full of risks."

31

A Severing of Heads

TEN MEN IN GRIM suits stalked down an alleyway. They were armed and in a hurry. Heavy sledges rested on their shoulders, or axes in hands. The Chinatown Police Squad was on a mission. Sergeant Price led the pack, and Jim Mason, former lumber yard laborer, was the first to slam his sledge against the reinforced door. It shuddered, shattering the stillness, echoing through the Quarter like a gong.

It was also a signal. Riot climbed a fire escape, and Tim followed on his heels. Their ascent ended at the third story. Riot sheathed Ravenwood's stick through the back of his waistcoat, and climbed a drain pipe that took him to the roof. A skylight gaped. He dropped through.

The booming thunder of a barrage shook the walls, reaching to the roof of the building. Riot stood in an attic.

Dingy pallets and bunks filled the space, but it was empty of the living.

A tumult of boots and slippers scurried under the floorboards, abandoning the sinking ship. Riot rushed to an access hatch. A hatchet man appeared through the hole, dragging a slave girl. Riot swung his stick. The heavy knob connected with the hatchet man's chest, but it hit mail and padding, and the man drew the weapon for which he was named. He leapt into the attic, swinging with fury. The blade chopped, Riot leaned back, caught himself, and thrust his stick into the man's face like a spear. Blood blossomed. Quick as lightning, he delivered two more blows to his opponent's head. The hatchet man fell to the sagging planks.

Riot left the girl to Tim, and rushed down to the next floor. Through the walls and thudding feet, he heard the front door burst open. A mob of boots flooded the tong headquarters, and the racket pushed a knot of men up the stairs.

The lead hatchet man made a familiar motion. Riot reacted. He drew with his left hand, and fired. The hatchet man's neck bubbled with blood, but he still managed to squeeze off a shot. Fire raced along Riot's arm. In return, he swung his stick at the man's hand. The revolver clattered to the ground. But Riot didn't stop there. The heavy silver knob hit a man's head, and another crumpled to the floorboards.

A silk-clad man carrying a satchel raced away. His eyes were wide with fear, and Riot ran after him in time to see the man toss the satchel out of a window. The scribe followed his load, climbing onto a rickety balcony.

As the scribe climbed down to the next balcony, Riot folded himself through the window. Wood groaned, and sagged, and rusty nails pulled away from their anchors. Riot scrambled down the death trap as it gave. The entire thing splintered, and he fell. The ground came fast, and he landed with a squelch, hitting muck and God knew what.

A movement caught his eye. Gritting his teeth, he drew his spare revolver, but mud splattered his spectacles. Gunshot barked against the bricks, and Riot threw himself to the side. He calmly wiped his sleeve across his spectacles, and, squinting through the streaked lens, returned fire. His bullet pegged the scribe, but the man kept running.

Riot grimaced. Mud was only so soft.

"You all right?" Tim called from the window.

Pain laced his thigh and upper arm as he slowly extracted himself out of the muck. His feet held. "Only a graze, I'd wager," he called back.

Riot plucked the abandoned satchel from the ground, and limped around to the front of the building. The front door gaped, hanging on its hinges. Sounds of destruction echoed in the alleyway. The police squad was inside, smashing everything in sight—every piece of furniture, every decorative mirror and fragile vase. All was rendered to splinters and dust. They intended to send a message to the peddlers of flesh, loud and clear.

Atticus Riot sat in the Consul General's office, nursing a cup of tea. His arm stung, his bones ached, and he was fighting to stay awake after the early morning raid. Ravenwood sat with an interpreter, and Consul General Chang politely looked over their shoulders as they sifted through the contents of the satchel that Riot had recovered.

"I'll say one thing for the tongs, they keep excellent records," the Consul said. Chang was a prim man in his late fifties. Veins of silver gracefully streaked his black hair, and threaded down his long queue. He adjusted his spectacles.

It was an odd assortment of records. The receipt for a bag of rice was listed with the sale of a slave girl—a casual buying of flesh that was given no more thought than the purchase of rice. Their rackets were carefully recorded in a long list. Protection money paid to the tongs by honest shop owners and free prostitutes. Anyone in the Quarter who refused to pay was generally found in pieces.

Chang sighed. "But I'm afraid none of this is new." His face was impassive, but his eyes held anger and frustration. San Francisco pinned the tongs to his shoulders, and rendered him powerless to do a thing.

"Is there any mention of where the selling takes place?" Riot asked.

Chang pointed to a series of characters. "The Queen's Room. It moves from place to place."

"How do the buyers know where to go?" Riot asked.

Chang interlaced his hands behind his back. He stood ramrod straight, and although he was the same height as Riot, he had a presence that filled a room. "The turn of a teacup, the placement of a vase in a window, the tilt of a mirror, the braid of a queue... these criminals have a complex system of symbols and signs. When we learn one form of code, they change it."

"Have you tried trailing the buyers?"

Chang nodded. "The highbinders are careful. Very careful. There are eyes everywhere. We suspect that many on the Chinatown Police Squad are still accepting payouts. In the past, they even acted as guards while the bidding was taking place, barring everyone from an alleyway."

Ravenwood looked at Riot. "Perhaps we should concentrate our efforts on stopping the flow of cargo."

Riot gave a slight nod. He knew just how to do that.

Atticus Riot leaned back in his chair, and pulled his hat low. He was a patient man. In his mind's eye he imagined William Cook placing one chip after another as the dealer surreptitiously fed cards from a rigged box. Swift bets were placed, counters moved on the abacus, and a flurry of deft, cheating hands flew over the table.

An honest game of faro was as rare as an honest politician.

It didn't take half the night for Riot's bait to lure Cook from the tables. It barely took an hour. Madeline was a woman who knew men, and the prospect of luring one upstairs in exchange for a full night's wage was too tempting an offer to let pass. Or maybe it was the simple fact that Riot had asked her politely. Politeness, in his opinion, should never be underestimated.

The door to the room opened with a woman's giggle. Madeline pulled in a man who looked more than eager. Cook followed the prostitute like a bull to the slaughter, giving a wild little whoop in response to her laugh. Madeline fell back on the bed, and Cook tossed his hat aside, his eagerness pressing at his trousers.

Riot waited, wondering when the man would notice him. But men weren't known for their perceptiveness when a woman had her legs spread wide. Cook was half undressed before Riot decided to clear his throat.

Cook jerked in surprise, and swiveled around. His face turned varying shades of red with anger and shame in equal parts.

"Hello, Mr. Cook."

Cook was transfixed by the gun in Riot's hand. He raised his hands. And Riot frowned. "You can button yourself up."

The man hastily did as he was told, and Riot looked to Madeline, who was playing her part of innocent surprise. "I think you should leave, ma'am." He nodded towards the dresser, and she took the payment as she hurried out, but not before she threw him a wink and a smile. The door closed.

"What the damnation are you playing at?" Cook asked. His hands weren't raised now, but Riot wasn't worried. Madeline had skillfully persuaded Cook to remove his coat and therefore his revolver.

"I only want to talk." Riot slid his No. 3 into its holster. "It's been awhile, hasn't it? You can sit on the bed."

Cook did as he was told. "What do you want with me? I told you everything I know. That murdering fellow is set to be hanged."

"I'm here to avert a disaster."

"Of what sort?"

"Your imminent arrest."

Cook shot to his feet. "My what?"

"You'll find a squad of patrolmen and a ruined head-quarters when you go to collect your payouts tonight."

The color drained from Cook's face.

"Your money has fled." Those three words knocked Cook back onto the bed. "Your wife's savings, too. Now I'm not a married man, never have been, but I wager she'll be none too pleased when she finds out you spent all her hard-earned cash. She'll leave you, I'm sure. And make her own way just fine. You're a piss poor gambler, and the women you've been buying won't want a thing to do with you once your cash flow disappears. Your playing days are over, Mr. Cook."

Cook gave a nervous sort of laugh. "Are you here to gloat, or do you have a proposal? If you think I'd be fool enough to testify against the tongs, then you're dead wrong."

"Nothing so dangerous," Riot purred. "I've something else in mind."

"What might that be?"

"I want names. Names of all the custom agents and quarantine officers accepting bribes."

Cook shook his head.

"Fair enough. I don't much care that you'll go down with them, because that is exactly what I'll see is done."

"You don't have proof."

"I can be a persuasive witness in a courtroom," Riot said with a smile. "The photographs will help, too. The Kodak is an amazing invention, don't you think?"

"Are you blackmailing me?" Cook asked with outrage. As if a man who helped sell girls to slavers had any moral ground on which to stand. He didn't even question Riot's bluff.

"Think of it as letting things play out," Riot said smoothly. "Once the money runs dry, so will your lifestyle. Tell me what you know, and I'll see to it that you're offered a bargain, because you're just one replaceable cog in the scheme of things. What I really want is the people who run things."

32

The Visit

Monday, November 23, 1896

THOUGHTS OF COURT CASES and witnesses flew through Riot's head as he climbed the steps to Ravenwood's house. The Quarantine Station and Customs Office Scandals were proceeding nicely. The main players had been charged, and proof hadn't been hard to come by. If all went as it had been going, the tongs would lose their advantage.

Riot opened the door, and walked inside. His hand went straight to his revolver of its own accord. Two effigies hung from the chandelier—one white-haired, and the other black-haired. There was a noose around each neck, and a Chinese poster hung from their ankles.

Riot walked right past the straw representations of himself and Ravenwood. He hurried deeper into the house, searching each room. The door to Ravenwood's consultation study was open. Broken glass lay on the floor, and Ravenwood was stooped over a chair, plying his long-time housekeeper, Mrs. Shaw, with whiskey. The old woman was pale, but she looked more irritated than anything else. Ravenwood, on the other hand, fussed over the woman with uncharacteristic gentleness.

"Only a warning—no damage done," Ravenwood said without glancing his way.

Tim poked his head through the jagged door. "Some warning." He brandished a half dozen sticks of dynamite. "Set to blow half the house off its foundations." The old man cackled.

Riot failed to find any humor in the situation. He stalked back to the effigies, and tore the posters down. Each was a classical *chun hung* bearing their respective names.

Hip Yee proclamation. The members of Hip Yee tong (the Temple of United Justice) offer a warning to Ravenwood Detective Agency. If you continue to interfere with our business affairs and murdering honored men of our association, you will not only be killed but you will bring death on family, fathers, brothers, and sisters. We will offer $500 to any able man for taking the life of witnesses who testify in the Customs Office Case. And $1000 for the killing of Atticus Riot and Zephaniah Ravenwood. We write this notice and seal by us for certainty.

Riot felt a presence beside him. He was about to turn, to tell his partner that this was his fight—he'd involve his name no more, but Ravenwood's voice drawled into the entryway.

"I look nothing like that. My beard is not so wild."

Riot looked at the man. His blue eyes danced with amusement.

"I'll be sure to let them know."

"I don't think that's wise. I'd hate to bury you, my boy,"

Ravenwood said.

"You know I'm a careful sort."

Ravenwood harrumphed, and Riot moved to cut down the straw men.

Steel shutters slammed shut, doors were barred, and the streets of Chinatown emptied with uncanny speed as a man walked through the maze of alleyways.

The man had an unhurried, easy strut. His hat was cocked, his spectacles gleamed, and his coat was thrown back, displaying two revolvers. Not worn low on the hip, but in holsters at his waist, a casual reach as if a gun were a pocket watch.

The man was dressed for death, and he dragged an odd sort of train. Two effigies and a line of dynamite sticks bumped over the cobblestones in his wake. He could feel eyes on him, watching him pass with the kind of fear reserved for the truly insane.

Atticus Riot turned down Sullivan's Alley. It was empty save for a few hatchet men. They watched him with something close to amusement. The *boo how doy* respected boldness. A trio of men stood guard in front of a restaurant. Thin cigarettes hung from their lips, and their hands were tucked in the wide, loose sleeves of their blouses.

Riot glanced at the window. The tea handle was turned out, the placement just so on a table in the window. He ignored the hired fighters, and took his parade through the front doors. The hatchet men followed, and the owner hurried towards him, bowing repeatedly. "Please, no violence."

"I'll be as civil as they are," he walked up the stairs to find a knot of bodyguards and six men seated around a table. Rice, soup, and seafood steamed from their dishes. A meeting of tongs. He could not place them all, but he recognized the leaders of Gee Sin Seer and Hip Yee. The latter controlled the slave market, and the former was known for its total disregard of human life.

Riot didn't waste time with pleasantries. He yanked on the rope, and let his load whip forward. Effigies and dynamite thudded on the table, scattering porcelain. "I thought it only polite to return your things," he said in Cantonese.

The bodyguards reached for their weapons, but the leader of Hip Yee held up a hand. It was the only flutter of movement. Aside from that single gesture, the six men at the table remained stoic and expressionless. Not even a lash fluttered.

"And this." He took out their letter of warning and held it to a candle. Ink and rice paper curled, and he dropped the flaming paper on the table. Right on top of the string of dynamite.

The leaders did not move. And as the flame grew closer to the dynamite, the tension in the restaurant crackled as Riot stared at the current leader of Hip Yee.

One of the bodyguards cracked. He rushed forward, patting out the flames.

"If you come to my home again, I'll come to each and every one of yours." Riot's words hung in the air as he surveyed the room, willing one of them to draw a weapon. When no one moved, he turned and strolled out the door.

"You're chasing the grave," Abigail Parks said, as she reached for a cigarette.

"Same as I've always done." Riot pulled on his union suit. He felt eyes on his back, and glanced over his shoulder at the supine woman. A bit of ash fluttered to her breast. Her fingers shook, and she was staring at him as if he were contagious.

"One day you'll trip right into that grave, and take everyone around you down, too."

"I'm usually the one Death favors."

"What kind of talk is that?" she asked. Her eyes shifted to the jumble of leather holsters and cold steel on the nearby table. He never went far without his guns; even to bed.

"Nothing," he said, with a sigh. Danger hit him that way. Fear turned to excitement, and excitement left him restless. He had walked out of Chinatown and found himself at Park's Place. But after spending an hour in Abigail's bed, he wasn't relaxed. And he'd not share the particulars of his wild youth with her. Only a handful of people knew of that.

"Do you think the tongs will keep clear of you?"

"It was intimidation; nothing more." He was sure of it.

"When do the trials start?"

Riot tugged on his trousers, and her eyes lingered over the undone buttons. "A week. We have our witnesses holed up safe. The customs ring will be all but smashed."

"You know these things sprout back like weeds."

"I know," he said. "But if you were one of those slave girls, wouldn't you want that done?"

"I'd likely take a knife to the bastard," Abigail said. More ash fell between her breasts, touching the top of a long scar. She'd taken a knife to her husband. Only after years of abuse, and taking one in her own gut. He'd killed their unborn child, assuring that Abigail Parks would never have another.

"When are you planning to leave?" Riot asked.

"A month from now." She crushed her cigarette in the ashtray. "I think I'll head north, or east, maybe south." She gave him a rueful smile.

"If you need anything—"

"I can take care of myself." Abigail looked at the photograph of her husband. "Jesus, I still love that God-awful man. What kind of woman am I?"

Riot didn't have an answer. He dressed and left, and never saw her again.

33

Chasing a Curiosity

Tuesday, December 15, 1896

ATTICUS RIOT WALKED INTO the study and lowered himself into his customary chair. He was grateful for its support. It was close to two in the morning, but he was too tired to move. He sighed, and laid his head back. It had been a long night—they were all long of late, running together in a blur.

The fire lulled his lids closed.

"Your bed is upstairs," a voice reminded from across the room. Riot didn't even bother to crack an eye. From the way the words carried, he guessed Ravenwood was at his desk.

"There's no fire up there."

"I'm sure Mrs. Shaw will light one."

"I'm not about to wake a seventy year-old woman to light my fire at this hour."

Ravenwood grunted.

A few minutes later, a glass was pressed into his hand. Riot cracked an eye open as Ravenwood laid a thin ledger on the table by his chair, and sat. There was a drink in his hand. The man rarely imbibed, and the sight of a brandy in his partner's hand woke him up like an electric charge.

"Is something amiss?"

Ravenwood was quiet. His brooding gaze turned to the flames. "I think these waters are deeper than they appear."

Riot studied the man over his glass. "Is greed ever shallow?"

"It should be, shouldn't it?" Ravenwood asked. There was a puzzled tilt to his head like an inquiring owl. "How was your raid tonight?"

Riot grimaced. "We arrested ten. Half will likely walk free. Three highbinders were killed, and one Chinese Vigilance member. He was a good man." Riot took a long draught of brandy. "Many were wounded; more escaped, but there were six newly-arrived girls who'll live free. For now."

Ravenwood nodded with approval. "Were any records recovered?"

"Not officially." Riot stood, feeling far older than his thirty-some years. He retrieved the recovered ledgers. "Tim cracked a safe during the chaos. We're still not sure about some of the men on the police squad. I figured I'd learn what I could first." He plopped the ledgers on the table beside Ravenwood.

Ravenwood flipped through the books, but they were written in Chinese characters. "What do they contain?" Ravenwood asked.

"Receipts for girls, bribe collection, and payouts—the same as usual," Riot answered. He removed his spectacles and rubbed his eyes. "I'll look over them tomorrow, or I should say today, and take them to the Consul later. What have you occupied yourself with?"

"Chasing a curiosity." Ravenwood stood, and placed a hand on Riot's shoulder. "Get some rest, my boy. It can wait."

Riot was already half there. He may have mumbled something, but he'd never know. It was the last time he'd sit across from the man.

34

Downward Spiral

Wednesday, December 16, 1896

A CURIOUS CROWD GATHERED around the steps of the courthouse. Every mob had a mood that could change at the drop of a hat or a single thrown punch. Currently, this crowd felt boisterous rather than angry.

Riot stood on the courthouse steps, searching the gathered crowd. His coat was tucked back, displaying his revolvers. Tim had a dozen men in the mob, and a dozen more police officers made a nice showing. Still, things were known to happen at courthouses. It wouldn't be the first time a lone gunman shot a judge, attorney, or witness in the face in broad daylight.

Well into the Quarantine Station trials, William Cook had testified. He'd done his part, and now it was Riot's job to see the man safely home.

Ravenwood walked out of the building with Cook and

Monty Johnson. Reporters rushed forward, hurling questions at the trio. But Monty pushed them back, and the ones who came too close found that the aging white-haired detective favored a weighted stick. Ravenwood made liberal use of that stick as he propelled Cook into a waiting hack. He climbed in after.

Just as Riot started to climb in, a messenger broke through the mass. He handed Riot a Western Union envelope. He tore it open, read it, and handed it to Ravenwood through the carriage window.

"I'll see him home," Ravenwood said.

The esteemed Consul General paced his study. It was uncharacteristic for the scholarly gentleman, but as Riot read the letter that had been sent from the governor of California, he began to see why.

"We have destroyed the tong headquarters. We risk our lives daily. Every single man in this building has a *chun hung* on his head. Yet, *your* government says I am to blame, along with the Six Companies."

Riot frowned at the last. The Chief of Police had recently threatened to deport every Chinese if Consul General Chang did not stop the tongs. As if the man had not been trying to eradicate the criminal tongs for years.

"My informants say the Wah Ting San Fongs and Sen Suey Yings have joined with the Hop Sings against the Suey Sings," Chang said. This latest war had been started over a woman, and a perceived slight. "I wonder how the Police Chief would feel if he were held responsible for eradicating all crime in the Barbary Coast."

Riot chuckled. "Only an act of God would dislodge that infestation. It's always easier to point fingers at someone else."

"Yes," the Consul nodded. "I will never forget. Politicians think we *heathens* are the cause of all trouble in San Francisco. And yet when I try to deport the highbinders, your benevolent societies resist, claiming that *we* are the barbarians. The tongs are a disgrace to China. They deserve to be deported and beheaded."

Riot spread his hands in surrender. "You're preaching to the converted, Consul Chang."

Chang composed himself, and sat. "I have posted a warning to the highbinders. A *chun hung* full of threats. But with my hands tied, there is little backing the threat."

"Maybe they'll kill each other," Riot said.

Chang shook his head. "I have hoped the same, but as long as money is involved, there will always be drifting young men to join their ranks."

"How can I help?" Riot asked.

A glint entered Chang's eye. "I have heard a whisper about the Queen's Room."

A sky of clotheslines sagged with blouses and unmentionables. Riot moved under the lines with purpose. There were no 'look-see' men positioned outside the building. No Chinese for that matter. The alleyway was empty.

Danger pricked the back of Riot's neck. He walked past the doorway, and turned down a narrow alleyway, while a dozen other men trickled towards the main doors from side streets.

Mason and Johnson came from the other end of the lane, brushing the dingy brick with their wide shoulders. Riot nodded to the big Chileno—Mason had been invaluable in the recent months. When the agency hired him, he'd offered to work for the same wages, since he wanted to help the girls anyway, but Ravenwood and Riot wouldn't have it. He was a rare kind of man.

Mason dragged over a crate filled with trash. Riot climbed on top, and caught the first rung of the fire escape of a building next to the one that was their target—a leaning hotel. The metal groaned, but the bolts held.

The hotel's own fire escape was on its front, impossible to climb without drawing attention. Chinatown was a warren of passages that the tongs made use of. When a raiding party went in through the front of a building, they'd stream out a dozen different exits. In order to catch the highbinders, Riot needed to plug holes.

As he climbed the fire escape of the building beside the hotel, the entire mangle of rust shuddered. He paused, holding his breath as it creaked and groaned. The anchor moved in its hole, scraping against the bolt, but the maze of metal held as Mason and Johnson began to climb.

The families and bachelors holed in their rooms averted their eyes from the windows as he passed. The less they saw, the better. Hatchet men were quick to silence witnesses.

He climbed to the top, and onto the flat roof. Riot consulted his watch. Ten minutes. Moving quickly, he walked across the roof to the edge on the other side. The hotel was only a few steps away. Without looking down at thirty feet of open air, he steeled himself, and hopped the two feet from his building to the hotel roof. As wood creaked under his shoes, he turned on the edge, and carefully lowered himself to a window ledge.

He tried the shutters. The rickety slats gave, and he slipped into a small room, startling two old men and four younger ones stuffed inside.

They had the look of laborers who were holing up in Chinatown for the winter. Exhaustion ringed their eyes, and their hands were hard with calluses. Riot put a finger to his lips.

"What room number is this?" he whispered in Cantonese.

They shook their heads in unison. Then an older man whispered something in a dialect that he could not place. The young men's eyes went wide with fear.

"What did he say?" Riot asked. But the younger men shook their heads.

Riot picked his way over to the door, and pressed an ear to the wood.

"Four minutes," whispered Monty at his shoulder. He had a good solid billy club in hand and a pistol on his hip.

Distant voices drifted through the hotel, traveling through flimsy wooden doors. Riot cracked the door and peeked into the hallway. It was dark and filthy. And empty. That emptiness pricked a nerve of danger. The room across bore a charcoal mark of seven. That was their room —the supposed Queen's Room.

Four minutes later, a rush of boots poured through the ground-level door, shaking the building with noise. Riot rushed out of the room, stick ready, and braced himself for a tide of highbinders and slave dealers. But no one appeared.

He stepped aside for Mason, and the bigger man applied his shoulder to room seven. The rickety wood gave. A burst of thunder filled the hallway. Mason crumpled with a spray of blood, and fire burned into Riot's shoulder. Scatter shot.

Before the gunman could cock his shotgun again, Riot dragged Mason away from the doorway. There was too much blood. He wasn't moving.

Keeping low, Riot thrust his revolver around the door jam, and peeked into the room. His throat clutched. Fighting down a slash of pain, he lowered his gun, and stepped into the room. The blood in his body went cold, and the pain in his shoulder moved into his throat.

A shotgun had been rigged with a tension cord that was triggered by the opening of the door. But that was secondary. An effigy hung from the ceiling of the empty room. The body had been blown clean off when the shotgun fired, and now only the head and shoulders hung from a noose. The straw man bore an unmistakable resemblance to Ravenwood.

"He's dead," Monty said as a stampede of boots joined them. Words were spoken, but they might as well have been in a different language. There were voices, and angry faces moving in and out of his vision, but he couldn't hear words; he could barely breathe. His line of sight narrowed to a dim tunnel as he read the *chun hung* nailed to the effigy.

Atticus Riot turned from the room and ran, leaving a trail of blood to mark his path.

He did not remember acquiring a horse, but he rode it hard, and his breath came as heavy as the horse's.

A single light shone on the porch of the Ravenwood estate. The house was as dark and brooding as ever, and the sight of it chilled his bones. He dismounted before the horse stopped, let the reins drop, and ran to the front porch. He slipped his key into the lock.

Riot stepped into the entranceway. "Ravenwood!" he yelled. His revolver was in hand, and he stepped into the first parlor. A single light drew his eye through the second parlor and into the dining room like a moth to flame.

Zephaniah Ravenwood stared from the tabletop.

Riot's throat clutched. He put a fist to his mouth. He could not remember walking closer. But he was there, standing in front of his partner's head. Streaks of blood marred the walls, as if some child had painted on the wallpaper. There was so much blood. It pooled in the silver tray, and dripped onto the floor.

Riot's spectacles clouded. He tore his eyes away from horror. The world spun so badly he wanted to drop to his hands and knees, and hold on tight. But he didn't. As he followed the trail of blood and footprints into the hallway, he was aware of the weight in his hand. His revolver was poised, his hand as steady as they came.

Mrs. Shaw lay on the floor. Bruises covered her frail body, and her skull was crushed. She had been murdered in her nightgown. The house was overturned, the study in shambles—ravaged like Riot's life.

Ravenwood's eyes kept flashing in his mind's eye. Dull and pale, the light had gone out, the glaze had set in, there was nothing left of his brilliant mind.

Riot followed the blood like cookie crumbs. It led into the conservatory. Glass crunched under his boots. The shards were coated with blood. Beakers and chemicals stained the floor. The bunsen burner was still on, bright and flickering in the dim. It looked like a bear had gone on a rampage.

And then he saw the rest of his dear friend. His mentor, his partner, the only person he had ever thought of as a father. Ravenwood's death had not been clean. There was signs of a struggle. His body lay in one place, and his hand in another, still clutching his weighted stick.

Tears burned Riot's eyes. He picked up his friend's

walking stick. The silver was coated in red, staining the delicate etchings. Clutching that stick, he holstered his revolver, and walked calmly to his room.

Men sat around a table playing dominos. A shot rang out. Screams interrupted the game, and a volley of gunshots filled the room. Bodyguards sprang to their feet, reaching for guns, but death had already found them. Riot didn't bother to keep count.

The Undertaker's Friend fired to kill, wielding two guns with equal precision in a cloud of smoke. A highbinder fired, and Riot jerked as he turned his left gun on the man, keeping his right on another. Two trigger fingers, and two more dead.

Three more men charged into the room. He aimed for their heads, quick and proficient. A killer without mercy. One of his bullets only grazed a shoulder as the highbinder moved to the side. The tong member threw himself at the white man in highbinder's clothes.

A bullet knocked the hatchet man back, lodging in his mail shirt. The man kept coming. A blade slashed across Riot's chin, but he didn't feel it. He was cold with grief, but mostly rage. He pulled the trigger point blank into the man's groin. The highbinder fell, and Riot walked on, calmly reloading.

Police whistles filled the streets below. Women screamed, and Atticus Riot stepped into a room to confront Hip Yee's leader—the man who peddled young flesh like sacks of rice. Riot raised his guns and fired two bullets into his head. The leader fell, and something hard pounded Riot's back. Two bullets bit into the chainmail beneath his disguise.

He whirled, as a third bullet pierced his mail coat and bit his shoulder. Riot staggered forward, dropping one of his revolvers. He squeezed off a shot at his attacker. Blood gushed from the man's throat, and Riot blinked past the haze of blood and carnage. As a swarm of police descended on the building, he caught sight of a skewed wardrobe, and followed the sounds of fleeing people.

The passage spit him out in a grocer's. He bumped against a stack of crates, caught himself on a rice sack, and staggered out a back door. The alleyway was narrow and dark, the night sky swallowed by rookeries and clotheslines.

A shadow moved, and Riot's hand whipped up, but he caught himself. A beggar huddled in the alleyway—an old wrinkled man. Riot lowered his gun, and started towards the main street. But a shot rang out. It bit into his thigh, and his leg gave out. He spun, with revolver close to his side, but the shooter was quicker. Another gunshot rang in the alleyway. It hit him square in the chest. A boot flashed in front of his eyes. His gun rattled to the ground, and his mail shirt dug into his flesh with burning pain. He couldn't draw breath.

A young man stood over him. A scar, like a tear, dripped from his right eye. His would-be killer pointed a Colt at his face, and grinned from under his broad-brimmed hat. The boy's eyes glittered with glee. Riot tried to move, but his limbs seemed far away.

His life didn't pass in front of his eyes; his only thought was one of relief. The boy started to squeeze the trigger, and at that moment a swift shadow came from the side. The gun barked, and Riot's spectacles shattered.

35

Of Kings and Pawns

Wednesday, March 6, 1900

HER COMPANION FILLED THE night with a lifetime of pain, of horrors, and butchery that no man or woman should see. Isobel listened to his story in silence, with only one desire—to take this caring, noble-hearted man far away from this city, clear across the ocean to the other side of the world. But Atticus Riot had been there; had done just that. And he had come back.

When Ravenwood's house loomed from the fog, they crept in through the front door and went up the stairway, shutting themselves in the turret room. She waited in darkness while Riot fiddled with a gas lamp. Light chased back shadows, revealing a wall of bookshelves, a large fireplace and bed, and a neat row of hats on a wardrobe. She shuddered—not from the cold, but from his last memory.

Riot placed his cap on a hook, shrugged out of his

peacoat, and turned to the fireplace. He did not look at her.

Another person might have offered sympathy, and reassurance that he had done everything he could have, or perhaps judgment. But Isobel was not that other person. Her mind was racing, sifting and rearranging facts.

"Take the bath. Take your time," he said without looking at her. His voice was hoarse from talking.

She opened her mouth to argue, and closed it with a click. It was an excellent suggestion—a bath would give her time to think. But she had one question, one pressing thought.

"What did the hatchet man say to you tonight before he lost consciousness?" she asked.

Riot was in the process of laying a fire, and now he grew very still. "He said, 'We did not kill your partner. Please, I need your help.'" Riot looked up at her, and in the light of the room she could see the turmoil in his eyes.

"Do you believe him?"

"I don't *want* to believe him, Bel." Riot looked away, and busied himself with a matchbox. His hands trembled.

On her way to the adjoining bath, she trailed her fingertips along the nape of his neck, letting her touch linger for a second more than necessary. A gesture of reassurance. But whether it was for him or for her, she did not know.

Ensconced in white porcelain, Isobel turned the taps on hot, and glanced at her reflection in the mirror. She was a mess. Her lip was bruised and bloodied, her nose sore, and dried blood added a dash of color to her blouse. Sand was everywhere. She shed her clothes, and stepped into the steam. As she sank into the water, she very nearly whimpered. It was bliss.

With thoughts racing, she scrubbed the grit from her skin, drained the tub and poured a fresh bath, and then laid her head back to think. A knock interrupted her speculations. As she opened her eyes, she realized the water had gone cold.

Isobel cleared her throat. "Yes?"

"I thought you might like a fresh change of clothing," a muffled voice said from behind the door. "I was also beginning to worry you fell asleep, and drowned."

Isobel glanced at the bloody, sandy mess on the floor. "One moment," she called. Muscles protesting, she pulled herself out of the tub and padded unsteadily across the tiles. Before cracking the door, she grabbed a towel.

"And what would you have done if I hadn't answered?"

Riot kept his bespectacled eyes on her face. "Assumed you had drowned."

"Very nearly," she admitted. "You think of everything, Riot." She took the neatly folded pile of clothes from his hands, and closed the door.

There were two sets of clothing in the pile—one fit to leave and the second fit for staying. Ever the gentleman, she thought. Isobel chose the latter pile, slipping into the nightshirt and wrapping a familiar robe around her. It was the same she'd worn the last two times she'd stayed the night. Borrowing his robe was becoming a habit, and even after being laundered it smelled of him.

Clothed in warmth, Isobel walked into his room, and curled into Ravenwood's throne-like chair. A glass of amber liquid waited for her on the table. Riot sat across, firelight dancing in the glass of his spectacles.

As she sipped her brandy, she studied the man—the wing of white in his raven hair, the silver in his beard, and the deep brown eyes that were so very far away. He had washed while she bathed, and now wore a fresh, white shirt. His cuffs were rolled up, his collar undone.

Those eyes turned on her, but his gaze was not intrusive. It was full of grief, and resignation. Whatever she had to say to him, he would accept.

Facts first. "Are there any other gaps in your memory?" she asked.

"The next thing I remember is waking up in a hospital. I felt... detached. Tim was there, but I didn't know who he was. It took me three days to remember his name. He said he found me at a Chinese undertaker's in Ragpicker's Alley."

Isobel suppressed a wince by taking a sip of brandy. That alleyway was notoriously filthy.

"I think he knew exactly what I did." Riot frowned at the fire. "He knew I kept a set of highbinder clothing for when subterfuge was required in the Quarter; instead, he told me that I had either been abducted by Ravenwood's murderers, or I'd been ambushed on my way home from the Queen's Room raid. The newspapers blamed the Suey Sings for the Hip Yee assassinations."

Isobel frowned, and glanced at the waiting chess board on the short table between their chairs. She leaned forward, and began arranging pieces, placing the black king dead center, straddling four interconnecting lines.

"Beheading isn't really their style, is it?" she asked, keeping her gaze fixed on the board. "It's more John the Baptist than Celestial."

Riot let his head fall against the back rest. He removed his spectacles, and rubbed his eyes. "Criminals are beheaded in China every day. Traditionally the tongs used hatchets, but now they favor a Colt .45. There are, however, a few hatchet men who hold to tradition."

The black king was meant to be Ravenwood, but she decided it was the wrong place for him. Isobel nudged the black king off to the side, and replaced it with an ivory king—a symbol she used for her blackmailing husband.

"God dammit," she cursed.

Riot's hand dropped in surprise. "What?"

"Is Kingston my ex-husband, my widower, or still my husband?" What was she supposed to call the scoundrel?

He cocked his head at her. As always, Riot kept up with her course change, never questioning why. "Is blackmail really an acceptable marriage proposal?"

"Law is blind."

"By law you're dead," he reminded her.

"That could change in a flash."

"It could, and might," he admitted.

"What's your dead partner saying now?"

"That I'm dense."

She snorted. "Tell him to go to hell."

"I'm fairly sure he's somewhere between."

Isobel glared at the ivory king; it wasn't even on a proper square.

"Who is that?" Riot asked.

"I don't know, but I've used the piece for Alex before." She glanced at him, and blushed. "In my mind, it seemed to fit. He's a manipulating, conniving bastard, and something doesn't add up about what you told me."

"It used to add up."

"But you're not sure anymore?"

"I don't think I've had the courage to look at it close enough."

She clucked her tongue. "You don't lack courage, Riot. I figure the body protects the mind as same as it does any other part. When someone twists an ankle, they limp to protect the injured limb. And even after it's healed, one tends to keep on limping."

"So I'm limping?"

"Yes, because you were in pain, and now you're finally testing that foot out." She frowned at the black king, and decided it wasn't the proper piece for Zephaniah Raven-wood. Not knowing precisely why, she replaced it, assigning him the role of black bishop. Satisfied, she set the king beside its ivory twin in the center. "The question I keep asking myself, is why did the tongs wait until after the Quarantine Scandal was well under way? Cook had already testified, the whistle was already blown. Why kill Ravenwood *after* the scandal was exposed?"

"Revenge?"

"That's not really the tongs' modus operandi, is it? From what I've heard, they tend to lean towards manipulating the law and bribing attorneys when it comes to whites."

Riot inclined his head. "True, but *chun hungs* have been collected on whites. Regardless, I wasn't planning on stopping with that trial."

"No, I imagine you weren't." She looked at the man who was everything opposite of cowardly. "But if the goal was to halt your investigation, why didn't they target *you*?"

"I should have been the first through that door, Bel."

"Maybe so, but you're not really a sledge man, are you?"

Riot scratched his beard in thought. "I'm not," he conceded. "But why on earth would they kill Ravenwood, and leave me alive?"

It was a good question. The Queen's Room was clearly a trap, designed to keep Riot out of the way. "Maybe they

320 * Sabrina Flynn

thought Ravenwood was the head?" She winced at the word, and cleared her throat. "The erm... spearhead."

Riot shook his own head. "Ravenwood always left me to deal with the courts. And I was the one who'd threatened the Hip Yee tong."

Isobel considered his words. He had a point. Anyone could see that Riot was the trigger man of the partnership. He carried himself with all the calm grace of a sunbathing tiger. Poke that animal, and it would strike. She had known that the moment she met him. And she had marveled at it. The confidence of the man was magnetizing.

"How many people knew about your stunt in the restaurant?" she asked.

"Word travels fast in the Quarter."

"So it's safe to say most everyone." Her mind spun, and pieces began to form a pattern. She placed an ivory knight beside the black bishop—the unknown assassin who'd slaughtered Ravenwood. "How many people knew you were a gunfighter?"

Riot paused. "What are you hinting at, Bel?"

She hesitated, not liking the answer at all. But she was never one to back down, no matter how difficult something might get. In answer, she carefully picked up a black pawn, and placed it between the ivory king and the black one. That piece was Riot.

He abruptly surged to his feet, and gripped the mantel. His knuckles were white, and the skin above his beard was taut. Isobel stood, and moved to his side.

"I'm not sure, Riot," she said softly. "But if the hatchet man in your carriage house is telling the truth, the possibility that another tong used you to bring down a rival is there."

He didn't move. And her heart twisted. She hated what she was suggesting—that an unknown person (or persons) had manipulated Riot to kill.

Isobel placed a hand on his arm. "As far as I'm concerned anyone who deals in flesh sold their right to live long ago."

"A vigilante is a hair's breadth away from a murderer."

"Maybe so, but unless you're planning on putting a bullet in our injured prisoner, you're not there yet."

He placed a hand over hers, and squeezed it gently. "I wouldn't dream of it; he may have answers."

"That's the spirit," she whispered, searching his eyes. "I hope he lives. I'd like to find out why Jin is protecting him. I doubt he's her brother. Do you think he was out there on the dunes hoping to abduct her? Maybe he's tricked her into thinking he was there to help?"

"Stealing slave girls is common enough between tongs. Most tong wars are started over an abducted slave girl."

"Is Doctor Wise as skilled as he sounds?"

"He is," Riot said without hesitation. "He saved my life."

"How will he feel about treating our prisoner?"

"Doctor Wise, or You On Chung, runs a free clinic on the edge of the Quarter. He has a long history of defying the tongs and fighting for Chinese rights in the courts. He won't be bullied by the tongs, but he'll treat a tong man without prejudice."

"Good." Her gaze drifted to the chessboard, to that ivory king gloating in the center. "If you were handling legal matters and going on raids, what was Ravenwood doing?"

Riot cocked his head. "Working on other cases, or research, I imagine."

"But you don't know for sure?"

"No," he admitted.

"What was the other possibility he mentioned?"

Riot opened his mouth, then shut it with a click.

"I don't suppose you could ask him?"

He grimaced. The voice in his head was conveniently silent. "I don't think it works like that. He's an unhelpful ghost."

"He's a conjuring of your own psyche—your unconscious mind doesn't have the answers, so neither does he."

"Have you been reading Freud?"

"I have, actually." Her lips quirked in a smile. "*Studies in Hysteria*. If deeply repressed conflicts can cause physical symptoms, why can't they conjure phantoms?"

"So in a word—insanity?"

"Aren't we all just a little bit off?"

"You're trying to make me feel better."

"It's not working?"

"The fact that you're still here means more than you can imagine."

She looked long and deep into his eyes. Without fear, without distrust, as unhurried and calm as a windless ocean. "We'll find answers, Riot," she said softly. "One way or another."

For the next hour, they sat in the two chairs by the fire and talked. Riot gently interrogated her about her captivity. She left out nothing. And Riot obliged when she asked after his other cases, Artells and Sarah Byrne, filling in the gaps that Lotario had left out in his narrative. Somewhere in that time, her lids grew heavy, and when the clock chimed four, Riot stirred from his chair.

"Bel," he said, placing a hand on her shoulder. "Take the bed."

She yawned. "I'll head to my room."

"It's taken."

"Oh." As tired as she was, that thought was hard to comprehend. So without argument she shuffled towards the bed, shed her robe, and burrowed under the covers. A thought swam to the surface of her muddled brain. "I was promised arms," she said distantly.

Shortly, in the daze of exhaustion, she heard the rustle of clothes, and felt the bed sag. Isobel reached across the space, and took his hand. He lay on his back, on top of the covers with his own blanket.

"I'm sorry I got you into this," she murmured.

"I was involved long before you. The past never stays quiet for long."

Isobel thought of her own past, and shivered. Feeling adrift in a sea of feathers, she edged closer, resting her forehead against his shoulder and her knees against his thigh. Riot held himself very still, but after a few moments, she felt him relax. He shifted slightly, and slid an arm under her head, drawing her close. She melted into that welcome pillow.

"I don't sleep easy, Bel." He sounded halfway to sleep.

"Neither do I," she whispered.

36

His Queen

SUNLIGHT STREAMED THROUGH A crack in the curtains and a fire crackled in her ears. Isobel was loath to move, to fully wake. A dim warning in the back of her mind promised bruises and sore bones. She felt like a brick on a feather pillow.

Reluctantly, her mind passed from gentle drifting to stark clarity. Softness cradled her, and the scent of clean linen calmed her. She opened her eyes, and blinked. The bed was empty. Had she dreamed those reassuring arms?

With a yawn, she carefully rolled over, and studied the empty space. The outline of his body was barely discernible on the quilt. But it was there. Along with the Queen of Hearts on his pillow. Isobel smiled, plucked the card from its resting place, and plopped onto her back. She studied the card in the light of the room.

She had seen severe queens that would make her mother nod with approval, and others that would raise a brow at impropriety. Most queens were shapely and airy, but not the one in Riot's preferred deck. His Queen of Hearts had a cunning air about her. There was a mystery in her eyes that was every bit as entrancing as the Mona Lisa.

She laid the card on her breast, and looked around the room. A set of neatly folded clothes sat on a nearby chair. Two sets in fact: one male and one female. Riot truly did think of everything. He just didn't know who she wanted to be today. But good God, how long had she slept? She squinted across the room to the mantle clock. Past noon.

"Insufferable," she muttered. But when she swung her legs off the bed and tried to stand, a burst of pain reminded her why she had slept so long. The past three days had caught up to her. Her bruises had blossomed, and she moved like a woman triple her age. Grimacing, she limped over to Ravenwood's chair. It was progress.

She uncovered a plate on a tray, and started salivating over bacon. As she ate, she wondered which set of clothing she should don. Mr. Morgan would be simple, unless she intended to talk with Dr. Wise and Jin, which she did. But if she left the room as Miss Bonnie, there might be raised eyebrows.

Life was far too complicated.

Isobel glanced towards the window. She could climb down the drain pipe, but the thought made her cringe. Climbing down took more effort than climbing up, and as much as she dreaded admitting it, she was exhausted.

In the end, she chose impropriety, and donned a simple skirt and blouse. Most of the residents seemed to keep to themselves, and she hoped that anyone who saw her would assume she was another elusive boarder.

Isobel cracked the door, and eyed the hallway that skirted the winding stairway. It was empty. She stepped onto the landing, gently closed the door, and made it almost all the way downstairs without encountering a living soul. A young lady sat primly on the bottom step. She faced the front door, and had a sketch book balanced on her stockinged knees.

Isobel tried to pass her on the stairway, but the girl looked up, her eyes narrowing in a thoughtful way. "Morning, Miss."

"Bonnie." Isobel was too tired to smile. "You must be Sarah Byrne." The newspapers had taken great care in describing her upturned nose and the spattering of freckles across her cheeks.

"Are you a relation of Mr. Amsel?"

Isobel nearly jumped out of her skin. "Who?" she squeaked.

"Lotario Amsel," Sarah said, turning her sketch pad around so Isobel might see. It was an illustration of her twin. Young (and old) women had a habit of falling in love with him. Dogs and cats, too, for that matter. He was an insufferable flirt in any gender he assumed. "He was kind enough to escort me around the city yesterday afternoon. We're to go to Golden Gate Park tomorrow."

Unfortunately, Miss Bonnie was not related to Lotario. She was related to his alter ego, Madame de'Winter, but any connection between Miss Bonnie and Lotario could put them both behind bars for the rest of their lives.

"Everyone has a twin, they say," she said breezily. "Enjoy your outing." Isobel hurried away from the girl. There was nothing worse than a precocious child.

What on earth had Lotario been thinking, coming here as himself? If she and her brother were seen together, the evidence would be damning.

Isobel's flight towards the grocer's door did not go

unnoticed. When she passed the kitchen, she heard a pleasant, "Good afternoon, Miss Bonnie."

She stopped, cleared her throat, and took a step back, poking her head in the kitchen. Miss Lily sat at the family table with needle, thread, and a pile of clothes to mend. There was a keen look in her eyes, but then that was usually the case.

Isobel stepped into the woman's domain. It gleamed with cleanliness, and smelled of herbs. "Afternoon."

"Let me know if you're still hungry."

'Still hungry'... not, 'would you like breakfast?' In those polite words, Lily acknowledged that she knew where Isobel had slept. She was a sly one.

"The breakfast you left was plenty. And please thank your daughter for the loan of her clothes."

Lily smiled, as she deftly worked her needle. "Those clothes are spares. Mr. Riot had me purchase various pieces a few weeks ago in case we had unexpected guests." Considering that they fit Isobel perfectly, it wasn't difficult to deduce who it was he'd had in mind.

Lily eyed her bruises. "Would you like some ice?"

Isobel touched her swollen lip. "That would probably be best. You wouldn't happen to have face powder to cover up the bruises?" The absurdity of the question struck her a moment later.

"I don't have any light enough for your complexion, but I'll ask the other women boarders. Miss Dupree is sure to have some." Lily set down her sewing, and went to the ice box.

"Thank you," said Isobel. "I don't mean to trouble you." God knew the woman had enough to do.

"No trouble at all. I've been there myself, Miss Bonnie. The best thing I did was leave." Lily took an ice pick to the block, chipping away as she talked—quick, strong, and precise. Lily filled a cheese cloth with chunks of ice, tied the top, and handed it to Isobel. "No man is worth it."

Isobel pressed the ice to her nose and lips. "I'd hardly call them men if that were the case. This was nothing more than an unfortunate bicycling accident."

"Hmhmm, if you say so, Miss Bonnie."

"Poor Tobias, I bet he can't get anything past you."

"No, he cannot."

"Call me Charlie. All my friends do."

"And all of mine call me Lily—the ones that don't really know me."

Isobel smirked from behind her ice pack. "I suppose you know about our guests in the carriage house?"

"That I do."

"I'm embarrassed to admit that the girl did this to me."

Rather than find that amusing, Lily sighed. "It's a shame—no child should have that look in her eyes."

"No," Isobel agreed.

"I hope she'll let you and Mr. Riot help her."

"So do I."

So much for not attracting attention, Isobel thought as she walked across the yard to the carriage house. She found Tim stomping around the wagon, oiling spokes. "How's our patient?" she asked.

"Alive," he grunted.

"Is Riot here?"

Tim glanced at her, and paused. "Nice shiner."

"Compliments of that hellion masquerading as a girl."

Tim chuckled. "She has a glare on her. Me and Miss Lily have been keeping her here with food. I'm not sure she's ever slept or ate before." There was sadness in his voice. "She won't let Wise or me near her. In my experience, it's best not to push feral children, but maybe a woman can get farther with her."

Isobel wasn't going to hold her breath. She had no idea how to deal with children. They were small, conniving oddities who were vastly underestimated, so she tended to treat them like scheming adults.

"I'll try," she said, without much hope. From what Isobel had gathered, Tim had helped a very young Riot once upon a time. She wondered how many other children he had pulled from the gutters.

"And no, A.J. isn't here," Tim said, wiping his hands roughly on a rag. "He checked in with Wise, and took off without a word."

"He didn't tell you where he was going?"

"Never does."

Isobel muttered an oath. It *was* vexing to be on the other side of the coin. Leaving Tim to his tinkering, she walked upstairs, and found Jin sleeping in the same chair as the night before. Daylight hadn't improved her appearance, but judging from the tray and the polished plate, the girl seemed to have a hearty appetite.

Wise was also sleeping in a chair, in that time-honored position of every doctor—at the bedside of his patient. She quietly stepped beside the narrow bed, and looked down at Wong Kau. The bonds around his wrists and ankles didn't elicit even a twinge of sympathy. Although they currently weren't needed. He was pale, and slept like the dead. But the slight rising and falling of his breast assured her that he wasn't there quite yet.

"Time and patience will decide his fate," a soft voice said.

Isobel glanced to the side. Doctor Wise studied her from his chair. He hadn't moved, but his eyes were open, and from the depth of those dark pools, she had a feeling that his name suited him. He rose smoothly, and gestured towards the doorway.

When they were out of earshot, she asked, "The bullet?"

"Thirty-eight caliber." Wise produced the mash of metal, and dropped it in her palm. "His jacket is lined with chainmail and padding. The bullet lodged in his pectoral, against his clavicle at an angle." Wise mimed shooting a gun with his hand, angled up from his waist. "I think it was fired at close range. Possibly during a scuffle."

"Has he said anything?"

"Only feverish murmuring. He keeps repeating a woman's name—Mei."

Isobel glanced back into the small room. Another girl? Unfortunately, feverish murmurings weren't very reliable. This Mei might be dead or entirely fictional.

"And what of your injuries, Miss Bonnie?"

Isobel blinked. "Pardon me?"

"Atticus told me that you're in need of medical attention."

"Oh, did he?" She nearly growled. "Where is he?"

"I'm afraid changing the subject will not protect you from a doctor's concern."

"It's only a split lip and a knocked nose."

"And numerous kicks to your stomach. May I?" He held out his hands.

"Nothing is broken." She did growl this time.

"You are as distrustful as that child. Most women are not comfortable with a Chinese doctor. I understand."

"I don't like *any* doctor near me—Chinese *or* white."

Wise smiled. It transformed his face from a wise sage to a benevolent uncle, and he leaned in close, lowering his voice. "She won't let me near her either. I had hoped that your cooperation would ease her trepidation."

Isobel glanced at the chair, and saw a pair of eyes peeking around the back. They narrowed at her.

"Fine, but make sure you tell her how brave I am."

"That was the plan."

Isobel grudgingly submitted to Wise's examination. He took her pulse, frowned over her wrists and cleaned them again. Then he asked a string of questions that irritated her immensely.

"Are you cramping?"

"No."

"Blood in your urine?" he asked.

"Yes.

"Is this tender?"

She grunted as he pressed on her stomach.

"Here?"

She tried not to wince.

"When was your last menstrual cycle?"

"It doesn't matter," she bit out.

A snort rose from the armchair.

"Vomiting?" he asked.

"No," she said with a click of teeth.

His brows drew together. "Have you been feeling queasy?"

She shrugged.

"Hungry?"

"Yes."

"Would you like to discuss this in private?"

"No." Isobel sat up, putting an end that line of questioning. "It's a shame Jin is *too scared* to be examined by you."

"It's understandable," Wise said. "I see it too often. The

more defiant the child, the harsher the keeper. Breaking a girl's spirit is paramount to the trade." There was pain and resignation in his voice. "Girls such as Jin have known nothing but severe abuse."

Isobel glanced at the wounded hellion. She was watching them with suspicious eyes, turning the bracelet around her wrist over and over again. Isobel was reminded of animals she had seen pacing their cages in zoos.

"Do they ever heal?"

Wise smiled. "Yes. Some. With time and love."

The warmth and hope in his voice was unmistakable. He reminded her of her own father.

"Do you have children?" she suddenly asked.

"I do," he said. "Two daughters. They are the joy in my world. And my wife, the heart."

"They're fortunate to have you for a father, Dr. Wise."

"I am the fortunate one, Miss Bonnie."

An ache filled her own heart—for her own father, aging and grief-stricken. She swallowed it down. "What will become of Jin?"

"I do not know," he said. "I have no idea if she has family."

The child in question was still watching, still glaring.

"I suppose we'll drop her off at one of the missions," Isobel said. Jin's eyes widened, and heat flushed her face. But only for a second, before she ducked back behind the big chair.

Isobel pounced, moving to the side of the chair. "You *do* speak English." She loomed over the girl.

Jin blinked innocently. "*No sabe.*"

"*No sabe* my ass."

Wise cleared his throat, and Jin's eyelashes flickered.

Isobel crossed her arms. "Don't play innocent with me.

You understand me perfectly well. I noticed last night when my partner mentioned that fellow in there is a hatchet man."

Jin bolted out of the chair. She was quick, and halfway to the stairs when Isobel tackled her. "I won't go back to the mission!" she screeched in perfect English. "You can't make me, *Faan Tung*!"

Isobel hoisted the girl off her feet, and more kicks pummeled her legs. Tim raced up the stairs, and Wise moved to assist, receiving scratches for his efforts. Teeth sank into Isobel's hand, and she lost patience. She simply dropped the child onto the floor. Jin thudded onto the floorboards, and scrambled to her feet. The girl retreated, and took up a crouched stance, preparing to fight the three adults with her last breath.

"No one is keeping you here," Isobel growled. "If you want to help your *brother* then you need to talk to us like a civilized human-being. If not, then go." She thrust her finger towards the stairway.

Jin's eyes blazed. She pressed her lips together, thrust out her chin, and stalked off, disappearing down the stairs.

"Let her be," Isobel said, when Tim made to go after her. "If her stubbornness gets her brother killed, it's her fault." Isobel yelled the last towards the stairway. Frustrated, tired, and temperamental, she gathered her handbag.

Wise held up a halting hand. "Miss Bonnie, I was about to recommend a day of rest."

"I can't."

Tim looked skyward.

"At least wait for me to prepare some herbs," Wise said. "My tea will help with internal swelling."

"I have to check on something."

"Look," Tim said, glancing from the doctor to her. "Someone has to watch the hatchet man in there. Wise has to go, and I have some telegrams to send. What do you need? Maybe I can do it."

Isobel blinked at the suggestion. She was accustomed to doing everything on her own. The thought of help had never occurred to her. "I need to check with a runner in front of the Call building. If he's not there, then I need to check messages at the nearby Western Union."

"Name?"

"Bill Cody. The stinky one."

"Got it." Tim thrust a shotgun in her hand, grabbed his coat, and bolted, leaving Isobel no choice. As Wise headed off to make his medicinal tea, she sank into the chair beside the man who'd shot Riot. His life, she decided, was as strange and complex as her own.

37

The Year of the Rat

ATTICUS RIOT LEANED CASUALLY on his stick, hands crossed on the engraved silver, as he watched police patrolling a barricade of barbed wire. The fence ran down the sidewalk, blocking off a Chinese grocer's, dipping back in for a boarding house for whites and a saloon, and then jutting back out to barricade a silk merchant.

Chinatown was under quarantine. The bubonic plague had come to San Francisco, or so a quarantine officer by the name of Joseph Kinyoun claimed. The newspapers, however, were far more skeptical, calling him mad, or a man with a political agenda.

A group of residents stood behind the barbed-wire, facing off with a number of police. Barred from reaching their jobs, locked in with a killing disease, their faces were grim—desperate even.

As Riot climbed Sacramento Street, he mused on the apparent prejudice of rats. How nice of them to stay away from white businesses. At the top of the hill, Riot stopped in front of a familiar door and used the much abused knocker. A slat slid to the side.

"Atticus Riot to see Miss Cameron."

The eyes behind widened, and a second later the door flew open. "Mr. Riot!" He could not help but smile as a grown girl of eighteen pulled him inside.

"Hello, Ling," he said, removing his hat.

She gripped his hand with both of hers. "We were so worried about you," she said in a rush. "I saw the newspapers and knew you returned. How are you?"

"Better," he said. "Although currently I'm in shock. The weed has blossomed into a rose." She was beautiful, and the joy that filled her eyes filled his heart. He squeezed her hands. But the smile in her eyes dimmed a moment later as they settled on his temple.

"A touch of death," she murmured in Cantonese. White was a mourning color in China.

"Only a touch," he said easily.

"I was so worried about you."

"I'm sorry I left without saying goodbye, Ling. I wasn't quite recovered."

"But you are now?"

"As much as any girl within these walls recovers."

She nodded with understanding. No more words needed saying.

"Is Miss Cameron still here?"

"Of course. She is the superintendent now."

"Not surprising at all."

Ling nodded. "Her blood is in these bricks."

"It wouldn't be the same without her."

"No," she agreed. "Did you hear about Miss Culberston?"

"I'm afraid I did," he said. "I was sorry to hear of her

passing." She had died in ninety-seven—nearly three years ago—from internal injuries. Years before, she had been kicked in the stomach by a rescued slave girl in a rage, and she never fully recovered. Riot couldn't help but think about Isobel, and he swallowed down his worry, focusing on Ling's next words.

"It was a bad time for Miss Cameron—for all of us."

"I'm sorry." He looked around the front hall. "I see life goes on?" Flowers filled the hall, along with red banners wishing fortune and happiness.

Ling beamed. "It does."

"What's the occasion?" he asked.

A blush spread over her cheeks. "I'm getting married."

Riot blinked.

"Next year. This was a celebration of the engagement. Will you..." she paused in thought. "What is the term? Give me away?"

Riot's throat caught.

"That is the custom, I believe?"

He could only nod.

"It's only that I wouldn't be here without you, Mr. Riot. And..."

"I'd be honored, Ling."

"It is fate. As it was before."

How many years had it been? She had been but a child when he'd helped her. Truth be told, she had rescued herself, and had run straight into a pair of policeman for help. Unfortunately, they had promptly seized her, and marched her straight back to the brothel and her keeper's hands. It was mere luck that placed him in that alleyway, at that moment, and he had taken issue with the officers. Violent issue.

"Is he a good man?"

She smiled, showing off a pair of dimples. "He is. Miss Cameron is very careful when arranging marriages. He is a merchant from Sacramento. Very fine, and kind like you."

"I'm happy then." There was an itch in the corner of his eyes, and he hastily removed his spectacles to wipe away the moisture as he followed Ling down a hallway.

Miss Cameron had not changed in the three years since he'd seen her last. Although some of the steel in her spine now laced through her dark hair. It was strange to find her sitting behind the desk instead of Miss Culberston.

"Atticus." His name was a breath, and Miss Donaldina Cameron greeted him with open arms. He returned the embrace, and she stepped back, gripping his forearms to get a better look at him. "The beard suits you."

"Lends me some refinement?"

She chuckled. "Definitely less wild looking."

"The last vestige of my youth," he said with a sigh.

"Somehow I doubt that… I heard you traversed the world."

"I did."

There was an appraising glint in her eye. "All things end at the beginning, it seems."

He expressed his condolences.

"It was… difficult at first," she admitted. "But we made it through with the Lord's help. Margaret was ailing and in pain for a long while, but she's at peace now." Her eyes traveled upwards. "Looking down at us no doubt."

"I'm sure she's pleased as ever with you."

"I don't know about that," she replied wryly. "You know I did some traveling of my own?" Donaldina glanced at her office. Little had changed since he was last there. The thick journal still sat on her desk. He suspected the names of hundreds more had been added in the years he had been gone. "But I couldn't leave for good; I couldn't abandon these girls—nor my calling." Her hand strayed to the thick journal.

"Admit it, Dolly, you were bored."

"It's partially true," she said with a laugh. "Never the same day twice."

"Would you like some tea?" Ling asked.

"Please."

Ling hurried off, leaving the two alone.

"Are you recovered from your injuries?" Donaldina's gaze traveled to the white streak of hair slashing across his temple.

"As much as I can be," he admitted. "My memories have recently come back."

Her brows shot up. "Only recently?"

He nodded. "I received a shock in the form of running into the hatchet man who shot me."

Donaldina sat down at her desk. Her hands flat on the top as if bracing herself for ill news. "Did he try to assassinate you again?"

Riot shook his head, and gave her the facts.

"Wong Kau," she repeated, softly.

"Have you heard of him?"

"I have. He's a notorious *boo how doy*. I wouldn't be surprised if shooting you earned him a fair amount of prestige. Do you believe him?"

"About Hip Yee not murdering Ravenwood?" Riot tapped his finger on the silver knob in thought. "I don't know."

"Will he survive?"

"He was alive this morning. He kept murmuring a woman's name, Mei, over and over."

Donaldina turned in her chair, and rifled through a desk drawer. Her eyes were alight with surprise. When she found what she desired, she pushed a note across the desk. "I received this a few weeks ago."

Honored Jesus Woman,
A concubine of Hip Yee leader is being held above store 929 Dupont Street. Mei. Please rescue.

"Did you go?" Riot asked.

"Of course I did." Donaldina looked offended by any other idea. "But she wasn't there."

"It could have been a trap."

"Every rescue could be my last," she said. "The risk hasn't stopped me before. But don't worry—I took Sgt. Price."

"I'm surprised he hasn't made lieutenant yet." William Price was an outstanding officer on the Chinatown Police Squad when Riot had joined in on the raids three years before.

"Oh, he was promoted to lieutenant in ninety-eight, then demoted back down to sergeant the following year, because he hadn't 'suppressed the Chinatown scandals yet.'"

Riot sighed, and looked at the ceiling. "It appears the police commissioners haven't changed, but I'm glad to hear he's still in town."

"And he's as determined as I am to stop the slave trade. I might be optimistic, but I think we might actually be making a dent."

"It's that Scottish stubbornness in your blood."

"Defiant to the end," she agreed.

Riot glanced at the note. The hand was precise and

careful, but unfortunately Mei was a common enough name. It might even be a milk name. Could this note have been about Sao Jin, and could the hatchet man have been sent to retrieve her? It was common for Chinese to have four or more names: an official name, a courtesy name, a nickname, a milk name, an American name, and a school name. One for every stage of life.

"I do remember a girl by the name of Sao Jin—let me find it," Donaldina murmured, as she flipped through her journal. "I suppose you saw the barbed-wire around the Quarter?"

"I did."

Ling walked in with a tray, and poured three cups. Riot took the green tea with a murmured thanks, and she sat in the chair beside him.

"Do you think it's the plague?" he asked.

"I don't know," Donaldina admitted. "The fellow they found was a bachelor living in the Globe Hotel on Dupont Street."

Riot winced. It was a flophouse known as *Five Stories* that sheltered hundreds of workingmen in its cramped cells.

"Rumor says it was the clap," Donaldina said, without the flutter of a lash. Treating girls with venereal disease was an everyday occurrence at the mission.

"There's been many dead rats though," Ling said.

"There have," Donaldina agreed. "An alarming number since January. The newest Consul, Ching Yen Fun, issued a complaint with the city, but as usual nothing was done."

"The coming of the devil of plague/Suddenly makes the lamp dim,/Thin it is blown out, Leaving man,/Ghost and corpse in the dark room," Riot recited.

Donaldina tilted her head in question.

"The poet Shih Tao-nan. Rats are bad luck."

"Very bad," Ling agreed.

"Entire households will clear out at the sight of a dead rat in China, but in the Quarter, there's nowhere to go," Riot explained. Discrimination prevented Chinese from living anywhere but Chinatown.

"Ironic that it's the Year of the Rat. Although I try to enlighten the children, they are still superstitious." She gave a pointed look at Ling.

"This year has been *horrible*, Miss Cameron," Ling defended. "Surely you cannot deny that?"

"Coincidence does not equal bad luck," Miss Cameron corrected. "But you're right. I don't know if you've kept up to date, Atticus, but the tong wars have been so brutal that the Police Department has canceled holiday celebrations. It's been the quietest New Year since I've been here."

Riot frowned. The Lunar New Year was usually a festive celebration with fireworks and parades, heralding in a new year. It meant a lot to the Chinese—to the entire city, truth be told, with whites flocking to the streets to join in the festivities.

An ill year indeed.

"Let's hope the city doesn't panic and resort to burning down Chinatown, like what happened in Honolulu," Riot said.

Donaldina shook her head. "I can only pray. This current Consul General is a cunning man and a skilled diplomat. I can well imagine what's been going on in the embassy. Meanwhile, half the city is without its workers— servants, cooks, launderers, childminders, delivery, grocers —all barred from going to work. I'm sure the Palace Hotel is in chaos."

San Francisco's relationship with Chinatown was a long one, of both love and hate.

"Here it is." Donaldina turned the journal towards him, and stabbed a finger at an entry two years earlier. "Ah, yes. Sao Jin came here seeking refuge. She was a quiet thing, and save for her name we couldn't get her to talk. I remember she had bruises on her cheek and eye— not nearly as bad as you've described. Her parents came with the police that very day, with a writ of *habeas corpus* and identity papers. I tried to hide her, of course, but the mother was particularly sharp-eyed, and they dragged her away."

"Were they her actual parents?" It was not uncommon for aunts, uncles, or neighbors to simply claim an or- phaned child as their own.

"I don't know. I looked for the child, but never heard another word about her." There was pain and regret in her eyes. Every failure bubbled over in her voice: every lost child, every death from the disease of a trade that had been forced upon the girls, and every long night spent beside a deathbed. "I'm glad you found her, although it sounds as if the years have not been kind."

"I remember her," Ling said. "She stole apples from the pantry, and glared at everyone in the house. She punched one of the other girls, too."

"That hasn't changed, at least," Riot said.

"Odd that she would turn up in Ocean Beach. Do you think that hatchet man abducted her, and she's simply too frightened to leave him?"

"We're trying to find out. I hope she'll be persuaded to talk."

"You will help her. I know," Ling said, with a smile. "I can ask the new arrivals if they know of her, or this Mei."

Riot nodded. "I'd appreciate that."

"And I'll pass the word along to my informants. Maybe something will turn up. But be careful, Atticus. It sounds as if you're climbing into a lion's den again."

"I've been down there for some time."

"Then I'll ask the Lord to shut their mouths," Donaldina said.

"I prefer my No. 3."

She smiled. "I'll pray all the same.

The door to Ravenwood Agency was unlocked. Riot entered, expecting to find Montgomery Johnson in a chair, sleeping; instead, Matthew Smith sat dutifully at his desk. His blond hair was neatly combed, and he was freshly shaven and bright-eyed. The ex-patrolman wrote carefully, his tongue (Riot was amused to see) protruding slightly from his lips. A sure sign of absolute focus.

Smith glanced up, and quickly laid down his pen to stand at near attention.

"At ease," Riot said dryly. The younger detective cleared his throat, and appeared to make an effort to relax. "How is Mrs. Artells?"

"Everything seemed fine, sir."

"Call me, A.J. I'm not your commanding officer."

"Right, er—A.J." The name appeared to make him uncomfortable.

"'Mr. Riot' works, too."

Smith looked relieved. "I beat Mr. Artells back to the cabin, and kept a lookout from when he first arrived. Everything seemed quiet and amiable. No shouting. I could see them talking at the table in the kitchen. They were holding hands. Mrs. Artells was humming the next morning, and they went for a picnic and swim—all very romantic."

"Is it?" Riot asked.

The question gave Smith pause. "I think so. Women like that sort of thing, don't they?"

"Some women." Riot placed his hat on its hook, and frowned. Had Isobel enjoyed their afternoon swim? She had not seemed particularly moved. Relaxed, yes. Enjoying herself, definitely. But what stirred *her* passions?

His thoughts drifted back to Isobel earlier that morning —and lingered there. The feel of her in his arms, the smell of soap on her skin, waking up beside her. If he had dallied a moment longer, he would have roused her in quite a different manner. But this was not casual. He didn't want to rush things—not with her. She was not a bored divorcee, or an independent widow looking for a charming bedmate. This was—

"Should I not have left, sir?"

"What?" Riot pulled his mind back into focus.

"The Artells," Smith said. "Should I not have left?"

"No, that was fine. It sounds as if Mr. Artells behaved himself. Any luck on locating Mrs. Parks?"

"Who?"

Riot stopped in the middle of hanging up his coat. "Didn't Monty tell you?"

"No."

He sighed.

Smith shifted on his feet. "Monty told me to watch the office because he was on a case. There's some messages on your desk."

Riot walked towards his office, and Smith raised his voice from the other room. "That Kingston fellow keeps calling. He won't talk to me on account of me being an imbecile." Alex Kingston had not developed a high opinion of Monty and Smith during the investigation into his missing wife.

"Noted." Riot closed the door, and turned to the stack of papers. He shuffled through the mess on his desk: case notes, telegrams, messages from reporters requesting an interview with Sarah. But there was no message from Monty. Riot had an overwhelming need to discover what had become of Abigail Parks.

Feeling sentimental? Ravenwood asked.

"I thought you left." He didn't look up, didn't want to know if he'd see a phantom, or some mental conjuring of his madness sitting in the chair across.

Isobel deserved better than an old man with a ghost on his heels.

I'm observing your blundering investigation, his dead partner said.

"Perhaps you should contribute," he said sharply.

Ah, my boy, you know why I can't. I'm the scratch in that skull of yours; the niggling thorn prickling your thoughts. Ravenwood lengthened every word, drawing out each syllable with a click of teeth.

Are you running from that intriguing woman?

"I am not," he said.

You confided in her, shared your bed, and now you're here.

"I'm trying to discover who killed you."

Ah.

The sound was irritating. Riot looked up, but the chair across the desk was empty. Still, he asked the question plaguing his mind. "What *were* you doing while I was handling the Quarantine Scandal?"

No answer. Of course not. Before his wounded mind decided to conjure a pink elephant, Riot picked up the telephone receiver and pressed the lever. "The Law Offices of Alex Kingston."

Minutes passed, and questions grew. What had Ravenwood meant when he mentioned another possibility? The man had had enough research projects for two lifetimes. He'd kept meticulous notes with which to dispute the findings of 'incompetent' criminalists in the rising field of forensics (which had been most everyone in Ravenwood's opinion).

Riot had been assuming that his partner was doing what he always did. But what if Ravenwood's death had nothing to do with the tongs? What if someone just wanted him out of the way, and used the tongs as a scapegoat? The way Timothy Seaward used the missions and tongs as cover to carry out his hellish bloodlust. The city itself did that very same thing—politicians blamed the Quarter for disease, crime, and the loss of every white man's job. But who else would have killed Ravenwood, and why?

"Riot." A sharp, deep voice crackled down the line. He tried not to think of this brute of a man blackmailing Isobel into his bed. Riot swallowed down that cold rage, and buried it deep, like any skilled gambler.

"Kingston," he said easily. "I hear you're looking for me."

"I have a job for you. Artells told me he was pleased with your work. A shame you couldn't find *my* wife in time." Straight to the point.

"You don't sound like a man wanting to hire me," Riot said.

Kingston grunted. "I like you. You don't back down."

He has no idea, Ravenwood said, with a rasping chuckle.

"I'd hardly be on this side of the veil if I did."

"From what I hear, you've sent a fair number of men to

be fitted for a pine suit. I like that."

Kingston would.

"You're familiar with the Lee Walker case. You found his niece."

"I did," confirmed Riot.

"I need you to investigate Walker. I'm representing Claiborne, and I want you to personally look into this matter." From the muffled way he spoke, Riot could well imagine the cigar thrust between his thick lips.

"I'm currently working on another case," Riot said. "I'll put a man on it, however."

"I want *you*. And I won't take no for an answer." It was a near growl.

"Is there a reason for the rush?"

"I don't want this to reach the courts. Better to nip it in the ass beforehand. Is there a reason why you're questioning me?"

"I'm a detective—that's my job."

"Then damn well do it."

Before Riot could deny his request a second time, Kingston slammed the telephone down. Riot jerked the receiver away from his ear, and frowned at the crackling line. He had been slowly working his way into Kingston's circle, and here was a chance to get closer. It was tempting to report Lee Walker to the authorities. If Walker avoided the courts, the man might go free, *or* Kingston would press charges, and Sarah would be dragged into her uncle's mess.

The outside door opened. Low voices came from the main office. A moment later Monty Johnson stomped inside without knocking, and Riot waited.

"I found your woman," Monty grunted. So he *had* taken on the job himself. "It wasn't hard. A few old timers remembered her well. They were fond of her at Park's Place."

"Where is she?"

"In the Odd Fellow's Cemetery."

38

A Tangled Web

RAVENWOOD MANOR CLUNG TO the side of a hill. A thing of turrets, and a confusion of design. It dominated the block as if to threaten visitors away. That wasn't working today, however. Cameron Fry was sulking across the street, but it wasn't the young reporter who caught Riot's attention—it was another, the same man who'd lurked under a lamppost the day before. The man leaned against his post, smoking and watching the house without any attempt at subterfuge.

The man tipped his hat, and Riot angled towards him, heading across the street, but Cameron Fry got eager, intercepting him in the middle.

"Mr. Riot," Fry said.

He kept walking, eyes on the smoking man. "In a minute, Fry."

The reporter fell silent, and kept on Riot's heels, his journalistic instincts sensing something grave in the air.

"Can I help you?" Riot asked the lurker. He was a few

inches taller than Riot, but most men were. Everything about the man was bland, from his bowler to his brown hair to the cut of his suit. Unremarkable in every way. Even his eyes. They appeared half-glazed as he sucked on his cigarette. The lurker took a lazy drag, and blew out a slow cloud of smoke. It raised Riot's hackles.

"No, sir." Slow and steady, without inflection. Definitely a predator. His coat was open, and he rested a hand on his right hip, but smoked with his left. A gun was sure to be hidden on that side.

"You look lost," Riot said.

"I'm enjoying your fine neighborhood. A nice family you have there." The smile barely moved his drooping mustache.

Riot was as relaxed and poised as the smoking man. Danger took him that way—like the calm before the storm. "That's a neighborly thing to say," Riot said. "You enjoy your day. A man never knows when it might be his last."

"Amen to that. Women and children, too."

Riot stared at the man, not in threat, but patience, waiting for him to say more. It unnerved most; they usually reacted, or left.

"You have a pleasant day, Mr. Riot." The smoking man tipped his hat, and strolled away.

Riot watched him until he disappeared around a corner.

"Who was that?" a voice asked.

Riot glanced at the reporter. "I don't know."

Fry licked his lips, and fiddled with the pen in his hand. "Why didn't you ask his name?"

Riot smirked. "I doubt he's the type to give it freely."

"What was that all about? He's been standing there all

morning."

"Trouble, Mr. Fry. He's trouble. I'd stay clear if I were you."

"Is that why you have those two goons out front?"

Those 'two goons' were slouching in plain view in front of the house. They watched as Riot came their way. One was bulky, the other wiry. Riot had sent both of them to San Quentin.

"That young fellow giving you problems, Mr. Riot?" the big man asked.

Fry's feet stuttered, and he angled himself to the opposite side, putting Riot between him and the big man.

"No, he isn't, Meekins." The bulky man was built like a Japanese wrestler. His hair, currently pulled back in a ponytail, was long and stringy, and he never bothered with a waistcoat.

"Oh." Meekins frowned. "Should I have let him pass?"

"No."

Meekins cracked his knuckles.

"*That* man tried to kill me," Fry said to Riot. "If I wasn't an amiable fellow, I'd have summoned the police. I could still press charges."

Riot arched his brow at the reporter. "Fry, if he had tried to kill you, he would have succeeded."

Meekins had had an awful temper once upon a time. Riot had encountered the 'tough-for-hire' during an investigation, and subsequently been the target of his drunken wrath. Meekins later confided to Riot that jail was the best thing that ever happened to him. When he sobered up, he found Jesus, and embraced the first half of his name. The man might be meek, but he was still a bull waiting to charge.

His thin partner mumbled something.

"I've been good, Mr. Payne, thank you."

Before San Quentin, Payne had built up a reputation worthy of his name. The man had a love of blades and revolvers. An agile bounty hunter who had once hog-tied a wanted man and taken him to jail—only to discover it was the wrong man. Luckily, for the sake of his neck, the wanted poster had been for alive and not dead.

Riot started to walk up the lane.

"Mr. Riot!" Fry called, too wary of the guards to step off the sidewalk. Riot stopped, and waited. "If I could have a chaperoned interview with Miss Byrne, I'd be in your debt. Someone's bound to keep trying anyhow. Wouldn't you rather I do the interview than some unscrupulous fellow? I have four sisters."

The young man was neatly dressed, and had a smile he liked to flash. Riot would be surprised if a word he'd just said were true.

"It'd be a sure-fire way to get rid of me, too. Otherwise, I'll dog your every move."

"I'd advise you to stay off my property."

"Oh, I will, but I'll be waiting. Persistence is my middle name."

Riot cocked his head with amusement. "Cameron Persistence Fry," he tasted the words. "It sounds like a character from Jane Austen."

"Who?"

Riot sighed, and Payne mumbled something low with a nearly unintelligible accent from his hometown in Maryland. "I agree, Mr. Payne, no class these days. Don't you read, Fry?"

"Newspapers."

"I have a proposition for you, Fry. Read one of Jane Austen's novels, give me a proper summary, and then I'll ask Miss Byrne if she'll consent to an interview."

"I would recommend *Pride and Prejudice*," said Meekins. "Makes a man think."

"An excellent recommendation," Riot agreed. He had regularly visited Meekins in prison, lending him a stack of books each time to better his education.

Fry scribbled down the name. "I'll hold you to that, sir. I'll be back—you can count on it."

Riot didn't doubt that. He walked up the lane without looking back. The yard and carriage house were quiet. There was no clunking, cursing, or sounds of deranged banging coming from its innards. That stillness was alarming.

And it triggered a memory—the smell of blood, and glazed, staring eyes. Instinctively, he drew his revolver, and hurried through the barn doors.

Riot swallowed down his dread, and took a step inside the carriage house. There was no blood, there were no murdered friends. He took a shaky breath, and climbed the stairway, careful not to step on the boards that he knew creaked.

The workshop was empty, and he moved into the living area. Sao Jin was not in the big chair by the stove. Finding the kitchen empty too, he headed towards the small room in the back.

Wong Kau lay in the bed, pale and deathly still, while Isobel sat in the chair beside his bed. She was slightly slumped. Before reason could take hold, Riot holstered his gun, and rushed forward, placing two fingers under her jaw and feeling for a pulse.

The heart is a most irritating and irrational organ, Ravenwood grumbled.

Isobel cracked an eye open. "Worried?"

"A little," he said faintly. She opened her eyes fully, and tilted her face towards his. His fingertips lingered over her pulse, and she smiled up at him.

"I figured it was you when I didn't hear the stairs creak." She shifted the blanket, uncocked her Shopkeeper, and wedged it back into her pocket.

She reached up and took his hand, brushing her lips along his knuckles. The touch drove all reason away, and his mind went momentarily blank; he even forgot the hatchet man in the bed.

Gripping his hand, she used it to pull herself up. She moved stiffly, and concern trumped all else. "Did Doctor Wise examine you?" he asked.

Isobel frowned, wrapping her blanket around her shoulders like a shawl. "I can't believe you put him up to that."

"You would have done the same."

"I'd have tied you to the bed, Riot."

"I look forward to it."

Her breath caught, and then a mischievous quirk raised the edge of her lip. He wanted to pull her close and kiss that quirk. And she well knew it. She was waiting, of course, waiting with a raised brow in challenge.

"I'll hold you to that." She slipped a card from her sleeve—the Queen of Hearts—and tucked it into his waistcoat pocket. "If only we didn't have an audience."

The words were a reminder of time and place. And he wished the same—wished that his past hadn't caught up to him at that moment. Riot remembered to breathe, his chest swelling, as her hand smoothed the fabric over his breast.

"Jin ran off," she said, snapping him from his daze.

"Unfortunate," he murmured. "But I didn't imagine

she'd stay."

"Well, I certainly didn't help things," she said with a sigh. "I'm not the motherly sort." Isobel narrowed her eyes at him. "Where have you been?"

He glanced over her shoulder at Wong Kau. His breathing was shallow, but steady. Riot placed a gentle hand on her back, and directed her out of the room, away from the hatchet man. When she sank into a plush chair by the stove, he went over to the kitchen and poured two glasses of water.

"I'm fairly sure I've aged twenty years in three days," she said, accepting his offering. Riot's back and shoulders ached as well, from carrying Kau across the dunes. But Riot hadn't been hog-tied and beaten beforehand, so his discomfort wasn't nearly as acute.

He pulled over a wooden chair, and sat. "I like to think I am a bit more fluid than you are, just now."

She sniffed at the water. "I hope you added brandy to this."

"A whole heap."

She smirked, and drank the plain water. As did he, stalling for time.

"You're not going to make me wait, are you?" she finally asked.

"Wait for what?"

"For you to start talking. It's clear you discovered something."

"Is it?" he asked.

"To me."

"I must be out of practice and losing my poker face."

"It's not your face that's rusty. It's..." she tilted her head, "more like how I can sense the mood of the ocean."

"Every sailor claims that," he said dryly.

"I will not be thrown off course," she said, and waited.

He obliged. "I stopped by 920," he said, and filled her in on what he had gleaned.

"That explains why Jin had such a violent reaction when I threatened to put her in a mission. She likely thinks she'll be handed back to the very people she ran from. She speaks English, you know."

His brows shot up. "*Does* she?"

Isobel inclined her head, and then made a frustrated sound in the back of her throat. "I don't have a maternal bone in my body, but it boils my blood to see those scars on her face, especially knowing the police were involved in handing her back."

"I wouldn't be so sure about your lack of maternal instinct."

"I don't have one," she persisted. "What do you think happened to her after she was taken from the mission?"

"Who knows. They may have been her parents, or not. And it's not terribly uncommon for parents to sell a daughter so they can return to China."

"Barbaric," Isobel growled.

Riot sat back, crossing his legs. "Is it much different than the custom of marrying off a daughter to a wealthy family in 'civilized society'?"

"I don't much care for that either."

"I didn't imagine you would," he said with a quick smile. "Slap whatever name you want on it, but there's little difference. Whether it's dowries, an outright sale, or pushing your daughter towards a financial gold mine to pad the family fortune—strip away the finery, and it's all the same. In English society, most mothers parade their daughters around like fine wares."

"Thank God I wasn't raised in England. God forbid a

woman might work."

"Not all women, nor men, have your tenacity."

"I'll take that as a compliment." She cocked her head. "Do mothers throw their daughters at you?"

"Since I inherited Ravenwood's estate the attempted engagements have tripled."

"A wealthy American with the manners of an English gentleman. A catch indeed."

"Only until you get to know me."

She snorted. "The same could be said of most so-called *gentlemen*."

"A pity," he sighed. "I hate to be another fish in the barrel."

"You're far more interesting than the other ones."

"*The miserable have no other medicine, but only hope.*"

"Far from miserable, Riot." She looked at him sideways. "Do you memorize Shakespeare so you can quote verses to all your women?"

"My harem swoons whenever I quote sonnets."

"I'm beginning to think you might have a harem," she mused. "You've knocked us off track again, Riot."

"Are you sure it was me this time?"

"*Men were deceivers ever*," she muttered. "If it weren't for men like Doctor Wise, whose daughter is the apple of his eye, and my father, I'd lose all hope for the male sex."

"I hope I'm included in that list."

"I have yet to meet your harem," she quipped. "I imagine there are quite a few headstrong women in your life."

He clucked his tongue. "A gentleman never tells, Bel."

"You told me about Abigail Parks."

"It seemed relevant."

"Why?"

"I don't know," he admitted. He thought of her grave.

The date on the stone said she died a week after Raven-wood. There had been a bouquet of hothouse roses at her gravesite. She had hated roses. And now he knew for a certainty that he was avoiding the subject, that he was hesitant to speak of Abigail's death aloud. "I find myself examining everything in those months. I'm seeing webs where there are likely shadows."

"You've got a mixed-up puzzle, Riot," she said softly. "We need to separate the pieces."

"Easier said than done."

"It only takes stubborn patience, and you have that in spades."

He removed his spectacles, and rubbed his eyes. "My supply is running thin of late."

"I hope you're not looking to me to be the patient one of this partnership?"

"You're more of a wrecking ball," Riot said.

"I like that image." There was true pleasure in her voice. "So what has you so uneasy?"

"Abigail Parks is dead."

Isobel narrowed her eyes in thought, as if she were shifting pieces around on a chessboard. Most would automatically express sympathy, but not Isobel—interrogation was more her style.

"How'd she die?"

"Murdered in a robbery."

Isobel frowned. "At the saloon?"

"Yes."

"Was she shot?"

Riot shifted. "Her skull was crushed with a slung shot. From the sound of it, she put up a fight."

"I'm so sorry, Riot."

He frowned into his glass. "We were two ships passing

in the night. Still, for three years, I imagined her enjoying life—raising chickens in some quaint village, or serving drinks in Montparnasse."

"I would have liked to meet her. She sounds like my kind of woman."

"I didn't know her very well," he admitted. "Our relationship was one of… convenience. Both of us valued our independence."

He could feel her eyes on him. Could practically feel her thinking. There was an energy that buzzed around Isobel as palatable as an electric charge.

"Do I dare ask?"

"Haven't you just?" she returned.

He threaded his spectacles over his ears, and looked expectantly at her.

"I'm seeing shadows, too," she confided. "Maybe everything *is* tangled. It *feels* like it, doesn't it?"

"I don't see how Abigail could be tied up in all this."

"I wouldn't be so sure of that."

"I was lying in a hospital bed when she was murdered. She wasn't involved in any of my affairs, and no one knew we were intimate."

"When did Jim Parks get out of prison?"

"He was set to be released in March of eighty-seven."

"Maybe a friend of his found out?"

Riot shifted. "Maybe so, but why not kill me? A pillow over my face would have done the job, nice and quietly."

Isobel pursed her lips in thought.

"Park's Place isn't on the best side of town," he pointed out.

"No, you're right, it isn't," she conceded. "It's likely nothing more than my suspicious mind. After dealing with Kingston for months, I've begun to see connections everywhere."

"It happens to the best of us."

Isobel tapped her fist against the armrest. "I should have chased Jin down. If Kau dies, she'll be our only chance to discover the truth of what happened that night."

"You did the right thing, Bel," he said quietly. "These girls are wounded badly. Trust is scarred, and it doesn't come back easy. The slave girls that Donaldina rescues are distrustful of everyone. And they have every right to be. The worst thing you can do is corner them. That's why Miss Culberston stopped snatching them straight out of a brothel—it's best to give them a say in the matter. Otherwise they fight like cornered wildcats, and it only makes things worse. Jin will come around when she's ready."

"*If* she finds her way back."

"She might not have gone far," he said. "Jin appears to be attached to Wong Kau in some way—seems to care about whether he lives or dies. Maybe she's waiting to question him, too."

"It's possible," she agreed.

"I'll send a telegram to 920. Miss Cameron's network of informants will be our best chance of finding her, if she ran to the Quarter."

Isobel looked to the small room, to the hatchet man fighting for his life on the cot. "I doubt there's much information flowing through the quarantine barricades."

"You'd be surprised."

"Do you think Kau is the one who wrote the note to 920?"

"I don't know."

"There's a lot of that going around." Her hand tightened around her glass—the frustration plain in her voice. "I've been resisting the urge to shake Kau awake and demand answers."

"Time and patience, Bel."

"You know I hate waiting."

"You're not waiting—you're on guard duty. And I'll leave you to it."

Isobel glared; he smiled.

"Where are you going?" she asked.

"I'm going to plumb the depths of Ravenwood's attic."

"Oh, in that case," she wrapped her blanket around her, propped her feet on a stool, and settled into the plush chair, "I think I'll make a sacrifice, and continue guarding our prisoner."

"Always the hero, Bel. Can I get you a fortifying brandy before I leave?"

"I'd best keep my wits about me," she said with a sigh.

"In case you change your mind, Tim keeps a medicinal bottle in that cabinet over there." He stood to leave, gathering his hat and stick.

"Riot."

The sound of his name stopped him at the stairs.

"I can't remember the last time I slept so well," she said softly.

It took him a few moments to find his voice. "Neither can I."

39

Pirates and Indians

A SHARP SCRAPING CAME from the ceiling, and then thudding footsteps. A moment later, a voice shouted, *Argh*! followed by a rapid *bang bang bang*. The noise shook the plaster from the ceiling. Riot paused, eyeing the blossoming crack. The wall shuddered, and Riot hurried to the end of the hallway. He opened the wide access hatch, and climbed the narrow staircase.

"I'll get you, Savage!" a growl filled the attic space.

Riot glanced through the railing slats to find a cowboy, an Indian, and a pirate. Maddie wore a feathered headdress and warpaint, and she wielded a broom like a spear, thrusting it towards a sloped ceiling and brandishing a feather duster as a shield in the other hand.

A pint-sized cowboy appeared, swimming in a Stetson and wearing an old leather holster on a belt that wrapped around his waist three times. Tobias waved a rabbit shooter at her.

Before Riot could react, a pirate leapt into the fray.

Sarah Byrne had a prospector's hat turned sideways, an eyepatch, and a rusty sword.

Broom handle and saber clunked together.

From the disarray and opened crates, it was clear this battle between Indians, cowboys, and pirates had been raging for days.

Riot stepped fully into the attic. Sarah saw him first. The momentary surprise distracted her from the fight. Her inattention earned her a smack on the arm from the broom. "Ow!"

Tobias pointed his rifle at his sister, and Riot hastened forward, snatching the gun from his hand. He quickly checked the chamber. It was empty.

Natural selection, Ravenwood said with a chuckle.

"Put that saber down, Sarah," he barked.

The sword clattered to the ground, nearly taking off a toe. Riot closed his eyes, briefly, wondering how children ever managed to reach maturity with fingers, toes, and limbs intact.

The children stood stone still for a second. Sarah blinked innocently. Maddie started shaking with fear, and Tobias bolted.

"Tobias White, get back here, or I'll tell your mother."

The boy stopped dead in his tracks, eyes rolling like a panicked horse.

"You mean you're *not* going to tell her?" Tobias asked.

"It depends," Riot said. "Go stand next to the pirate."

Tobias darted over to the other two, half hiding behind his quivering sister. She put her arm in front of the boy, as if preparing to shield him from whatever was to come. Her reaction did not escape Riot's notice, and he was careful to keep his voice low and calm.

"I'm sorry, Mr. Riot," Maddie said. "I know we ain't

supposed to be up here. It's my fault. Tobias and Sarah don't know any better." The words came out in a rush. Her usually careful pronunciation flew to the winds in her panic, but despite her fear she stood as proud and straight as her mother.

"I don't mind you three playing up here," Riot said. "But leave the blades, knives, guns, and whatever other weapons you find alone. Is that clear?"

Three heads nodded as one.

"And you, young man." He pointed at Tobias, who had his hands thrust into his pockets and had developed a pronounced slouch. "Never point a gun at someone unless you intend to kill him. That goes for all of you."

"I wasn't trying to kill her. It was empty."

"It doesn't matter. Empty or not, don't point a gun at someone."

"But you pointed one at me," Tobias said, indignant.

Riot looked at the boy; Tobias went instantly still. "And it's fortunate you're still alive, young man. Do you all understand?"

There was a trio of 'Yes, sir.'

"Maddie, Tobias, don't you two have school?"

Brother and sister glanced at each other. Maddie spoke up. "Ma teaches us, sir."

"And Mr. Tim," added Tobias.

"I mean a real school."

"Ma don't want us going. She says it's too easy for someone to find children there," Tobias said.

"*Doesn't* want us going," Maddie corrected. Her poise was nearly restored, but she kept a white-knuckled grip on her broom. The girl, like her older brother Grimm, had likely dealt with her share of angry men.

Riot gently rested the rifle against a nearby crate.

"Why's that?" he asked, sitting on the crate.

Tobias shrugged.

"There are a lot of houses in the city, sir. But not many schools," Maddie said.

Riot understood everything she wasn't saying. If he were looking for a specific child living in a large city, he'd go straight to the schools. It would be far easier to locate a child there.

Let one child in, and they multiply like rats. Insufferable children, Ravenwood grumbled. The voice of memory was gruff, but there was little bite to the words. Riot resisted the urge to point that out to his dead partner.

"I'll speak with your mother," he said instead. "Perhaps we can arrange a teacher to come to the house."

Tobias groaned, Maddie brightened, and Sarah looked suddenly sad. No doubt she missed her own school and friends.

"Right now, I need your help," he said, giving the three a distraction. "I'm looking for notebooks, journals, anything that has writing inside it."

Sarah brightened. "There's a few crates full of books and things."

"That's a good place to start. Bring all the books you can find, and stack them here." He pointed to the center of the attic. "There might be some hidden inside clothing, too."

The children scattered, and Riot took a moment to put the headdress respectfully back in its place. Too many memories lurked in this attic.

In less than ten minutes a large stack of books filled their pretend battlefield. Riot looked at the growing stack, and blew out a long breath. He pulled over a chest, sat down, and picked up the first leather-bound journal. A lifetime of case notes, research notes, and diary entries awaited his perusal.

"Mr. Riot?" Tobias still wore the over-sized Stetson.

"Hm?

"You ever shot an Indian?"

Riot looked up from the journal. "When they've shot at me," he said truthfully. "But that goes for any man."

"The Chickasaw slaughtered my grampa," Sarah said. "You can't trust an Indian."

"Is it fair to lump them all together?" Riot asked.

"'Course it is, else you'll be scalped," Sarah said.

Tobias nodded sharply. "That's right."

"I've known plenty of Indians who I counted as kin. A person should be judged by his actions, not by the color of his skin."

"But they're savages," Tobias argued.

"Some people say that about negroes," Riot reminded.

"My gramma said that all the time," Sarah confirmed.

"We are not!" Tobias seethed.

"Ma says you are sometimes," Maddie said.

The boy ignored his sister, and looked at Sarah. "Anyway, we're not near as bad as the Irish."

Sarah's eyes widened, and her nostrils flared. The prim young lady looked about to charge the boy.

Riot held up a calming hand. "*When the debate is lost, slander becomes the tool of the loser.* So let's be civil about this. If people say negroes and the Irish," he looked pointedly at Sarah, "are savages, and you both know you're not—why doesn't the same apply to Indians?"

Sarah looked at Tobias. The children didn't say a word.

"*Even your silence holds a sort of prayer,*" Riot quoted in Apache. The children's eyes went wide.

Tobias was the first to react. "You speak Indian?"

"A little Apache, a good deal of Miwok. And a few words from some other tribes as well."

"You know a lot," Maddie said.

He smiled. "Not near enough."

"But... Indians aren't the same as us, are they?" Tobias blurted out.

"Aren't they?"

"Well, they're not as smart," Tobias said.

Riot glanced at Sarah and Maddie. "Are women as smart as men?"

"They sure aren't," Tobias said.

Both girls glared. Maddie slapped the back of her brother's head. "You're not even half as smart as Ma."

"He said girls—not Ma."

"Would you say your mother is as smart as a man?"

"Yes," Maddie said.

Sarah appeared skeptical. "Wouldn't it depend on the man?"

"And there you have it," Riot said. "People, no matter their color, education, or gender, all have their strengths and weaknesses. But in general, most everyone can learn anything given a chance."

"You have a funny way of thinking, Mr. Riot," Tobias said.

"It's the detective in me." He wasn't about to explain to the trio that since his mother was a crib whore, he didn't know the race of his own father. So he could be mixed with just about anything.

"I want to learn about detecting," Sarah said.

Tobias' chest swelled. "Sometimes I help Mr. Riot."

"That you do, Tobias. And a fine job you've done. Detective work only takes a keen eye and the ability to work your way through a problem. Along with the patience to wade through an ocean of old journals," he added dryly.

The children leapt back into their scavenger hunt before he could rope them into that task. When every crate, nook, and cranny had been checked, they left him to the tedious task of sorting. He piled Ravenwood's journals into a neat stack. They were all the same—slim, leather notebooks filled with the man's neat, precise hand. The penmanship made Riot's hands cramp just looking at it. And worse, it made his head ache. Ravenwood's writing was a mixture of short hand, code, and cryptic symbols.

With a grimace, Riot turned the journal sideways. It didn't help. A ghost from his past chuckled into the dusty space.

"Mr. Riot?"

The intrusion brought him around. He searched the dimness, looking for the source of the voice. He hadn't realized Tobias and Sarah were still in the attic. They were lying on their stomachs in the far corner, looking out the top of a rounded window that was halfway between floors.

"Call me A.J.," he said automatically.

"My Ma wouldn't approve," Tobias said.

Sarah made a frustrated noise. "There's someone hiding in the bushes."

Riot dropped the journal, and hurried over to the two. He got right down on his belly between them. The decorative glass was colored, save for a few small panes that Tobias was peeking through.

"In the corner there, under the willow, by my fort."

"You have a fort in the corner of the yard?" Riot asked.

"Ma said it was all right."

"Personally, I'd aim for a tree house."

Tobias stilled in deep thought.

Don't encourage the child, Ravenwood grunted.

Nothing moved down below in the yard, but the trees and bushes offered ample cover. He needed a better perspective. Riot hopped to his feet, and hurried down the stairs with Sarah and Tobias on his heels. On his way to the grocer's door he stopped by the kitchen and snatched up the latest offering of muffins from the stove, then shot outside.

Riot walked through the drape of drooping vines, and passed into the clearing under the willow's branches. A curved bench hugged the trunk—a cool spot for the rare San Francisco heat wave. Faint prints confirmed his suspicion, and he followed them towards the far corner of the yard, behind the carriage house.

Tobias darted to his fort. "Someone pinched my things!"

Bushes rustled, and a swift form leapt from behind shrubs, grabbing the top of the fence, feet braced to fly right over the top.

"There's a large, hungry dog on the other side of that fence," Riot said calmly in Cantonese. It was a ten pound Chihuahua. The most ferocious kind of dog there was.

Jin froze, caught with indecision.

"I, on the other hand, have a plate full of hot muffins. They're like sticky buns without the sticky part."

She glanced over her shoulder, gaze darting to the two children at his side, and finally the plate in his hand.

"You know Chinese, too?" Tobias asked.

"Cantonese," Riot corrected.

"Who is he?" Sarah asked.

"A guest." He emphasized the last.

"Well, he stole my lock picks," Tobias said.

"You are *not* supposed to have lock picks," Riot said, firmly.

Tobias shut his mouth.

He was going to have to have a talk with Tim. Riot shoved that thought aside, and focused on the escaping girl. "If I were you, Jin, I'd play nice, and take a muffin to bribe your way past the feral beast waiting to devour you on the other side of the fence. But that's just me," he said, taking a bite of a muffin. They truly were divine. "Or you could try a muffin. It's your choice."

Jin ground her teeth. With a growl, she dropped to the dirt, crawled through the bushes towards them, and stood. She was still as dingy as when they'd found her.

Keeping a suspicious eye on Riot, she edged forward, and snatched a muffin from the plate. Riot handed the plate to Sarah, and walked over to inspect Tobias' fort. An old blanket served as a bed. It was neatly folded, and in need of a wash. A crude shelf took up one side of the wall, filled with a child's prized collection of discoveries: shells, rocks, an old key, a rusty spring, and various animal bones.

"You're a regular magpie, Tobias."

"None of it's stolen," Tobias said.

Sarah joined them, and wrinkled her nose. "It smells."

"It needs a woman's touch," Riot agreed. "Maybe some flowers."

"No, it does not," Tobias said. "It only smells to girls. And they're not allowed inside."

As the children fell to arguing, Riot glanced over his shoulder. Jin had cupped her muffin in both hands, and was nibbling the top off, as she watched his every move. She was likely wondering why he hadn't grabbed her and marched her straight back to the carriage house.

"I hope you'll make an exception for our guest," Riot said. "I think she feels more comfortable in here."

Tobias frowned at her. "He isn't a girl. He's a boy."

Sarah cocked her head, as if another angle would help her decide on Jin's gender.

"What happened to his face?" Tobias traced his own cheek, mimicking the scars that marred Jin's. "How'd he get those? And why do Chinese wear that funny braid?"

Jin took a step back.

"I've always wondered that, too," said Sarah between mouthfuls.

"It's called a queue," Riot explained. "The Manchu forced the Han to wear them as a sign of submission. Now it's a source of pride."

"Well, it's funny," Tobias said. "What's his name?"

Jin threw her muffin at Tobias. "I am *not* a boy. And I can understand you perfectly!"

Tobias blinked. "He speaks English!"

"Better than you, *Wun Dan*."

"What did he call me?"

Riot decided not to translate 'cracked egg'. Instead, he gently pushed the small boy back a step. "We can't help you, unless you talk, Jin," he said in Cantonese. "Every hour you stay silent is a wasted one."

"That *faan tung* couldn't find a Joss stick in a temple."

She was angry, hurt, and fuming that Isobel had discovered her cave. Isobel was an easy target for the child to vent her rage on.

"Do you think the same of me?" he asked, as he walked closer, looking her straight in the eye.

Jin didn't answer, but neither did she back away.

"Do you know what the tongs call me?"

She shook her head.

"*Din Gau*," he said, stopping in front of her. "Do you know why?"

Jin jerked her head.

"Because they fear me."

She might not understand kindness, but she knew fear.

"If you want my help, I expect you to make yourself presentable. Sarah will show you to the bath, and afterwards you can come talk with me. Are we clear?"

Her lips pressed into a thin line. When she jerked her head again, he turned and walked away.

"You want me to hitch up the hack?" Tim's voice drifted from the dim interior of the stable.

"I have two legs," Isobel said, as Riot rounded the corner. She ran straight into him, and he leaned back as her fist came up. Air brushed his cheek.

Isobel blinked. "Jesus! I'm going to put a bell on you, Riot."

"Watson wouldn't even tolerate that."

"I can't decide if I'm relieved you dodged my punch, or annoyed."

"Both are acceptable."

"There are some unidentified corpses that arrived at the city morgue this morning. Two men, one woman." She stepped to the side and started towards the doors. She was bristling, charged with energy.

"A hack would be worth the wait, Bel," he called to her back.

She stopped, thought, and turned. "In case the trail leads elsewhere."

"Exactly." He was more concerned about her injuries than the trail leading elsewhere, but casting doubt on her current physicality would only make her more determined to walk.

"I'll go find Grimm," Isobel said.

Tim glanced at him, nodded, and got to work, opening the corral door for the horse. Riot retrieved the saddle and breeching. He found the smell of leather and the weight of tack strangely comforting. It was simple and uncomplicated, something tangible to hold in his hands.

"Look, A.J., I'm sorry—for what's it's worth," Tim said, slipping the bridle over the mare's nose. "But I'd do it again. You just weren't ready, wounded like you were. You didn't even know who the hell I was."

Riot busied himself with the saddle. "A part of me knew, or at least suspected. Knowing is different though."

"So we're square?" Tim asked.

Riot glanced at his old friend. "With a few bent edges."

"Not as bad as the time I shanghaied you, right?"

"Don't tempt fate, Tim."

The old man cackled. "I got fifty dollars for your head, too."

As Riot smoothed the horse's coat, the edge of his lip raised. "I hated your guts for an entire year. But it was the best thing that ever happened to me."

Tim nudged him in the ribs with an elbow. "I steered you true."

"In a roundabout way." It was hard to stay mad at the man who'd handed him his first pair of spectacles.

Isobel returned with Grimm, who climbed into the seat, and took up the reins. Riot opened the door for Isobel, and helped her into the carriage. "Tim, keep an eye on the place. There was a man lurking across the street—a gunfighter if I'm any judge."

Tim grunted. "Any idea what he's about?"

"Take your pick. He might be here for Jin, hired to kill our patient, or involved with Sarah's uncle in some way."

"You never could stay out of trouble."

"And Jin's staying in Tobias' fort, so don't get spooked and shoot her."

Isobel's brows shot up. "She is? How'd you find her?"

"I'll explain later," he said. "Any word on Walker?"

Tim shook his head.

"What about Freddy the horseman?"

Tim slapped his bald head. "I swear my mind is going, some days. I did actually track him down while I was out talking with Isobel's runt. Gawd does that boy smell."

"I pay him well," Isobel said.

"He's sharp, that one. I wager he's scouting the sewers for trinkets."

A thoughtful look came over her face.

"Anyhow, I found Freddy outside the Palm. Slick fellow, all oiled, and decked in flash. I wager he was an ex-jockey, or aiming to be by his build. So I get talking about horses, of course, and he's bragging himself up." Tim reached for his pipe, and knocked it against his palm, dislodging ash and dottle. "He said he knew horses, and boasted about having a 'knack'. But when I asked him about Lee Walker, he closed up like a clam, and shot out of there real quick."

Isobel half leaned out of the carriage. "Was it because the horse lost?"

"I don't know," Tim said. "But he looked uneasy to me. Made an excuse, and left real quick. You want me to poke around the race tracks?"

Riot climbed into the hack. "Make friends first. I don't want to raise suspicion. Where there's money, there's men willing to kill."

"From time immemorial," said Tim.

"Before I go, do you have any idea what Ravenwood was doing during the Quarantine Scandal trials?"

Tim shut the carriage door. "I knew that man for forty years, and didn't have a rat's ass what he did most of the time."

Isobel snorted. "Eloquent, Tim."

"Ma'am." Tim tipped an imaginary hat, and slapped the carriage door. "City morgue, Grimm."

The carriage lurched forward.

Isobel was quiet as the carriage rattled over cobblestones, no doubt mulling over Tim's conversation with Freddy the horseman. It was a new piece to add to their muddled pile, but not a significant one.

She had covered her bruised eye and split lip with makeup, and looked like a harried woman with an angry husband. Riot wasn't her husband, but he was angry in that cold, brewing way of his. He wanted to knock down the door of that brick building, and put a gun to Parker Gray's temple. In his younger days he might have, but experience and age had tempered his trigger-fingers.

Barely, Ravenwood grunted.

He ignored the voice, and focused on the feel of Isobel's arm brushing his own. That was real; that was tangible.

"So you found my stray?" she asked.

"Tobias and Sarah found her, to be exact. She never left. She was hiding out in Tobias' fort."

Isobel closed her eyes in relief, like a silent prayer. But when she spoke, there was no warmth in her voice. "And here I thought I had the monopoly on 'ungrateful wretch'."

"Sorry to disappoint, Bel, but she's not here to hear your insult."

"I'll make sure to repeat it when she is," she said dryly.

"Do you think she'll still be there when we return?"

"I left her in capable hands. Hopefully the other children will ease some of her fear."

"Unlikely." She sucked on her bruised lip.

"Not much faith in children?"

"It's not that," she said. "Only that *I* wouldn't trust us if I were her."

"You trusted me," he reminded.

"That was different. I had a blade to your ribs."

He chuckled. "You pinned my weakness straight away."

"I'm no damsel, Riot. Although your damn eyes were irresistible."

"Were?"

She looked boldly into them now. Without hurry, without a flutter of unease. "Still are," she whispered. "Are you planning on kissing me before or after our visit to the morgue?"

"Dinner, theatre, and a polite kiss doesn't work for you?"

"Morgue, murder, and imminent danger are more my style."

He smirked. "I had noticed."

"Ever perceptive." She leaned into him. "Before I drown in those eyes of yours, I was thinking that the only thing that's keeping Jin in place is that she might not know where she is."

"I won't argue that."

"Do you or Tim have any contacts in Chinatown?"

"Not directly. Informants are hard to come by in the Quarter. When a resident reports on tong activity, his neck is on the chopping block—literally. Generally informants operate through notes. When Donaldina and the Consul receive a note, they usually don't know who delivered it."

"Rescuing slave girls seems risky."

"It is." Riot thought of the Queen's Room trap, and Mason meeting his end on the floor of a dingy hotel. Most of the time the informants were genuine, and the girls for whom Chinese residents risked their lives were indeed waiting. The risk was there, but the failure of not acting was far more keenly felt.

"From what you told me, it seems that most of the tong headquarters and leaders are known," she said. "Why doesn't the Consul round the highbinders up and ship them back to China for trial?"

Riot frowned, as he idly traced the pattern on his walking stick. "The former Consul General tried that very thing. As did the ones who came before. But I'd wager there's a good number of politicians and lawmen who profit from the illegal affairs in Chinatown."

"Never been proved?"

"A few have been caught, but they were minor cogs in the wheel. There's the other side of the coin, too—well-meaning activists and charitable societies make a racket every time the Consul threatens to ship a highbinder to China."

"Why would anyone want to prevent criminals from being deported back to their own country?" Her disbelief was apparent.

"Because there's no trial—only a swift beheading."

"Oh."

"In my experience the vast majority of tong members join for safety," he explained. "I've found three different affiliation markers on one man. A lot of men join in the hopes of being left alone. Every merchant, grocer, and ragpicker is prey to the tongs. Joining their ranks might seem like a way to escape their brutality."

"So the Consul is tasked with cleaning up Chinatown, but his authority has been stripped away, and he has no real power to do a thing?"

"In a nutshell," Riot confirmed. "It used to be that the Chinatown Police Squad took payouts, but Donaldina says Price is doing a fine job of stamping out blatant corruption. There's always someone willing to take a pay-out on the white police force though. The Consuls generally keep their own staff of detectives and police—a sort of vigilance committee like in the early days of San Francisco. Some have even posted their own *chun hungs* on high-binders."

"How'd that go?"

"It scared the highbinders for a short time, but then they came back. Boldness is their calling card," he said. "A few years ago there was a hatchet man who walked on stage at the Chinese theatre, during a performance, and delivered a quieting dose of lead to the cymbalist—a suspected informant for the Consul. No one saw a thing, of course. If anyone had identified the shooter, they'd have been next."

Isobel was quiet for a time, as she pondered his words. The city rolled by, and Riot watched her residents—the poor, the joyful, the desperate—each and everyone with a story of his own.

"Why a rabid dog?" she asked suddenly.

"Tongs use code words," he explained. "A 'big dog' is a shotgun; a 'puppy' is a revolver; powder and bullets are 'dog feed', and 'Let the dogs bark' is a command to kill."

"Ah, you're a wild gun."

"It seems so."

"That explains why those men who held me didn't want you involved."

No criminal would. Ravenwood and Riot had both had a reputation for felling professional criminals and brutes alike.

"I see why you did what you did, Riot," she said. "You were cornered same as me—same as Jin."

"Only I had a number of guns."

"As I recall, I had one too when you met me. You neatly took care of that issue, however." She rubbed her wrist to emphasize her point. "There's simply no justice in the courts."

"I hope there will be one day," he said, placing a hand over her wrist. She wore gloves, but he could feel the layer of bandage underneath.

"Hope." It was a bitter word. "There's something I don't think of often."

"You don't hold any out for yourself?"

"I do not. Never have," she confirmed. "Unless you count hoping I'll go out with a bang."

"I'd say you're living each day like that."

"Eat, drink, and be merry, for tomorrow we die," she quoted.

"There's one issue with that."

"Only one?" she asked wryly.

"One day you'll eat your fill, and drink yourself drunk, and wake up in the mess of your life and realize you're still alive."

Isobel looked into his eyes. "Is that how you feel?"

Riot took a breath. "I did. When that young hatchet man pointed a gun at my head, all I can remember is feeling a profound sense of relief. And then I came to. My life was still a mess."

"Mess or no, I'm glad you're alive."

"And I'm glad you are."

She smiled. "My mother used to say that I had a whole army of angels and saints watching over me. Maybe they kept you alive for my amusement."

Riot laughed, the carriage rolled to a stop in front of the city morgue, and with a smile on his lips he stepped down and offered her a hand. "I live to serve."

The city morgue was stark and solid. Not much more was needed for the dead and those left behind. Riot stepped up to the desk clerk. "My client is here to view the unclaimed," he said in a hushed voice.

A sob tore from Isobel's throat. It was muffled by the handkerchief she pressed to her face. Somehow she had summoned tears, smudged her makeup, and looked like a truly distraught woman. He marveled at the transformation.

"A missing loved one?" the constable asked.

"Her husband," he confirmed.

The constable pushed a ledger towards him, and he signed his name Jack Rackham in a nearly illegible scrawl. Another muffled noise came from Isobel, but this time it sounded suspiciously like a laughing snort rather than distress.

"If you'll sign too, ma'am."

"Let's not tax her anymore than necessary," Riot said. "She's liable to smear the ink."

Her shoulders shook.

"Yes, of course." The constable waved them on, and Riot offered his arm, as he led her towards a doorway.

"Rackham?" Isobel said, from beneath her handkerchief. "You're hardly a calico, Riot."

"It seemed fitting to keep with your pirate theme."

"I'm thrilled you noticed." She held his arm a little tighter.

The temperature dropped with the stairs, and the smell hit a moment later. It would have floored lesser constitutions. The unclaimed lay on the floor in two long rows. A thin sheet covered each.

A cheerful man came hurrying up. His complexion was the color of codfish and his ears looked as if they were melting. "Don't mind the smell, Miss, or so I'm told. I'm Mr. Sims, and I'm blessed with no sense at all." Judging from the strain put on his apron, his loss of smell had not hindered his appetite. "You can peek under the covers there. Each one is a surprise, is what I say. And don't worry —the dead don't feel. Right from the good book, that is. It's the living that hurts, isn't that right?" He was all smiles, and led them towards the first corpse. "Good you have a friend. I've had some fainters. Never good on these stone floors." As he rambled on, he swept back the first sheet, and continued, left and right, down the line of corpses, revealing each with a macabre sort of relish.

Riot glanced at Isobel, who looked as disturbed as he felt.

"It's terrible about all these unclaimed people," she said with a trembling voice, as she walked down the line.

"We find most of them names," Mr. Sims said cheerfully. "Though some remain a mystery. Common in a big city such as this. People are always coming and going, with no kin to their name. Most neighbors don't even stop to introduce themselves—not like across the bay."

"Are you a medical examiner?" Riot asked, as he bent to get a closer look at a man with a bashed in face.

"Me?" Sims snorted. "No, I just haul bodies around, but I've seen a good deal. Most tell me how they die. Take that poor besotted soul there. Poison."

"This man?" Isobel asked.

"No, that woman behind you. You can tell by the burns around her lips. 'Course they don't let me crack them open. Got to be a doctor for that—in the cities at least. Some towns let anyone who's willing have a go. It's a shame about the last coroner, though. Him being a physician and all. He was thorough, he was."

Isobel sighed softly. Riot knew that her feelings about August Duncan were conflicted. Murder was rarely as simple as good and evil.

"What do you make of the new coroner who's replaced him—Weston, isn't it?"

"Hmmhmm."

"You don't have a high opinion of him?" Riot asked.

Sims guffawed, short and loud, but its echo lingered. "I value my job, sir. That's all I'll say. And you may want to put a strong hand on the lady's arm, this one isn't pretty."

"Are any of the dead pretty?" Isobel asked.

"Well, yes," Sims said. "They have a certain peace to them." He flipped back the last sheet. And his eyes glittered, watching Isobel with anticipation. Sims had clearly spent far too much time with the dead.

"No," she whispered. "He's not pretty at all." But her words were at odds with her actions. Isobel quickly bent over the corpse. Judging from the dent on the top of his skull, she had found her man.

"Is that your husband?" asked Sims.

"I thought he was at first," Isobel said.

Riot crouched beside her, studying the corpse's face. Death was never pleasant, and this man was no exception.

"I know this man," Riot whispered in her ear. Her brows shot up in question, but he shook his head. Not here, that gesture said. He turned to Sims and asked, "Where was this one found?"

"In an alleyway off of David Street down by the docks," Sims supplied. "A bad place to walk at night. Seedy as they come. Do you know him, by chance?"

"Hard to tell with the discoloration." If he told Sims what he knew, he would be asked to sign an official document, or worse give testimony at a coroner's inquest. Attention was the last thing they needed.

"Oh, yes, course it is, but you learn to read the signs." Sims huffed over, and bent slightly, putting his hands on his knees, to study the corpse. "I'd wager he's been dead for two to three days. Hard to tell with the cold. And what with the body being moved. You can tell that by the discoloration on his stomach. He lay there for a good while. There was sand on his clothes, and in the wound, too. A hatchet or axe, if you ask me. And from the angle of that blow, I'd say he was on his knees when he was struck. But he had a gun in his hand. There was gunpowder stain on his fingers. No gun was found with him, though. Odd, if you ask me. Since there's no sand in the docks, I doubt he died there. From his knuckles and such, it's clear he's a pugilist, or knows his way around a fight. I'd of said he died in a boxing ring, but those are usually hard-packed dirt, or a mat. I think he was killed near the ocean, along the Golden Gate or the dunes would make most sense."

Both Isobel and Riot stared at the heavy-set man with mouths slightly agape.

Sims stopped, and closed his mouth, clearing his throat. "I'm saying too much, aren't I?" he asked. "I've a bucket, ma'am, if I've made you sick. No one invites me to a meal anymore 'cause I have this blabbering tongue of mine."

"No, no, I'm quite fine. You have a remarkable gift." Isobel said with feeling.

The man blushed crimson. "I just talk to them. They're peaceful company. I hate to bury them unnamed, so I give them one myself if they're not claimed."

"Did you find anything in his clothes?" Isobel asked.

Sims shook his head. "Picked clean, and left to rot. That's the way of the alleys. Even his boots and coat was taken."

Riot stood, and helped Isobel to her feet. "If you ever decide to run for coroner, I'll vote for you, sir." He offered a hand, and Sims shook it with a wheezing laugh.

"That's hilarious, sir. People like myself are always the last to be picked for anything except the jobs no one will take. Before this I was a gravedigger, but I slipped one day, and ended up in the grave I was digging." He chuckled at the irony. "Hurt my back and knee, and couldn't manage no more."

"Sorry to hear that," Riot said. Although he thought the man's talents had been wasted in a graveyard.

"Oh, it's not so bad. I just get to talk to them above ground now," Sims said with a short giggle. He patted the dead man's arm, and straightened, and Isobel and Riot excused themselves, leaving Sims with his dead friends.

Riot handed Isobel into the hack. "Hold for a bit, Grimm," Riot said to the young man, before climbing inside.

A pair of impatient gray eyes were staring at him with the intensity of a dagger blade. "His name is Andrew Ross," he explained.

"Andrew Ross?" she repeated.

"That's the name he went by when I knew him. He was a hired gun."

"Good riddance, then?"

"Indeed."

"Well, I doubt I have half a brain," Isobel said, ripping off her gloves. "It never occurred to me that the calling cards might not be his own."

"Or a nom de plume," Riot offered.

"True, but he didn't really strike me as the type for subterfuge."

"The dead aren't very clever," he admitted.

She snorted, and let her head fall back on the padding. "I suppose he could have changed his name, or been posing as someone else. I do it every day... Or he might have pinched a billfold, or robbed the real Lincoln Howe. But we have no way of knowing. And if we start asking after Lincoln Howe, we could attract the wrong kind of attention."

"I agree—we'll have to be careful. And patient."

A low growl came from her throat. "I want to go back to that brick building."

"And do what?"

"Get inside of it. Find that cigar man, and drag him out."

"Then testify that he abducted you?"

She opened her mouth, and closed it. "My death has its complications, doesn't it?"

"A great many." Too many, he added silently. Even if she were willing to expose herself by testifying against those men, her reputation would be called into question every step of the way. "Something will turn up, Bel." Some of his cases had taken years to solve. That kind of case, no doubt, would drive Isobel insane.

"What do you know about Andrew Ross?" she asked.

"Ross used to be part of the Chinatown Police Squad

under a Sgt. Jesse Cook—the most hated squad captain in the history of the Quarter. He had a temper, and was known to grab the closest Chinese—innocent, young, or old—and beat him to a bloody pulp when he was angry. His squad tended to follow his lead. After a new squad sergeant took over, I heard Ross was signing up for strike-breaking and boxing matches. It's an official way to get violent without legal consequences."

"Lovely," she muttered. "Kau likely did society a favor."

"He's no shining moral compass himself."

"I doubt anyone is."

"Miss Cameron comes fairly close."

"I hope to meet her."

"I'm sure you will one day."

"In the meantime, I have an idea."

He looked at her in question.

"I believe I know a way to investigate Andrew Ross, or Lincoln Howe, without raising suspicion. On us, at any rate."

"So reassuring, Bel."

She showed her teeth. "An admirer of mine at the Call."

"Should I be jealous?"

"Yes, he's a big, charming Scotsman," she said, with a wistful, dreamy sigh. "He's offered me dinner at the Palace, and whatever might follow."

"Does this charmer of yours have a name?"

"You're a detective, I'll let you discover that."

"I'm hesitant to let you out of my sight."

Isobel reached into his waistcoat pocket, and slipped out the card she had placed there earlier. "I'll make sure and return it," she whispered, lips brushing his ear. And like a soft breeze, she was gone.

40

A Nose For News

"ANDREW ROSS?" MCCORMICK RUBBED the side of his nose, leaving behind a smudge of ink. "Sure I know him. I've seen him down at the Pavilion, and at just about every boxing match besides. Why do you ask?"

"His name came up for a piece I'm working on—*The Effects of Boxing on the Male Physique.*"

Mack cracked his knuckles. "I've done my fair share of boxing. I'd be happy to let you conduct an in depth interview." He leaned a massive elbow on the edge of his desk, and smiled. Or at least, she thought he was trying to smile. He looked more like a panting wolf.

Isobel had stopped earlier at her apartment in Sapphire House to change into something more presentable. So a flowery hat sat on her auburn wig, and a pair of delicate pince-nez were perched on her nose. She wore a fitted coat, blouse, long gloves with tiny buttons, and a matching skirt that hugged her in all the right places, before flaring at the knees. The effect was not lost on Mack

McCormick.

"Should I require a volunteer, you'll be the first to know." An impish sort of impulse overtook her (which was all too common). "During my last story I discovered that pugilists are most in need of *Doctor Sanden's Electric Belt and Suspensory for Weak Men*."

"You like goading me," he growled.

"Isn't that what you're doing with me?"

"It's called seduction." There was a glint of amusement in his eyes.

"Oh, I hadn't noticed," she said, taking out her hand mirror. She flipped it open and consulted the glass, running a finger along the line of her lip. She had watched Lotario do that very thing numerous times.

"Who is the ruffian, Charlie?" Mack leaned in closer. She silently cursed her attempts at flirtation. Hidden bruises put a damper on the act. "I'll use him as a sand bag."

"I fell off a bicycle, Mack."

"Right." He leaned back in his chair, and crossed massive arms. "So what did you pretty yourself up for? What's your angle today? I was about to go stand around the quarantine fence and watch bruisers beat heathens back into their pen."

"They put a fence around the gymnasium?" she asked.

He chuckled. "They probably should. And throw us some of those electric belts while they're at it."

She smiled at his self-depreciation. Mack delivered verbal blows, but he accepted their return with good humor.

"Andrew Ross," she said, nudging him back on track. "Do you know what he does for work? Where he lives? Does he have a favorite saloon or gymnasium?"

"How important is it to you?"

"You mean is it worth dinner with you?"

"I had more in mind."

"It's not worth *that*, Mack."

He turned pink. "No, I didn't mean—" He blew a breath past his mustache. "I mean not that I'd turn you down."

"You're digging a pit over there."

He took a deep breath, glanced around the corral at the other reporters typing away, and leaned closer. "It's clear you have a nose for news, Charlie. I was only wondering if you'd throw me a bone every so often."

"Is money tight?"

"Isn't it always for the working man?"

"And woman."

"You all add to the competition," he mumbled.

"I like to think we make things interesting," she said with a smirk. "Besides, it's not as if you'd touch a 'Sob Sister' story."

"True."

"But I'll do better than a bone. I'll let you into the kitchen."

His bushy brows shot up, and he bristled like a mastiff on the hunt.

"Andrew Ross is lying in the city morgue with an 'unidentified' tag on his toe," she confided. "Clear murder."

"How do you know it was murder?"

"He has an axe impression in his skull."

"How do you know it's him?"

"A girl has her secrets, but I can't investigate him. Don't ask why," she hastened when he opened his mouth. "You're a regular at the matches, and you're known as a reporter. And I can hardly infiltrate the gentleman clubs and gymnasiums. You're the best man for the job."

Mack huffed. "So you expect me to do all the legwork, and you take all the credit?"

She shook her head. "I don't want my name anywhere near this story. All I want is for you to share what you learn. And in exchange, you get an exclusive on a murder before the others catch wind of it. I suggest you speak with a fellow by the name of Mr. Sims in the morgue. He has a better idea of where he died than where he was found."

"Sounds fishy."

"Would it be worthy of a story if it wasn't?" she asked.

He frowned.

"You can make whatever you want of it," she said. "But I'm fairly sure there are some shady men involved in this."

"Murder isn't exactly a society soiree."

"Fair warning, is all."

"You're a queer one, Charlie."

"You have no idea."

The night was young, and Riot's revealing story had been forefront in her mind. Small wonder he had left San Francisco behind. She wondered if his departure had prevented his own assassination. Or worse, was Riot still a target in whatever web he had fallen into? That worried her.

She disappeared into the newspaper archives as Miss Bonnie, and emerged as Mr. Morgan. The fading light and rush of commuters was ideal for her male disguise, and she drifted into seedy streets stirring with the nightlife of the Barbary Coast.

Bright electric lights flickered to life with the falling sun. Saloons, bagnios, and dance halls opened their doors, and music filled the sidewalks. In an hour the halls would be bursting. This was the hour between—when twelve blocks rose from ashes to fiery life like a mythical phoenix.

Park's Place was located near the docks, and Isobel thought she might have visited it once or twice. But nights masquerading as a fresh-faced man tended to run together, especially when Lotario and drinks were involved.

There was already a crowd. Men and women gathered in the saloon, mingling and talking. A few women were clearly on the lookout for their next john, while others gathered at a table, enjoying a meal before a long night of work. The place was exactly as Riot had described it—a former dive turned nearly respectable.

The aroma made her stomach growl. She walked to the bar, and tossed down fifteen cents. It bought her a plate of roast chicken, green beans, and cornbread, and a beer that wasn't watered down. Simple but good.

Isobel hunkered down at the bar and dug into her dinner, listening and observing as more people crowded in. She didn't know why she had come here. Intuition, curiosity, or a need to bring some reality to Riot's history—to imagine him as he'd been three years before, exhausted after long nights of combing slave dens for a child-killer. And feeling helpless. Craving human contact, looking for a morsel of comfort in the arms of a woman who did not love him.

As she ate, she watched the mirror behind the bar. Old friends greeted each other with warmth, and a few old men seemed rooted to the table where they sat. She watched sailors fresh off the boat waltz in with a lady on each arm, and an emaciated man using his fingers to clean every crumb off his plate. She assessed them all in a flash, until a slash of red over the door caught her eye. It was nearly lost in shadow.

Isobel swiveled, and looked across the room. Knick-knacks filled the saloon, lining shelves and hanging from walls—tokens left by sailors and visitors from all around the globe. But that octagon hanging above the entrance drew her like a moth to flame. A *bagua*. Only it was turned around, so the mirror faced the wall.

"What's caught your eye?"

The smooth voice made her throat go dry. She nearly jerked, but swallowed her response, glancing casually over a shoulder. "You have a fine collection of... just about everything."

A man stood behind the bar. The first thing she noticed were his eyes. They were not kind eyes, but passionate and fiery and possessive. This saloon was *his*. And he was proud of that fact. It wasn't enough for him to have his name on the deed; he had marked it with blazing words on the front. The second thing she noticed was his missing right ear. Abigail must have been left-handed, or desperate. His size registered next. Not in a towering way like her bull of a husband Kingston, but the girth of his shoulders. He was built like a keg.

"Patrons sometimes bring me a trinket or two from their travels," Parks was saying. "They don't forget this place."

"Best saloon food I've ever had," she said, and meant it.

"We only hire the best. The locals call this the Palace of the Docks."

"Ever think of changing the name?"

His eyes turned hard. "No."

Isobel took a sip of her beer, and thought it best to steer in another direction. "What is that round thing over the door?"

"You've a good eye," he said, as he dried a glass with a

clean rag. There was a hard edge to the man, the kind that came with honing, like a sharpened blade. "It was a gift from my dear departed wife."

"Sorry to hear." There was true grief in his eyes, and it was an odd sensation seeing that emotion there. Isobel knew his history—that he had stabbed and maimed the very woman he claimed to love.

"Such is life," he said with a sigh. "But you're young yet. It's all still fresh and new for you."

"With food like this, it's hard not to be enthused."

He chuckled, a cold sort of rattle, and then tossed down his rag, and thrust out his hand. "Jim Parks."

"Henry Morgan," she introduced. "Give my compliments to the chef."

Only Parks didn't let go of her hand. He stayed right there, staring her straight in the eye, squeezing her bones tight. Isobel's instinct was to squeeze harder, and stare right back, but she played the uneasy young man, looking back to the *bagua*, so he was left holding her hand at an awkward angle. He let go, and she resisted the urge to rub the blood back into it.

"I've seen that in Chinatown before," she said. "But I can't make heads or tails of that Celestial garble."

"It's a *bagua*."

"Why's the mirror turned towards the wall?"

"That's the way they're supposed to be," he explained. "It keeps out evil, deflects spirits from coming in and such. A wall won't stop a spirit."

"Is this place haunted? Maybe the ghosts are cooking supper?" Isobel glanced over the bar, looking for hiding spirits, but Parks didn't share her amusement. A flash of anger ripped across his eyes, and he squeezed the glass in his hand until she thought it might break.

"Don't mock what you don't know. The dead don't leave us."

"No, sir," she hastened. "Sorry, I don't mean to offend. It was thoughtful of your wife to give you such a fine gift."

"That's what I told her. She gave me this, too." Parks traced the scar running down the right side of his face and flicked a finger at his missing ear. "Is that fine, too, *Miss*?"

Isobel tensed for a second, and then raised her mug to him, gulping down the beer. It was thick and foamy, and she barely tasted a drop of it.

41

The Plea

THE MAN'S CHEST MOVED steadily. Up and down, without a shudder. Sao Jin had watched him breathe for three days. She had nursed him—a dreaded *boo how doy*. No, he could not be, she thought. How could she have helped an enemy?

Jin did not know whom to trust; her only friend was lost.

She closed her eyes, clenched her fists. Rage had kept her alive, kept her burning. It had kept her *fighting*. That white woman had ruined everything. Taken her away from the dunes—away from Mei.

Wong Kau's lips moved. They were cracked and pale, and his eyes fluttered open. He tried to lick his lips, but his tongue was clumsy. With a low growl, Jin soaked a clean cloth in the pitcher. She wrung it out lightly, then squeezed it gently over his mouth. Water slipped between his lips, and he drank, swallowing, growing in strength. What would he become when he recovered? What if Mei had been mistaken—what if this man had not been trying to help them on the dunes?

Wong Kau's hand came up, or tried to, but his bonds stopped him short. He whispered something. She bent closer, straining to hear. "*Wun...ah Mei*," he rasped. "*Wun... ah Mei*." Was it a plea, or an order from his tong?

Footsteps approached from outside. Jin swiveled, preparing to face whoever entered, in whatever form. It was the white-bearded old man.

Tim glanced at her. "I see the children got you into a bath. Not so bad, right?" When she did not answer, he tried another question. "How's he doing?"

Jin said nothing. No one really wanted her to speak— they only asked questions to discover if her spirit had been broken. When she answered, inevitably they would try to break her again. So she simply remained silent.

Tim placed his hand on Kau's forehead, and looked down into the younger man's eyes. "You'll live, then." He sounded displeased, as if he had silently added, 'For now.' "Be careful with the amount of water you give him. I'll have Miss Lily warm up some chicken broth."

He was a small man, but quick. Jin did not trust him. White men pretended to be civil to make themselves feel better. But all were the same. She preferred the ones who were not two-faced. At least she knew what was coming when she missed a smudge on the floor, or did not move fast enough.

"I can't believe I'm playing nursemaid to this fellow," Tim grumbled. "He shot my boy." The man scratched his bald pate, glaring down with murder in his eyes at the *boy how doy*.

Jin did not know whether she'd help Kau if the old man tried to kill him—the *boy how doy* had ruined her life.

Blue eyes settled on her again. "He say anything yet?"

Find Mei. Find Mei.

Jin shook her head. She would do as the *boy how doy* said, not because he'd requested it, but because she wanted to.

42

Love and Ciphers

WATCHMEN PATROLLED RAVENWOOD ESTATE, and bright lights glared from the windows. Wanting to avoid meeting the men and having to explain herself (or risk getting shot), she circled the block, and hurried up steps to a house that butted up against the grounds. It was on a steep slope below the manor, and its fence was particularly high. Walking down the narrow side lane to its small back yard, she shimmied up a drainage pipe, and stretched out her leg to reach the fence.

Isobel easily made the transition, and balanced along the fence until she came to a higher one. She scrambled up that and dropped over the side, landing in Ravenwood's yard, in the corner with the willow tree and Tobias' fort.

The small exertion reminded her that she was not at her best. She adjusted the ditty bag on her shoulder, and crouched, giving herself time to watch the yard and catch her breath. It was tempting to sit for a time, but she forced herself to move.

Small noises came from within the fort, and she edged slowly forward, stopping at the entrance. "Jin?" she called softly. "It's me—*Faan Tung.*" At that moment, Isobel agreed whole-heartedly with that 'good-for-nothing' sentiment. What had she been thinking when she'd gone to Park's Place? Bartenders were known for their powers of observation, as surely as prostitutes and gamblers.

Eyes glinted through a window from the dark interior.

"It's me." She removed her cap. "Can we talk?"

No answer. Isobel withdrew the candle she carried, and struck a match. Slowly, she pushed the hatch open. Her little light filled the interior of the fort. It was a fine one, and Isobel suspected Tim had had a hand in helping Tobias build it.

Jin tilted her head, eyes narrowing. She held an open clasp knife, likely pinched from Tim's workshop.

"You look like a man." There was puzzlement in Jin's voice.

Curiosity was the failing of every rebel. Isobel knew that for a fact. A small, freshly made up cot, and a thick blanket took up half the space. Shelves of knickknacks and treasures filled the rest, and a tray laden with rice and a teapot sat on a stool.

Jin did not offer her any.

"I find it best to move around the city disguised as a man at times," Isobel said, ignoring the blade in the child's hand, as she crawled through the hatch. She put her back to the far wall, and ran her fingers through her short black hair. It would need trimming soon. The thought of cutting it again brought a pang of loss. She was becoming sentimental. Intolerable.

She set the candle between them. "How's your *brother*?"

"Why don't you go see?" Jin tucked her legs up on the

cot, wrapping her arms around them protectively.

Fear, Isobel decided. Fear and rage. She eyed the scars crisscrossing the girl's face, and wondered what others were lurking underneath her clothes. The thought made her sigh. Being the adult of the pair, she had hardly behaved as one.

"Look, I'm sorry about earlier today," Isobel said. "It's been a hard few days for both of us. You have no reason to trust me, I know. But now you know something about me —that I run around the city dressed as a man. That could get me arrested." Not entirely true. Only if she were caught wearing men's clothes. "I'm trusting you with that knowledge."

She let that sink in for a moment. But she had no idea how far it was sinking.

"I'm not going to take you to a mission. You can sit here and grow old if you like, but you'll have to pay Tobias rent and Miss Lily for food. I'm sure she has some work for you. Whatever it is that happened on the dunes, we *will* find out one way or another. I already know about the man who was killed in a struggle."

Jin tightened her grip on the knife, confirming her deduction.

"I know about the big Chinese man, and I don't like him, or anyone else from that brick building. When I was hog-tied in that basement and beaten, they wanted to know where 'the girl' was. I'm assuming they meant you."

The hellion pressed her lips together. She could give Riot a run for his money. Isobel swallowed down an urge to growl; instead, she channeled Riot, and waited for more. But silence never seemed to work for her. Maybe it was because Riot gave the impression of settling in to wait for years. Or maybe it was the sound of his voice—deep and calm, seducing a person to talk. When he fell silent the absence of his voice was keen.

"I'll leave you to it, then. I need to change into my 'Miss Bonnie' outfit." Isobel pushed her ditty bag outside, and started to back out.

"Why do you disguise yourself?" the girl asked, closing her knife and tucking it into a pocket. Her English was only lightly accented, and full of iron.

"I'm a detective."

Jin scoffed. "Girls are not detectives."

"A girl who does as she pleases can be. I don't wait for permission from other people. And I doubt you do either."

"You know *nothing* about me." The words were pure venom.

"The meaning of those scars on your face is as plain as words in a book. It's the title to the book, only I don't know what's inside it yet—I don't know if you have more to you than fear and anger."

"I am *not* afraid." Her eyes were defiant, but her fingers strayed to the bracelet at her wrist, turning it and plucking at the beads.

"Of course you aren't, Jin," Isobel said. "I've told myself that same lie for years."

Isobel left, but she could feel eyes on her back as she trotted across the yard, towards the manor. Without missing a step, she grabbed the drainpipe that climbed the house, and followed its course to Riot's window.

Up was easier than down, and she'd had a full day of rest. Still, she was regretting her choice halfway up the side of the house.

Isobel clenched her jaw, ignored her shaking arms, and kept climbing, striving towards the light that spilled from Riot's window. It was cracked, and the curtains had not yet been drawn. She reached for the side of the window frame, gripped the edge, stretched one of her legs, and found purchase on a bit of trimming. Taking a steadying breath, she braced herself, and was reminded of every bruise and strain from the past three days.

The reminder of the large man and his kick-happy foot brought a flare of irritation, and a surge of strength. Isobel made the transition from pipe to window, and promptly slipped. She caught herself, barely. Making a racket, she quickly hoisted herself up, then rested the upper half of her body on the windowsill.

Riot sat in his armchair, bent over the small table with pen in hand. "You know I do have a door," he drawled without taking his eyes off the notepad.

"I thought this was it," she said. "May I come in?"

Riot stood, and opened the window the rest of the way. It was obvious he had stopped by a barber. His beard was newly trimmed and immaculately sculpted, and his raven hair gleamed in the fire's light.

"Such a polite burglar." She accepted his hand, and when she was on *terra firma*, he looked her up and down. "Dare I ask what Mr. Morgan has been up to?"

Isobel removed her cap, and dropped her ditty bag on the floor. "Probably best not to ask."

"Ah," Riot said. "A drink, then?"

"That would be lovely." But before he left to fetch her a drink, she pulled the Queen of Hearts from her pocket, and held it up, poised between two fingers. "As promised."

His eyes smoldered as he slipped the card from her finger tips, and pressed his lips to the back of her hand. She forgot to breathe. The card disappeared into a pocket, and he looked into her eyes, still holding her hand. His skin was warm from the fire, his collar undone, and his sleeves rolled to his forearms.

"You're shaking, Bel," he said. "Sit down."

Isobel didn't have the breath to argue. As he turned towards the cupboard, she sank into Ravenwood's chair with a sigh of relief.

The chess pieces on the table had not been moved. The two kings, black and white, and the little pawn in front, were stark reminders of their task. She knocked her mind back on course, and focused on an open, leather-bound journal. There was a stack of similar journals on the floor.

Numbers filled the pages. Along with occasional Latin terms, Chinese characters (or so she assumed), and an amalgam of other languages written in a meticulous hand. She glanced at Riot's notes. A series of numbers (that included a space) was circled: 1415 7181523208. And beside the numeric sequence were two simple words: No growth.

She frowned, working through the sequence. "Are these laboratory notes in cipher?"

"Hell froze over, thawed, and dumped the slush on my table," he said with feeling. Riot took a long draught of his brandy, before bringing one to her.

"Brandy won't help with the deciphering," she said.

"It may."

Isobel smiled, and touched her glass to his. "Then drink more, my friend."

"I'd need the whole bottle to counteract the headache these journals give me." It was close to a growl, and the sound sent a charge through her body, leaving her flushed. She took another sip of brandy.

"It... uhm," she cleared her throat, "seems like a simple substitution cipher."

"That one is," he said, sitting in the chair across. "One for 'A'. Two for 'B', and so forth. But it's not consistent. Some paragraphs contain a more complicated variation."

"Exciting."

"That's one word for it," he said dryly.

"You aren't looking forward to deciphering these journals?"

Riot pressed the cool glass to his temple, and sank back against the chair. "Ciphers generally make my head throb."

Isobel cocked her head. "Why?"

"I remember everything I read, Bel. It's a knack, or a curse, depending on how you look at it. It gives me an edge as a gambler."

"Really?" She leaned forward. "You mean you have a photographic memory?"

"I don't know about that. But it's fairly decent."

"And here I thought you spent inordinate amounts of time memorizing poetic prose to impress your harem."

Riot chuckled. "I can't imagine a harem would leave much free time for reading."

She snorted.

"I didn't learn to read until I was somewhere between hay and grass," he explained in a more serious tone. "I've been making up for lost time ever since."

This room, his room, was filled with books on its shelves. Books made her feel at home—they calmed her, and so did he.

"So why are these journals different?"

"I remember what I read, but I can't make sense of these, so everything stays garbled in my head. It's a bit like having an itch you can't scratch."

She frowned at the page. After a moment's considera-tion, she grabbed his notebook and pen, and scratched a note onto a blank page. With great care, she tore it from the book, folded it neatly, and when she was satisfied with the crispness of the edges, she handed it to him.

Riot set down his glass, and took his time unfolding her note. She watched him carefully as he read the three words in her message. He looked up from the slip of paper.

"So you won't forget," she said softly.

"I could hardly forget these."

Isobel smiled, and raised a slim shoulder. "I figured I'd throw you a line."

"Consider me saved." He folded the paper, and tucked it in his breast pocket, over his heart. Hope had manifested into something tangible.

"I'll decipher these for you—unless you're in a hurry?"

It took a few moments for her words to sink in. Riot shook his head. "The journals have been sitting in the attic for the past three years. I don't think there's much rush."

"Why have you decided to look at them now?"

"I'm not sure, Bel," he admitted. "The world is a bit tilted at the moment."

"Welcome to the sea."

"My sea legs are rusty."

"You'll get them back. I know you will. In the meantime, you have me to lean on."

Riot balanced his glass between his finger tips, and looked down into the amber liquid. "I appreciate that." He took a breath. "Your question the other night made me think."

"The horror."

He smirked. "I have no clue what Ravenwood was doing. I was hoping his journals might shed some light on the matter."

She frowned at the stack. It would take a long while to

wade through the ciphers. But Isobel loved a good puzzle, and she wanted to know more about the man who once sat in the chair she had claimed as her own.

"I'll work on them when I can."

"I'll take a few, too. I can hardly let you do all the work."

"Why?" she asked. "Mr. Morgan is your employee. You can have him go fetch you coffee every morning."

"I could," he agreed. "But I'd rather fetch Miss Bel tea in bed every morning."

"My God, Riot, you're going to turn me into a spoiled heiress."

"I thought you were?"

She threw a knight at him, but he caught it left-handed, and flashed a quick grin. "Have you eaten?" he asked.

Isobel thought of her dinner, and the conversation that had made her ill. She decided to change the subject. "How is Wong Kau?"

The humor left his eyes. Isobel regretted her question immediately. She liked to see Riot smile, to see the chip in his tooth. And she loved to watch him laugh—a thing felt more than heard.

"He's out of danger," Riot said. "Last time I checked, Wong Kau was being spoon-fed broth."

Isobel grunted. She wondered how she'd feel if Kingston were being cared for and spoon-fed in a room in her family's home. One thing she knew for certain, she'd not be handling the situation as well as Riot was.

"I can talk to Kau. You don't need to be there," she offered gently.

"Did you learn Cantonese while you were away?"

"Dr. Wise could translate," she said.

"He returned to the Quarter. He wanted to be back at his clinic."

"I imagine he was worried about his family, too."

"They live just on the edge. His wife is white. She's a teacher at one of the missions."

Isobel arched a brow. "What about the anti-miscegenation laws?"

"They were married in New York. He went there to get his doctorate, and came back with a wife. Their marriage isn't recognized here, but San Francisco has never been much concerned with fornication. Still, he's been ostracized from both cultures. Fortunately, the mission where his wife teaches and the sick who come to his clinic are of a more practical mind."

And Isobel thought her life was difficult.

Riot turned the glass in his hand, watching the movement of liquid. "Would you back down?" he asked, without meeting her eye.

"From what?"

"From talking with Wong Kau if you were in my shoes."

"I can't answer for certain—I've never been shot in the head."

He winced. "I can't even ponder that thought."

"Don't get protective on me, Riot," she chided.

Riot met her gaze. "No more than you are with me."

"*Touché.*"

"I had planned on questioning him when you returned, or maybe I was hoping for a supporting arm—some 'strength in union.'"

"Then we might as well get it over with." She set her glass down, and started to stand.

"Before we go, I talked with Alex Kingston today."

Isobel froze, then sat back down.

"He hired the agency to investigate Lee Walker on behalf of his client Claiborne. Demanded, more like. He wouldn't settle for anyone but me."

"Ever the blunt object—that's my poor widowed husband." Isobel tried not to think of the blustering, bully of a man. A long drink did nothing to help. "What are you going to do? Divulge what you already know, or keep it to yourself?"

Riot ran a hand over his beard in thought. "I'm not sure, Bel. It's been on my mind, though. I'm hoping the inquiries that Tim sent east will turn up something decisive. On one hand, it would put me in good with Kingston, and on the other hand... it might rob a girl of her only kin."

"Depending on the jury, Walker might only serve two years for attempted fraud, or none at all if they're sympathetic."

"It's his collectors that I'm worried about," Riot admitted. "There wasn't near enough money in his bank account to pay off his debts. And I wouldn't be surprised if he owed far more to unscrupulous parties."

"Parties of the dangerous sort?"

"Danger and money usually go hand in hand."

"And if he's only penniless?" she asked.

The edge of Riot's lip raised in a wry smile. "I'm hardly one to judge."

"I won't argue that," she said with a laugh. "A harmless con for an uncle who preys on filthy rich silver barons is spades better than a house with a prostitute, a deranged leprechaun, a cross-dressing non-lodger, and a gambler turned detective."

"Far from a proper environment for a young lady," he

agreed, setting his drink aside.

"Yes, well, proper environments are also boring."

"Speaking of proper..." He stood, and retrieved his tie and collar. As he set about putting himself back in order (not that she minded), she debated whether to tell him about her foolish visit to Park's Place. Jim Parks had been unnerving, to say the least.

"I noticed that you changed the subject when I asked if you'd eaten," Riot said from across the room. He was standing in front of the mirror, tying his tie, and he caught her eye in the mirror's reflection.

Isobel sighed, and drifted closer. "I think your knack for mind reading would be far more useful to a gambler than a good memory."

Riot arched an eyebrow, waiting.

She took a breath, and dove in. "After I spoke with my Scotsman, I stopped by Park's Place."

His fingers stilled on his tie, and he turned. Before he let the thing unravel, she stepped forward, and deftly finished the knot to buy herself some time.

"He saw right through my male guise," she said. Riot tensed, and worry and fear flashed in his eyes. "It wasn't until the end of our conversation that he addressed me as *miss*," she explained. "I wasn't threatened, but it was unnerving. The thing of it was, there was a *bagua* hanging above the entrance, but the mirror was facing the wall instead of the room. When I asked him about it, he told me it had been a gift from his wife."

Riot considered her words. "I never asked where she got that thing. I assumed she bought it in Chinatown."

"More than likely, but it struck me as odd," she said. "Parks is certainly uneasy about his ghosts." Now that she'd said it aloud, she felt foolish. And Riot seemed to sense her thoughts.

"He likes to toy with people. He was likely doing the same with you."

"Are you sure he was released in March of ninety-seven?" she asked.

"By that time I was halfway to England."

"Could he have been released early?"

"Meekins and Payne might know," he said. "Abigail may have given it to him before he tried to kill her. Even after the knife attack, for whatever reason, she still loved him."

Isobel tried to imagine loving a man who had put a knife through her belly. She could not.

43

A Good Cause

SAO JIN GAZED INTO the night. She eyed the long pipe that *Faan Tung* had climbed, before disappearing into *Din Gau*'s window. As much as she hated to admit it, the woman was different—strange for a white woman. But she did not know what to make of the man. He was dangerous. And kind. It made no sense to her.

It did not matter. *Faan Tung* had given her ideas.

A large shadow walked slowly through the yard—a guard. This one had sharp eyes. The grocer's door opened, and light filled the yard, illuminating the guard and two other figures—the man and woman. *Faan Tung* was dressed as a woman again. So strange. They walked across the yard and stopped to talk with the guard.

Jin crept forward, darting from under the bushes to the barn, edging along until she came to the corner. She held her breath and listened.

"I knew Parks in prison," the big man was saying. "He tried to provoke me."

"What did he do?" asked Riot.

The big man scratched his nose. "I don't want to say in front of the lady."

"I've heard it all before," said Isobel.

Meekins looked to Riot for confirmation, and when he nodded, the man continued. "He started a rumor that me and Payne were... a bit closer than cell mates. The other prisoners, and even some guards, started calling us impolite terms."

"Stick and stones may break my bones, but words stab to the heart?" Riot asked.

"They do, but that wasn't so bad," Meekins said. "He started messing with my books, though I couldn't prove a thing. Ripping out pages..."

Isobel made a sound somewhere between a gasp and a growl.

"...and I even found one in the latrine."

"But you weren't provoked?"

"No, sir," Meekins said proudly. "Parks was always doing things like that to others, too. It's what finally got him put in solitary."

"Do you know when he was released?"

Meekins shrugged. "March 1897, is what I heard. He'd boast to us all how he only got two years for slashing his woman good. But I can ask Payne, he was mates with some guards. I mostly kept to my books."

Departing words were exchanged, and the man and woman disappeared into the carriage house. Before the guard could regain his night vision, Jin darted across the yard on silent feet. She dove under a bush, and slithered to the side of the house. Crawling on her belly, she skirted the foundation until she came to a long rectangular window that was at ground level.

The window was open, the light was on, but the room was empty. When Tobias and Sarah had shown her to the bath, the boy had given them a tour of the house, including his own room.

"Your room stinks," Sarah had said, with a wrinkled nose. The two had fallen into arguing, and Jin had hopped onto the bed and opened the window.

"Problem solved," she'd said.

She was happy to see that Tobias had either taken Sarah's suggestion to heart, or simply forgotten about his window.

Jin pushed her small bag through the window, and slithered in after. Gravity pulled her down, and she hooked her feet on the sides of the window frame. For a moment, she dangled headfirst over his narrow bed, and then unhooked her feet, and fell. At the last moment, she tucked her body, hit the mattress, and rolled off, landing on her feet.

If *Faan Tung* could be a man, then so could she. Jin moved over to Tobias' chest, and opened it, pulling out trousers, shirt, and coat. She quickly slipped into the boy's clothes, and tucked her braid under a floppy cap. His boots did not fit her feet, but his trousers mostly covered her slippers. And no one ever looked at a child's shoes.

Jin stole his lock picks for a second time, and added them to her bag filled with muffins, scones, and a clasp knife she had taken from the old man's workshop.

Hurried foot thuds came down the hall. Her heart leapt. She quickly stuffed her own clothes inside the bag, and stood on her tippy toes to shove it back through the window.

"Tobias White, I'll tell Ma!" Maddie's voice pierced the walls. The rapid pounding grew louder, and Jin jumped, catching the edge of the window. Using the wall, she pulled, and scrambled her way up. Her belly touched the dirt that butted up against the window, and she kicked her feet, as she clawed at the ground.

A hand latched around her ankle. "Thief!" Tobias screeched. "Maddie! Ma—"

Jin kicked out. Her foot connected with something, and the boy cursed. Both hands latched around her foot, and he braced against the wall, yanking her back hard. She fell on top of him. Both children jumped up, ready to fight.

"You're lucky I'm a gentleman, or I'd punch you back." Blood poured from his nose. Heavier footsteps hurried down the hallway, and Jin became frantic. Desperate, she grabbed the boy's collar and hissed, "Keep quiet and I'll let you come."

Before he could speak, she scrambled under his bed, and pressed herself against the far wall.

"Tobias, what happened?" It was his mother's voice.

Silence answered, as a swish of skirts approached.

"I tripped is all."

Jin bit her lip with relief.

"Serves you right," said Maddie. "You put a snake in my bed!"

"Did not," he said.

"Did too," Maddie insisted.

From beneath the bed, Jin saw an array of feet. She recognized Sarah's shoes, and at this distance could see the girl's puzzled face. "It was just an itty bitty garter snake," Sarah said.

"Maybe *she* did it," Tobias said, triumphant. "Always got to blame the negro."

Sarah's mouth fell open.

"Tobias White, I'll have no such talk from you," his

mother said. Jin tensed. It was the kind of threat that usually was followed by a beating. But no such thing happened. "Did you put that snake in Maddie's bed?"

Tobias scuffed his boot on the polished wood. "No, Ma'am."

Miss Lily took a deep, patient breath. "Did you *coax* that snake into her bed?"

"Yes, Ma'am."

"I'd get a strap, but God's already punished you with that nose. Let me see that." Tobias shuffled closer.

"Ow, Ma!"

"Well, it's not broken," Miss Lily said. "There'll be no dessert for you, and you'll stay in this room until morning. I want you to do your letters. Is that clear?"

"Yes, Ma'am."

The door closed, and Jin peeked from beneath the bed. Tobias glared down at her from behind a handkerchief.

"Thank you," she whispered.

His face softened, and he sat on his bed. "Don't know why I protected a thief."

"Because it is for a good cause."

He looked dubious.

"I must go."

"Where to?" Tobias asked.

"To help a friend in trouble."

Tobias frowned. "Mr. A.J. can help with that."

Jin shook her head. "It's too dangerous." She caught the window ledge again.

"You said I could come," he hissed.

"Your mother said stay." She pulled herself up, and slipped outside into the cool night. But before she'd got very far, she heard a faint rustling, and looked over her shoulder. Tobias was there, following in the dark.

"I'm coming," he hissed.

With a sigh, Jin checked for the guard, and darted back across the yard, to the far corner. Her unwanted companion followed, but when she reached the fort, another stood in the dark. Sarah Byrne crossed her arms.

Jin skidded to a stop. Eyes wide. "*Bai!*" she hissed.

"I saw you under that bed," Sarah said. "I knew something was happening. Where are you two off to?"

"To find her friend," Tobias answered before Jin could tell her to mind her own business. She shot the boy a glare.

"I don't think we're supposed to be out at night," Sarah said.

"It's for a good cause," said Tobias.

Jin growled under her breath, and stalked over to the fence. Big dog or no, she intended to cross that other yard. She rested a log against the fence, and used it as a step to catch the top of the fence.

"Where are you going?" Sarah asked, again.

"You cannot come," Jin whispered.

"I traveled clear across the world on my own," Sarah said defiantly. "And I'll holler if you don't tell me."

Jin glanced over her shoulder. "I will tell you when we get there."

44

The Hatchet Man

EVERY STEP FELT LIKE lead. His hand shook, and he gripped his stick like a lifeline.

Click.

The sound echoed between his ears. It sounded real. It *felt* real. As if he were on his back in the muck once again. He could feel his blood running over his skin. Could see the boy grin. And the ringing that followed was so loud it drowned him.

Atticus Riot could still feel that bullet rattling around his head, slicing a path across his skull. And in his nightmares, he didn't know what was real and what was simply terror. The lines were blurred, and that loss of control unnerved him—but not as much as walking up those stairs to Tim's workshop.

What would he do if Wong Kau told him who had really slaughtered Ravenwood? How would he feel knowing he had killed the wrong men?

Thus far, Riot had avoided looking at the man—had

pretended the highbinder wasn't lying in the bed, or imagined he was simply dead. It was easier that way. But now he intended to talk with the face that haunted his nightmares. His waking hours, too. Memories exploded in his skull like a hammer hitting a primer.

Riot stopped on the stairs, halfway to the top. He took reassurance in the cool metal and weight of his walking stick. In the months following his shooting, he had actually needed it to walk. And now it had become a mental crutch.

"Did your knees give out on the stairs, Riot?" Isobel's voice broke through his uneasy mind. She stood on the step below, waiting.

"Old man that I am." The words came out rough and shaky.

Isobel stepped onto his own cramped stair, and placed a hand over his shaking one. There was strength in her grip. "Second thoughts?"

"I'm only glad you're here."

"Let's face your demon, then."

He nodded, and the steps flew by, until he was standing outside the room. Tim leaned in the doorway, arms crossed, glaring at his recovering prisoner. He glanced over his shoulder as they approached. "Wise made me swear to keep an eye on you when you interviewed him."

"Was Ewan worried I'd string him up by his thumbs?" Riot asked. He kept his voice light and easy, though he felt far from it.

"Probably wanted to give me something to do so I wouldn't," Tim grunted. "Anyhow, Kau is fed and watered."

Riot nodded, and stepped into the room. Tim and Isobel hung back, giving him space. A wave of disorientation hit him. It was disconcerting having their positions reversed, and his fear seemed a silly thing.

The hatchet man sat upright, resting against a mound of pillows. His arm was in a sling, and his chest was heavily bandaged. Wong Kau looked straight at Riot, and he returned the stare. The cocky youth of three years before was all but gone, replaced by a grave man, who looked at him as warily as a wounded tiger.

"You know my name, I believe," Riot said. "But I'm not entirely sure of yours." He was curious which name the man would use. And whether Jin had been telling the truth.

"Wong Kau." He was pale, and weak, but his voice was strong. "I do not regret shooting you, *Din Gau*. I would do it again. We are warriors. That is our way." There was resignation rather than defiance in those words. "I will not apologize for that night, but I will beg for your help now."

Riot frowned, wondering if he had heard that right. He felt rather than heard Isobel's frustration. To stall for time, he translated. Hearing the words in English cemented them in his mind.

"Why would you need my help?" he asked.

Kau looked like he might be ill. Steeling himself, he raised his chin, and explained, "Four months ago, Sing Chung Lee, leader of Hip Yee, arranged a celebration in honor of his new acquisition—a beautiful new concubine from China. All of Hip Yee were invited. She was as beautiful as he boasted.

"I admired her with the other men, at first. But whereas they looked away, I could not take my eyes from her. And when I left, I kept seeing her eyes, and the way she moved. It was like a dream; she became my obsession.

"At first I thought it was because of her beauty and

poise, and me, a man, but there was something more—as if we were connected. I began to think of excuses to visit Sing Chung Lee's home, and one day I realized the truth. His concubine was my little sister, Mei, grown into a woman. I ask... No, I will beg, that you find her and rescue her, or permit me to go free so I can try to save her again."

Riot translated, but the irony was too much for Isobel. She snorted, and he didn't blame her one bit.

Wong Kau narrowed his eyes at her. "Fate is laughing at me, too." His gaze dropped, his voice lowered. "How many girls, how many daughters and sisters, have I forced into a life of shame? But this is *my* sister, *my* blood."

"Funny how things suddenly matter when it's your own kin," Riot said.

"I cannot change the past," Kau said. The words struck Riot; he had thought the very same thing on more than one occasion. But he was wary. Hatchet men were cunning, and Kau was in a severely compromised position.

"It was my responsibility to bring honor and money to my family, but when I arrived in the Gold Mountain, I found desperate men, back-breaking work, and a hateful city. But in Hip Yee, I found brothers."

"At the cost of innocent lives," Riot bit out.

"Now I regret it—now that my sister has been abducted from China and sold into slavery," Kau said. "When I realized all this, I vowed to save her, even knowing that it is certain death." The strength in his voice had fled. He looked defeated, and exhausted.

Riot did not trust himself to read the man, a source of terror for so long. Too much history clouded his judgment. And this hatchet man in particular was feared in the Quarter. That kind of reputation did not come easy.

"What were you doing on the dunes?" he asked.

"I sent a message to the mission on the hill. I asked the White Devil to save Mei. I watched as the police and white woman raided Chung Lee's home, but he must have suspected me, he must have moved her. It took many weeks for me to find her again. I discovered that he had placed her in a brothel—Chi Gum Shing—The Forbidden Palace. She now made money for him. But when I tried to enter, tried to hire her so I might speak with her, the guards were suspicious of me.

"Eventually I arranged to have a message delivered to her through another prostitute. I hoped my note would ease Mei's despair. To know that her brother Kau was searching for her. When I returned, the woman told me she had delivered the message, but Mei had been moved again—to a brick house near the ocean.

"I watched the building night and day, living in a hole in the sand. I tried to disguise myself as a grocer, a cook, and a groomsman, but each time I was turned away." His hands clenched the blanket, white-knuckled, fierce with frustration, although his face revealed nothing.

"Does your tong own the Forbidden Palace and the brick house?"

"No—I had never heard of the brick house before. But I know that Hip Yee does not own the Forbidden Palace, nor do we collect money from it. I hear it is owned by a white man."

"Did your leader sell her?"

"I do not know," he said. "But on the night I decided to enter the brick building by force, I saw her face in a window. I thought it must be a sign of good fortune. The next thing I knew, she and a small girl were climbing from the third story. They ran, and I chased them, but men from the brick building were chasing them, too. One of the men grabbed Mei, and I attacked. But I was shot during the struggle."

"And then you buried a hatchet in his skull," Riot said.

"Yes."

"He's dead," Riot said.

Kau nodded. "Good."

Isobel bristled, and a flash from her steely eyes chilled the room. "Why shouldn't we hand you over to the police? How many girls have you destroyed? How many innocent grocers and laundrymen have you threatened and beaten? And yet you have the gall to judge *that* man?"

Riot translated, and Kau jerked his head towards her. "Who is *that* woman?"

"You're not in any position to ask questions, Mr. Wong," Riot said calmly. He kept his voice low, and did not translate. "Treat her with respect, or I won't hand you over to the police. I'll hand you to your tong."

Kau paled. "It was only a question," he said quietly. "I have already lost face—*mien tzu*—a severe loss. I saw it in the eyes of my Hip Yee brothers while I was searching for Mei. Sing Chung Lee suspected me already. Shooting you brought me much honor, and now I have lost it with you here. It is fate, the yin and yang, the way of life. Perfectly balanced."

"Why didn't you finish the deed three years ago?"

"I would have," Kau said. "If it were not for your friend."

"My friend?"

Kau's eyes twitched with surprise. "Your friend disguised as a beggar waiting in the alley that night. He threw a knife, and hit my arm as I pulled the trigger." Kau pointed to a long scar on his arm. "He attacked me, and, thinking that I had killed you, I left."

Riot kept his expression neutral, waiting to see if Kau would say anything else, but the man's mind wasn't on three years before. It was on his sister.

"I do not care what happens to me now—only that Mei is safe. That my mother and father do not know of her shame."

"The only people who are neck deep in shame are the men who abducted and abused her," Riot said. "What do you know of the young girl?"

"I know nothing of her. After I was shot, Mei told her to help me." Kau swallowed, his lips dry. Riot poured him a glass of water, and loosened one of his bonds. When he had finished drinking, he plucked the glass from his hand, and tightened the ropes.

Kau nodded his thanks, and continued. "As the small girl supported me, Mei ran back to the men who were still following. She knew they were after her. She did it to save us. Otherwise, I would have been killed, and the small girl taken again. And without the girl's help, I would have died from my wound, but I am already lost. Mei can still be saved, though."

"I was trying to save slave girls when you murdered my partner. I'll find Mei, but not for you," Riot said.

A shudder of relief shook Kau's body, and he nodded.

"You told me that your tong didn't kill my partner."

"We did not."

"Why should I believe a word you say?"

"I swear to you that no Hip Yee hatchet man was given the task," said Kau. "But believe me there were many who wished for that honor after you invaded our headquarters."

"Your tong broke into my home, planted dynamite, and hung effigies from the chandelier with notes threatening to kill us both."

"Yes, we did. To scare you," Kau confirmed. "But we did not kill him."

Riot stared him straight in the eye, and Kau held his gaze without deceit, without guile. "If Hip Yee didn't kill Ravenwood, then who did? Was it Gee Sin Seer?"

"I do not know."

"I don't believe you," Riot said through clenched teeth.

"Do you think we would have let you live? Do you think we would have been so unprepared to meet you? You came into our headquarters, and caught us off-guard while we were celebrating. No one was expecting it. Even now, no one knows who killed your partner."

He slapped his palm against the knob of his stick, turned and walked out of the room, and headed straight for the stairs.

"Riot?"

The voice brought him up short. It stopped him just inside the stable, and he waited, staring out into the crisp night. It was cold and clear, and the moon hung low. The scents of simple hay and leather grounded him. And the fingers that lightly touched his arm.

"Another walk?" Isobel asked.

"Maybe," he said hoarsely, placing a hand over hers.

"You don't actually believe him, do you?" Tim asked when he caught up.

"I don't know what to believe," Riot snapped.

Tim froze, his eyes widening a fraction.

Riot took a steadying breath. "There *was* a beggar in that alley."

"It might explain how you got to an undertaker's," Tim

said in a quieter voice. "I always wondered that."

"It might." Riot tried to remember the beggar's face, but it had been dark, and the man had been clothed in rags and filth.

"I don't see why he'd lie about the beggar," Isobel said. "Kau has more reason to say he spared your life out of mercy in hopes you'll offer him the same."

Riot had to agree.

"As far as the present, there was a note," she reminded. "Miss Cameron showed it to you."

"But that could have been sent by someone else," Tim argued. "For all we know this Mei was abducted by another tong, and Wong Kau was sent to get her back."

"Could be," Riot acknowledged. "It still doesn't change the fact that there's a woman being held against her will."

"According to *him*." Tim spat. "Are you planning on charging into that place with guns blazing?"

Riot didn't answer his old friend.

"You sure you want to walk into this, A.J.? Even if it's not a trap, it'll take you into a viper's nest."

"I'm afraid I've already fallen into that nest," said Isobel. "And I've dragged Riot in, too."

Tim snorted. "No, you haven't even come close. You're not in it until they bring out the hot irons." The old man spat again, and stomped back upstairs.

Riot removed his hat, and rested his head on wood, closing his eyes. He felt a hand on his back. "I didn't even ask for a description of her," he murmured.

"Beautiful. Answers to the name of Mei. It's a start," Isobel said softly.

He straightened. There was no question in Isobel's eyes. She knew what he'd do. And *he* knew that if he didn't look for this girl, real or fictional, she would continue without him.

"We'll be looking for a needle in this viper's nest, Bel."

"Which viper should we start with?"

"I intend to talk to Jin. Now that we know more, perhaps she'll confirm his story, or at least deny it."

"That's harsh, Riot. I wouldn't call her a viper, precisely. She's more like a red-eyed rabbit with a good kick and large teeth."

He looked sideways at her. "I think you're growing fond of your stray."

"What's not to love?" Isobel asked dryly. But when they poked their heads into Tobias' fort and found her missing, the look of worry in Isobel's eyes was unmistakable.

45

Jail Break

"I DON'T THINK THIS is a good idea."

Jin glanced at the dark boy. All she could see were the whites of his eyes, and an occasional flash of teeth. "I did not ask you to come."

"I agree with Tobias." There was a tremor in the older girl's voice. Already, Sarah had nearly fallen off the back of the streetcar that they'd hitched a ride on. And when the conductor confronted them, she'd nearly spilled everything before Jin dragged her into the dunes.

"I did not *want* you to come," Jin reminded.

Tobias blew a breath past his lips. "Well, we're here now."

"I still think you should have told Mr. Riot," said Sarah.

Jin sniffed, and turned her gaze back to the brick house. They were on their bellies behind a dune, looking over its crest. Windows spilled out light, and horses came and went. The shutters were closed, save for one set. It prickled the back of Jin's neck, and made her think of a mouse trap.

"So your friend is in there?" asked Tobias.

"Yes," Jin said, firmly. She did not know for certain, but she had to believe that she would see Mei again.

"Why don't we just knock on the front door, and ask if we can see her?" asked Sarah.

"It is a house of shame, with bad men. The only children they take inside are—"

Sarah gasped, and Jin rolled her eyes, thinking the girl must be related to *Faan Tung*. But Jin did not say more. She would not be like the women who had tormented her. "It is a bad place," she said instead.

Tobias shook his head. "My Ma is gonna whip me."

Jin glanced at the boy in surprise. "Miss Lily whips you?"

"She hasn't yet, but I've never done nothing like this."

Jin smirked. "I did not think so."

"Think what?"

"Your mother seems very nice."

"You haven't seen her mad."

"I'm sure." Jin shifted, trying to ease the discomfort of the scars on her back. It made her think of Mei, of her herbs and ointments that soothed the pulling flesh. Mei had seen her, not as a house slave to be thrown away, but as a friend. Mei had shown her kindness—and no one had done that in a long time.

Jin roughly wiped the stinging sand from her eyes. Gritting her teeth, she pushed herself up. Trap or no, she would go. "If I am not back before dawn, tell Mr. Riot and that *other* woman."

Before her companions could protest, Jin darted across the sand, and scrambled over the fence. The open window called; one way or another, she would find Mei.

Tobias watched Jin run to a corner of the building, and use two walls to shimmy her way up to a second-story window. She slipped inside, but he didn't like it. Not one bit.

"I don't like this," Sarah confided in his ear.

The children looked at each other. Tobias crinkled his nose. Sarah huffed, and they darted towards the iron fence as one. Tobias blew out all his breath and squeezed through the gaps, but being older, and taller, Sarah couldn't manage. She jumped towards the top of the fence, but it was too high.

"I'll be back," Tobias hissed. Just as he turned, a screech flew out the window, and a shadow passed over its front. The window slammed shut, and the interior shutters followed with a bang.

Tobias dropped to his stomach with a word that should have led to a mouthful of soap. Tense, and ready to run, he watched that window and held his breath. But the only thing he heard was the crashing surf. He looked over at Sarah, who had dropped to the sand, too. Her eyes were wide under the moon.

Before he thought better of it, Tobias exploded towards the house with a burst of frantic speed. He darted across the carriage yard, and shimmied up the corner. Only Jin had made it look easy. Tobias slipped, and frantically lunged towards the windowsill. He caught the ledge on the tips of his fingers, his boots scraping against the brick for purchase. He stuck out one leg, stretched his toes, and braced himself on the opposite wall.

Tobias slowly pulled his head up an inch, and peeked

through the window. There was light creeping through the slats, but he couldn't see much. A bed, a chair, and a door. The room looked empty.

Below, a door opened. And Tobias froze. Heart thundering, arms shaking and fingers aching, he held on for his life, as a man strode quickly across the yard. He disappeared into the carriage house. A second later, the door opened again.

"Psst, Bill."

The first man stuck his head back out of the carriage house.

"Tell him to hitch up the wagon, she's too lively for a horse," the second man ordered. This one had a cigar between his lips. He inhaled slowly, blew a puff of smoke out into the night, and disappeared back inside the brick building.

As soon as both men disappeared, Tobias' fingers slipped. He hit the sand with a thud, and crumpled. Arms and legs trembling with fear, he scrambled towards the carriage house just as a thin man led a horse from the barn. Tobias made himself part of the bricks, dropping to the sand and pretending to be a board.

Could they hear his heart? He was sure of it—sure he'd be snatched, and then his Ma would find out, and he'd be in a whole heap of trouble.

Minutes passed as the men hitched up the wagon. The first man was loud and muttering, complaining about heathen whores, but the thin man was quiet, never answering or commenting in return. He was watchful though. And Tobias swore those eyes focused on him more than once.

The back door opened again, and the cigar-smoking man walked out, carrying a bundle over his shoulder. It was dark, but the moon was bright, and Tobias could see the sack squirming and writhing on the man's shoulder.

The man tossed his bundle into the back of the wagon with a hollow thud, and yanked the tarp over the bed, cinching it tight. "Take her back to those incompetent chinks, and tell them they best stick her in one of their hospitals, or we'll be displeased. I don't want to hear about this little shit again."

The cigar-smoking man stalked off, and slammed the back door. Bill climbed into the driver's seat, and picked up the reins, and Tobias slithered forward, bracing himself to run. The wagon rolled off, and the quiet man stood, watching it roll away.

Tobias had to take his chance. He darted forward—hoping the quiet man would stay that way—and ran for the back of the wagon. If there was one thing Tobias White excelled at, it was hitching rides on anything with wheels.

46

The Brick House

A SHADOW MOVED ON the moonlit road. Isobel and Riot reined in their mounts, and squinted into the night. The horses danced as they watched the shadow. It was a girl— her braids flying behind her as she ran.

"Sarah," Riot breathed. He dug in his heels, and Isobel followed suit. When he reached the girl, he dismounted before his horse had fully stopped. Sarah ran into his arms, and he held her with his right, while he drew his revolver with his left hand.

"Tobias... Jin...men... the building." Sarah was wheezing, panting, and near to collapsing, and her words came out in desperate gasps. A run from the brick building was over two miles.

"Calm down, Sarah," Riot said. "Take your time."

"Is someone chasing you?" Isobel asked, as she grabbed Riot's horse by the bridle.

Sarah shook her head, and Riot holstered his gun as quickly as he had drawn it. He placed his hands on her shoulders, and held her at arm's length, looking into her tear-filled eyes.

"What happened?" he asked.

Sarah quivered. "I shouldn't have gone. I'm sorry—"

"You're not in trouble, Sarah. Just tell us what happened." As usual, Riot pinned her panic, and she calmed enough to tell them.

As she listened to Sarah's story, Isobel clenched her jaw, and, sensing her anger, her horse danced to the side. She should have pressed Jin, should have watched the girl more closely, should have sent the police into that damn building. She slapped the regrets out of her mind. There was no changing a chess board once the pieces were in play. The only path was forward.

"Why a hospital, Riot?" she asked.

He looked at her, and gave a slight shake of his head. Not here; not now.

"Can you ride?" Riot asked Sarah.

"I'm from Tennessee. Of course I can ride."

Riot took his reins, and swung up into the saddle. And Isobel caught his eye. "I know a safe place she can wait." It was an odd sensation, knowing what he was thinking. She had only ever felt that way about her twin.

Riot reached down, offering Sarah a hand.

"I'm not wearing a proper riding dress, sir."

"It's dark enough that no one will notice."

Sarah gripped his hand, and he swung her up into the saddle behind him, before urging his horse into a run. Soon trees gave way to sand dunes, and distant lights along the shoreline. Puffs of warm air billowed around the horses' nostrils, and Sarah shivered behind Riot as they trotted past the brick house and its electric lights.

Isobel led the way to the Falcon's Clubhouse, and

frowned at the light behind the curtains. She hadn't count-ed on anyone being inside. With a muttered curse, she dismounted, tied a mooring hitch to the rail, and knocked on the door. Footsteps approached, and a head peeked out through the curtains. It was Margaret. Thrilled, Isobel waved, but there was puzzlement in her friend's eyes. A second later, Isobel remembered that she had changed into the guise of Mr. Morgan when they'd discovered the chil-dren missing.

"It's Charlie," she mouthed, removing her cap. Mar-garet's eyes widened, and she disappeared. The locks slid to the side, and the door opened.

"Thank God it's you," Isobel said, hugging the woman.

"Why are you dressed—" Margaret stopped as Riot and Sarah approached. He had bundled her in his over-coat.

"Madame." Riot removed his hat with a flourish. "I'm Atticus Riot, and this is Sarah Byrne." His voice purred in the night, as warm and smooth as whiskey. Margaret stam-mered out her name, realized she was in her nightgown, and quickly closed the collar of her robe.

"A pleasure, sir," she said. "Has something happened?"

"Some children are in danger," Isobel said. "I need you to watch this girl. If we're not back by morning, take her to Ravenwood estate in Pacific Heights."

"Yes, of course I'll watch her, Charlie. But why did you cut your hair, and why are you dressed as a man?"

"There's no time to explain."

The light from the horse car shone on Isobel's face for the first time, and Sarah got a clear look at her. "Mr. Am —" Isobel clamped a hand over Sarah's mouth before she uttered the dreaded word 'Amsel', and shoved her towards Margaret. "It's Miss *Bonnie*." She grabbed the door handle, and shut it firmly on two very confused faces.

"Thank God you don't have a twin, Riot," she growled, as they skirted the clubhouse towards the dunes.

"Are you positive I don't?"

"Ari would be delighted," she said.

Together, they circled the brick house, surveying the property and getting a feel for the land. They stopped on the carriage house side, and lay on a dune, peeking over the crest.

"What's a hospital?"

She felt his quiet anger. "When a slave girl falls ill, usually from a venereal disease, they're placed in an airless shed with a single pot of paraffin and a bowl of rice— sometimes laced with poison. A 'doctor' goes to check on them in three days, and if they aren't dead, then he makes sure they are."

Isobel glared at the brick building, and itched to tear the place down. "We could start a fire, and see who comes out."

"We could," Riot said. There was a lot that he left unsaid in those two words. He drew his No. 3 and checked the chambers.

"You're right. Fire is always risky," she conceded.

Isobel recalled Lotario's terror and her mother's cold calm as she'd ripped curtains off rods to beat at the flames. Isobel had learned about the dangers of starting fires at an early age. She changed her plan. "You can sneak in through the back door, and I'll take the high road."

"I intend to knock on the front door," he drawled.

"Knock?"

"Too civil for you?"

"Well, it's awfully boring, Riot."

"I doubt this will be."

✣

The door opened, and Atticus Riot helped it along with a sound kick. It caught the man behind the door in the nose. Taking advantage of his surprise, Riot grabbed the doorman's collar, and yanked him forward, sending him sprawling down the front steps.

With an open invitation, Riot walked inside, shut the door, and slid the bolt in place, turning to survey grandeur. The front hall cried out wealth: colored glass, twining metal, the finest marble, and a pair of Herculean sconces of brass men holding giant orbs over their heads. They looked like gargoyles on the wall.

A wide stairway led straight ahead, and two rooms branched off from the main hall. The room to the left appeared to be a viewing room, with a long ornate couch for the line up, and several screens.

Riot swept off his hat, hung it on a hook, and with a twirl of his stick walked into the room on the right—a sitting room. An older gentleman snored in an armchair by the fireplace. Riot made himself comfortable. He turned an armchair to face the front hall, set down his stick, and poured himself a whiskey.

The first furious knock from the doorman thundered through the building, and the gentleman in the armchair snorted awake. He was past graying and near to white, and appeared to enjoy his food more than exertion.

"A drink, sir?" Riot asked.

"Yes, I think I will. A whiskey, if you please." The man had a slow drawl to his voice, thick and lazy, with barely a movement of his lips.

As the volley of knocks became increasingly desperate, he poured the gentleman his drink. Riot set the shot glass on the table beside the man, unbuttoned his own coat, and sat in the chair with a view.

A moment later, a trio of fit men tripped down the stairs in various states of undress. A brawny fellow, hairy as a bear, had barely managed to pull on the bottom half of his union suit.

"Why the blazes is Jon outside?" This from a shirtless man who had a distinct British drawl. Riot placed him from Oxford. But his attention was focused on Parker Gray, who glanced in the room as he rushed past. In a club like this, the fine clothing Riot was wearing tended to blend with the scenery.

Riot took a sip of his whiskey as they opened the door. A string of Cantonese cuss words flew into the front hall.

"What the hell happened?" the furry man asked.

"*Din Gau* is here," the Chinese doorman spat.

The older gentleman in the chair chuckled from his belly, raised his glass to Riot, and took a sip. The front hall fell silent.

Parker Gray stalked into the sitting room with his toughs on his heels. He had managed to get on trousers and suspenders, and nothing else. The customary cigar in his hand had been replaced by a Colt Peacemaker. There was murder in his eyes. But Riot had already drawn his No. 3. He held it casually, aimed at Gray's chest.

"I wouldn't do that if I were you," Riot said.

"There's four of us," Gray said.

"I agree; you'll need more men." Riot took another sip of his whiskey, watching the four men over the glass. He knew what they were thinking—he could see it in their eyes. They knew his reputation, and they were wondering how much of it was true.

The older gentleman shifted in his armchair, sitting

upright and straightening his waistcoat. "Gray, why don't you be civil? You'd already be dead if Mr. Riot had that in mind."

Riot glanced at the man. He had mistaken wealth and age for passivity, and underestimated the snoring gentleman. This man was not Gray's equal—he was his superior.

"He hit me and threw me out the door," Jon said.

"By my reckoning, you hit your own goddamned door, and tripped down the stairs," the older man said with a chuckle.

Jon fumed, but Gray lowered his gun, and then thrust it through his waistband.

The old man took a sip of his whiskey. "Could I get a cigar, Mr. Jon?"

Gathering himself with all the grace of an English butler, Jon moved to the cupboard and produced a cigar box. The older gentleman took one, clipped the end, and lit it, sucking on the fine cigar while Jon offered one to each of the other men. Riot declined, and holstered his gun.

"Well, this has been most amusing," the older gentleman said, rising to his feet. "I'll leave you to clean up your mess, Gray." He inclined his head to Riot. "Most amusing."

"And your name, sir?" Riot asked.

"I think not," he said with an avuncular wink. The older man left, still chuckling, a sound that made Riot more uneasy than the man with a gun.

"What do you want?" Gray demanded.

"I want to have a civil conversation with you, but your leering friends there are ruining the atmosphere."

Gray jerked his head, and the two men left. He stuck his unlit cigar between his lips, and sat in the vacated chair.

Jon remained, standing off to the side, hands folded behind his back.

Riot waited for Gray to light his cigar. When a billow of smoke rose over his head, Gray sat back, and put an ankle on the opposite knee. Men who sat like that generally wanted the world to know that they were in charge—it always reminded Riot of a rooster puffing its feathers.

"Now that we're settled, why did you barge into my club?" Gray asked.

"I did ask politely a few days ago."

"Like I said, this club is by invitation only." Gray looked him up and down. "I don't take you for a stupid man, Mr. Riot. I'm sure you've worked out that this is a sporting house. Are you that hard up for a woman on the dunes that you practically kicked in my door?"

"I've never had to pay a woman for the pleasure of her company."

Gray showed his teeth. "You must be real desperate then."

"Real men don't buy women."

"Are you going to thump your bible at me?"

"No," Riot said. "Lead is my preferred method of delivery."

"Is that a threat?"

"Only information."

"The only information I want is the answer to why you're here."

"I think you know," Riot said.

Gray sucked on his cigar, and blew out a ring of smoke in short puffs. "This is about that agent of yours, isn't it?"

Riot inclined his head.

"As soon as I found out she was a woman, I treated her real civil-like," said Gray. "And out of respect for you, I released her. I'm sure you'll appreciate that."

"I am appreciative."

Gray eyed him, waiting for the next move, but Riot didn't make one. He didn't answer the question in Gray's eyes: *Then why are you here?* Riot's silence was thoroughly frustrating the man.

"The man who roughed her up wasn't one of mine," Gray said.

"I already know that." He let Gray shift for a minute, and then he spoke into that silence. "This clubhouse is in the business of selling flesh. It's a middleman for wealthy members who don't want to soil their shoes by setting foot in a known brothel. And you simply cater to their whims— whatever those might be."

Gray paused, the smoke around his face moving fitfully. "It is," he confirmed.

"Your members value discretion," Riot continued. "I can understand that—you don't want to draw attention to your club here."

"That's right."

"Then you'll be eager to help me with my search."

"What search is that?" Gray asked.

"There were two girls in your clubhouse. Both Chinese. There was a girl named Mei, and a younger one who was recently taken away in the back of a wagon."

Ash gathered on the end of Gray's cigar. He seemed to have forgotten about it. Riot leaned forward. "Tell me where they are, Mr. Gray, and I'll leave you to your business."

Gray smashed his cigar in the ashtray, and left it there. "We don't own any girls, Mr. Riot. As soon as the girl climbed in the window we left open, I had her returned to her kin. I don't know where they took her."

"You're forgetting that I'm not stupid," Riot said. "She left in your wagon, which was driven by your driver, with orders from you to throw the 'little shit' in a hospital."

Gray's eyes blazed.

"Reach for that gun. I beg you," Riot said with a click of teeth.

Gray didn't move.

"Trust me, Mr. Gray. You don't want this dog sniffing around your tree. You know it as well as I—you knew it that day you interrogated my agent. And you know it now. Where did your men take those girls?"

"We're middlemen," Gray said. "Protection goes both ways."

"I only want the girls."

"You don't know who you're dealing with."

Riot smiled like a wolf. "You think I care?"

Gray only smirked, reaching for his smoldering cigar, grounding it further into the ashtray. "I think you care about that agent of yours."

"I care about each and every one of my agents. And I care about those girls."

"I'm sorry to say, Mr. Riot, but life can be dangerous."

"The Hip Yee tong discovered that, too."

Gray's eyes twitched, and his hand stilled.

"Reach for it," Riot urged.

A full minute passed with only the tick of a clock to keep them company. The odds flashed through Gray's eyes —the risk, the glory, and then the realization that he'd be dead at the first twitch of movement.

Riot took a risk. "I'm not the only one in a precarious situation, Mr. Gray. You answer to the same men you brandished at me. It's plain to see you fear them. The gentleman who was sitting in that chair of yours will be watching to see how you handle this situation. Will you handle it quietly, or draw attention to your members? You know my reputation—I have a long history of shedding light on *very* dark places."

"They took the girls to the Dog Kennel. Bartlett Alley. There's an iron door in a courtyard behind the mill."

The British fellow walked slowly into view, his hands raised. The reason for his cautionary entrance became apparent a moment later. A gun was pressed to his back. Isobel stepped into the room, gaze darting from Gray to Riot.

"Everything all right, Riot?"

"We were just finishing up our conversation." He stood smoothly, and plucked Gray's gun from his belt. He emptied the cartridges, pocketed them, and placed the gun on the table.

"Civility seems to have escaped your agent," Gray said.

"I'm far from civil," Isobel said. "But then neither were your hoodlums in the basement."

"They were only guests, *Miss* Morgan."

Isobel tipped her cap.

Gray looked her up and down. "I didn't get a chance to tell you the other day—you have a fine pair of breasts."

Riot's grip tightened on his stick, but the comment was intended to goad. He swallowed down his reaction, and let the words slide over him. But Isobel didn't let it slide.

"Why, thank you," she said, sounding genuinely pleased.

Riot glanced at the woman. Rare, unique, and contrary in every way.

"By the way, they're not here. I mean my breasts are," she corrected. "But not the girls."

The Englishman with a gun pressed against his back

chuckled, and Riot nearly laughed. He dared not meet her eye. "We'll take our leave then. Mr. Gray, pray we don't cross paths again."

"You should be the one praying on your knees."

Riot clucked his tongue. "Now, now, never provoke a rabid dog. Your superior wouldn't be pleased."

Gray had no more words for him, and Isobel and Riot took their leave. As they walked down the front steps, Isobel had her gun aimed on the front door. It wasn't until they'd retrieved their horses at the Falcon's Clubhouse that Riot breathed easy.

"Did you discover anything more?" Riot asked, as they rode towards Chinatown.

Isobel snorted. "Only the wide and varied fetishes of so-called gentlemen."

"Were there any underage girls or boys?"

"No—not tonight. Not obvious, at any rate." While he had been away, the age of consent had been raised from fourteen to sixteen. Small victories at least. "Still, I wish I could scrub out the inside of my skull after looking through some of those peepholes. I think I've been away from the Barbary Coast for too long."

"Odd that they'd have peepholes in a place that boasts discretion," he mused.

"Maybe there's blackmail involved. They were fairly well concealed."

"Apparently not well enough."

"I have a knack." She hesitated a moment. "You, erm… don't have any odd appetites, do you?"

"I do have one."

She arched a brow in question.

"Recently discovered." Riot nudged his horse into a run, and tossed the words over his shoulder. "A taste for a certain woman dressed as a man."

Isobel laughed, and urged her horse after him.

47

Willing Bait

TOBIAS WHITE CLUNG TO the back of the wagon as it bumped over the road. Keeping an eye on the driver, he tugged at the corner rope of the tarp, and when it flapped free, he crawled inside the bed.

"Jin?" he whispered in the blackness. His fingers brushed the coarse sack, and prodded it until it moved. "Jin?"

A foot kicked his hand. And he quickly went to the other end, tugging off the sack that was over her head. She had a rag stuffed in her mouth, and he pulled that out, too.

"Don't worry, I'll get you out of here."

"No, you will not," she hissed.

Tobias thought he must have heard her wrong. He started working on the knots.

"Stop it." She bumped him away with her shoulder. "I let them capture me."

"Why would you do something stupid like that?"

"I need to find Mei," she whispered. "They will take

me to her now."

"I don't know about that."

"If not, I will escape." Even laying down in the darkness, Tobias could well imagine that stubborn tilt of her chin.

"How are you going to escape?" he asked.

"I could have gotten out of these ropes at any time."

"Could not."

"Could too."

"Fine, I'll leave you here," Tobias huffed.

"Wait."

He hesitated. "What?"

"You might as well loosen them for me."

Tobias grumbled, but did as she asked. "You're crazy."

He saw a flash of teeth. "No. I am cunning."

"Starts with the same letter. Close enough."

The wagon rolled to a stop, and Tobias watched from under the tarp as the driver talked to the police in front of a barricade. There were barrels with flames spouting off foul smoke. It smelled like they were burning rotten eggs.

Money passed between driver and police, and the barricade was moved to let the wagon through. As it rolled past, Tobias shot daggers at the police from his concealment. But that glare widened into amazement and fear as the streets transformed. Burning barrels of rotten eggs were interspersed with paper lanterns and golden braziers. Chinatown. Tobias had been there once, the year before, for New Year's celebration, but that festive atmosphere was a dim memory compared to the somber mood on the streets tonight.

Men milled past the wagon, looking grim and angry,

roaming with nowhere to go. The wagon stopped in front of a narrow lane. Red lanterns cast sinister shadows on the surrounding bricks. The driver hopped down, and Tobias quickly climbed out the back and slipped underneath the wagon.

He watched the driver knock on the door of a building with a balcony and curling gold eaves strung with a whole row of lanterns. The door opened, and the driver spoke to the man inside. A minute later, a large Chinese man came out the front. He stomped over to the wagon, and threw back the tarp. Tobias heard the big man dragging Jin over the bed.

With the slight load on his shoulder, he walked down the narrow lane and disappeared into darkness. The wagon rolled forward, and Tobias lost his cover. Exposed in the middle of the street, Tobias had no choice—he darted after the big man, keeping low and to the shadows like a mouse darting between legs.

The lane cut through a building, making it more like a tunnel. Stairs dropped at the end of the passageway. A man in a wide hat stood at the end of the passage, watching as other men walked past. A moment of panic took over Tobias, and he dropped to his belly, pressing himself against the wall. A man stumbled over his foot, and another nearly stepped on him, but no one looked down. They were swaying gently with drink and singing under their breath.

The big man stopped to talk with the guard, and while the guard reached for a cigarette, Tobias scrambled forward, nearly tripping down the stairs.

There was an entire courtyard down those stairs. A sea of laundry lines and smoke filled the night sky, and a warren of doors lined the four walls. Men in broad-brimmed hats came and went from doors with barred windows that circled the courtyard. Tobias slipped through a broken railing slat, and dropped to the hard-packed earth.

A woman looked out from one of the barred windows. She looked straight at him, and Tobias tensed, ready to run. But the woman didn't make a sound. She only sucked on a long, thin pipe as if bored.

Tobias watched as the big Chinaman walked across the courtyard. The other men scrambled out of the way as he neared, and he stopped in front of a door that looked like the entrance to a bank vault. He knocked once on the iron. Waited. Knocked three times, and waited again. Another two knocks opened the door.

The man stepped inside, and the door slammed shut. Tobias blew out a sharp breath. He had never felt so hopeless and small in all his life. The man had taken Jin in there, and Tobias White didn't know what he should do next.

48

The Angry Angel

"WHY ARE WE STOPPING here?" Isobel eyed the solid brick building on the top of the hill. 920 Sacramento Street. She knew it from Riot's past, and little more.

"Chinatown is surrounded by barricades and police," Riot reminded.

"Is there an entrance into the Quarter through here?" They had stabled the horses in a nearby corral, and walked up to the mission.

"No, a guide." He lifted the knocker, and banged it against the plate three times. Minutes passed while Isobel shivered, listening to the echo of distant voices and watching smoke drift over buildings. It smelled of sulfur.

A slat opened, and a light illuminated them. Isobel shielded her eyes, blinking as the door opened. A tall, sturdy woman in a blouse and skirt ushered them inside. Tendrils of auburn hair hung limp around her face, dark circles ringed her eyes, and her sleeves were rolled up to her elbows.

"What is it, Atticus?" There was a note of exhaustion in her voice.

Riot didn't waste time with pleasantries. "Two girls are being held in the Dog Kennel behind an iron door. We need to get into the Quarter."

Donaldina Cameron glanced at Isobel as she dried her hands on a towel.

"This is Mr. Morgan. He's as trustworthy as me."

"High praise. A pleasure, sir."

Isobel nodded.

"I know that den, Atticus. It's very secure." Even as she spoke, she tossed down the towel, and rolled down her sleeves.

"I don't plan on bashing down the door with a sledge," he said. "It's Mei and Jin."

"I thought Jin was with you?"

"She was," he said. "Not anymore."

"You can tell me over a cup of tea later."

"I can see you're in the middle of something. You don't have to accompany us, I only need a route."

"I know a way in. I used it yesterday to rescue a sick girl, but I have to go along, too. Wait here a moment." Donaldina walked from the front hall, and disappeared down a hallway. A face peeked from behind a corner. A tiny Chinese girl in a wide-sleeved tunic watched them with curious eyes.

"Kay, go back to bed," Donaldina's voice drifted from the hallway. The girl darted across the front hall to a stairway, and hurried upstairs with a giggle. Donaldina marched back into the front hall with hat, coat, and gloves. A delicate young woman followed in her wake.

"Do not worry, *Lo Mo*, I will nurse her."

"You can only try."

Ling nodded, and smiled at Riot as he gave her shoulder a quick squeeze. Without a word, Donaldina charged into the night. For a missionary woman in skirts, she moved quickly down the steep hill, and Isobel was hard-pressed to keep pace.

Donaldina turned a corner, and hurried towards the thick smoke that hung over buildings like a persistent cloud. The moon shone dimly through the haze, and scents of rotten eggs, incense, and too many humans living too close wafted down the street.

Even as an adolescent, Isobel had been wary of the narrow alleys that led off the main streets of Chinatown. Men in broad-brimmed hats had watched her every move, as they stood smoking, guarding narrow lanes with unknown names. Isobel had boldly entered a few, but for the most part she had steered clear of the more dangerous-looking men. Yet there she was, being led by a missionary woman in a skirt towards those very same alleyways.

They shot straight down Sacramento, past two police barricades on Stockton and Waverley Place, and stopped in front of a Chinese herbalist, sandwiched between a white grocer and a saloon.

Donaldina knocked on the door, and they waited in front of the store, listening to music and laughter drifting over from the saloon. A face appeared in a window behind Chinese characters, and a moment later the door opened. Isobel was hit with the scents of earth and spices as a man ushered them inside. The front of his head was shaved, and the rest of his hair was gathered in a long braid down his back. He wore a spartan silk robe that clung to his torso.

The man offered a low bow. "Miss Cameron."

"I'm sorry to bother you a second night in a row, Mr.

Woon, but I need to make use of your closet and skylight again."

He smiled, and extended his arm towards the back of the store. "I am happy to help." From what Riot said, every time residents aided Donaldina, they were putting their necks on the chopping block.

Isobel followed the others through the narrow shop. Cabinets with small drawers lined the walls, each drawer meticulously labeled in cryptic lines.

"How is the girl from last night?" Woon asked.

"Not good, I'm afraid. It wasn't the plague after all, but appendicitis. The health officials were very disappointed. I don't think she'll survive the night—the doctor can't do anything more."

Woon frowned, and nodded. "At least she will die with her sister by her side, and not in the gutter where you found her."

"There is that."

He escorted them upstairs, into a simple room. A woman waited there, with an infant on her hip, and a small boy stared bleary-eyed from his room. The woman beamed at Donaldina and the two greeted each other with a hug. Woon spoke to his wife, and she considered Riot and Isobel with thoughtful eyes. More words flew back and forth, and she and her husband hurried off to another room.

Woon soon appeared with clothes draped over his arm. He issued each an outfit. "The same as you wore yesterday, Miss Cameron."

"It suited me fine."

"I will say again, things are very bad in the Quarter. There is little food, no one can go to work—many men are becoming desperate, and desperate men have no fear."

"That didn't stop me before."

He chuckled. "All of Chinatown is talking of you bullying the ambulance past the barricade."

"I do not bully, Mr. Woon." But she said it with a wink, and he chuckled again, gesturing towards a room.

"Do you happen to have padding or a chain shirt?" Riot asked.

The question took Woon aback. "No, nothing like that, sir." Woon looked thoughtfully at Riot as he exchanged jackets, but said nothing more.

Isobel turned, and shrugged out of her jacket, donning the quilted one with wide sleeves and toggles. It was dark enough not to worry about trousers and shoes. At least she hoped so.

As they placed the stiff, broad-brimmed fedoras on their heads, Donaldina emerged in a similar outfit, though she had retained her skirt and had an umbrella in hand.

Woon led them to an upper story, and opened a skylight to the roof. "May your God watch over you."

Isobel glanced at Donaldina, wondering if they'd have to lift the woman, but once again she surprised Isobel. Donaldina pulled herself through, and Isobel followed.

A sea of sloping angles, chimneys, and flat roofs stretched in smoke and moonlight. Ominous red light glowed from cracks between buildings. It looked like a scene from *Dante's Inferno*.

As soon as Riot joined them on the rooftop, Donaldina hurried through the maze, hopping over gaps, and balancing along narrow edges with admirable speed. The journey was dizzying, and Isobel lost all sense of direction in the murk and smoke.

Donaldina stopped on a roof that looked no different than any other. She bent, and wrenched open a hidden hatch. Riot dropped inside, and Donaldina followed. Isobel braced herself on the opening, legs dangling, and grabbed for the hatch. As she fell, it closed.

The space was cramped and dark, but their guide moved with confidence. A voice called out, quick and threatening in Cantonese.

"It's me, Chu," Donaldina whispered into another trapdoor.

"Ah, come, come quick." A man with a cleaver ushered them into a room.

"I'm afraid I'm making use of your home again."

"No problem," he said in broken English. "Happy to help. Please, whatever you need. You bring girl back this way?"

"I'm not sure."

He nodded profusely as he led them to a stairway. "I help hide if you need."

"Thank you, Chu." She opened the door quickly, ushered Riot and Isobel out, then closed it. The second Donaldina's feet touched the muddy ground, she opened her umbrella and hunched down. It gave her the appearance of a bent old woman.

"Do you know where you are?" Donaldina asked.

Riot nodded.

"The guard won't let me into the Kennel, but I'll go around back, and see if I can find an alternate route."

"I wouldn't mind some help from the Police Squad."

Donaldina nodded. "I'll get Price, then." The mission woman didn't wait for an answer, but stepped out of the lane into a stream of people, hobbling over the boardwalk under her umbrella.

Riot pulled up his collar, and kept his chin down, hiding his beard as they walked. Barrels of sulfur smoldered in the streets. Red lanterns lined the murk, shining dimly in the smoky air. They did little to press back the night. The entire Quarter seemed to be holding its breath, and men roamed the larger streets looking restless and angry.

"I have no idea where I am," Isobel whispered in Riot's ear. It was an admittance. She hated not knowing, and prided herself on her sense of direction, but she was only familiar with the main streets of Chinatown, where toy merchants entertained children in bright silks, and lanterns and festive banners decorated the shops. This was not one of those streets.

"West." He inclined his head in that direction, and she felt instantly grounded. "Don't make eye contact with anyone, and keep your head low."

She had been planning on doing just that. As they walked through the streets, towards an unknown goal, Riot started singing, low and slurring, in Cantonese. He staggered here and there, and Isobel followed suit, adopting the gait of a slightly tipsy man.

No one paid them any mind.

"There it is," Riot murmured under his breath.

A highbinder lounged in the front of a lane, smoking and watching a brothel across the way. The place was bright and ornate, and looked like paradise on earth compared to the dismal wooden rookeries surrounding it. Isobel would wager her cutter that it was the Forbidden Palace.

Singing under his breath, Riot turned into the narrow lane. The lookout hardly glanced their way. They were in more of a tunnel than a lane, passing beneath two buildings whose balconies were intertwined. Stairs led down into a courtyard ringed by leaning rookeries and basement-level cribs. Men milled in the courtyard, talking, smoking, and perusing flesh.

A low, discreet door disappeared down another series of steps, and another lane across the alley cut through the buildings. The sky was a smoky mixture of sulfur, incense, and laundry lines, and foul air nearly choked Isobel. She eyed the plank and iron door as Riot walked across the courtyard, towards the other lane. Only when they'd turned the corner did they discover the lane was a dead end, leading to a cesspit. Rats scurried on the edges. Considering the entire Quarter was barricaded due to a suspected plague death, Isobel was hard-pressed not to recoil.

"Damn," she whispered. And then turned to survey the mix of brick and wood. "I can make it to the roof."

"I'm not sure that will lead into the den," Riot said, gazing out into the courtyard.

"What else are we supposed to do? Knock?"

"It's worth a try."

"So is climbing." San Francisco had burned numerous times, and the builders were fond of reusing melted brick. The misshapen bricks made for convenient handholds and footholds. But a small sound off to the side interrupted her inspection.

Isobel drew her gun, but Riot beat her to it. His gun was already cocked and aimed at the moving pile of refuse on the ground. A pair of eyes opened, and the outline of a boy took shape.

"Tobias," Isobel breathed.

He scrambled forward, eyes darting to the open courtyard. "I knew you'd both come!"

Isobel hissed at him to be quiet.

He lowered his voice. "Please don't tell my mother about this."

"Did you see where they took Jin?"

"Through that iron door. I don't know how to get in though. A big man carried her inside. I was going to try and knock like the rest of them do, but I didn't know what to do after I got inside. And I don't much look like a Chinaman."

"How do they knock?" Isobel asked.

"Once. Then they wait for five seconds. I counted. And then three times, real quick. Then wait again. Then twice, and the door opens. It's kind of like the special knock I use with Grimm so Maddie won't bother us."

"You're a genius, Tobias," Riot said.

The boy beamed. "I'm not in trouble?"

"We'll talk about that later." Riot pulled out a police whistle, and handed it to the boy. "Do you think you can sneak out of this courtyard?"

"I'm coming with you."

"It's too dangerous—more dangerous than you sneaking out of this courtyard alone."

It was a dilemma, but Isobel had to agree. She didn't want to leave Tobias there anymore than she wanted to take him inside.

"I don't know where I am," Tobias said.

"Head straight out those stairs, take a left, and keep going until you hit a street. Turn right at the street, then the first left you come across. That's Dupont Street. Keep going until you hit the police barricade on Sacramento. Tell them you're on an errand for Donaldina Cameron and that she'll be furious if they don't let you through. If you can get past, head straight up the hill. There's a big brick building at the top. Tell them you're a friend of mine."

Tobias looked at the whistle. "What am I supposed to do with this?"

"If someone starts chasing you—run and blow it like your life depends on it. The police should come. And if you throw around Donaldina Cameron's name, they should at least take you to a cell, if not the mission."

Tobias snorted. "They took money from the wagon driver, and let him right in. I don't trust the police."

"There's a lot of men who'll do things for money, but there are good ones, too. Same goes for the police. Not all are corrupt."

Tobias looked dubious.

"Get going. We'll make sure you get out all right."

Tobias nodded, and, keeping to shadows and ducking under crib grates, he skirted the courtyard as swiftly as a mouse. He climbed up the stairs, and Isobel held her breath, listening. But there were no shouts, or sounds of a scuffle. With the barricade in place, the guards weren't very vigilant.

Riot looked at her. "Ready?"

"I'm never ready for any of the trouble I get into, Riot."

49

Rats and Ruin

SURPRISE WAS EVERYTHING. AT the first pounding of a sledge on a door, the highbinders would scatter with their cash, opium, and women through a warren of secret passages. It was far simpler to pose as natives.

Riot knocked on the iron door, repeating the pattern that Tobias had relayed. Isobel waited, exposed, with the sensation of watching eyes pricking the back of her neck. A shuddering breath of nerves swept past her lips, and Riot turned slightly, catching her eye from beneath his broad-brimmed hat. His beard rather ruined the native effect.

When the door opened, Riot stepped inside, and his fist came up fast. The punch stunned the doorman for a split second, long enough for Riot to draw his gun, and point it at the man's face. He walked him backwards against the wall, and Isobel shut the door.

Unlike the outside, the inside was a world away from filth—teak and polished wood and curved railings. A sickly

sweet smell that lay somewhere between flowers and al-
monds drifted from a side hallway. Opium. Isobel had tried
it once, but didn't much care for anything that muddled
her mind.

A stairway climbed to the right, and the hallway that
stank of opium went off to the left.

Riot asked something in Cantonese. The guard's eyes
twitched to the side, towards the stairway. "Thank you,"
said Riot, and reversed his revolver, bringing the stock
down hard on the man's head. He crumpled.

Isobel dragged the man to the side of the long hallway.
Opium fiends were less likely to notice a man passed out
on the floor. She walked to the end, and peeked through
the beaded curtain. It was dark, and the sickly sweet scents
were overwhelming; the occupants were far away, drifting
in a dream of pleasure. There were a few women inside,
lounging with men, but they were of the same age as
Isobel, not younger. An old man moved from client to
client, refilling their pipes when one was held up.

Before the man caught sight of her, she reversed direction. Riot was already at the top of the stairs, and she
hurried to catch up. Murmuring conversation drifted from
an archway. A reinforced door was propped open, revealing a large room. Men sat at the tables smoking, and deftly
moving ivory tiles around on tables. A haze of smoke hung
over their heads, and Isobel stifled a cough.

Riot didn't even pause. On silent feet, he moved up
another set of stairs to the third story. Isobel was halfway
up the stairway, when a man appeared above. There was
no hesitation, no pause. As smooth as if he'd been planning it, Riot pressed a gun to the man's ribs, but it did little
good.

"*King chak!*" the man shouted. *Police!* The alarm was

accompanied with a whirlwind of movement. The man twisted to the side, spun, and brought up his leg, smacking his heel against Riot's face. And the entire gambling hall erupted with a noise of scraping chairs and thudding boots.

"Arrest them!" Isobel barked in her deepest voice.

Instead of pressing his attack, the kicking man raced down the hallway, and Riot gave chase. As the gambling hall door slammed shut, Isobel climbed the stairs two at a time. She reached the top in time to see a foot disappear through a hatch, while another group raced through a door at the end of a long hallway. Riot was on their heels.

A woman cried out in Cantonese, and Isobel bolted in that direction, charging through the doorway after Riot. It led into a room of carpets and silks, and another hallway. She kept running.

The building was a honeycomb of trapdoors and rooms that made no sense, but Riot appeared to have a destination in mind. He raced through a decadent room, and kicked in the first door in a long line of them. Isobel sped past, and started on the last, throwing her shoulder against a door. She bounced off, and staggered back.

It felt as if she'd hit a brick wall, and then the hinges registered in her mind. They were all wrong. The door was false.

"Mei!" Riot called, disappearing into yet another doorway. Feeling half a step behind, she got there in time to see him disappear through a trap door in the floor. She flew to the opening, raced through another room, up a flight of stairs, and burst out onto a rooftop.

A woman screamed, Riot stepped off the edge of the roof, and Isobel rushed to the side of the building. A girl in a flimsy silk shift huddled on one side of a fire escape, while Riot grappled with a large highbinder. The man was familiar to Isobel. She had an imprint of his foot on her stomach.

The highbinder had a hatchet in hand, and Riot had both of his locked around his opponent's wrist, trying to keep the blade at bay, while he was pounded with kicks. The man laughed, and bashed his head into Riot's face.

Isobel aimed her gun, and fired. The pinging echo of metal registered a split second before fire laced across her thigh. Her shot had ricocheted off the railing. She bit back a curse, thrust her gun into her pocket, and leapt down onto the fire escape. Her wounded leg gave out, and she landed with a thud on her side.

Sparks flew as the hatchet scraped along a rusty rail. Riot drew his gun, smoke filled the space between, and he was slammed back against a railing. The entire fire escape shuddered, and groaned. His revolver fell, clattering against metal as it spiraled its way down. An anchor snapped, and the hulk of metal tilted at a severe angle.

Both men lost their balance. Riot bent precariously back against the railing, and the big highbinder was thrown his way. His opponent took advantage of momentum, and locked his hands around Riot's throat.

The need to get that man away from Riot was overwhelming. Isobel grabbed the highbinder's long queue, and wrapped it around a metal support. She put her feet against the wall, and heaved with the strength she used to hoist a mainsail. It wrenched the highbinder backwards. He lost his footing, and fell against the stair with a thud. A rapid-fire series of groans and snapping sped down the side of the building, as the anchors on one side gave way entirely.

Isobel scrambled for purchase, as hatchets and guns

slid over the grate, and clattered their way down. Mei started to slide, too. She grasped weakly at the rails, but her fingers slipped. As she slid, Isobel grabbed her around the waist, and held on tight.

The metal shuddered. Riot grunted, and Isobel looked down the sloping fire escape. He dangled off the edge. His fingers were hooked on the metal grating, and the high-binder brought up his foot to stomp down on Riot's hand. Anchored by his queue, the highbinder was careless of his balance, not at all at risk of falling. He stomped on Riot's hand again.

Isobel hooked the girl's arm around a railing, and reached into her pocket, taking out her Tickler. As the metal shuddered with every stomp and grunt of pain, she started sawing on his queue. The highbinder's heel slammed down again, and Riot fell. The hair gave way, and the highbinder pitched forward, tumbling over the railing as well.

Both men disappeared into the darkness between buildings, and a crash roared from that Stygian lane.

Isobel's heart stopped. She couldn't breathe, could not think. Every inch of her had fallen into that darkness. Mei lost her grip, and slipped, and Isobel reacted, grabbing her around the waist again. The girl was light, and weak, and rescuing her gave Isobel something to do. Bracing her feet, she punched at a flimsy wooden shutter. The wood splintered, revealing the interior—a small, cramped room of a rookery. A man stood in front with a broom handle raised. Behind him stood a woman and two children, cowering in the corner.

"Help us," Isobel said.

The man glanced at Mei, and stepped forward, pulling her inside. As soon as Mei was safe, Isobel scrambled down the twisted ladder of metal.

"Riot?" With a shaking hand, she pulled out her candle and matches. It took two failed attempts before she managed to light one. She called his name again. And then she saw him, lying on his back in the muck of the lane— bloodied, battered, and not moving. Isobel hurried over to him, skidding to a stop and dropping to her knees. She stuck her candle in the mud, and took his head in her hands, bending over him. Blood dripped from a gash in his forehead, staining his collar.

"Riot!" She pressed her hand over the gash. His chest rose as he sucked in a breath, and the eye that was able, opened.

Her heart began to beat again. She pressed her lips to his, blood and all, and when she pulled away he blinked in surprise.

There was puzzlement in that eye. "Who are you?"

The question hit her like a punch to the gut. She stared for long moments, stunned, and reeling. No answer came to her mind. And then he winked.

"You bastard," she said, slapping his chest.

Riot winced. "Ow," he said through gritted teeth.

"Sorry—no I'm not." She glared down at him, and then kissed him again.

"Marry me, Bel?" he murmured against her lips.

She pulled away. "You're delirious. How's your hand?"

"Probably broken." Riot slowly sat up, and with her help climbed to his feet. "I think I should stay away from fire escapes," he said, reaching into a pocket to retrieve a pristine handkerchief with his good hand.

As he wiped the blood from his face, she studied the brick wall, retracing his path. He must have caught the window underneath, and then slipped. No small surprise with his bloodied hand.

A thud echoed in the stillness. Isobel remembered where and when she was, and scrambled for the revolver in the muck. She aimed it straight at the noise. It came from a small shack jutting from the rookery. The roof was half-caved in. Had the big highbinder fallen in there? Another thud shook the board, and it cracked.

"*Yiu!*" a small voice growled.

The board shuddered again, and Isobel lowered her gun. As Riot fumbled for his spectacles, Isobel limped over to the shaking shack. She picked up a metal railing slat that had fallen with the fire escape, and wedged it between two boards. With a bit of a pressure, the board cracked from its nails, and she helped it the rest of the way with a good tug.

As Riot approached with her little candle, the light illuminated the interior. Sao Jin stood in the shack, fists raised, braced to charge. A single bowl of rice lay scattered on the floor, along with an unshackled chain. Blood dripped from her nose, and her nostrils flared.

"Did you pick that lock?" Isobel asked, impressed. Her own lock picking skills were advancing at a less than desirable pace.

"No, I broke it with my teeth, *Faan Tung*."

"Impressive," Isobel said. "Maybe you should use those teeth of yours on the wood, too."

"I could have gotten out," Jin said defiantly.

"I'm sure you would have, but I figured you'd want to see Mei sooner rather than later."

Jin's eyes widened, not with rage, but with relief, and something close to hope.

The following hours were a blur. First, Isobel found herself bouncing in the back of an ambulance, with Mei laying on the cot, and Jin clutching her hand. Mei was weak, and exhausted, and her feet were bloody and swollen, deep lacerations crisscrossing her soles, but her eyes remained fixed on her young friend.

Then they were ushered into 920, and the moment the door shut, a small army of Chinese women and girls carried a string of food, hot tea, blankets, and bandages their way. Tobias was there, too—talking and gesturing as wildly as a hyper squirrel. Danger took some that way. Noting his excessive energy, Donaldina put Tobias to work straightaway, and that quieted him for some blissful minutes.

As Riot gave his report to Sergeant Price and Donaldina Cameron, Ling hovered over him, cleaning the gash on his forehead. Isobel sat in a daze, leaning against the wall, half-listening and feeling as if she were melting into the bricks.

When the squad of police had come charging down the fire escape and into the alleyway, she had nearly bolted until Riot grabbed her arm. Police made her uneasy when she was in her male garb. Worse, Sgt. Price struck her as a man with sharp eyes.

"We were able to round up a few of the highbinders, but Big Queue wasn't one of them," Price was saying. He was a taciturn man with a fine mustache.

"He's slippery for a big man," Donaldina said.

"And notoriously dangerous," Price said. "You're lucky to be alive, A.J."

"He is *barely* alive," Ling corrected. "How are you going to give me away if you die?"

"I swear I will wait to die until after your wedding, Ling."

She sighed, and wrung out her cloth. As she dipped the

cloth in her disinfectant, her eyes flickered to Isobel, and widened with alarm. "*Ai ya!*" Ling exclaimed. "You are bleeding."

A small puddle was forming around her boot. Riot moved immediately to her side, took a knife from his jacket, and widened the hole in her trousers. A round hole in her thigh was leaking blood.

"Who shot you?" he asked.

Isobel frowned in thought. She felt muddled and distant, and poked at the hole with her finger. It hurt. When she remembered her ricocheting shot, she cleared her throat. "A, erm… highbinder from across the way." It was fortunate she'd only had a Shopkeeper, and not a Peacemaker. In the struggle, in the fear, in the rush of the moment and the wave of relief, she had forgotten all about the pain in her thigh.

Riot cocked his head. "I don't recall a second highbinder."

"He was there," she said firmly.

"Ah, yes, the one on the *railing*."

Isobel glared.

"We'll summon a doctor," Riot said.

Her fingers brushed the lump of lead under her flesh, and she bit back an oath. "I can make it home, Riot. It's not deep."

"We can make up a room for you," Donaldina offered.

"No really, some hot water and pliers will do."

The women ignored her. "I'll get hot water," Ling said.

"And I'll let the doctor know," Donaldina said. He was currently with Mei. As both women left, Price excused himself after getting Riot's promise that he would stop by the Chinatown Police Headquarters at a later date.

Alone, sitting on a bench, Riot laid his head back.

"Well, that didn't go as planned."

"Does it ever?"

His splinted fingers brushed her thigh. "No," he admitted. "It never does."

50

Restless Detectives

Thursday, March 7, 1900

THE SUN WAS FULL by the time Isobel, Tobias, and Riot dragged themselves back to Ravenwood manor. While Riot left to check in with Tim and tell Kau that his sister was safe, Isobel limped into the kitchen, and Tobias tried to skulk right past his mother's domain.

"Tobias White," Lily said. "Get back here this instant." The boy dragged his feet every inch of the way, until he stood next to Isobel.

She was relieved to see Sarah sitting safely at the table. Margaret had returned her, and was sitting with the others sipping tea. As soon as she caught sight of Isobel, she rose, and hurried over. "You look the worse for wear... erm?" Margaret glanced at Sarah, who had rushed over too.

"Mr. Amsel?" Sarah asked. The poor girl was utterly confused. Damn Lotario, and his careless ways.

"Henry Morgan," Isobel introduced.

"Oh, like the pirate?" asked Margaret.

"But you look exactly like Mr. Amsel," Sarah persisted. As soon as Sarah said the name, Margaret's eyes narrowed in thought. And then recognition.

"Remarkable, isn't it?" Isobel patted the girl's shoulder, resisting the urge to knock her over the head.

"What happened?" Margaret asked, trying to distract the precocious girl.

"I'll tell you later." She squeezed Margaret's hand. "Everything that you're probably already thinking."

But Sarah wouldn't be put off that easily. "You look exactly like Miss Bonnie, too."

"She's my cousin."

Tobias snorted. "As if you're foolin' anyone, Miss Bonnie."

His mother smacked the back of his head, and Grimm chuckled silently. Lily shot her children a firm look. "We are who we say we are, isn't that right?"

Isobel sighed. She had not been very careful. "I'm tired, and the bullet hole in my leg is starting to hurt. I apologize for attempting to deceive you all. But if it gets out that I'm running around dressed as Mr. Morgan, and look anything like that other fellow..." She looked pointedly at Sarah. "I'll either end up in jail, or an asylum. Can you all keep my secret?"

"We all have things we don't want aired in the light, *Mr. Morgan*," Lily said. "It won't leave this room. Isn't that right, Tobias?"

The boy looked at his toes. "Yes, ma'am."

Isobel wanted to disappear. She wanted to melt into the floorboards. Why had she made friends? Why had she inserted herself so carelessly, without plan or plot, into this household?

"I can't thank you enough for retrieving my boy," Lily said. "Have a seat, and I'll get you some breakfast."

"I'm not fit for this kitchen," Isobel said.

"Oh, don't worry," Maddie snickered. "Tobias is going to clean it spotless with a toothbrush."

"Honestly, we wouldn't have rescued the girls if it weren't for Sarah and him." That wasn't entirely true, but despite (or due to) Tobias' sharp eyes, Isobel found she had a sudden soft spot for adventurous children on the verge of being grounded for life.

"I'll have a talk with him about that later. Maddie, would you please go pour Mr. Morgan a bath, and make up his room. Sarah can stay in yours if need be."

"Yes, ma'am."

"You should have seen it, Ma." The boy was bouncing in his seat.

"Hush," Lily said. "Sarah's told me some of it already, and I'm not sure I want to hear about the rest of the trouble you got yourself into."

"It was terrifying," Sarah said, softly.

Margaret put a hand around the girl's shoulder, and hugged her close. "You did fine."

With everyone safe, Isobel murmured her apologies and gratitude, and shuffled towards the stairs. She paused in the front hall, staring at the door. She should leave this house and never come back. There were too many discerning eyes, too many caring hearts.

Isobel grabbed the knob, preparing to leave them in peace, but a rasping creak of a stair pulled her back. She looked to the stairway, expecting to see Maddie, or another mysterious boarder, but it was empty. Old houses often whispered to their exhausted guests.

She glanced upwards, to the chandelier that had once

held two effigies with death threats dangling from their ankles. And from there, she walked into the sitting room, and stared through the second parlour, into the dining room.

The table gleamed as she drifted closer. But instead of a head on a platter, there was a simple bouquet of wild flowers. This house knew danger. It knew death, and even if she left, it would know it again. Atticus Riot sat in the center of a web that had been spun long before she came along. Everyone in this house was in danger; everyone had something to hide. She felt it in her bones. But it was home. And one does not run away from that.

Digging in her mental heels, Isobel climbed the stairs, and went into the hallway bath.

"Thank you, Maddie."

"I'll bring in some fresh clothes. You want me to take away the ones you're wearing?" The girl wrinkled her nose. "I'll send them straight to the launderer."

"I suppose."

"Er, unless you're wanting to be Mr. Morgan again?"

"Miss Bonnie will do."

After the girl left with a bundle of torn and filthy clothing, Isobel sank into the steamy bath. Hot water might have had something to do with her tendency to end up at Ravenwood manor. It was an irresistible lure, and she'd been too exhausted to resist it.

She scrubbed until the water was murky, drained the tub, and refilled it again. When her skin glowed, she lay back and stared at the ceiling until the water turned cold. A third bath was tempting, but she doubted she'd ever be able to drag herself out.

Wrapping Riot's old robe around her, she walked into one of the adjoining bedrooms, and lay on the narrow bed. But sleep eluded her. The sun was bright and shining, and she had passed the point of sleep. She was restless, and questions rattled around her head.

With a frustrated growl, she tossed back the covers, and walked softly to the door. She cracked it open and peered into the hallway. The house was quiet; it seemed empty. Most people, she remembered, spent their lives in daylight —not during those hours when the fog was at its thickest.

Isobel dressed in a skirt and blouse, and limped quickly towards Riot's room. She knocked softly, wondering if he had succumbed to exhaustion from the night, or if he was as restless as she. There was no answer. She started to turn away, but stopped, and tried the door handle instead. It opened.

Atticus Riot stood in front of a cold hearth. A glass of water was in his left hand, and his right hung at his side, two fingers wrapped together in heavy bandage. She slipped inside, closed the door and turned the key, but he didn't stir. His hair was damp and wild, and his beard as immaculate as ever. He wore a shirt, but it was unbuttoned and his braces hung at his waist, as if he had given up dressing partway through. She eyed the bruises blossoming on his ribs.

"Are you going somewhere, Riot?" she asked. Her voice brought his head up, and he reached for his spectacles. He looked lost in his own room.

"I didn't feel much like sleeping." His voice was at odds with his words. He sounded tired enough. She should have gone with him to see Kau.

"May I come in?"

"You don't need to ask." As she closed the distance, he quickly set down his drink, and started buttoning up his shirt with one hand.

"Did everything go all right with Kau?"

"He's grateful," Riot said. "He'd like to visit his sister before he leaves."

"Leaves? You mean straight to jail?" She eyed the plaster on his forehead, wondering if he'd hit his head as hard as she first feared.

"I'm certainly not going to turn him in for killing a man like Andrew Ross. Self-defense or no, a court won't think twice about hanging a Chinese for killing a white man, and as for the rest," he gestured vaguely at his head, "I believe in second chances."

"What about the girls he turned into slaves?"

"Kau has a *chun hung* on his head, Bel. Every hatchet man in the West will be gunning for him. I doubt he'll make it far."

"And if he does?"

"Who am I to judge another man? I've done some things in my time that would get me hanged as sure as any other."

"That's noble of you," she said. "I'd definitely want you sitting behind a desk with a gavel if it were my trial."

"I'm hardly impartial where you're concerned."

"I think that goes for a lot of men and women. You're a fair man, Riot. But do you believe Kau? That his tong wasn't behind Ravenwood's murder?"

"Whatever happened, I'm convinced that he truly believes they're innocent." He looked back to the cold hearth. "I may never know the truth of what happened that night."

"There's a whole heap of questions left," she said with a sigh. "I feel like we only scratched the surface on that clubhouse in Ocean Beach. Why was Andrew Ross carrying around cards with Lincoln Howe's name? And what *was* Ravenwood working on?" Those questions had been spinning in her mind while she bathed, and were making her as restless as the sea before a storm.

Riot turned slightly towards her. "Is that why you're still on land? There's still a mystery left?"

She smiled. "Partly."

"The other reason?"

"Did you forget that note I gave you?"

"Those words are etched in my mind, and on my heart, Miss Bel."

"Good." She closed the distance, and slowly unbuttoned his shirt. She placed her hand on his chest, over that heart, and soaked up the warmth of his flesh. She felt his breath catch, saw his pupils dilate with desire, and sensed his muscles tense with energy.

She pressed her lips suddenly to his. Her teeth scraped his lip for a second, and she pulled away like a fish flirting with a hook.

"Are you worried I'm drowning again?" he asked.

"Yes," she whispered. "I wanted to give you something simple to focus on."

"Consider me focused."

"Good, I was wondering if you remembered proposing to me?"

"You said I was delirious."

"Were you?" she asked.

Riot leaned forward, his beard brushing her cheek as he whispered in her ear. "Marry me, Bel?" Her knees went weak.

"I'm dead, Riot."

"Then haunt me," he said with feeling.

"Don't you have enough ghosts?"

"I prefer you."

"You still haven't kissed me."

"Haven't I?"

"Not properly."

"May I?" he asked politely.

"I thought you were going to surprise me?"

"Only a fool would surprise you."

The edge of her lips quirked. It was too much. Tired, drained, with all his defenses down, Riot gave in to impulse. He kissed that quirk, and pulled her close, his mouth coming down on hers. It was slow and deep, and all consuming. And when his teeth scraped against a spot just below her ear, it traveled through her body like a jolt. Her neck arched, and she inhaled sharply, aching for more.

Riot smiled against that spot on her neck. "I thought so," he murmured. It was a deliciously dangerous sort of purr.

Isobel drifted in an ocean. It was warm, and soft, and she moved up and down with each gentle swell. Her mind was still, as calm as a windless sea. And the heart beating under her ear lured her back to the surface.

She loved the sound of that heart.

"So this is how it's supposed to be," she breathed. "I see what all the fuss is about now."

Sunlight shone through the cracks in the curtains, but the air was crisp and cool, and it brushed her skin. Strong arms tightened around her, and Riot buried his fingers in her short hair. Only to wince. She kissed the bruise over his collarbone.

"Broken fingers, a gunshot wound, and a near concussion aren't generally involved." His voice was deep and soothing in the stillness.

"We managed."

"You can slap that on my gravestone."

She snorted, and stretched, reaching for the blanket that had ended up on the floor, along with their clothing. She pulled it over them, and settled on her back, with her head resting on his arm.

They drifted for a time, with the lazy kind of warmth that made her forget where she ended and he began. Isobel felt herself edging towards sleep. But at the last possible moment, her mind rebelled, tossing out a question that she had no answer to.

"Atticus James Riot." She tasted the name on her lips as she had tasted his skin only minutes before. "Did your mother have grandiose ideas for you?"

A lazy chuckle shook his body. "You're going to laugh at me," he said, rolling onto his side. His fingers idly circled her hip bone. It was divine.

"Never."

"I might believe you if you didn't have that glint in your eyes," he said.

"You're imagining things." She waited, enjoying his lazy exploration.

Color rose in the skin above his beard. "I named myself," he admitted.

Rather than laugh, Isobel felt a pang in her breast. She swallowed it down.

"I thought it sounded important," he continued. "For as long as I could remember everyone called me A.J. And I never thought to ask what it stood for. By the time I did my mother had already died."

Isobel wished she had laughed before—to soften the gravity of his words. She rolled onto her side to meet his eyes, slipping a leg between his own.

"Andrew Jackson? Andy Jacob?" she mused aloud.

Riot gave a crooked grin, showing off his two chipped teeth. She liked those teeth, and that smile.

"No, wait. I have it. Abe Jeremiah," she announced.

Riot propped his head on his good hand, waiting for more, brown eyes dancing with amusement.

"Aubrey John," she said with an official air. "That is most definitely it."

He kissed the hollow of her throat, and she closed her eyes. The next name was a simple sigh.

"What about Riot?" she asked breathlessly.

"I got my surname from a penny dreadful."

A burst of laughter filled the room.

51

A Blossom in the Wind

Friday, March 8, 1900

SAO JIN SAT AT Mei's bedside. The young woman *was* beautiful—unearthly, even in sickness.

"Jin refuses to leave her side," Donaldina said, softly. "I finally had a washbasin brought in here."

Jin hadn't looked at any of them when they entered; instead, she held Mei's hand like a lifeline. And Mei held hers.

The young woman's feet were propped up, lathered in a green salve that smelled of herbs.

"She'll recover with time," Donaldina said.

"How is the girl you found the night before?" Isobel asked.

Donaldina shook her head. "She died this morning."

"I'm sorry to hear," Riot said.

"At least she died with her sister." Donaldina gave him

a weak smile, and he nodded in return, grasping her hand momentarily in support. Isobel wondered how many abused and discarded girls had died in this house, and how many had these mission women nursed back to life?

Mei stirred, and her eyes opened. She shifted, smiling weakly at Jin. Then her large, dark eyes fluttered over to the trio in the doorway. Mei beckoned them in with a soft word.

Jin glanced at Isobel. "*Faan Tung.*"

"*Wai Daan,*" Isobel returned, sticking out her tongue.

Mei gasped, and said something quick and reprimanding in Cantonese. Jin lowered her eyes, and nodded. And Mei blushed, offering an apology that Riot translated. "Please, forgive her. She is young and angry, and has known nothing but hate for many years."

"I understand," Isobel said. "Unfortunately, I don't have any excuse for my tongue."

"You are too kind," Mei said softly. "Thank you for rescuing us."

"You nearly rescued yourself," Riot said. "You were halfway there on the beach that night. It was very brave of you to go back to the men—to save Jin."

Mei shook her head. "I feared for Jin. We *had* to escape. She was a *Mui Tsai*—house slave—but it was only a matter of time before they started selling her to men. They would have placed her in a low crib, or worse sent her to a mining camp. I could not live with that." A mining camp was the most brutal kind of life there was for a slave girl. Girls there did not live long.

"I was shocked to see Kau again."

"So he *is* your brother?" Riot asked.

Mei inclined her head. Even sitting in bed, propped on pillows, she looked like a queen holding court. "When I received his message in the brothel, I could not bear to hope that it was really him, and then we were moved again."

Mei lowered her eyes. "Jin has told me everything—everything that you have done for her and Kau. And everything that my brother did to you, Mr. Riot." Her gaze flickered to the white stripe slashing through Riot's raven hair. "Kau was a kind older brother. He was a good man. Please, I beg you, not to think ill of him. Many of these men are like scared boys—lonely and aching for their home. They are as trapped as I was."

Not quite, Isobel thought when Riot had translated, but the girl's compassion struck her straight to the heart. Even after all she had been through, Mei still saw the good in others. It was admirable, and courageous, and the girl was far better than Isobel could ever be.

"Were you sold to someone other than Sing Chung Lee?" asked Riot.

Mei shook her head. "He became bored with me, and placed me in the Forbidden Palace to make money. And then the brick house. After we tried to run, the white men were angry with my keeper, and sent me away in shame," Mei continued. "I was happy to know that they had not found Jin, though. She caused them much anger." She smiled at her younger friend, and squeezed her hand. "Sing Chung Lee was furious with me for losing his tong's face. He had my feet whipped, so my beauty would not be marred, but my feet would remember if I should ever think to run again."

Tears glistened in her eyes, and Jin murmured something, bending forward and pressing her forehead against Mei's hands.

"You're safe now, Mei," Donaldina said. "If you like I'll

draw up adoption papers. You can stay here as long as you wish."

But the kind words had the opposite effect on Jin. The girl sprang to her feet, her features twisting with rage. "You lie! You gave me to the police!" Jin screamed. "To the woman who sold me as a *Mui Tsai*! You will give Mei to the men." Her hands balled into tight fists.

Donaldina blinked in surprise. She had had no idea that the girl spoke English. The surprise lasted for a moment, before Donaldina raised her hands in peace. "Jin, I can only offer you my sincere apologies. Some police, attorneys, and judges take money from the tongs. They are corrupt, and they use the law against us. But that's no excuse—I failed you that day." There was pain in her voice. "You're not the first child I have failed, and I doubt you'll be the last. There wasn't a day that went by I didn't think of you—that I wasn't looking for you. You are not the first girl to be taken from me under the guise of the law. All I can say is that I *am* sorry. You can stay with Mei if you like, or go. No one is forcing you to remain."

Jin lifted her chin. But the reality slowly sank in. Where else would she go? Her chin lost some of its defiance. "I will stay with Mei."

Donaldina nodded. "I'll start sorting out the paperwork, then."

"Mei," Riot said. "Your brother Kau would like to see you when you are ready. Do you want to speak with him?"

"Yes," Mei breathed. "Please, I need to speak with him. I will go to him if it is better."

"You need to stay off your feet until you heal," Donaldina said. "And I'll not let a highbinder inside these walls—repentant or not. It would undermine the safety and trust that we work hard to build with our girls."

Isobel could understand that completely. Worse, what if one of the girls recognized Kau—what if he had beaten or bought them. It would strike terror in a survivor.

"When you're healed, then," Riot said. "I'll arrange a meeting."

"And after the adoption papers are drawn," Donaldina added.

A scream torn from rage and grief shattered the peace of the house. It bounced off the bricks, and slammed into the room. Isobel tensed, as voices raised, and footsteps padded quickly down the hallway. Another raging howl, and a crash joined the tumult.

Ling darted into the room. "*Lo Mo! Lo Mo!* Ini is having a fit again."

Something crashed, wood splintered, and Donaldina took Riot's hand, and then Isobel's. There was a twinkle in her eye. "A pleasure to meet you, sir." With a breath, she plunged back into the hallway, and Ling poked her head inside.

"Do not worry; some girls rage. It will pass." Ling backed out, and closed the door as angry screams echoed through the house. Isobel was struck by the despair and joy these bricks had seen. She looked at Jin. The girl's teeth were clenched.

"Jin," Isobel said. "You're angry, too. And rightly so. But I still don't understand why the cigar man was so keen to get you when they already had Mei."

"What?" the girl spat. "I am not pretty enough?" Jin traced the scars on her cheeks, and fluttered her eyes.

"You know as well as I that men aren't overly concerned about looks," she said bluntly.

The direct answer stole some of Jin's wind. She deflated, and nodded, looking thoughtful.

"That man—when he tossed you in the wagon—he told the driver to have your keeper throw you in the hospital. They wanted you dead without dirtying their own hands," Isobel said. She let that sink in for a moment. "Did you overhear something in that house, or see something?"

Jin raised a shoulder. "I saw and heard many things."

"What?"

"Groaning, moaning, grunting—do you want me to repeat every piggish word?" Jin smirked, but neither Riot nor Isobel reacted to her vulgarity.

"I mean anything of import," Isobel said.

"Men talking money. Men talking women. Men talking horses. Smoking, and drinking, and shooting balls around a table. All they ever do."

"Some men are more civilized," Isobel said.

"A shallow pool has many appearances."

"Then what were these men reflecting? What business? What horses?" she pressed.

"I heard many names," Jin said.

"Do you remember any of them?"

"I remember *everything*," Jin hissed.

She felt Riot's fingers brush her elbow. A gentle reminder to tread carefully. This was about the time he should take over, before she lost patience and said something that would make Jin shut up like a clam. She glanced at him, giving him his cue.

"Jin, we're trying to help you," he said calmly. "The couple who took you from this mission—they used the law against you. Now you have the chance to return the favor. The more we know, the more likely we can use the same law against the men in that brick building."

The words oiled the gears in her calculating eyes. But whereas Isobel simply moved pieces around a board, Sao

Jin had a fire lit in her eyes that Isobel found disturbing in one so young.

"Do you want me to tell everything now?"

"Can you write?" Riot asked.

"Not Chinese," Jin said. "It is very hard, but English is simple. I learned ABCs very fast."

"We'll get you some paper, and while you sit with Mei, you both can write down every name, every place, every conversation you can remember. Will you do that?" Riot asked.

"Yes."

"Good."

Mei looked to the trio of English speakers in confusion and frustration. Riot quickly translated the gist of their conversation, and Mei glanced at her young, angry friend. She said something, and from the way Riot tensed, Isobel knew it was of import. It was her turn to wait while an incomprehensible conversation flowed around her.

When they fell silent, Riot shifted, considering what he had heard. "Mei reminded Jin that she had seen someone in the Forbidden Palace—a white man with a trim beard like mine, except blond, and longish hair. He was straight as a board, and very precise. Jin heard him referred to as *Si Fu*—the Master. He seemed to be the owner of the establishment."

"A white man owns that place?"

"I doubt his name is on anything official."

"I doubt his name is the Master," she said. "Although maybe he's named himself, too."

"Far more pretentious than mine."

"Only a pinch, Riot." Mention of yesterday and last night distracted him for a moment, and the way he looked at her made her heart gallop with the same memories.

She cleared her throat. "Was there, uhm, anything else?" She felt suddenly breathless.

His eyes turned hard along with his voice. "When the Madam saw that Jin had seen him, she flew into a rage, and beat her."

Emotion turned sour in Isobel's throat. "Maybe Kau knows something more."

"Maybe." He sounded doubtful.

Another question to add to her growing list. Isobel felt like a fly trapped in a web that was ever expanding, and now she was waiting for the spider to make an appearance.

"I will start now," Jin said. "How much paper do you have?"

52

The Soothing Sea

Sunday, March 11, 1900

ATTICUS RIOT HELPED MEI down the plank, and lifted her into the cutter. She could walk with help. Barely. But every day her brother spent in San Francisco put him at risk. The time was now, or never.

Mei leaned heavily against Riot's arm, and let her gaze travel over the bay. She closed her eyes, feeling the ocean air against her cheeks. Color had returned to her, and Isobel was struck by the woman's beauty. Despite everything that had happened to her, she glowed from within.

"Your brother is in the cabin," Riot said to her. "Are you sure you want to see him?"

"I do."

As Isobel scurried back and forth along her cutter preparing to set sail, Mei inhaled the scent of freedom "My father and mother lived by the sea," Mei said. "You will love it when we are back in China, Jin. When we return to my village by the sea."

Jin crossed her arms. She sat in the cockpit, looking stubborn and angry, watching Isobel out of the corner of her eye.

Isobel surveyed the bay. It was early morning, and the sky was strangely clear. The sea was as flat as glass near the wharf. But farther out the water rippled from the constant breeze that blew in through the narrow Golden Gate.

A flood tide pushed the fenders against the wharf, and the harbor was packed full with boats. There'd be no sailing from dock.

"Jin, can you untie that dinghy?" she asked as she walked to the bow with a long line. The girl did not move. "If you can't," she called over her shoulder, "I understand. It's not easy, and you don't know a thing about sailing."

Isobel could feel the dark-eyed glare burn into her back, and then soft footsteps vibrated her deck. Isobel smiled to herself, as she started flaking the line down the deck. When Jin had freed the dinghy, Isobel tied one end of the line to a bow cleat, and walked to the stern. Gathering the kedge anchor and its rode, she carried it back, and secured the other end of the line to the anchor rode with a sheet bend.

"Now comes the hard part," Isobel said, lightly. "How much can you lift?"

"Anything you can," Jin said.

"Good. Hold this." She handed the anchor to the girl, who staggered under the thirty pound weight.

Isobel quickly directed her to the rail, and helped her rest the anchor there. Having nearly dropped it, Jin tensed, as if expecting a blow, but Isobel quickly wrapped the line around a pin, and took it from her hands, and carefully lowered the anchor, letting it dangle off the bow.

"Wait here," Isobel said easily. She lowered the dinghy into the water, and climbed overboard. Picking up the oars, she rowed forward, and grabbed the kedge anchor. "Unwind that warp."

Jin looked puzzled.

"The line…erm, the rope around the pin," Isobel explained.

Jin did as she was told, and Isobel placed the anchor in the dinghy. "Do you want to come?"

Instead of answering, Jin climbed over the rail before she could stop her. Isobel quickly grabbed her around the waist, and sat her down. "Don't get your feet tangled in the warp."

She took up the oars, and started to row, and Jin watched, as the line attached to the cutter's bow cleat slithered after them in the water.

"What are you doing?" Jin finally asked.

"There's no wind, no room, and the tide is coming in, knocking the Lady against the wharf. This is called kedging. We'll go out a good distance, drop the kedge anchor, and then go back to the Lady, and haul her out to deeper waters."

"It is a lot of work," Jin said. "Why don't you take the ferry?"

"We figured Mei would like to spend some time with her brother. It might be the last time they see each other." She did not add that the ferries were likely being watched, and that hatchet men with guns were searching for Wong Kau.

Jin wrinkled her nose. "I do not want anything to do with a highbinder. I should have let him die. I do not care what Mei says, they are bad men." Her fingers kept plucking at her sleeve, fraying the threads. Jin always wore long ones, and Isobel wondered what those sleeves hid.

"But you didn't."

"Mei asked me to watch him, so I did."

"And that was good of you," Isobel said. "Mei seems happy."

"Yes."

"How do you like the mission?"

"I hate it."

"It's a home," Isobel said.

"It is a cage." Jin scowled, defying her to argue, but then she softened. "Mei is there, though."

"I don't much care for walls, either," Isobel admitted. "That's why I love sailing."

"Will you teach me?" It was the first hint of hope, the first stirring of interest Isobel had glimpsed in the girl. Her eyes were fixed on the anchor, though. As if that flutter of hope pained her too much.

"If you want, but you might not like it."

Jin looked up, eyes widening in surprise. "I will like it."

"You might get sick."

"I will not." The words weren't defiant, but full of conviction. That, too, gave Isobel hope.

"There's something I should warn you about though."

"What is that?"

"It's about the sea."

Jin waited.

"Even a rotten egg can hatch out here."

The girl cocked her head, and cast her gaze towards Angel Island, to the seagulls circling the fishing trawlers. Jin pressed her lips together, and scraped her palm across her eyes. She said nothing more.

In the hours that followed, Jin took in everything. Eager to help and learn, and haul double her weight in work.

When the sails were full, and the water rushed steadily around the hull, Isobel let her take the tiller while she made adjustments to the jib sail. The girl kept her steady, as if born to the sea.

The trip across the bay was pleasant, and peaceful. Kau and Mei emerged, and sat on the cabin trunk and talked. She smiled often, and her laughter bounced across the waters.

And during that time, Riot opened the basket that Miss Lily had prepared earlier. Isobel smiled at him as he handed her a plate of cold cuts, cheese, and fruit.

"I could get used to a galley cook," she said when he produced a bottle of red wine.

"I do a fair job of lighting fires, too."

Isobel looked into his eyes. "You certainly do."

Riot popped the cork, and sat beside her. Isobel basked in his company, and Jin kept the Lady steady while they ate. The girl's hands seemed to be glued to the wood, and no matter how they tried, she would not be persuaded to let go long enough to eat, until Isobel showed her how to tie the tiller in place.

But the journey was bittersweet. When Isobel piloted her cutter into a nameless inlet near Vallejo, it was time for brother and sister to say their goodbyes. Kau handed his sister a small fortune, and left with a slight nod to Riot, who returned it just as stiffly.

Tears ran down Mei's cheeks as Isobel pointed the Lady towards San Francisco. Riot gently coaxed the distraught girl below deck to rest.

"We made the lists," Jin said. She had been completely silent for most of the afternoon, watching Mei with her brother. Isobel had not known what was going through her mind. She was a difficult one to read.

Jin reached into her padded jacket, and held out a bundle of folded papers. The stack was tied with twine. Isobel draped an arm over the tiller, and accepted the bundle.

Burning with curiosity, Isobel glanced towards the bow, saw a clear path, and asked Jin to hold her steady. When the girl had a firm grip on the handle, Isobel moved to the cover of the hatch, half perching on the companionway as she started to read the stack. The letters were deep and slanting, and tore through the pages in places.

"I wanted to be sure," Jin said. It was clear as day that writing this down had not been easy for her. Her spelling could have used some work, but overall it was legible.

"I'm sure it will—" A name on the list caught her eye. She looked sharply at Jin. "This man, Lei Wok Air, what did you overhear about him?"

53

The Uncle

CAMERON FRY LEFT WITH a spring in his step, and a note-book clutched to his chest. An exclusive interview was reason for celebration. Sarah Byrne had turned her Southern charm on full, dazzling the young reporter. More importantly, she hadn't mentioned a thing about her ordeal the week before. For that, Riot breathed easy. Almost.

"Sarah, can I speak with your uncle alone?" Riot asked.

Lee Walker had insisted on being present for the interview. He had put on a good performance as a concerned uncle, but Riot hadn't bought any of it. And he still wasn't buying it.

Sarah stood, and nodded. And as she walked out, Riot closed the doors on Tobias, who had eavesdropped on the entire interview.

Riot turned to find Walker studying the inkblots, biological drawings of animals, and human nervous and skeletal systems on the wall. Ravenwood had had an odd sense of decor, and Riot hadn't bothered to have them taken down.

"I know Sarah isn't keen on coming home with me today, but I assure you, Mr. Riot, she will be safe with me," Walker said without turning to face him. His arm was still in a sling, and for some inexplicable reason, he walked with a cane now. A narrow bandage wound around his head, too.

"In fact," Walker drawled, "she'll live like a queen, and want for nothing."

"*If* you win your case," Riot said. "If you don't, you'll still be digging into your Levis."

Walker turned from a pinned butterfly in a frame, and faced him. "I see you've been looking into my affairs." His voice was hard.

"It's a habit of mine," Riot said easily.

"Every man falls on hard times once in a while."

"But not every man falls into a gold mine *twice*."

Walker's hand tightened around his cane. "I don't like your tone, Mr. Riot."

"Of course you don't. You prefer horse races, saloons, gambling halls, and whores." Riot sat down in an armchair, and crossed his legs.

"I'm no different than any other man. And I don't much like the idea of Sarah staying with you any longer. It's clear as day from the bruises on your face that you ran into some rough trouble."

"I fell," Riot said dryly.

"I'll take my leave, and I'll take my niece." Walker reached for the doors.

"You best stay, Mr. Walker."

He spun. "And why is that?"

"I know about your accident in Chicago. You were hit by a rail car, and dislocated your shoulder. You sued the city for a hefty sum."

Walker's hand fell away from the door. "It was an unfortunate accident."

"I don't know about that. You were compensated well."

"Bad luck turned good. And as before I hope to settle all my debts."

"It never came out—during that trial—that you were an escape artist in the Ringling Circus."

Walker licked his lips. "What do you want? Do you want a cut? Is that it?"

Riot shook his head. "I don't care that you're trying to get change from a silver baron. I do, however, care about Sarah's welfare. I'm looking for information."

"Information? I don't follow."

"Your name came up in another investigation of mine. In connection with a Mr. Parker Gray."

Walker paled. He looked like a man with a gun to his head—the hammer cocked and ready, and Riot's finger already squeezing the trigger.

"I don't want to know any names. These aren't the type of men you rat out."

"I imagine not, but I've been hired by Claiborne's attorney to investigate you. One word from me, and you won't have a penny in your pocket to pay them. No more home, no more manservant—"

"Manservant?" There was genuine confusion in Walker's eyes.

"The Chinese man who answered your door while you were in the hospital."

"I don't have any Chinese servants. I have a housekeeper who comes once a day, that's it."

"He was in your home. Maybe he was sent to collect, and you lucked out again."

Walker shook his head. "I'm settled at the tracks."

Riot cocked his head. "How so?"

"I had this fellow at the Palm—Freddy. He always had good advice, and never steered me wrong, but this last time... his banker turned out to be a dud. I wagered more than I had, and lost everything and then some. It was going to be my last bet—I swear. I wanted to set Sarah up real nice."

Riot waited.

"I found two men waiting inside my house one night. They said if I wanted to clean my slate I had to do something for them. They knew about my past—knew about the settlement in Chicago—and they wanted me to do it again. With Mr. Claiborne."

"Did they pick the property?"

Walker nodded.

"What did these men look like?"

"A big, pugilist-type fellow. Busted nose, big knuckles— and another fellow, black hair, a sculpted beard, and a cigar, but it wasn't lit. He just chewed on it."

"Have they contacted you since you pulled off the accident?"

He shook his head.

"Did they provide the attorney?"

"They gave me his card. It was his idea to leave Sarah waiting at the ferry building."

A spineless, witless con man. And a lying one. "You're not telling me the whole truth, Walker."

"Why would I lie to you?"

"Because you're scared witless."

"They knew everything about me!" Walker hissed. "And they knew about Sarah."

"So you were set up? How much of a cut do they get?"

"My debt at the tracks was canceled the moment I fell down that shaft," Walker said. "And I get ten percent of what's left after the attorney gets his retainer fee."

"Why do you think they went to all that trouble for a settlement that might or might not be won?"

"I don't know," Walker said, desperate. "Like I said I didn't ask questions."

Riot considered the man, and he swallowed nervously under that unwavering gaze. "Here's the thing, Walker. It only took a few telegrams to discover that you injured your shoulder in Chicago, and that you received a hefty settlement for it. Now at best, Kingston will play it off as a previous injury that you aggravated when you fell down his client's cellar. At worst he'll put two and two together, and dig into your past a bit more. My money is on the latter. Fraud will get you two years, but there's a chance that Claiborne won't want his name dragged through the papers anymore than it already has been. In fact, Kingston mentioned that very thing. If you drop the case, I doubt Claiborne will press charges."

"I have other debts."

"You owe tailors, saloons, grocers—they're not the type to break your knees. I suggest you secure a job for yourself."

"But," Walker stammered, "I haven't worked in years."

"It's like riding a horse."

"I'll split my earnings with you. I'll give you fifty percent of my cut."

"When I don't turn up a single thing, Kingston will hire another detective. These men you're dealing with aren't dense."

"I'll take my chances in court," Walker said. "And if I don't win the settlement, I'll get a loan, and earn my way at the tables."

"That's no life for Sarah."

"It will be. I'll provide for her."

"It's a precarious life. Drop your settlement, and start fresh, Walker."

Walker stood abruptly. "I'll be taking my leave, and I'll be taking Sarah home with me now. If what you say is true, then Kingston is likely to offer me a deal out of court before he finds out the truth."

A muscle in Riot's jaw twitched. He had no legal sway over the girl. "She's welcome to stay here until you settle your affairs."

"I don't think so, Mr. Riot."

"Then you can be sure I'll be checking in."

"Thank you, Mr. Riot," Sarah Byrne said. Her voice was muffled by his waistcoat, and her arms were around his waist. He smoothed back her hair, and looked down to see her smiling up at him.

"I'll be around to visit. You know how to find your way here." He had made sure of that.

Lee Walker picked up her suitcase, and ushered her towards the waiting hack. Riot stood on the sidewalk, watching as he helped Sarah inside. She, at least, appeared optimistic, and something her uncle said made her smile.

Walker shut the door, and ordered the hack forward without looking at Riot. The hack passed a familiar bicycle, and Riot saw a hand wave from the carriage window. The bicyclist waved back. Riot stood waiting until the hack disappeared, and Isobel had skidded to a stop in front of the manor.

She wore a simple straw hat and was dressed in a riding suit: snug jacket, tie and blouse, and riding breeches tucked into the top of tall leather boots. Her cheeks were fairly glowing with exertion, and perspiration curled the hair around her ears. The black dye was fading, and he wondered if she'd dye it again soon.

"Did he take your deal?" she asked.

"He intends to try his luck in the courts."

Isobel made a sound as she tugged off her gloves. "How much will you tell Kingston?"

"Only that Walker had a prior settlement. The case has already made its way across country. Whether or not I tell Kingston, someone else is bound to recall the suit in Chicago. It might as well be me." He told her the rest of the conversation. And she whistled low.

"Deep waters, Watson." Her brows drew together in frustration. "There's so much we still don't know."

"You found your body, and we rescued two girls. Not a bad day's work."

She lifted a shoulder. "I suppose not. Still, a good many questions remain. The foremost being where to start?"

"I'm sure you have our course laid out."

"A number of them, actually."

Riot nearly kissed her there in the lane, in broad daylight; instead, he held her eyes with his own and thought he'd drown. A number of long, pleasurable nights passed in that space. And a rare blush that only he was privy to spread over her cheeks.

Noting her limp, Riot gripped her handlebars, and took over walking her bicycle up the lane.

"Have you read the newspaper this morning?" she

asked.

"I haven't had the time. I breakfasted with Sarah, and then sat in on the interview with Cameron Fry."

"How did the new Austen fan conduct himself?"

"He was as gracious and polite as could be."

Isobel nodded with approval as she reached into her satchel and pulled out a newspaper. She pointed to an article.

Infamous Hatchet Man Wong Kau Gunned Down in Sacramento

The article claimed the Suey Sings had carried out the assassination, and added his name to a growing list of dead in the ongoing tong wars. But most newspapers couldn't be bothered with differentiating tongs, so they simply lumped the whole jumble into two different ones.

"I'm not surprised," Riot said after he finished reading.

"Well, I intend to set this story right," Isobel said. "Setting your shooting aside, and the years in between and before, Kau did die for his sister. I think people ought to know that. Don't you?"

"Are you asking my permission, Bel?"

She snorted. "Don't flatter yourself. I'm only making sure you're all right with it. Kau didn't shoot me in the head."

"I don't mind."

She pulled him to a stop. "Are you sure?"

"I've put some of my own ghosts to rest." There was a tremor in his voice. "Kau's face haunted my dreams for years. But all this has shed light on dark places—cleared some of the unknown and the fear that always came with it. It's a shame, though."

"His death?"

Riot nodded. "I would never begrudge a man his redemption. Although, it rarely ends well."

"Doesn't it?" She brushed his temple with her fingertips.

"*Just as a snake sheds its skin, we must shed our past over and over again,*" he murmured.

She cocked a brow at him.

"Buddha," he said. "No matter how many times we start over, our past comes back to haunt us. And when we stop running, it usually bites us."

"I *do* keep coming back," she agreed.

"I certainly don't mind you coming around."

"I bite, too."

The edge of his lip raised in a half-grin. "Careful, Bel. Or I'll forget we're standing outside."

"The horror of it."

There in the lane, under the sun, he buried his fingers in her hair and tasted her lips. "I think we had better get upstairs," he murmured.

"You're brilliant."

"Is that why you haven't gone to sea?"

She smiled, and whispered in his ear. "I forget I'm not sailing when I'm with you."

Emotion caught in his throat. "For better or worse?" he asked softly.

"Through any storm that comes our way."

"Mr. Riot?"

They both stepped away from the other, and Riot cleared his throat, watching Mr. Payne hurry up the carriage drive. "Yes?"

"I've some news."

Isobel looked perplexed. The man's mumble was a language of its own.

"About?"

"You asked after Jim Parks."

"I did."

"I checked with a friend of mine from prison. He was a guard there. Nice fellow, only he said Parks wasn't put into solitary; he swears he was released three months early."

"What?"

"That's what he said. Released on good behavior."

54

Before the Storm

Sunday, March 18, 1900

TENDRILS OF SILVER WRAPPED around grave-markers, caressing stone. It was the hour before dawn, when the sun still slept. A gray half-light and a bitter cold clung to the grass, winter green and glistening with frost. And on a hill sat an oak, spreading its limbs over a dear departed friend.

A dark shape twined his way through the gravestones. Riot watched the man from the cover of a mausoleum. The roses in the man's hand looked black in the half-light. He stopped in front of a headstone. Riot knew the etchings on that stone by heart.

Abigail Laurent Parks
Devoted Wife
June 1862 - December 1896

The man crouched and laid the bouquet of roses on

the grave. Then he stood. Riot gave him a moment. Love could manifest itself in horrific ways at times. When the man reached inside his pocket for a cigarette, Riot stepped from his concealment, moving with the fog like the wraith whispering in his mind.

"Hello, Parks," he said, softly.

Jim Parks spun on his wife's grave. His hand reached towards his hip, but when he saw the cultured man in a fancy suit and with bandaged fingers, he relaxed. He struck a match on his wife's headstone, and lit the cigarette dangling from his lips.

"Atticus Riot," Parks said, shaking out the match. He let it fall to the earth. "Are you visiting my wife's grave like you visited her bed after you sent me to prison?" Parks blew out a stream of smoke, agitating the air.

"She tried to divorce you after you stabbed her, but you refused to sign the papers."

"Until death do us part," Park said with relish. "She was mine. And still is." He ground his foot into the grave, and flicked the ash there.

"Is that why you killed her? I'd ask if it was because of me, but you tried to kill her before I ever met her."

Parks chuckled, and turned slightly. "What's that you're saying? Me? Kill Abby?" He gestured at the dates. "Written in stone. I was in prison, Riot. You and your partner put me there for marking what was mine."

"Is that why you killed Ravenwood, too? Revenge?"

Parks laughed. "You are full of accusations. You know, I heard you went a bit mad." He pointed his cigarette at Riot's head, and mimed shooting a gun. "Seems I heard correctly."

The man's voice was loud, and it bounced in the fog. It was an unnerving sound. "I can see Ravenwood's gravestone from here. Funny how they died so close together, isn't it?"

"I don't share your amusement," Riot replied. "I find it suggestive, however."

"*Suggestive*," Parks tasted the word. "I like that word. You were always well spoken. You know what Abby used to call men like you?"

Riot didn't answer.

"Little pricks in lace." He flicked more ash on her grave. "Compensation, she used to say."

Riot waited in silence, and his stillness agitated Parks. "So what, are you here to gloat over my grief?"

"I'm waiting for you to finish your thought. It's rude to interrupt."

"It's rude to sneak up on a man, too."

Riot glanced to the side, around the bone orchard. It was empty, and so very quiet. "There's plenty of open ground here. Hard to startle a man."

"You didn't startle me," Parks said, showing his teeth. "I'm just waiting for an apology now."

"An apology for what?"

"For your accusations."

Riot shook his head. He was less than ten feet from Parks, and he could see his eyes clearly. "You were released early, but it was a hushed affair. Your release took place at night."

"I was in solitary confinement. Whoever fed you that lie must be mistaken."

"You were *supposed* to go into confinement, but instead you were released on 'good behavior'."

"You're mad."

"So are a number of eye witnesses," Riot returned. "I also have a regular at your bar who swears up and down that he saw you the night Abigail was murdered."

Rage entered Jim Parks' eyes. The kind of rage that drove a man to stab his own wife.

"My witness is in a safe house, and enjoying himself immensely." Also sobering up, but Riot left that part out.

Parks smirked. "So you have drunks and convicts who say I magically fluttered away from prison in the dead of night."

"I also looked at the coroner's report for her death, and compared it with Ravenwood's and Mrs. Shaw's. I wasn't surprised to find the same knuckle pattern of bruises. You know knuckles leave a print as sure as a boot, which also matched. You see the man who killed Ravenwood was wearing a slipper-type shoe with no tread, sort of like a stocking. It looked like bare feet, but the size matches yours."

"Circumstantial."

"A judge signed your release—in secret. How much would you wager that that judge will throw you to the dogs at the first sign of trouble?"

It was Parks' turn to be quiet.

"Now, I don't think you arranged for yourself to be released. I think you had help, Parks. I think you're one tiny cog in a larger machine. In exchange for killing Ravenwood, I think you were set free and got your saloon prettied up. Not a bad deal."

Parks flicked his cigarette down. The stub smoldered in the frost. "The thing about a Bone Orchard is there's no one to hear a thing. Only miles of dead." Parks casually moved back his coat, revealing the gun on his hip.

"And here I figured you'd pound me to death."

"Like you said, knuckles leave a print."

"Why did you kill Ravenwood?"

"I was paid for it, and there wasn't a risk as long as everyone thought I was in prison. I only had to make it look like a chink did it. I'd have done it for free, though."

"Who hired you?" Riot asked.

Parks chuckled. "I guess you'll never know." He flinched, and Riot drew with his left hand. A single bark echoed in the silence. Parks dropped to his knees, clutching his stomach.

Riot strolled forward, pushed him back, and stepped on his hand. Parks had been reaching for the gun on his hip.

Parks panted, and spat, but the bloody spittle fell on his own chin. "You're a dead man, Riot. You just shot me in cold blood."

"No," Riot said. "I just shot a slow man who fancied himself a gunfighter."

Parks coughed. "Are you going to finish the job?"

Riot shook his head. "I'll let the Law do that."

Parks rolled, and pawed at the gravestone, leaving bloody smears on the stone. "I'll die with her, then."

"I know plenty of men who have survived a gut shot with this caliber."

Parks groaned.

"Your own wife survived your knife in her gut," Riot reminded. "In case you're wondering if my aim was coincidence—it wasn't."

"You're a dead man," Parks spat through bloody teeth.

"We already went over this."

"Sing Ping King Sur," Parks spit out each word.

Riot cocked his head. "What?"

Panting into the dirt, Parks squeezed his eyes shut, fighting against pain, and wishing for death. "Those words killed Ravenwood, and they'll do the same for you."

As Riot digested his words, Parks moved. A knife flashed in the man's hand. Before Riot could stop him, Parks drove the blade between his own ribs, straight to his heart. Blood soaked the earth, down into his wife's grave, and Riot was left with those killing words.

To Be Continued
Conspiracy of Silence
(Ravenwood Mysteries #4)
Coming 2018

Historical Afterword

IT'S SAID THAT LIFE is stranger than fiction. And that is definitely true. I take facts, and I weave them into my stories, but it's usually the more unbelievable elements in my books that are factual. A rule of thumb while reading *Ravenwood Mysteries* is that if it seems far-fetched it's probably true, or at least based on fact.

Researching this book was amazing. And overwhelming. I came across so many larger-than-life people, and things that were stranger than fiction. But what I managed to work into this book was only the tip of the iceberg.

The Beach Ghost was taken straight out of the Call newspaper archives. There *were* corrupt police and custom officers taking bribes, and countless trials were held over the smuggling of slave girls and dishonest officials.

The bubonic plague and barricading of Chinatown really did happen, and the plague would continue to be an issue up to the 1906 earthquake, and beyond. After Wong Chut King died in his bed at the Globe Hotel, politicians dragged their feet and tried to discredit health officials, so that the words "bubonic plague" wouldn't soil San Francisco. That would have risked port closures and hit them right in the pocketbook. Because health officials were impeded by greedy politicians, the bubonic plague gained a foothold in America's wildlife, and is an ongoing issue to this day.

There was, in fact, a girl of seven, Elsie Engstrom, who travelled from Germany by steamer, and took a train from New York to San Francisco alone to live with her uncle.

The stories that the tongs told slave girls about the house on the hill and the white devils (missionary women) eating girls are true. The dynamite at the mission house, the effigy of Donaldina Cameron and her sneaking past the quarantine barricades to save a girl dying in the street of appendicitis, and the circumstances surrounding Miss Culberston's death are also true. Along with the varied forms of brutalization of slave girls and very young house slaves.

The story of Mei and Kau is based on an actual account of a feared hatchet man named Kim who gave up everything to rescue his sister Mae. He sent a note to the mission, but when Donaldina tried to rescue her, she was gone. Kim eventually had to disguise himself as an old man to gain entrance into an opium dealer's home behind a steel door. He shot the man and took his sister, spiriting her away to the mission. He fled San Francisco, and was shot dead by his own tong in Fresno as he stepped off a train.

Poverty, hunger, and harsh conditions drove many young Chinese men from China's Canton province to California—to the Golden Mountains. They considered themselves sojourners rather than immigrants, traveling temporarily to America in hopes of making money to send back to their impoverished families.

What they found was bitter work, cramped living conditions, and extreme prejudice. The cry of *Chinese Must Go!* was a common sentiment throughout San Francisco's history. And to make matters worse, the Supreme Court ruled in 1862 that a Chinese could not testify against a white man, meaning they were subject to the whims of hoodlums, thieves, and murderers without any possibility of justice.

Dreams were quickly replaced by harsh realities. And a Chinese-English phrasebook hinted at those realities. Imagine traveling to a new country and memorizing these phrases:

I cannot trust you.
He took it from me by violence.
They were lying in ambush.
He was murdered by a thief.
He committed suicide.
He was choked to death with a lasso by a robber.
He was starved to death in prison.
He was going to drown himself in the bay.
He tried to assassinate me.
He was smothered in his room.
He was shot dead by his enemy.

In 1865, fifty Chinese laborers were hired by the Central Pacific Railroad on a trial basis. Railroad officials soon realized they could pay Chinese workers less than their Irish counterparts, and began recruiting Chinese laborers for mining camps. Leland Stanford, who once denounced Chinese immigrants, suddenly started pushing for the immigration of 500,000 Chinese men. It was Chinese laborers who risked their lives building the first Transcontinental Railroad enduring harsh winter conditions, with little food, low wages, and a casual disregard for their lives.

When the railroad was complete, thousands of ex-railroad workers and ex-miners found their way to San Francisco's Chinatown. Since harsh immigration laws actively sought to prevent Chinese men from establishing families by severely limiting Chinese women from immigrating, Chinatown became a bachelor society, full of thousands of young men with no family ties. By the 1880s, Chinese men outnumbered Chinese women by twenty to one.

The word 'tong' simply means 'hall' or 'gathering place'. They were organizations of volunteers who originally were formed to help immigrants with legal matters, immigration advice, and provide a brotherhood to thousands of men with no families. But a new form of tong sprouted up—criminal tongs that dealt in fear, slavery, opium, and gambling.

And into this massive population of men with no women... the Yellow Slave Trade was born.

Having been sold by their family or abducted, or by boarding a ship thinking they would be reunited with their husbands, thousands of girls were smuggled into the country and sent straight to the Queen's Room where they were stripped and sold to the highest bidder. Any who resisted were beated with bamboo sticks or branded with hot irons. And once these girls began 'working', the ones who showed even a spark of defiance against their new life were chained to beds or forced into a stupor with opium.

The average lifespan of a singsong girl (as they were called) was only about five years after they were sold into sexual slavery. When a singsong girl became sick, she was sent to small, dismal room in a Chinatown back alley known as a 'hospital'. Once inside the hole, she was forced to lie down on a small shelf, and given a single bowl of rice, a cup of water, and a metal oil lamp. She generally died from starvation or by her own hand. Whether she was dead or alive when the 'doctor' returned... he always left with a corpse.

The sex slave trade was a profitable business for the tongs in California. A girl from China generally cost around $40. When she arrived in San Francisco, she was sold for around $300-500 in the market. The average return on a girl once the parade of men started lining up to use her was $3000 dollars. The average cost of a 'crib whore' was 25 to 50 cents with a special rate of 15 cents for boys under 16.

I'll let you do the math on the number of men an average crib whore 'entertained' in five years.

In fact, boys visiting prostitutes was so common that one doctor remarked on the staggering number of young boys with venereal disease.

Sexual slavery was one of the cornerstones of the tongs' existence, along with the opium trade and gambling. These tongs employed salaried soldiers called *boo how doy*, or killers. These were the professional hatchet men. And they were bold. It was common for hatchet men to assassinate a blacklisted person in front of multiple witnesses, and in some cases even the police. One hatchet man walked onto stage during a theatre performance in a Chinese Theatre and shot the cymbalist before casually walking away.

As a result of the ruthless tongs, Chinatown was under a crushing weight of terror and silence. Any resident of Chinatown who dared to testify against a highbinder or tong had a *chun hung*, or a reward poster, plastered all over Chinatown with his or her name on it. It was as good as a death sentence.

Although slavery was against the law and a few people had tried to help these girls over the years, it was a seemingly hopeless fight because San Francisco was built on graft. The tongs paid protection money to white government officials, including mayors, lawyers, custom officers, and policemen. And the tongs would often exploit a loophole in the law itself, forcing a mission (with pressure from the police) to hand a runaway girl back to her slavers.

It wasn't until 1895 when a sewing teacher entered the fight that any real progress was made. That's right. A Presbyterian sewing teacher who worked at a mission put the infamous, fear-inspiring tongs on the run.

Her name was Donaldina Cameron, and in a few years she would become a living legend. You may have heard of one of her descendants: David Cameron, the former Prime Minister of England. The girls she rescued called her Lo Mo—Old Mother. And the newspapers called her the Angry Angel of Chinatown, while the hatchet men, who came to fear her, called her *Fahn Quai*, or White Devil.

Donaldina did what no honest policeman or the Chinese Six Companies could manage to do: she struck hard and repeatedly at the tongs' foundations—the slave trade.

This 'beloved, gentlemanly missionary' was described as having 'the equivalent of carbon steel in her make up.' She may have been armed with a detailed map of Chinatown drawn by cartographer Willard B. Farwell; she was said to be able to find her way blindfolded to every hidden den. And when Donaldina made her 'calls' to rescue girls, she usually brought along a trio of brawny policeman armed with axes and sledgehammers. As you can imagine, these rescue raids were not without risk.

She had a nose for trap doors, hidden panels, and secret stairways. And she was known to climb out windows onto rickety fire escapes in pursuit of a girl being whisked away.

During the 1900 Bubonic plague and subsequent quarantine of Chinatown, Donaldina slipped through the tight quarantine lines using sky lights and roofs to rescue girls as knowingly as the highbinders themselves.

But once she spirited the girls to her mission, the danger wasn't over. The tongs' pet lawyers used the law and police to retrieve the girls. When the police came looking for a slave girl with warrants and fake charges, Donaldina would insist 'she's not here' and pray that the police wouldn't look under the rice sacks in the dark space behind the basement gas meter.

She accepted the fact that she had to break the letter of the law in order to uphold the spirit of it. And when one of her rescued slave girls was jailed on trumped-up charges, she willingly and proudly occupied the same cell to keep the girl out of highbinder hands.

Despite great danger to herself, she was credited with rescuing over 3,000 girls. With the help of police, law-abiding Chinese, immigration officials, the Consul General, and eventually the 1906 earthquake and fire, she was able to put the tongs in retreat.

During an interview with Miss Cameron in 1961, she gave her reason for leading police into the brothels and fighting the highbinders in court. Her reason was simple: Because no one else would.

Sex trafficking is still a thriving criminal business throughout the world, and modern day heroes continue to fight a seemingly hopeless battle, doing what few will do—fighting for those with no voice.

Below is a list of some of the research books on my shelf, in case you are interested in non-fiction reading of the time and place:

Fierce Compassion: The Life of Abolitionist Donaldina Cameron —K. & K. Wong

The Barbary Plague: The Black Death in Victorian San Francisco —Marilyn Chase

Hatchet Men: The Story of the Tong Wars in San Francisco's Chinatown — Richard Dillion

My Own Story —Fremont Older

The Making of 'Mammy' Pleasant: A Black Entrepreneur in 19th Century San Francisco — Lynn M. Hudson

SamFow: The San Joaquin Chinese Legacy —Sylvia Sun Minnick

Alice: Memoirs of a Barbary Coast Prostitute —Ivy Anderson and Devon Angus

The Barbary Coast: An Informal History of the San Francisco Underworld — Herbert Asbury

Black San Francisco: The Struggle for Racial Equality in the West, 1900 -1954 —Albert S. Broussard

Acknowledgements

Books may be written by a single person, but they are polished by many hands, or in this case sharp eyes. I don't speak Cantonese, and I would likely mispronounce every single phonetic transcription in this book. Cantonese, with 6 to 9 tones (compared to Mandarin's 4 tones), is a difficult language to learn. All of the phonetic transcriptions in this book are due to the efforts of Gina Sze. She was gracious enough to share her knowledge and time with me, and for that she has my gratitude.

To Ken Littlefield for making sure that Isobel's kedging efforts were done correctly with all her knots in order. To my editors, Merrily Taylor and Tom Welch, for putting up with my struggling grammar efforts. To Alice Wright, the queen of consistency, for making sure there were no gaping plot holes. To my beta readers, Lorene Herrera, Selena Compton, Annelie Wendeberg, Rich Lovin, and Erin Bright. Your insights are invaluable, and much appreciated.

To my husband and children. I'm pretty sure they were on the verge of asking me to stop writing during the hair-pulling ordeal that was the first draft. Thank you for your understanding, and for listening to my writerly hardships.

And finally, thank you to all my readers for your continued support.

Glossary

Bai! - a Cantonese expression for when something bad happens (close to the English expression, 'shit')

Banker - a horse racing bet where the bettor believes their selection is certain to win

Bong 幫 - help

Boo how doy - hatchet man - a hired tong soldier or assassin

Capper - a person who is on the look out for possible clients for attorneys

Chi Gum Shing - 紫禁城 - Forbidden Palace

Chinese Six Companies - Benevolent organizations formed to help the Chinese travel to and from China, to take care of the sick and the starving, and to return corpses to China for burial.

Chun Hung - a poster that puts a price on someone's head

Dang dang - wait

Digging into your levis - searching for cash

Din Gau - 癲狗 - Rabid Dog

Dressed for death - dressed in one's best

Faan tung - 飯桶 - rice bucket - worthless

Fahn Quai - White Devil

Fan Kwei - Foreign Devil

Graft - practices, especially bribery, used to secure illicit gains in politics or business; corruption.

Hei Lok Lau - House of Joy - traditional name for brothels in old days

Hei san la nei, chap chung! - 起身呀你個雜種！- Wake up, you bastard!

Highbinders - general term for criminals

Kedging - to warp or pull (a ship) along by hauling on the cable of an anchor that has been carried out a ways from the ship, and dropped.

King chak - the police

Lo Mo - foster mother

Mien tzu - a severe loss of face

Mui Tsai - little Chinese girls who were sold into domestic households. They were often burdened with heavy labor and endured severe physical punishments.

Nei tai - you, look

Ngor bon nei - I help you

No sabe - Spanish for 'doesn't know' or 'I don't understand'. I came across a historical reference to a Chinese man using this phrase in a newspaper article. I don't know if it was common, but it is a simple, easy to say phrase that English speakers understand.

Pak Siu Lui - White Little Bud

Si Fu - the Master

Siu wai daan - 小壞蛋 - Little Rotten Eggs - An insult that implies one was hatched rather than born, and therefore has no mother. The inclusion of 'little' in the insult softens it slightly.

Slungshot - A maritime tool consisting of a weight, or "shot," affixed to the end of a long cord often by being wound into the center of a knot called a "monkey's fist." It is used to cast line from one location to another, often mooring line. This was also a popular makeshift (and deadly) weapon in the Barbary Coast.

Wai Daan - 壞蛋 - Rotten Egg

Wai Yan - 壞男人 - Bad Men

Wu Lei Ching - 狐狸精 - Fox Spirit
Wun Dan - Cracked Egg
Wun... ah Mei - Find Mei
Yiu! - 妖! - a *slightly* less offensive version of the English 'F-word'.